# War and Peace

# War and Peace

## Books XI–XV

## Leo Tolstoy

MINT EDITIONS

*War and Peace: Books XI–XV* was first published in 1867.

This edition published by Mint Editions 2021.

ISBN 9781513281827 | E-ISBN 9781513286846

Published by Mint Editions®

 MINT
EDITIONS
minteditionbooks.com

Publishing Director: Jennifer Newens
Design & Production: Rachel Lopez Metzger
Project Manager: Micaela Clark
Translated by: Louise and Aylmer Maude
Typesetting: Westchester Publishing Services

# Contents

## Book Twelve. 1812

# Book Thirteen. 1812

BOOK FOURTEEN. 1812

BOOK FIFTEEN. 1812–13

BOOK ELEVEN

1812

# I

Absolute continuity of motion is not comprehensible to the human mind. Laws of motion of any kind become comprehensible to man only when he examines arbitrarily selected elements of that motion; but at the same time, a large proportion of human error comes from the arbitrary division of continuous motion into discontinuous elements. There is a well-known, so-called sophism of the ancients consisting in this, that Achilles could never catch up with a tortoise he was following, in spite of the fact that he traveled ten times as fast as the tortoise. By the time Achilles has covered the distance that separated him from the tortoise, the tortoise has covered one tenth of that distance ahead of him: when Achilles has covered that tenth, the tortoise has covered another one hundredth, and so on forever. This problem seemed to the ancients insoluble. The absurd answer (that Achilles could never overtake the tortoise) resulted from this: that motion was arbitrarily divided into discontinuous elements, whereas the motion both of Achilles and of the tortoise was continuous.

By adopting smaller and smaller elements of motion we only approach a solution of the problem, but never reach it. Only when we have admitted the conception of the infinitely small, and the resulting geometrical progression with a common ratio of one tenth, and have found the sum of this progression to infinity, do we reach a solution of the problem.

A modern branch of mathematics having achieved the art of dealing with the infinitely small can now yield solutions in other more complex problems of motion which used to appear insoluble.

This modern branch of mathematics, unknown to the ancients, when dealing with problems of motion admits the conception of the infinitely small, and so conforms to the chief condition of motion (absolute continuity) and thereby corrects the inevitable error which the human mind cannot avoid when it deals with separate elements of motion instead of examining continuous motion.

In seeking the laws of historical movement just the same thing happens. The movement of humanity, arising as it does from innumerable arbitrary human wills, is continuous.

To understand the laws of this continuous movement is the aim of history. But to arrive at these laws, resulting from the sum of all those human wills, man's mind postulates arbitrary and disconnected units. The first method of history is to take an arbitrarily selected series of continuous events and examine it apart from others, though there is and can be no beginning to any event, for one event always flows uninterruptedly from another.

The second method is to consider the actions of some one man—a king or a commander—as equivalent to the sum of many individual wills; whereas the sum of individual wills is never expressed by the activity of a single historic personage.

Historical science in its endeavor to draw nearer to truth continually takes smaller and smaller units for examination. But however small the units it takes, we feel that to take any unit disconnected from others, or to assume a beginning of any phenomenon, or to say that the will of many men is expressed by the actions of any one historic personage, is in itself false.

It needs no critical exertion to reduce utterly to dust any deductions drawn from history. It is merely necessary to select some larger or smaller unit as the subject of observation—as criticism has every right to do, seeing that whatever unit history observes must always be arbitrarily selected.

Only by taking infinitesimally small units for observation (the differential of history, that is, the individual tendencies of men) and attaining to the art of integrating them (that is, finding the sum of these infinitesimals) can we hope to arrive at the laws of history.

The first fifteen years of the nineteenth century in Europe present an extraordinary movement of millions of people. Men leave their customary pursuits, hasten from one side of Europe to the other, plunder and slaughter one another, triumph and are plunged in despair, and for some years the whole course of life is altered and presents an intensive movement which first increases and then slackens. What was the cause of this movement, by what laws was it governed? asks the mind of man.

The historians, replying to this question, lay before us the sayings and doings of a few dozen men in a building in the city of Paris, calling these sayings and doings "the Revolution"; then they give a detailed biography of Napoleon and of certain people favorable or hostile to him; tell of the influence some of these people had on others, and say: that is why this movement took place and those are its laws.

But the mind of man not only refuses to believe this explanation, but plainly says that this method of explanation is fallacious, because in it a weaker phenomenon is taken as the cause of a stronger. The sum of human wills produced the Revolution and Napoleon, and only the sum of those wills first tolerated and then destroyed them.

"But every time there have been conquests there have been conquerors; every time there has been a revolution in any state there have been great men," says history. And, indeed, human reason replies: every time conquerors appear there have been wars, but this does not prove that the conquerors caused the wars and that it is possible to find the laws of a war in the personal activity of a single man. Whenever I look at my watch and its hands point to ten, I hear the bells of the neighboring church; but because the bells begin to ring when the hands of the clock reach ten, I have no right to assume that the movement of the bells is caused by the position of the hands of the watch.

Whenever I see the movement of a locomotive I hear the whistle and see the valves opening and wheels turning; but I have no right to conclude that the whistling and the turning of wheels are the cause of the movement of the engine.

The peasants say that a cold wind blows in late spring because the oaks are budding, and really every spring cold winds do blow when the oak is budding. But though I do not know what causes the cold winds to blow when the oak buds unfold, I cannot agree with the peasants that the unfolding of the oak buds is the cause of the cold wind, for the force of the wind is beyond the influence of the buds. I see only a coincidence of occurrences such as happens with all the phenomena of life, and I see that however much and however carefully I observe the hands of the watch, and the valves and wheels of the engine, and the oak, I shall not discover the cause of the bells ringing, the engine moving, or of the winds of spring. To that I must entirely change my point of view and study the laws of the movement of steam, of the bells, and of the wind. History must do the same. And attempts in this direction have already been made.

To study the laws of history we must completely change the subject of our observation, must leave aside kings, ministers, and generals, and study the common, infinitesimally small elements by which the masses are moved. No one can say in how far it is possible for man to advance in this way toward an understanding of the laws of history; but it is evident that only along that path does the possibility of discovering the laws of history lie, and that as yet not a millionth part as much mental effort has been applied in this direction by historians as has been devoted to describing the actions of various kings, commanders, and ministers and propounding the historians' own reflections concerning these actions.

# II

The forces of a dozen European nations burst into Russia. The Russian army and people avoided a collision till Smolénsk was reached, and again from Smolénsk to Borodinó. The French army pushed on to Moscow, its goal, its impetus ever increasing as it neared its aim, just as the velocity of a falling body increases as it approaches the earth. Behind it were seven hundred miles of hunger-stricken, hostile country; ahead were a few dozen miles separating it from its goal. Every soldier in Napoleon's army felt this and the invasion moved on by its own momentum.

The more the Russian army retreated the more fiercely a spirit of hatred of the enemy flared up, and while it retreated the army increased and consolidated. At Borodinó a collision took place. Neither army was broken up, but the Russian army retreated immediately after the collision as inevitably as a ball recoils after colliding with another having a greater momentum, and with equal inevitability the ball of invasion that had advanced with such momentum rolled on for some distance, though the collision had deprived it of all its force.

The Russians retreated eighty miles—to beyond Moscow—and the French reached Moscow and there came to a standstill. For five weeks after that there was not a single battle. The French did not move. As a bleeding, mortally wounded animal licks its wounds, they remained inert in Moscow for five weeks, and then suddenly, with no fresh reason, fled back: they made a dash for the Kalúga road, and (after a victory—for at Málo-Yaroslávets the field of conflict again remained theirs) without undertaking a single serious battle, they fled still more rapidly back to Smolénsk, beyond Smolénsk, beyond the Berëzina, beyond Vílna, and farther still.

On the evening of the twenty-sixth of August, Kutúzov and the whole Russian army were convinced that the battle of Borodinó was a victory. Kutúzov reported so to the Emperor. He gave orders to prepare for a fresh conflict to finish the enemy and did this not to deceive anyone, but because he knew that the enemy was beaten, as everyone who had taken part in the battle knew it.

But all that evening and next day reports came in one after another of unheard-of losses, of the loss of half the army, and a fresh battle proved physically impossible.

It was impossible to give battle before information had been collected, the wounded gathered in, the supplies of ammunition replenished, the slain reckoned up, new officers appointed to replace those who had been killed, and before the men had had food and sleep. And meanwhile, the very next morning after the battle, the French army advanced of itself upon the Russians, carried forward by the force of its own momentum now seemingly increased in inverse proportion to the square of the distance from its aim. Kutúzov's wish was to attack next day, and the whole army desired to do so. But to make an attack the wish to do so is not sufficient, there must also be a possibility of doing it, and that possibility did not exist. It was impossible not to retreat a day's march, and then in the same way it was impossible not to retreat another and a third day's march, and at last, on the first of September when the army drew near Moscow—despite the strength of the feeling that had arisen in all ranks—the force of circumstances compelled it to retire beyond Moscow. And the troops retired one more, last, day's march, and abandoned Moscow to the enemy.

For people accustomed to think that plans of campaign and battles are made by generals—as anyone of us sitting over a map in his study may imagine how he would have arranged things in this or that battle—the questions present themselves: Why did Kutúzov during the retreat not do this or that? Why did he not take up a position before reaching Filí? Why did he not retire at once by the Kalúga road, abandoning Moscow? and so on. People accustomed to think in that way forget, or do not know, the inevitable conditions which always limit the activities of any commander in chief. The activity of a commander in chief does not at all resemble the activity we imagine to ourselves when we sit at ease in our studies examining some campaign on the map, with a certain number of troops on this and that side in a certain known locality, and begin our plans from some given moment. A commander in chief is never dealing with the beginning of any event—the position from which we always contemplate it. The commander in chief is always in the midst of a series of shifting events and so he never can at any moment consider the whole import of an event that is occurring. Moment by moment the event is imperceptibly shaping itself, and at every moment of this continuous, uninterrupted shaping of events the commander in chief is in the midst of a most complex play of intrigues, worries, contingencies, authorities, projects, counsels, threats, and deceptions and is continually obliged to reply to innumerable questions addressed to him, which constantly conflict with one another.

Learned military authorities quite seriously tell us that Kutúzov should have moved his army to the Kalúga road long before reaching Filí, and that somebody actually submitted such a proposal to him. But a commander in chief, especially at a difficult moment, has always before him not one proposal but dozens simultaneously. And all these proposals, based on strategics and tactics, contradict each other.

A commander in chief's business, it would seem, is simply to choose one of these projects. But even that he cannot do. Events and time do not wait. For instance, on the twenty-eighth it is suggested to him to cross to the Kalúga road, but just then an adjutant gallops up from Milorádovich asking whether he is to engage the French or retire. An order must be given him at once, that instant. And the order to retreat carries us past the turn to the Kalúga road. And after the adjutant comes the commissary general asking where the stores are to be taken, and the chief of the hospitals asks where the wounded are to go, and a courier from Petersburg brings a letter from the sovereign which does not admit of the possibility of abandoning Moscow, and the commander in chief's rival, the man who is undermining him (and there are always not merely one but several such), presents a new project diametrically opposed to that of turning to the Kalúga road, and the commander in chief himself needs sleep and refreshment to maintain his energy and a respectable general who has been overlooked in the distribution of rewards comes to complain, and the inhabitants of the district pray to be defended, and an officer sent to inspect the locality comes in and gives a report quite contrary to what was said by the officer previously sent; and a spy, a prisoner, and a general who has been on reconnaissance, all describe the position of the enemy's army differently. People accustomed to misunderstand or to forget these inevitable conditions of a commander in chief's actions describe to us, for instance, the position of the army at Filí and assume that the commander in chief could, on the first of September, quite freely decide whether to abandon Moscow or defend it; whereas, with the Russian army less than four miles from Moscow, no such question existed. When had that question been settled? At Drissa and at Smolénsk and most palpably of all on the twenty-fourth of August at Shevárdino and on the twenty-sixth at Borodinó, and each day and hour and minute of the retreat from Borodinó to Filí.

# III

When Ermólov, having been sent by Kutúzov to inspect the position, told the field marshal that it was impossible to fight there before Moscow and that they must retreat, Kutúzov looked at him in silence.

"Give me your hand," said he and, turning it over so as to feel the pulse, added: "You are not well, my dear fellow. Think what you are saying!"

Kutúzov could not yet admit the possibility of retreating beyond Moscow without a battle.

On the Poklónny Hill, four miles from the Dorogomílov gate of Moscow, Kutúzov got out of his carriage and sat down on a bench by the roadside. A great crowd of generals gathered round him, and Count Rostopchín, who had come out from Moscow, joined them. This brilliant company separated into several groups who all discussed the advantages and disadvantages of the position, the state of the army, the plans suggested, the situation of Moscow, and military questions generally. Though they had not been summoned for the purpose, and though it was not so called, they all felt that this was really a council of war. The conversations all dealt with public questions. If anyone gave or asked for personal news, it was done in a whisper and they immediately reverted to general matters. No jokes, or laughter, or smiles even, were seen among all these men. They evidently all made an effort to hold themselves at the height the situation demanded. And all these groups, while talking among themselves, tried to keep near the commander in chief (whose bench formed the center of the gathering) and to speak so that he might overhear them. The commander in chief listened to what was being said and sometimes asked them to repeat their remarks, but did not himself take part in the conversations or express any opinion. After hearing what was being said by one or other of these groups he generally turned away with an air of disappointment, as though they were not speaking of anything he wished to hear. Some discussed the position that had been chosen, criticizing not the position itself so much as the mental capacity of those who had chosen it. Others argued that a mistake had been made earlier and that a battle should have been fought two days before. Others again spoke of the battle of Salamanca, which was described by Crosart, a newly arrived Frenchman in a Spanish uniform. (This Frenchman and one of the German princes serving with the Russian army were discussing the siege of Saragossa and considering the possibility of defending Moscow in a similar manner.) Count Rostopchín was telling a fourth group that he was prepared to die with the city train bands under the walls of the capital, but that he still could not help regretting having been left in ignorance of what was happening, and that had he known it sooner things would have been different... A fifth group, displaying the profundity of their strategic perceptions, discussed the direction the troops would now have to take. A sixth group was talking absolute nonsense. Kutúzov's expression grew more and more preoccupied and gloomy. From all this talk he saw only one thing: that to defend Moscow was a physical impossibility in the full meaning of those words, that is to say, so utterly impossible that if any senseless commander were to give orders to fight, confusion would result but the battle would still not take place. It would not take place because the commanders not merely all recognized the position to be impossible, but in their conversations were only discussing what would happen after its inevitable abandonment. How could the commanders lead their troops to a field of battle they considered impossible to hold? The lower-grade officers and even the soldiers (who too reason) also considered the position impossible and therefore could not go to fight, fully convinced as they were of defeat. If Bennigsen insisted on the position being defended and others still discussed it, the question was no longer important in itself but only as a pretext for disputes and intrigue. This Kutúzov knew well.

Bennigsen, who had chosen the position, warmly displayed his Russian patriotism (Kutúzov could not listen to this without wincing) by insisting that Moscow must be defended. His aim was as clear as daylight to Kutúzov: if the defense failed, to throw the blame on Kutúzov who had brought the army as far as the Sparrow Hills without giving battle; if it succeeded, to claim the success as his own; or if battle were not given, to clear himself of the crime of abandoning Moscow. But this intrigue did not now occupy the old man's mind. One terrible question absorbed him and to that question he heard no reply from anyone. The question for him now was: "Have I really allowed Napoleon to reach Moscow, and when did I do so? When was it decided? Can it have been yesterday when I ordered Plátov to retreat, or was it the evening before, when I had a nap and told Bennigsen to issue orders? Or was it earlier still? ... When, when was this terrible affair decided? Moscow must be abandoned. The army must retreat and the order to do so must be given." To give that terrible order seemed to him equivalent to resigning the command of the army. And not only did he love power to which he was accustomed (the honours awarded to Prince Prozoróvski, under whom he had served in Turkey, galled him), but he was convinced that he was destined to save Russia and that that was why, against the Emperor's wish and by the will of the people, he had been chosen commander in chief. He was convinced that he alone could maintain command of the army in these difficult circumstances, and that in all the world he alone could encounter the invincible Napoleon without fear, and he was horrified at the thought of the order he had to issue. But something had to be decided, and these conversations around him which were assuming too free a character must be stopped.

He called the most important generals to him.

"My head, be it good or bad, must depend on itself," said he, rising from the bench, and he rode to Filí where his carriages were waiting.

# IV

The Council of War began to assemble at two in the afternoon in the better and roomier part of Andrew Savostyánov's hut. The men, women, and children of the large peasant family crowded into the back room across the passage. Only Malásha, Andrew's six-year-old granddaughter whom his Serene Highness had petted and to whom he had given a lump of sugar while drinking his tea, remained on the top of the brick oven in the larger room. Malásha looked down from the oven with shy delight at the faces, uniforms, and decorations of the generals, who one after another came into the room and sat down on the broad benches in the corner under the icons. "Granddad" himself, as Malásha in her own mind called Kutúzov, sat apart in a dark corner behind the oven. He sat, sunk deep in a folding armchair, and continually cleared his throat and pulled at the collar of his coat which, though it was unbuttoned, still seemed to pinch his neck. Those who entered went up one by one to the field marshal; he pressed the hands of some and nodded to others. His adjutant Kaysárov was about to draw back the curtain of the window facing Kutúzov, but the latter moved his hand angrily and Kaysárov understood that his Serene Highness did not wish his face to be seen.

Round the peasant's deal table, on which lay maps, plans, pencils, and papers, so many people gathered that the orderlies brought in another bench and put it beside the table. Ermólov, Kaysárov, and Toll, who had just arrived, sat down on this bench. In the foremost place, immediately under the icons, sat Barclay de Tolly, his high forehead merging into his bald crown. He had a St. George's Cross round his neck and looked pale and ill. He had been feverish for two days and was now shivering and in pain. Beside him sat Uvárov, who with rapid gesticulations was giving him some information, speaking in low tones as they all did. Chubby little Dokhtúrov was listening attentively with eyebrows raised and arms folded on his stomach. On the other side sat Count Ostermann-Tolstóy, seemingly absorbed in his own thoughts. His broad head with its bold features and glittering eyes was resting on his hand. Raévski, twitching forward the black hair on his temples as was his habit, glanced now at Kutúzov and now at the door with a look of impatience. Konovnítsyn's firm, handsome, and kindly face was lit up by a tender, sly smile. His glance met Malásha's, and the expression of his eyes caused the little girl to smile.

They were all waiting for Bennigsen, who on the pretext of inspecting the position was finishing his savory dinner. They waited for him from four till six o'clock and did not begin their deliberations all that time but talked in low tones of other matters.

Only when Bennigsen had entered the hut did Kutúzov leave his corner and draw toward the table, but not near enough for the candles that had been placed there to light up his face.

Bennigsen opened the council with the question: "Are we to abandon Russia's ancient and sacred capital without a struggle, or are we to defend it?" A prolonged and general silence followed. There was a frown on every face and only Kutúzov's angry grunts and occasional cough broke the silence. All eyes were gazing at him. Malásha too looked at "Granddad." She was nearest to him and saw how his face puckered; he seemed about to cry, but this did not last long.

"Russia's ancient and sacred capital!" he suddenly said, repeating Bennigsen's words in an angry voice and thereby drawing attention to the false note in them. "Allow me to tell you, your excellency, that that question has no meaning for a Russian." (He lurched his heavy body forward.) "Such a question cannot be put; it is senseless! The question I have asked these gentlemen to meet to discuss is a military one. The question is that of saving Russia. Is it better to give up Moscow without a battle, or by accepting battle to risk losing the army as well as Moscow? That is the question on which I want your opinion," and he sank back in his chair.

The discussion began. Bennigsen did not yet consider his game lost. Admitting the view of Barclay and others that a defensive battle at Filí was impossible, but imbued with Russian patriotism and the love of Moscow, he proposed to move troops from the right to the left flank during the night and attack the French right flank the following day. Opinions were divided, and arguments were advanced for and against that project. Ermólov, Dokhtúrov, and Raévski agreed with Bennigsen. Whether feeling it necessary to make a sacrifice before abandoning the capital or guided by other, personal considerations, these generals seemed not to understand that this council could not alter the inevitable course of events and that Moscow was in effect already abandoned. The other generals, however, understood it and, leaving aside the question of Moscow, spoke of the direction the army should take in its retreat. Malásha, who kept her eyes fixed on what was going on before her, understood the meaning of the council differently. It seemed to her that it was only a personal struggle between "Granddad" and "Long-coat" as she termed Bennigsen. She saw that they grew spiteful when they spoke to one another, and in her heart she sided with "Granddad." In the midst of the conversation she noticed "Granddad" give Bennigsen a quick, subtle glance, and then to her joys she saw that "Granddad" said something to "Long-coat" which settled him. Bennigsen suddenly reddened and paced angrily up and down the room. What so affected him was Kutúzov's calm and quiet comment on the advantage or disadvantage of Bennigsen's proposal to move troops by night from the right to the left flank to attack the French right wing.

"Gentlemen," said Kutúzov, "I cannot approve of the count's plan. Moving troops in close proximity to an enemy is always dangerous, and military history supports that view. For instance. . ." Kutúzov seemed to reflect, searching for an example, then with a clear, naïve look at Bennigsen he added: "Oh yes; take the battle of Friedland, which I think the count well remembers, and which was. . . not fully successful, only because our troops were rearranged too near the enemy. . ."

There followed a momentary pause, which seemed very long to them all.

The discussion recommenced, but pauses frequently occurred and they all felt that there was no more to be said.

During one of these pauses Kutúzov heaved a deep sigh as if preparing to speak. They all looked at him.

"Well, gentlemen, I see that it is I who will have to pay for the broken crockery," said he, and rising slowly he moved to the table. "Gentlemen, I have heard your views. Some of you will not agree with me. But I," he paused, "by the authority entrusted to me by my Sovereign and country, order a retreat."

After that the generals began to disperse with the solemnity and circumspect silence of people who are leaving, after a funeral.

Some of the generals, in low tones and in a strain very different from the way they had spoken during the council, communicated something to their commander in chief.

Malásha, who had long been expected for supper, climbed carefully backwards down from the oven, her bare little feet catching at its projections, and slipping between the legs of the generals she darted out of the room.

When he had dismissed the generals Kutúzov sat a long time with his elbows on the table, thinking always of the same terrible question:

"When, when did the abandonment of Moscow become inevitable? When was that done which settled the matter? And who was to blame for it?"

"I did not expect this," said he to his adjutant Schneider when the latter came in late that night. "I did not expect this! I did not think this would happen."

"You should take some rest, your Serene Highness," replied Schneider.

"But no! They shall eat horseflesh yet, like the Turks!" exclaimed Kutúzov without replying, striking the table with his podgy fist. "They shall too, if only. . ."

# V

At that very time, in circumstances even more important than retreating without a battle, namely the evacuation and burning of Moscow, Rostopchín, who is usually represented as being the instigator of that event, acted in an altogether different manner from Kutúzov.

After the battle of Borodinó the abandonment and burning of Moscow was as inevitable as the retreat of the army beyond Moscow without fighting.

Every Russian might have predicted it, not by reasoning but by the feeling implanted in each of us and in our fathers.

The same thing that took place in Moscow had happened in all the towns and villages on Russian soil beginning with Smolénsk, without the participation of Count Rostopchín and his broadsheets. The people awaited the enemy unconcernedly, did not riot or become excited or tear anyone to pieces, but faced its fate, feeling within it the strength to find what it should do at that most difficult moment. And as soon as the enemy drew near the wealthy classes went away abandoning their property, while the poorer remained and burned and destroyed what was left.

The consciousness that this would be so and would always be so was and is present in the heart of every Russian. And a consciousness of this, and a foreboding that Moscow would be taken, was present in Russian Moscow society in 1812. Those who had quitted Moscow already in July and at the beginning of August showed that they expected this. Those who went away, taking what they could and abandoning their houses and half their belongings, did so from the latent patriotism which expresses itself not by phrases or by giving one's children to save the fatherland and similar unnatural exploits, but unobtrusively, simply, organically, and therefore in the way that always produces the most powerful results.

"It is disgraceful to run away from danger; only cowards are running away from Moscow," they were told. In his broadsheets Rostopchín impressed on them that to leave Moscow was shameful. They were ashamed to be called cowards, ashamed to leave, but still they left, knowing it had to be done. Why did they go? It is impossible to suppose that Rostopchín had scared them by his accounts of horrors Napoleon had committed in conquered countries. The first people to go away were the rich educated people who knew quite well that Vienna and Berlin had remained intact and that during Napoleon's occupation the inhabitants had spent their time pleasantly in the company of the charming Frenchmen whom the Russians, and especially the Russian ladies, then liked so much.

They went away because for Russians there could be no question as to whether things would go well or ill under French rule in Moscow. It was out of the question to be under French rule, it would be the worst thing that could happen. They went away even before the battle of Borodinó and still more rapidly after it, despite Rostopchín's calls to defend Moscow or the announcement of his intention to take the wonder-working icon of the Iberian Mother of God and go to fight, or of the balloons that were to destroy the French, and despite all the nonsense Rostopchín wrote in his broadsheets. They knew that it was for the army to fight, and that if it could not succeed it would not do to take young ladies and house serfs to the Three Hills quarter of Moscow to fight Napoleon, and that they must go away, sorry as they were to abandon their property to destruction. They went away without thinking of the tremendous significance of that immense and wealthy city being given over to destruction, for a great city with wooden buildings was certain when abandoned by its inhabitants to be burned. They went away each on his own account, and yet it was only in consequence of their going away that the momentous event was accomplished that will always remain the greatest glory of the Russian people. The lady who, afraid of being stopped by Count Rostopchín's orders, had already in June moved with her Negroes and her women jesters from Moscow to her Sarátov estate, with a vague consciousness that she was not Bonaparte's servant, was really, simply, and truly carrying out the great work which saved Russia. But Count Rostopchín, who now taunted those who left Moscow and now had the government offices removed; now distributed quite useless weapons to the drunken rabble; now had processions displaying the icons, and now forbade Father Augustin to remove icons or the relics of saints; now seized all the private carts in Moscow and on one hundred and thirty-six of them removed the balloon that was being constructed by Leppich; now hinted that he would burn Moscow and related how he had set fire to his own house; now wrote a proclamation to the French solemnly upbraiding them for having destroyed his Orphanage; now claimed the glory of having hinted that he would burn Moscow and now repudiated the deed; now ordered the people to catch all spies and bring them to him, and now reproached them for doing so; now expelled all the French residents from Moscow, and now allowed Madame Aubert-Chalmé (the center of the whole French colony in Moscow) to remain, but ordered the venerable old postmaster Klyucharëv to be arrested and exiled for no particular offense; now assembled the people at the Three Hills to fight the French and now, to get rid of them, handed over to them a man to be killed and himself drove away by a back gate; now declared that he would not survive the fall of Moscow, and now wrote French verses in albums concerning his share in the affair—this man did not understand the meaning of what was happening but merely wanted to do something himself that would astonish people, to perform some patriotically heroic feat; and like a child he made sport of the momentous, and unavoidable event— the abandonment and burning of Moscow—and tried with his puny hand now to speed and now to stay the enormous, popular tide that bore him along with it.

# VI

Hélène, having returned with the court from Vílna to Petersburg, found herself in a difficult position.

In Petersburg she had enjoyed the special protection of a grandee who occupied one of the highest posts in the Empire. In Vílna she had formed an intimacy with a young foreign prince. When she returned to Petersburg both the magnate and the prince were there, and both claimed their rights. Hélène was faced by a new problem—how to preserve her intimacy with both without offending either.

What would have seemed difficult or even impossible to another woman did not cause the least embarrassment to Countess Bezúkhova, who evidently deserved her reputation of being a very clever woman. Had she attempted concealment, or tried to extricate herself from her awkward position by cunning, she would have spoiled her case by acknowledging herself guilty. But Hélène, like a really great man who can do whatever he pleases, at once assumed her own position to be correct, as she sincerely believed it to be, and that everyone else was to blame.

The first time the young foreigner allowed himself to reproach her, she lifted her beautiful head and, half turning to him, said firmly: "That's just like a man—selfish and cruel! I expected nothing else. A woman sacrifices herself for you, she suffers, and this is her reward! What right have you, monseigneur, to demand an account of my attachments and friendships? He is a man who has been more than a father to me!" The prince was about to say something, but Hélène interrupted him.

"Well, yes," said she, "it may be that he has other sentiments for me than those of a father, but that is not a reason for me to shut my door on him. I am not a man, that I should repay kindness with ingratitude! Know, monseigneur, that in all that relates to my intimate feelings I render account only to God and to my conscience," she concluded, laying her hand on her beautiful, fully expanded bosom and looking up to heaven.

"But for heaven's sake listen to me!"

"Marry me, and I will be your slave!"

"But that's impossible."

"You won't deign to demean yourself by marrying me, you. . ." said Hélène, beginning to cry.

The prince tried to comfort her, but Hélène, as if quite distraught, said through her tears that there was nothing to prevent her marrying, that there were precedents (there were up to that time very few, but she mentioned Napoleon and some other exalted personages), that she had never been her husband's wife, and that she had been sacrificed.

"But the law, religion. . ." said the prince, already yielding.

"The law, religion. . . What have they been invented for if they can't arrange that?" said Hélène.

The prince was surprised that so simple an idea had not occurred to him, and he applied for advice to the holy brethren of the Society of Jesus, with whom he was on intimate terms.

A few days later at one of those enchanting fetes which Hélène gave at her country house on the Stone Island, the charming Monsieur de Jobert, a man no longer young, with snow white hair and brilliant black eyes, a Jesuit à robe courte* was presented to her, and in the garden by the light of the illuminations and to the sound of music talked to her for a long time of the love of God, of Christ, of the Sacred Heart, and of the consolations the one true Catholic religion affords in this world and the next. Hélène was touched, and more than once tears rose to her eyes and to those of Monsieur de Jobert and their voices trembled. A dance, for which her partner came to seek her, put an end to her discourse with her future directeur de conscience, but the next evening Monsieur de Jobert came to see Hélène when she was alone, and after that often came again.

One day he took the countess to a Roman Catholic church, where she knelt down before the altar to which she was led. The enchanting, middle-aged Frenchman laid his hands on her head and, as she herself afterward described it, she felt something like a fresh breeze wafted into her soul. It was explained to her that this was la grâce.

After that a long-frocked abbé was brought to her. She confessed to him, and he absolved her from her sins. Next day she received a box containing the Sacred Host, which was left at her house for her to partake of. A few days later Hélène learned with pleasure that she had now been admitted to the true Catholic Church and that in a few days the Pope himself would hear of her and would send her a certain document.

---

* Lay member of the Society of Jesus.

All that was done around her and to her at this time, all the attention devoted to her by so many clever men and expressed in such pleasant, refined ways, and the state of dove-like purity she was now in (she wore only white dresses and white ribbons all that time) gave her pleasure, but her pleasure did not cause her for a moment to forget her aim. And as it always happens in contests of cunning that a stupid person gets the better of cleverer ones, Hélène—having realized that the main object of all these words and all this trouble was, after converting her to Catholicism, to obtain money from her for Jesuit institutions (as to which she received indications)—before parting with her money insisted that the various operations necessary to free her from her husband should be performed. In her view the aim of every religion was merely to preserve certain proprieties while affording satisfaction to human desires. And with this aim, in one of her talks with her Father Confessor, she insisted on an answer to the question, in how far was she bound by her marriage?

They were sitting in the twilight by a window in the drawing room. The scent of flowers came in at the window. Hélène was wearing a white dress, transparent over her shoulders and bosom. The abbé, a well-fed man with a plump, clean-shaven chin, a pleasant firm mouth, and white hands meekly folded on his knees, sat close to Hélène and, with a subtle smile on his lips and a peaceful look of delight at her beauty, occasionally glanced at her face as he explained his opinion on the subject. Hélène with an uneasy smile looked at his curly hair and his plump, clean-shaven, blackish cheeks and every moment expected the conversation to take a fresh turn. But the abbé, though he evidently enjoyed the beauty of his companion, was absorbed in his mastery of the matter.

The course of the Father Confessor's arguments ran as follows: "Ignorant of the import of what you were undertaking, you made a vow of conjugal fidelity to a man who on his part, by entering the married state without faith in the religious significance of marriage, committed an act of sacrilege. That marriage lacked the dual significance it should have had. Yet in spite of this your vow was binding. You swerved from it. What did you commit by so acting? A venial, or a mortal, sin? A venial sin, for you acted without evil intention. If now you married again with the object of bearing children, your sin might be forgiven. But the question is again a twofold one: firstly. . ."

But suddenly Hélène, who was getting bored, said with one of her bewitching smiles: "But I think that having espoused the true religion I cannot be bound by what a false religion laid upon me."

The director of her conscience was astounded at having the case presented to him thus with the simplicity of Columbus' egg. He was delighted at the unexpected rapidity of his pupil's progress, but could not abandon the edifice of argument he had laboriously constructed.

"Let us understand one another, Countess," said he with a smile, and began refuting his spiritual daughter's arguments.

Hélène understood that the question was very simple and easy from the ecclesiastical point of view, and that her directors were making difficulties only because they were apprehensive as to how the matter would be regarded by the secular authorities.

So she decided that it was necessary to prepare the opinion of society. She provoked the jealousy of the elderly magnate and told him what she had told her other suitor; that is, she put the matter so that the only way for him to obtain a right over her was to marry her. The elderly magnate was at first as much taken aback by this suggestion of marriage with a woman whose husband was alive, as the younger man had been, but Hélène's imperturbable conviction that it was as simple and natural as marrying a maiden had its effect on him too. Had Hélène herself shown the least sign of hesitation, shame, or secrecy, her cause would certainly have been lost; but not only did she show no signs of secrecy or shame, on the contrary, with good-natured naïveté she told her intimate friends (and these were all Petersburg) that both the prince and the magnate had proposed to her and that she loved both and was afraid of grieving either.

A rumor immediately spread in Petersburg, not that Hélène wanted to be divorced from her husband (had such a report spread many would have opposed so illegal an intention) but simply that the unfortunate and interesting Hélène was in doubt which of the two men she should marry. The question was no longer whether this was possible, but only which was the better match and how the matter would be regarded at court. There were, it is true, some rigid individuals unable to rise to the height of such a question, who saw in the project a desecration of the sacrament of marriage, but there were not many such and they remained silent, while the majority were interested in Hélène's good fortune and in the question which match would be the more advantageous. Whether it was right or wrong to remarry while one had a husband living they did not discuss, for that question had evidently been settled by people "wiser than you or me," as they said, and to doubt the correctness of that decision would be to risk exposing one's stupidity and incapacity to live in society.

Only Márya Dmítrievna Akhrosímova, who had come to Petersburg that summer to see one of her sons, allowed herself plainly to express an opinion contrary to the general one. Meeting Hélène at a ball she stopped her in the middle of the room and, amid general silence, said in her gruff voice: "So wives of living men have started marrying again! Perhaps you think you have invented a novelty? You have been forestalled, my dear! It was thought of long ago. It is done in all the brothels," and with these words Márya Dmítrievna, turning up her wide sleeves with her usual threatening gesture and glancing sternly round, moved across the room.

Though people were afraid of Márya Dmítrievna she was regarded in Petersburg as a buffoon, and so of what she had said they only noticed, and repeated in a whisper, the one coarse word she had used, supposing the whole sting of her remark to lie in that word.

Prince Vasíli, who of late very often forgot what he had said and repeated one and the same thing a hundred times, remarked to his daughter whenever he chanced to see her:

"Hélène, I have a word to say to you," and he would lead her aside, drawing her hand downward. "I have heard of certain projects concerning. . . you know. Well my dear child, you know how your father's heart rejoices to know that you. . . You have suffered so much. . . But, my dear child, consult only your own heart. That is all I have to say," and concealing his unvarying emotion he would press his cheek against his daughter's and move away.

Bilíbin, who had not lost his reputation of an exceedingly clever man, and who was one of the disinterested friends so brilliant a woman as Hélène always has—men friends who can never change into lovers— once gave her his view of the matter at a small and intimate gathering.

"Listen, Bilíbin," said Hélène (she always called friends of that sort by their surnames), and she touched his coat sleeve with her white, beringed fingers. "Tell me, as you would a sister, what I ought to do. Which of the two?"

Bilíbin wrinkled up the skin over his eyebrows and pondered, with a smile on his lips.

"You are not taking me unawares, you know," said he. "As a true friend, I have thought and thought again about your affair. You see, if you marry the prince"—he meant the younger man—and he crooked one finger, "you forever lose the chance of marrying the other, and you will displease the court besides. (You know there is some kind of connection.) But if you marry the old count you will make his last days happy, and as widow of the Grand. . . the prince would no longer be making a mésalliance by marrying you," and Bilíbin smoothed out his forehead.

"That's a true friend!" said Hélène beaming, and again touching Bilíbin's sleeve. "But I love them, you know, and don't want to distress either of them. I would give my life for the happiness of them both."

Bilíbin shrugged his shoulders, as much as to say that not even he could help in that difficulty.

"Une maîtresse-femme!* That's what is called putting things squarely. She would like to be married to all three at the same time," thought he.

"But tell me, how will your husband look at the matter?" Bilíbin asked, his reputation being so well established that he did not fear to ask so naïve a question. "Will he agree?"

"Oh, he loves me so!" said Hélène, who for some reason imagined that Pierre too loved her. "He will do anything for me."

Bilíbin puckered his skin in preparation for something witty.

"Even divorce you?" said he.

Hélène laughed.

Among those who ventured to doubt the justifiability of the proposed marriage was Hélène's mother, Princess Kurágina. She was continually tormented by jealousy of her daughter, and now that jealousy concerned a subject near to her own heart, she could not reconcile herself to the idea. She consulted a Russian priest as to the possibility of divorce and remarriage during a husband's lifetime, and the priest told her that it was impossible, and to her delight showed her a text in the Gospel which (as it seemed to him) plainly forbids remarriage while the husband is alive.

Armed with these arguments, which appeared to her unanswerable, she drove to her daughter's early one morning so as to find her alone.

Having listened to her mother's objections, Hélène smiled blandly and ironically.

"But it says plainly: 'Whosoever shall marry her that is divorced. . .'" said the old princess.

"Ah, Maman, ne dites pas de bêtises. Vous ne comprenez rien. Dans ma position j'ai des devoirs,"† said Hélène changing from Russian, in

---

* A masterly woman.
† "Oh, Mamma, don't talk nonsense! You don't understand anything. In my position I have obligations."

LEO TOLSTOY

which language she always felt that her case did not sound quite clear, into French which suited it better.

"But, my dear. . ."

"Oh, Mamma, how is it you don't understand that the Holy Father, who has the right to grant dispensations. . ."

Just then the lady companion who lived with Hélène came in to announce that His Highness was in the ballroom and wished to see her.

"Non, dites-lui que je ne veux pas le voir, que je suis furieuse contre lui, parce qu'il m'a manqué parole."*

"Comtesse, à tout péché miséricorde,"† said a fair-haired young man with a long face and nose, as he entered the room.

The old princess rose respectfully and curtsied. The young man who had entered took no notice of her. The princess nodded to her daughter and sidled out of the room.

"Yes, she is right," thought the old princess, all her convictions dissipated by the appearance of His Highness. "She is right, but how is it that we in our irrecoverable youth did not know it? Yet it is so simple," she thought as she got into her carriage.

By the beginning of August Hélène's affairs were clearly defined and she wrote a letter to her husband—who, as she imagined, loved her very much—informing him of her intention to marry N.N. and of her having embraced the one true faith, and asking him to carry out all the formalities necessary for a divorce, which would be explained to him by the bearer of the letter.

And so I pray God to have you, my friend, in His holy and powerful keeping—Your friend Hélène.

This letter was brought to Pierre's house when he was on the field of Borodinó.

---

* "No, tell him I don't wish to see him, I am furious with him for not keeping his word to me."

† "Countess, there is mercy for every sin."

# VIII

Toward the end of the battle of Borodinó, Pierre, having run down from Raévski's battery a second time, made his way through a gully to Knyazkóvo with a crowd of soldiers, reached the dressing station, and seeing blood and hearing cries and groans hurried on, still entangled in the crowds of soldiers.

The one thing he now desired with his whole soul was to get away quickly from the terrible sensations amid which he had lived that day and return to ordinary conditions of life and sleep quietly in a room in his own bed. He felt that only in the ordinary conditions of life would he be able to understand himself and all he had seen and felt. But such ordinary conditions of life were nowhere to be found.

Though shells and bullets did not whistle over the road along which he was going, still on all sides there was what there had been on the field of battle. There were still the same suffering, exhausted, and sometimes strangely indifferent faces, the same blood, the same soldiers' overcoats, the same sounds of firing which, though distant now, still aroused terror, and besides this there were the foul air and the dust.

Having gone a couple of miles along the Mozháysk road, Pierre sat down by the roadside.

Dusk had fallen, and the roar of guns died away. Pierre lay leaning on his elbow for a long time, gazing at the shadows that moved past him in the darkness. He was continually imagining that a cannon ball was flying toward him with a terrific whizz, and then he shuddered and sat up. He had no idea how long he had been there. In the middle of the night three soldiers, having brought some firewood, settled down near him and began lighting a fire.

The soldiers, who threw sidelong glances at Pierre, got the fire to burn and placed an iron pot on it into which they broke some dried bread and put a little dripping. The pleasant odor of greasy viands mingled with the smell of smoke. Pierre sat up and sighed. The three soldiers were eating and talking among themselves, taking no notice of him.

"And who may you be?" one of them suddenly asked Pierre, evidently meaning what Pierre himself had in mind, namely: "If you want to eat we'll give you some food, only let us know whether you are an honest man."

"I, I . . ." said Pierre, feeling it necessary to minimize his social position as much as possible so as to be nearer to the soldiers and better understood by them. "By rights I am a militia officer, but my men are not here. I came to the battle and have lost them."

"There now!" said one of the soldiers.

Another shook his head.

"Would you like a little mash?" the first soldier asked, and handed Pierre a wooden spoon after licking it clean.

Pierre sat down by the fire and began eating the mash, as they called the food in the cauldron, and he thought it more delicious than any food he had ever tasted. As he sat bending greedily over it, helping himself to large spoonfuls and chewing one after another, his face was lit up by the fire and the soldiers looked at him in silence.

"Where have you to go to? Tell us!" said one of them.

"To Mozháysk."

"You're a gentleman, aren't you?"

"Yes."

"And what's your name?"

"Peter Kirílych."

"Well then, Peter Kirílych, come along with us, we'll take you there."

In the total darkness the soldiers walked with Pierre to Mozháysk.

By the time they got near Mozháysk and began ascending the steep hill into the town, the cocks were already crowing. Pierre went on with the soldiers, quite forgetting that his inn was at the bottom of the hill and that he had already passed it. He would not soon have remembered this, such was his state of forgetfulness, had he not halfway up the hill stumbled upon his groom, who had been to look for him in the town and was returning to the inn. The groom recognized Pierre in the darkness by his white hat.

"Your excellency!" he said. "Why, we were beginning to despair! How is it you are on foot? And where are you going, please?"

"Oh, yes!" said Pierre.

The soldiers stopped.

"So you've found your folk?" said one of them. "Well, good-by, Peter Kirílych—isn't it?"

"Good-by, Peter Kirílych!" Pierre heard the other voices repeat.

"Good-by!" he said and turned with his groom toward the inn.

"I ought to give them something!" he thought, and felt in his pocket. "No, better not!" said another, inner voice.

There was not a room to be had at the inn, they were all occupied. Pierre went out into the yard and, covering himself up head and all, lay down in his carriage.

# IX

Scarcely had Pierre laid his head on the pillow before he felt himself falling asleep, but suddenly, almost with the distinctness of reality, he heard the boom, boom, boom of firing, the thud of projectiles, groans and cries, and smelled blood and powder, and a feeling of horror and dread of death seized him. Filled with fright he opened his eyes and lifted his head from under his cloak. All was tranquil in the yard. Only someone's orderly passed through the gateway, splashing through the mud, and talked to the innkeeper. Above Pierre's head some pigeons, disturbed by the movement he had made in sitting up, fluttered under the dark roof of the penthouse. The whole courtyard was permeated by a strong peaceful smell of stable yards, delightful to Pierre at that moment. He could see the clear starry sky between the dark roofs of two penthouses.

"Thank God, there is no more of that!" he thought, covering up his head again. "Oh, what a terrible thing is fear, and how shamefully I yielded to it! But they. . . they were steady and calm all the time, to the end. . ." thought he.

They, in Pierre's mind, were the soldiers, those who had been at the battery, those who had given him food, and those who had prayed before the icon. They, those strange men he had not previously known, stood out clearly and sharply from everyone else.

"To be a soldier, just a soldier!" thought Pierre as he fell asleep, "to enter communal life completely, to be imbued by what makes them what they are. But how to cast off all the superfluous, devilish burden of my outer man? There was a time when I could have done it. I could have run away from my father, as I wanted to. Or I might have been sent to serve as a soldier after the duel with Dólokhov." And the memory of the dinner at the English Club when he had challenged Dólokhov flashed through Pierre's mind, and then he remembered his benefactor at Torzhók. And now a picture of a solemn meeting of the lodge presented itself to his mind. It was taking place at the English Club and someone near and dear to him sat at the end of the table. "Yes, that is he! It is my benefactor. But he died!" thought Pierre. "Yes, he died, and I did not know he was alive. How sorry I am that he died, and how glad I am that he is alive again!" On one side of the table sat Anatole, Dólokhov, Nesvítski, Denísov, and others like them (in his dream the category to which these men belonged was as clearly defined in his mind as the category of those he termed they), and he heard those people, Anatole and Dólokhov, shouting and singing loudly; yet through their shouting the voice of his benefactor was heard speaking all the time and the sound of his words was as weighty and uninterrupted as the booming on the battlefield, but pleasant and comforting. Pierre did not understand what his benefactor was saying, but he knew (the categories of thoughts were also quite distinct in his dream) that he was talking of goodness and the possibility of being what they were. And they with their simple, kind, firm faces surrounded his benefactor on all sides. But though they were kindly they did not look at Pierre and did not know him. Wishing to speak and to attract their attention, he got up, but at that moment his legs grew cold and bare.

He felt ashamed, and with one arm covered his legs from which his cloak had in fact slipped. For a moment as he was rearranging his cloak Pierre opened his eyes and saw the same penthouse roofs, posts, and yard, but now they were all bluish, lit up, and glittering with frost or dew.

"It is dawn," thought Pierre. "But that's not what I want. I want to hear and understand my benefactor's words." Again he covered himself up with his cloak, but now neither the lodge nor his benefactor was there. There were only thoughts clearly expressed in words, thoughts that someone was uttering or that he himself was formulating.

Afterwards when he recalled those thoughts Pierre was convinced that someone outside himself had spoken them, though the impressions of that day had evoked them. He had never, it seemed to him, been able to think and express his thoughts like that when awake.

"To endure war is the most difficult subordination of man's freedom to the law of God," the voice had said. "Simplicity is submission to the will of God; you cannot escape from Him. And they are simple. They do not talk, but act. The spoken word is silver but the unspoken is golden. Man can be master of nothing while he fears death, but he who does not fear it possesses all. If there were no suffering, man would not know his limitations, would not know himself. The hardest thing (Pierre went on thinking, or hearing, in his dream) is to be able in your soul to unite the meaning of all. To unite all?" he asked himself. "No, not to unite. Thoughts cannot be united, but to harness all these thoughts together is what we need! Yes, one must harness them, must harness them!" he repeated to himself with inward rapture, feeling that these words and they alone expressed what he wanted to say and solved the question that tormented him.

"Yes, one must harness, it is time to harness."

"Time to harness, time to harness, your excellency! Your excellency!" some voice was repeating. "We must harness, it is time to harness. . ."

It was the voice of the groom, trying to wake him. The sun shone straight into Pierre's face. He glanced at the dirty innyard in the middle of which soldiers were watering their lean horses at the pump while carts were passing out of the gate. Pierre turned away with repugnance, and closing his eyes quickly fell back on the carriage seat. "No, I don't want that, I don't want to see and understand that. I want to understand what was revealing itself to me in my dream. One second more and I should have understood it all! But what am I to do? Harness, but how can I harness everything?" and Pierre felt with horror that the meaning of all he had seen and thought in the dream had been destroyed.

The groom, the coachman, and the innkeeper told Pierre that an officer had come with news that the French were already near Mozháysk and that our men were leaving it.

Pierre got up and, having told them to harness and overtake him, went on foot through the town.

The troops were moving on, leaving about ten thousand wounded behind them. There were wounded in the yards, at the windows of the houses, and the streets were crowded with them. In the streets, around carts that were to take some of the wounded away, shouts, curses, and blows could be heard. Pierre offered the use of his carriage, which had overtaken him, to a wounded general he knew, and drove with him to Moscow. On the way Pierre was told of the death of his brother-in-law Anatole and of that of Prince Andrew.

# X

O n the thirtieth of August Pierre reached Moscow. Close to the gates of the city he was met by Count Rostopchín's adjutant.

"We have been looking for you everywhere," said the adjutant. "The count wants to see you particularly. He asks you to come to him at once on a very important matter."

Without going home, Pierre took a cab and drove to see the Moscow commander in chief.

Count Rostopchín had only that morning returned to town from his summer villa at Sokólniki. The anteroom and reception room of his house were full of officials who had been summoned or had come for orders. Vasílchikov and Plátov had already seen the count and explained to him that it was impossible to defend Moscow and that it would have to be surrendered. Though this news was being concealed from the inhabitants, the officials—the heads of the various government departments—knew that Moscow would soon be in the enemy's hands, just as Count Rostopchín himself knew it, and to escape personal responsibility they had all come to the governor to ask how they were to deal with their various departments.

As Pierre was entering the reception room a courier from the army came out of Rostopchín's private room.

In answer to questions with which he was greeted, the courier made a despairing gesture with his hand and passed through the room.

While waiting in the reception room Pierre with weary eyes watched the various officials, old and young, military and civilian, who were there. They all seemed dissatisfied and uneasy. Pierre went up to a group of men, one of whom he knew. After greeting Pierre they continued their conversation.

"If they're sent out and brought back again later on it will do no harm, but as things are now one can't answer for anything."

"But you see what he writes. . ." said another, pointing to a printed sheet he held in his hand.

"That's another matter. That's necessary for the people," said the first.

"What is it?" asked Pierre.

"Oh, it's a fresh broadsheet."

Pierre took it and began reading.

His Serene Highness has passed through Mozháysk in order to join up with the troops moving toward him and has taken up a strong position where the enemy will not soon attack him. Forty-eight guns with ammunition have been sent him from here, and his Serene Highness says he will defend Moscow to the last drop of blood and is even ready to fight in the streets. Do not be upset, brothers, that the law courts are closed; things have to be put in order, and we will deal with villains in our own way! When the time comes I shall want both town and peasant lads and will raise the cry a day or two beforehand, but they are not wanted yet so I hold my peace. An ax will be useful, a hunting spear not bad, but a three-pronged fork will be best of all: a Frenchman is no heavier than a sheaf of rye. Tomorrow after dinner I shall take the Iberian icon of the Mother of God to the wounded in the Catherine Hospital where we will have some water blessed. That will help them to get well quicker. I, too, am well now: one of my eyes was sore but now I am on the lookout with both.

"But military men have told me that it is impossible to fight in the town," said Pierre, "and that the position. . ."

"Well, of course! That's what we were saying," replied the first speaker.

"And what does he mean by 'One of my eyes was sore but now I am on the lookout with both'?" asked Pierre.

"The count had a sty," replied the adjutant smiling, "and was very much upset when I told him people had come to ask what was the matter with him. By the by, Count," he added suddenly, addressing Pierre with a smile, "we heard that you have family troubles and that the countess, your wife. . ."

"I have heard nothing," Pierre replied unconcernedly. "But what have you heard?"

"Oh, well, you know people often invent things. I only say what I heard."

"But what did you hear?"

"Well, they say," continued the adjutant with the same smile, "that the countess, your wife, is preparing to go abroad. I expect it's nonsense. . ."

"Possibly," remarked Pierre, looking about him absent-mindedly. "And who is that?" he asked, indicating a short old man in a clean blue peasant overcoat, with a big snow-white beard and eyebrows and a ruddy face.

"He? That's a tradesman, that is to say, he's the restaurant keeper, Vereshchágin. Perhaps you have heard of that affair with the proclamation."

"Oh, so that is Vereshchágin!" said Pierre, looking at the firm, calm face of the old man and seeking any indication of his being a traitor.

"That's not he himself, that's the father of the fellow who wrote the proclamation," said the adjutant. "The young man is in prison and I expect it will go hard with him."

An old gentleman wearing a star and another official, a German wearing a cross round his neck, approached the speaker.

"It's a complicated story, you know," said the adjutant. "That proclamation appeared about two months ago. The count was informed of it. He gave orders to investigate the matter. Gabriel Ivánovich here made the inquiries. The proclamation had passed through exactly sixty-three hands. He asked one, 'From whom did you get it?' 'From so-and-so.' He went to the next one. 'From whom did you get it?' and so on till he reached Vereshchágin, a half educated tradesman, you know, 'a pet of a trader,'" said the adjutant smiling. "They asked him, 'Who gave it you?' And the point is that we knew whom he had it from. He could only have had it from the Postmaster. But evidently they had come to some understanding. He replied: 'From no one; I made it up myself.' They threatened and questioned him, but he stuck to that: 'I made it up myself.' And so it was reported to the count, who sent for the man. 'From whom did you get the proclamation?' 'I wrote it myself.' Well, you know the count," said the adjutant cheerfully, with a smile of pride, "he flared up dreadfully—and just think of the fellow's audacity, lying, and obstinacy!"

"And the count wanted him to say it was from Klyucharëv? I understand!" said Pierre.

"Not at all," rejoined the adjutant in dismay. "Klyucharëv had his own sins to answer for without that and that is why he has been banished. But the point is that the count was much annoyed. 'How could you have written it yourself?' said he, and he took up the Hamburg Gazette that was lying on the table. 'Here it is! You did not write it yourself but translated it, and translated it abominably, because you don't even know French, you fool.' And what do you think? 'No,' said he, 'I have not read any papers, I made it up myself.' 'If that's so, you're a traitor and I'll have you tried, and you'll be hanged! Say from whom you had it.' 'I have seen no papers, I made it up myself.' And that was the end of it. The count had the father fetched, but the fellow stuck to it. He was sent for trial and condemned to hard labor, I believe. Now the father has come to intercede for him. But he's a good-for-nothing lad! You know that sort of tradesman's son, a dandy and lady-killer. He attended some lectures somewhere and imagines that the devil is no match for him. That's the sort of fellow he is. His father keeps a cookshop here by the Stone Bridge, and you know there was a large icon of God Almighty painted with a scepter in one hand and an orb in the other. Well, he took that icon home with him for a few days and what did he do? He found some scoundrel of a painter. . ."

# XI

In the middle of this fresh tale Pierre was summoned to the commander in chief.

When he entered the private room Count Rostopchín, puckering his face, was rubbing his forehead and eyes with his hand. A short man was saying something, but when Pierre entered he stopped speaking and went out.

"Ah, how do you do, great warrior?" said Rostopchín as soon as the short man had left the room. "We have heard of your prowess. But that's not the point. Between ourselves, mon cher, do you belong to the Masons?" he went on severely, as though there were something wrong about it which he nevertheless intended to pardon. Pierre remained silent. "I am well informed, my friend, but I am aware that there are Masons and I hope that you are not one of those who on pretense of saving mankind wish to ruin Russia."

"Yes, I am a Mason," Pierre replied.

"There, you see, mon cher! I expect you know that Messrs. Speránski and Magnítski have been deported to their proper place. Mr. Klyucharëv has been treated in the same way, and so have others who on the plea of building up the temple of Solomon have tried to destroy the temple of their fatherland. You can understand that there are reasons for this and that I could not have exiled the Postmaster had he not been a harmful person. It has now come to my knowledge that you lent him your carriage for his removal from town, and that you have even accepted papers from him for safe custody. I like you and don't wish you any harm and—as you are only half my age—I advise you, as a father would, to cease all communication with men of that stamp and to leave here as soon as possible."

"But what did Klyucharëv do wrong, Count?" asked Pierre.

"That is for me to know, but not for you to ask," shouted Rostopchín.

"If he is accused of circulating Napoleon's proclamation it is not proved that he did so," said Pierre without looking at Rostopchín, "and Vereshchágin. . ."

"There we are!" Rostopchín shouted at Pierre louder than before, frowning suddenly. "Vereshchágin is a renegade and a traitor who will be punished as he deserves," said he with the vindictive heat with which people speak when recalling an insult. "But I did not summon you to discuss my actions, but to give you advice—or an order if you prefer it. I beg you to leave the town and break off all communication with such men as Klyucharëv. And I will knock the nonsense out of anybody"— but probably realizing that he was shouting at Bezúkhov who so far was not guilty of anything, he added, taking Pierre's hand in a friendly manner, "We are on the eve of a public disaster and I haven't time to be polite to everybody who has business with me. My head is sometimes in a whirl. Well, mon cher, what are you doing personally?"

"Why, nothing," answered Pierre without raising his eyes or changing the thoughtful expression of his face.

The count frowned.

"A word of friendly advice, mon cher. Be off as soon as you can, that's all I have to tell you. Happy he who has ears to hear. Good-by, my dear fellow. Oh, by the by!" he shouted through the doorway after Pierre, "is it true that the countess has fallen into the clutches of the holy fathers of the Society of Jesus?"

Pierre did not answer and left Rostopchín's room more sullen and angry than he had ever before shown himself.

When he reached home it was already getting dark. Some eight people had come to see him that evening: the secretary of a committee, the colonel of his battalion, his steward, his major-domo, and various petitioners. They all had business with Pierre and wanted decisions from him. Pierre did not understand and was not interested in any of these questions and only answered them in order to get rid of these people. When left alone at last he opened and read his wife's letter.

"They, the soldiers at the battery, Prince Andrew killed. . . that old man. . . Simplicity is submission to God. Suffering is necessary. . . the meaning of all. . . one must harness. . . my wife is getting married. . . One must forget and understand. . ." And going to his bed he threw himself on it without undressing and immediately fell asleep.

When he awoke next morning the major-domo came to inform him that a special messenger, a police officer, had come from Count Rostopchín to know whether Count Bezúkhov had left or was leaving the town.

A dozen persons who had business with Pierre were awaiting him in the drawing room. Pierre dressed hurriedly and, instead of going to see them, went to the back porch and out through the gate.

From that time till the end of the destruction of Moscow no one of Bezúkhov's household, despite all the search they made, saw Pierre again or knew where he was.

# XII

The Rostóvs remained in Moscow till the first of September, that is, till the eve of the enemy's entry into the city.

After Pétya had joined Obolénski's regiment of Cossacks and left for Bélaya Tsérkov where that regiment was forming, the countess was seized with terror. The thought that both her sons were at the war, had both gone from under her wing, that today or tomorrow either or both of them might be killed like the three sons of one of her acquaintances, struck her that summer for the first time with cruel clearness. She tried to get Nicholas back and wished to go herself to join Pétya, or to get him an appointment somewhere in Petersburg, but neither of these proved possible. Pétya could not return unless his regiment did so or unless he was transferred to another regiment on active service. Nicholas was somewhere with the army and had not sent a word since his last letter, in which he had given a detailed account of his meeting with Princess Mary. The countess did not sleep at night, or when she did fall asleep dreamed that she saw her sons lying dead. After many consultations and conversations, the count at last devised means to tranquillize her. He got Pétya transferred from Obolénski's regiment to Bezúkhov's, which was in training near Moscow. Though Pétya would remain in the service, this transfer would give the countess the consolation of seeing at least one of her sons under her wing, and she hoped to arrange matters for her Pétya so as not to let him go again, but always get him appointed to places where he could not possibly take part in a battle. As long as Nicholas alone was in danger the countess imagined that she loved her first-born more than all her other children and even reproached herself for it; but when her youngest: the scapegrace who had been bad at lessons, was always breaking things in the house and making himself a nuisance to everybody, that snub-nosed Pétya with his merry black eyes and fresh rosy cheeks where soft down was just beginning to show—when he was thrown amid those big, dreadful, cruel men who were fighting somewhere about something and apparently finding pleasure in it—then his mother thought she loved him more, much more, than all her other children. The nearer the time came for Pétya to return, the more uneasy grew the countess. She began to think she would never live to see such happiness. The presence of Sónya, of her beloved Natásha, or even of her husband irritated her. "What do I want with them? I want no one but Pétya," she thought.

At the end of August the Rostóvs received another letter from Nicholas. He wrote from the province of Vorónezh where he had been sent to procure remounts, but that letter did not set the countess at ease. Knowing that one son was out of danger she became the more anxious about Pétya.

Though by the twentieth of August nearly all the Rostóvs' acquaintances had left Moscow, and though everybody tried to persuade the countess to get away as quickly as possible, she would not hear of leaving before her treasure, her adored Pétya, returned. On the twenty-eighth of August he arrived. The passionate tenderness with which his mother received him did not please the sixteen-year-old officer. Though she concealed from him her intention of keeping him under her wing, Pétya guessed her designs, and instinctively fearing that he might give way to emotion when with her—might "become womanish" as he termed it to himself—he treated her coldly, avoided her, and during his stay in Moscow attached himself exclusively to Natásha for whom he had always had a particularly brotherly tenderness, almost lover-like.

Owing to the count's customary carelessness nothing was ready for their departure by the twenty-eighth of August and the carts that were to come from their Ryazán and Moscow estates to remove their household belongings did not arrive till the thirtieth.

From the twenty-eighth till the thirty-first all Moscow was in a bustle and commotion. Every day thousands of men wounded at Borodinó were brought in by the Dorogomílov gate and taken to various parts of Moscow, and thousands of carts conveyed the inhabitants and their possessions out by the other gates. In spite of Rostopchín's broadsheets, or because of them or independently of them, the strangest and most contradictory rumors were current in the town. Some said that no one was to be allowed to leave the city, others on the contrary said that all the icons had been taken out of the churches and everybody was to be ordered to leave. Some said there had been another battle after Borodinó at which the French had been routed, while others on the contrary reported that the Russian army had been destroyed. Some talked about the Moscow militia which, preceded by the clergy, would go to the Three Hills; others whispered that Augustin had been forbidden to leave, that traitors had been seized, that the peasants were rioting and robbing people on their way from Moscow, and so on. But all this was only talk; in reality (though the Council of Filí, at which it was decided to abandon Moscow, had not yet been held) both those who went away and those who remained behind felt, though they did not show it, that Moscow would certainly be abandoned, and that they ought to get away as quickly as possible and save their belongings. It was felt that everything would suddenly break up and change, but up to the first of September nothing had done so. As a criminal who is being led to execution knows that he must die immediately, but yet looks about him and straightens the cap that is awry on his head, so Moscow involuntarily continued its wonted life, though it knew that the time of its destruction was near when the conditions of life to which its people were accustomed to submit would be completely upset.

During the three days preceding the occupation of Moscow the whole Rostóv family was absorbed in various activities. The head of the family, Count Ilyá Rostóv, continually drove about the city collecting the current rumors from all sides and gave superficial and hasty orders at home about the preparations for their departure.

The countess watched the things being packed, was dissatisfied with everything, was constantly in pursuit of Pétya who was always running away from her, and was jealous of Natásha with whom he spent all his time. Sónya alone directed the practical side of matters by getting things packed. But of late Sónya had been particularly sad and silent. Nicholas' letter in which he mentioned Princess Mary had elicited, in her presence, joyous comments from the countess, who saw an intervention of Providence in this meeting of the princess and Nicholas.

"I was never pleased at Bolkónski's engagement to Natásha," said the countess, "but I always wanted Nicholas to marry the princess, and had a presentiment that it would happen. What a good thing it would be!"

Sónya felt that this was true: that the only possibility of retrieving the Rostóvs' affairs was by Nicholas marrying a rich woman, and that the princess was a good match. It was very bitter for her. But despite her grief, or perhaps just because of it, she took on herself all the difficult work of directing the storing and packing of their things and was busy for whole days. The count and countess turned to her when they had any orders to give. Pétya and Natásha on the contrary, far from helping their parents, were generally a nuisance and a hindrance to everyone. Almost all day long the house resounded with their running feet, their cries, and their spontaneous laughter. They laughed and were gay not because there was any reason to laugh, but because gaiety and mirth were in their hearts and so everything that happened was a cause for gaiety and laughter to them. Pétya was in high spirits because having left home a boy he had returned (as everybody told him) a fine young man, because he was at home, because he had left Bélaya Tsérkov where there was no hope of soon taking part in a battle and had come to Moscow where there was to be fighting in a few days, and chiefly because Natásha, whose lead he always followed, was in high spirits. Natásha was gay because she had been sad too long and now nothing reminded her of the cause of her sadness, and because she was feeling well. She was also happy because she had someone to adore her: the adoration of others was a lubricant the wheels of her machine needed to make them run freely—and Pétya adored her. Above all, they were gay because there was a war near Moscow, there would be fighting at the town gates, arms were being given out, everybody was escaping—going away somewhere, and in general something extraordinary was happening, and that is always exciting, especially to the young.

# XIII

On Saturday, the thirty-first of August, everything in the Rostóvs' house seemed topsy-turvy. All the doors were open, all the furniture was being carried out or moved about, and the mirrors and pictures had been taken down. There were trunks in the rooms, and hay, wrapping paper, and ropes were scattered about. The peasants and house serfs carrying out the things were treading heavily on the parquet floors. The yard was crowded with peasant carts, some loaded high and already corded up, others still empty.

The voices and footsteps of the many servants and of the peasants who had come with the carts resounded as they shouted to one another in the yard and in the house. The count had been out since morning. The countess had a headache brought on by all the noise and turmoil and was lying down in the new sitting room with a vinegar compress on her head. Pétya was not at home, he had gone to visit a friend with whom he meant to obtain a transfer from the militia to the active army. Sónya was in the ballroom looking after the packing of the glass and china. Natásha was sitting on the floor of her dismantled room with dresses, ribbons, and scarves strewn all about her, gazing fixedly at the floor and holding in her hands the old ball dress (already out of fashion) which she had worn at her first Petersburg ball.

Natásha was ashamed of doing nothing when everyone else was so busy, and several times that morning had tried to set to work, but her heart was not in it, and she could not and did not know how to do anything except with all her heart and all her might. For a while she had stood beside Sónya while the china was being packed and tried to help, but soon gave it up and went to her room to pack her own things. At first she found it amusing to give away dresses and ribbons to the maids, but when that was done and what was left had still to be packed, she found it dull.

"Dunyásha, you pack! You will, won't you, dear?" And when Dunyásha willingly promised to do it all for her, Natásha sat down on the floor, took her old ball dress, and fell into a reverie quite unrelated to what ought to have occupied her thoughts now. She was roused from her reverie by the talk of the maids in the next room (which was theirs) and by the sound of their hurried footsteps going to the back porch. Natásha got up and looked out of the window. An enormously long row of carts full of wounded men had stopped in the street.

The housekeeper, the old nurse, the cooks, coachmen, maids, footmen, postilions, and scullions stood at the gate, staring at the wounded.

Natásha, throwing a clean pocket handkerchief over her hair and holding an end of it in each hand, went out into the street.

The former housekeeper, old Mávra Kuzmínichna, had stepped out of the crowd by the gate, gone up to a cart with a hood constructed of bast mats, and was speaking to a pale young officer who lay inside. Natásha moved a few steps forward and stopped shyly, still holding her handkerchief, and listened to what the housekeeper was saying.

"Then you have nobody in Moscow?" she was saying. "You would be more comfortable somewhere in a house. . . in ours, for instance. . . the family are leaving."

"I don't know if it would be allowed," replied the officer in a weak voice. "Here is our commanding officer. . . ask him," and he pointed to a stout major who was walking back along the street past the row of carts.

Natásha glanced with frightened eyes at the face of the wounded officer and at once went to meet the major.

"May the wounded men stay in our house?" she asked.

The major raised his hand to his cap with a smile.

"Which one do you want, Ma'am'selle?" said he, screwing up his eyes and smiling.

Natásha quietly repeated her question, and her face and whole manner were so serious, though she was still holding the ends of her handkerchief, that the major ceased smiling and after some reflection— as if considering in how far the thing was possible—replied in the affirmative.

"Oh yes, why not? They may," he said.

With a slight inclination of her head, Natásha stepped back quickly to Mávra Kuzmínichna, who stood talking compassionately to the officer.

"They may. He says they may!" whispered Natásha.

The cart in which the officer lay was turned into the Rostóvs' yard, and dozens of carts with wounded men began at the invitation of the townsfolk to turn into the yards and to draw up at the entrances of the houses in Povarskáya Street. Natásha was evidently pleased to be dealing with new people outside the ordinary routine of her life. She and Mávra Kuzmínichna tried to get as many of the wounded as possible into their yard.

"Your Papa must be told, though," said Mávra Kuzmínichna.

"Never mind, never mind, what does it matter? For one day we can move into the drawing room. They can have all our half of the house."

"There now, young lady, you do take things into your head! Even if we put them into the wing, the men's room, or the nurse's room, we must ask permission."

"Well, I'll ask."

Natásha ran into the house and went on tiptoe through the half-open door into the sitting room, where there was a smell of vinegar and Hoffman's drops.

"Are you asleep, Mamma?"

"Oh, what sleep—?" said the countess, waking up just as she was dropping into a doze.

"Mamma darling!" said Natásha, kneeling by her mother and bringing her face close to her mother's, "I am sorry, forgive me, I'll never do it again; I woke you up! Mávra Kuzmínichna has sent me: they have brought some wounded here—officers. Will you let them come? They have nowhere to go. I knew you'd let them come!" she said quickly all in one breath.

"What officers? Whom have they brought? I don't understand anything about it," said the countess.

Natásha laughed, and the countess too smiled slightly.

"I knew you'd give permission... so I'll tell them," and, having kissed her mother, Natásha got up and went to the door.

In the hall she met her father, who had returned with bad news.

"We've stayed too long!" said the count with involuntary vexation. "The Club is closed and the police are leaving."

"Papa, is it all right—I've invited some of the wounded into the house?" said Natásha.

"Of course it is," he answered absently. "That's not the point. I beg you not to indulge in trifles now, but to help to pack, and tomorrow we must go, go, go! . . ."

And the count gave a similar order to the major-domo and the servants.

At dinner Pétya having returned home told them the news he had heard. He said the people had been getting arms in the Krémlin, and that though Rostopchín's broadsheet had said that he would sound a call two or three days in advance, the order had certainly already been given for everyone to go armed to the Three Hills tomorrow, and that there would be a big battle there.

The countess looked with timid horror at her son's eager, excited face as he said this. She realized that if she said a word about his not going to the battle (she knew he enjoyed the thought of the impending engagement) he would say something about men, honor, and the fatherland—something senseless, masculine, and obstinate which there would be no contradicting, and her plans would be spoiled; and so, hoping to arrange to leave before then and take Pétya with her as their protector and defender, she did not answer him, but after dinner called the count aside and implored him with tears to take her away quickly, that very night if possible. With a woman's involuntary loving cunning she, who till then had not shown any alarm, said that she would die of fright if they did not leave that very night. Without any pretense she was now afraid of everything.

# XIV

Madame Schoss, who had been out to visit her daughter, increased the countess' fears still more by telling what she had seen at a spirit dealer's in Myasnítski Street. When returning by that street she had been unable to pass because of a drunken crowd rioting in front of the shop. She had taken a cab and driven home by a side street and the cabman had told her that the people were breaking open the barrels at the drink store, having received orders to do so.

After dinner the whole Rostóv household set to work with enthusiastic haste packing their belongings and preparing for their departure. The old count, suddenly setting to work, kept passing from the yard to the house and back again, shouting confused instructions to the hurrying people, and flurrying them still more. Pétya directed things in the yard. Sónya, owing to the count's contradictory orders, lost her head and did not know what to do. The servants ran noisily about the house and yard, shouting and disputing. Natásha, with the ardor characteristic of all she did suddenly set to work too. At first her intervention in the business of packing was received skeptically. Everybody expected some prank from her and did not wish to obey her; but she resolutely and passionately demanded obedience, grew angry and nearly cried because they did not heed her, and at last succeeded in making them believe her. Her first exploit, which cost her immense effort and established her authority, was the packing of the carpets. The count had valuable Gobelin tapestries and Persian carpets in the house. When Natásha set to work two cases were standing open in the ballroom, one almost full up with crockery, the other with carpets. There was also much china standing on the tables, and still more was being brought in from the storeroom. A third case was needed and servants had gone to fetch it.

"Sónya, wait a bit—we'll pack everything into these," said Natásha.

"You can't, Miss, we have tried to," said the butler's assistant.

"No, wait a minute, please."

And Natásha began rapidly taking out of the case dishes and plates wrapped in paper.

"The dishes must go in here among the carpets," said she.

"Why, it's a mercy if we can get the carpets alone into three cases," said the butler's assistant.

"Oh, wait, please!" And Natásha began rapidly and deftly sorting out the things. "These aren't needed," said she, putting aside some plates of Kiev ware. "These—yes, these must go among the carpets," she said, referring to the Saxony china dishes.

"Don't, Natásha! Leave it alone! We'll get it all packed," urged Sónya reproachfully.

"What a young lady she is!" remarked the major-domo.

But Natásha would not give in. She turned everything out and began quickly repacking, deciding that the inferior Russian carpets and unnecessary crockery should not be taken at all. When everything had been taken out of the cases, they recommenced packing, and it turned out that when the cheaper things not worth taking had nearly all been rejected, the valuable ones really did all go into the two cases. Only the lid of the case containing the carpets would not shut down. A few more things might have been taken out, but Natásha insisted on having her own way. She packed, repacked, pressed, made the butler's assistant and Pétya—whom she had drawn into the business of packing—press on the lid, and made desperate efforts herself.

"That's enough, Natásha," said Sónya. "I see you were right, but just take out the top one."

"I won't!" cried Natásha, with one hand holding back the hair that hung over her perspiring face, while with the other she pressed down the carpets. "Now press, Pétya! Press, Vasílich, press hard!" she cried.

The carpets yielded and the lid closed; Natásha, clapping her hands, screamed with delight and tears fell from her eyes. But this only lasted a moment. She at once set to work afresh and they now trusted her completely. The count was not angry even when they told him that Natásha had countermanded an order of his, and the servants now came to her to ask whether a cart was sufficiently loaded, and whether it might be corded up. Thanks to Natásha's directions the work now went on expeditiously, unnecessary things were left, and the most valuable packed as compactly as possible.

But hard as they all worked till quite late that night, they could not get everything packed. The countess had fallen asleep and the count, having put off their departure till next morning, went to bed.

Sónya and Natásha slept in the sitting room without undressing.

That night another wounded man was driven down the Povarskáya, and Mávra Kuzmínichna, who was standing at the gate, had him brought into the Rostóvs' yard. Mávra Kuzmínichna concluded that he was a very important man. He was being conveyed in a calèche with a raised hood, and was quite covered by an apron. On the box beside the driver sat a venerable old attendant. A doctor and two soldiers followed the carriage in a cart.

"Please come in here. The masters are going away and the whole house will be empty," said the old woman to the old attendant.

"Well, perhaps," said he with a sigh. "We don't expect to get him home alive! We have a house of our own in Moscow, but it's a long way from here, and there's nobody living in it."

"Do us the honor to come in, there's plenty of everything in the master's house. Come in," said Mávra Kuzmínichna. "Is he very ill?" she asked.

The attendant made a hopeless gesture.

"We don't expect to get him home! We must ask the doctor."

And the old servant got down from the box and went up to the cart.

"All right!" said the doctor.

The old servant returned to the calèche, looked into it, shook his head disconsolately, told the driver to turn into the yard, and stopped beside Mávra Kuzmínichna.

"O, Lord Jesus Christ!" she murmured.

She invited them to take the wounded man into the house.

"The masters won't object. . ." she said.

But they had to avoid carrying the man upstairs, and so they took him into the wing and put him in the room that had been Madame Schoss'.

This wounded man was Prince Andrew Bolkónski.

# XV

Moscow's last day had come. It was a clear bright autumn day, a Sunday. The church bells everywhere were ringing for service, just as usual on Sundays. Nobody seemed yet to realize what awaited the city.

Only two things indicated the social condition of Moscow—the rabble, that is the poor people, and the price of commodities. An enormous crowd of factory hands, house serfs, and peasants, with whom some officials, seminarists, and gentry were mingled, had gone early that morning to the Three Hills. Having waited there for Rostopchín who did not turn up, they became convinced that Moscow would be surrendered, and then dispersed all about the town to the public houses and cookshops. Prices too that day indicated the state of affairs. The price of weapons, of gold, of carts and horses, kept rising, but the value of paper money and city articles kept falling, so that by midday there were instances of carters removing valuable goods, such as cloth, and receiving in payment a half of what they carted, while peasant horses were fetching five hundred rubles each, and furniture, mirrors, and bronzes were being given away for nothing.

In the Rostóvs' staid old-fashioned house the dissolution of former conditions of life was but little noticeable. As to the serfs the only indication was that three out of their huge retinue disappeared during the night, but nothing was stolen; and as to the value of their possessions, the thirty peasant carts that had come in from their estates and which many people envied proved to be extremely valuable and they were offered enormous sums of money for them. Not only were huge sums offered for the horses and carts, but on the previous evening and early in the morning of the first of September, orderlies and servants sent by wounded officers came to the Rostóvs' and wounded men dragged themselves there from the Rostóvs' and from neighboring houses where they were accommodated, entreating the servants to try to get them a lift out of Moscow. The major-domo to whom these entreaties were addressed, though he was sorry for the wounded, resolutely refused, saying that he dare not even mention the matter to the count. Pity these wounded men as one might, it was evident that if they were given one cart there would be no reason to refuse another, or all the carts and one's own carriages as well. Thirty carts could not save all the wounded and in the general catastrophe one could not disregard oneself and one's own family. So thought the major-domo on his master's behalf.

On waking up that morning Count Ilyá Rostóv left his bedroom softly, so as not to wake the countess who had fallen asleep only toward morning, and came out to the porch in his lilac silk dressing gown. In the yard stood the carts ready corded. The carriages were at the front porch. The major-domo stood at the porch talking to an elderly orderly and to a pale young officer with a bandaged arm. On seeing the count the major-domo made a significant and stern gesture to them both to go away.

"Well, Vasílich, is everything ready?" asked the count, and stroking his bald head he looked good-naturedly at the officer and the orderly and nodded to them. (He liked to see new faces.)

"We can harness at once, your excellency."

"Well, that's right. As soon as the countess wakes we'll be off, God willing! What is it, gentlemen?" he added, turning to the officer. "Are you staying in my house?"

The officer came nearer and suddenly his face flushed crimson.

"Count, be so good as to allow me. . . for God's sake, to get into some corner of one of your carts! I have nothing here with me. . . I shall be all right on a loaded cart. . ."

Before the officer had finished speaking the orderly made the same request on behalf of his master.

"Oh, yes, yes, yes!" said the count hastily. "I shall be very pleased, very pleased. Vasílich, you'll see to it. Just unload one or two carts. Well, what of it. . . do what's necessary. . ." said the count, muttering some indefinite order.

But at the same moment an expression of warm gratitude on the officer's face had already sealed the order. The count looked around him. In the yard, at the gates, at the window of the wings, wounded officers and their orderlies were to be seen. They were all looking at the count and moving toward the porch.

"Please step into the gallery, your excellency," said the major-domo. "What are your orders about the pictures?"

The count went into the house with him, repeating his order not to refuse the wounded who asked for a lift.

"Well, never mind, some of the things can be unloaded," he added in a soft, confidential voice, as though afraid of being overheard.

At nine o'clock the countess woke up, and Matrëna Timoféevna, who had been her lady's maid before her marriage and now performed a sort of chief gendarme's duty for her, came to say that Madame Schoss was much offended and the young ladies' summer dresses could not be left behind. On inquiry, the countess learned that Madame Schoss was offended because her trunk had been taken down from its cart, and all the loads were being uncorded and the luggage taken out of the carts to make room for wounded men whom the count in the simplicity of his heart had ordered that they should take with them. The countess sent for her husband.

"What is this, my dear? I hear that the luggage is being unloaded."

"You know, love, I wanted to tell you. . . Countess dear. . . an officer came to me to ask for a few carts for the wounded. After all, ours are things that can be bought but think what being left behind means to them! . . . Really now, in our own yard—we asked them in ourselves and there are officers among them. . . You know, I think, my dear. . . let them be taken. . . where's the hurry?"

The count spoke timidly, as he always did when talking of money matters. The countess was accustomed to this tone as a precursor of news of something detrimental to the children's interests, such as the building of a new gallery or conservatory, the inauguration of a private theater or an orchestra. She was accustomed always to oppose anything announced in that timid tone and considered it her duty to do so.

She assumed her dolefully submissive manner and said to her husband: "Listen to me, Count, you have managed matters so that we are getting nothing for the house, and now you wish to throw away all our—all the children's property! You said yourself that we have a hundred thousand rubles' worth of things in the house. I don't consent, my dear, I don't! Do as you please! It's the government's business to look after the wounded; they know that. Look at the Lopukhíns opposite, they cleared out everything two days ago. That's what other people do. It's only we who are such fools. If you have no pity on me, have some for the children."

Flourishing his arms in despair the count left the room without replying.

"Papa, what are you doing that for?" asked Natásha, who had followed him into her mother's room.

"Nothing! What business is it of yours?" muttered the count angrily.

"But I heard," said Natásha. "Why does Mamma object?"

"What business is it of yours?" cried the count.

Natásha stepped up to the window and pondered.

"Papa! Here's Berg coming to see us," said she, looking out of the window.

# XVI

Berg, the Rostóvs' son-in-law, was already a colonel wearing the orders of Vladímir and Anna, and he still filled the quiet and agreeable post of assistant to the head of the staff of the assistant commander of the first division of the Second Army.

On the first of September he had come to Moscow from the army.

He had nothing to do in Moscow, but he had noticed that everyone in the army was asking for leave to visit Moscow and had something to do there. So he considered it necessary to ask for leave of absence for family and domestic reasons.

Berg drove up to his father-in-law's house in his spruce little trap with a pair of sleek roans, exactly like those of a certain prince. He looked attentively at the carts in the yard and while going up to the porch took out a clean pocket handkerchief and tied a knot in it.

From the anteroom Berg ran with smooth though impatient steps into the drawing room, where he embraced the count, kissed the hands of Natásha and Sónya, and hastened to inquire after "Mamma's" health.

"Health, at a time like this?" said the count. "Come, tell us the news! Is the army retreating or will there be another battle?"

"God Almighty alone can decide the fate of our fatherland, Papa," said Berg. "The army is burning with a spirit of heroism and the leaders, so to say, have now assembled in council. No one knows what is coming. But in general I can tell you, Papa, that such a heroic spirit, the truly antique valor of the Russian army, which they—which it" (he corrected himself) "has shown or displayed in the battle of the twenty-sixth—there are no words worthy to do it justice! I tell you, Papa" (he smote himself on the breast as a general he had heard speaking had done, but Berg did it a trifle late for he should have struck his breast at the words "Russian army"), "I tell you frankly that we, the commanders, far from having to urge the men on or anything of that kind, could hardly restrain those. . . those. . . yes, those exploits of antique valor," he went on rapidly. "General Barclay de Tolly risked his life everywhere at the head of the troops, I can assure you. Our corps was stationed on a hillside. You can imagine!"

And Berg related all that he remembered of the various tales he had heard those days. Natásha watched him with an intent gaze that confused him, as if she were trying to find in his face the answer to some question.

LEO TOLSTOY

"Altogether such heroism as was displayed by the Russian warriors cannot be imagined or adequately praised!" said Berg, glancing round at Natásha, and as if anxious to conciliate her, replying to her intent look with a smile. "'Russia is not in Moscow, she lives in the hearts of her sons!' Isn't it so, Papa?" said he.

Just then the countess came in from the sitting room with a weary and dissatisfied expression. Berg hurriedly jumped up, kissed her hand, asked about her health, and, swaying his head from side to side to express sympathy, remained standing beside her.

"Yes, Mamma, I tell you sincerely that these are hard and sad times for every Russian. But why are you so anxious? You have still time to get away. . ."

"I can't think what the servants are about," said the countess, turning to her husband. "I have just been told that nothing is ready yet. Somebody after all must see to things. One misses Mítenka at such times. There won't be any end to it."

The count was about to say something, but evidently restrained himself. He got up from his chair and went to the door.

At that moment Berg drew out his handkerchief as if to blow his nose and, seeing the knot in it, pondered, shaking his head sadly and significantly.

"And I have a great favor to ask of you, Papa," said he.

"Hm. . ." said the count, and stopped.

"I was driving past Yusúpov's house just now," said Berg with a laugh, "when the steward, a man I know, ran out and asked me whether I wouldn't buy something. I went in out of curiosity, you know, and there is a small chiffonier and a dressing table. You know how dear Véra wanted a chiffonier like that and how we had a dispute about it." (At the mention of the chiffonier and dressing table Berg involuntarily changed his tone to one of pleasure at his admirable domestic arrangements.) "And it's such a beauty! It pulls out and has a secret English drawer, you know! And dear Véra has long wanted one. I wish to give her a surprise, you see. I saw so many of those peasant carts in your yard. Please let me have one, I will pay the man well, and. . ."

The count frowned and coughed.

"Ask the countess, I don't give orders."

"If it's inconvenient, please don't," said Berg. "Only I so wanted it, for dear Véra's sake."

"Oh, go to the devil, all of you! To the devil, the devil, the devil. . ." cried the old count. "My head's in a whirl!"

And he left the room. The countess began to cry.

"Yes, Mamma! Yes, these are very hard times!" said Berg.

Natásha left the room with her father and, as if finding it difficult to reach some decision, first followed him and then ran downstairs.

Pétya was in the porch, engaged in giving out weapons to the servants who were to leave Moscow. The loaded carts were still standing in the yard. Two of them had been uncorded and a wounded officer was climbing into one of them helped by an orderly.

"Do you know what it's about?" Pétya asked Natásha.

She understood that he meant what were their parents quarreling about. She did not answer.

"It's because Papa wanted to give up all the carts to the wounded," said Pétya. "Vasílich told me. I consider. . ."

"I consider," Natásha suddenly almost shouted, turning her angry face to Pétya, "I consider it so horrid, so abominable, so. . . I don't know what. Are we despicable Germans?"

Her throat quivered with convulsive sobs and, afraid of weakening and letting the force of her anger run to waste, she turned and rushed headlong up the stairs.

Berg was sitting beside the countess consoling her with the respectful attention of a relative. The count, pipe in hand, was pacing up and down the room, when Natásha, her face distorted by anger, burst in like a tempest and approached her mother with rapid steps.

"It's horrid! It's abominable!" she screamed. "You can't possibly have ordered it!"

Berg and the countess looked at her, perplexed and frightened. The count stood still at the window and listened.

"Mamma, it's impossible: see what is going on in the yard!" she cried. "They will be left! . . ."

"What's the matter with you? Who are 'they'? What do you want?"

"Why, the wounded! It's impossible, Mamma. It's monstrous! . . . No, Mamma darling, it's not the thing. Please forgive me, darling. . . Mamma, what does it matter what we take away? Only look what is going on in the yard. . . Mamma! . . . It's impossible!"

The count stood by the window and listened without turning round. Suddenly he sniffed and put his face closer to the window.

The countess glanced at her daughter, saw her face full of shame for her mother, saw her agitation, and understood why her husband did not turn to look at her now, and she glanced round quite disconcerted.

"Oh, do as you like! Am I hindering anyone?" she said, not surrendering at once.

"Mamma, darling, forgive me!"

But the countess pushed her daughter away and went up to her husband.

"My dear, you order what is right. . . You know I don't understand about it," said she, dropping her eyes shamefacedly.

"The eggs. . . the eggs are teaching the hen," muttered the count through tears of joy, and he embraced his wife who was glad to hide her look of shame on his breast.

"Papa! Mamma! May I see to it? May I? . . ." asked Natásha. "We will still take all the most necessary things."

The count nodded affirmatively, and Natásha, at the rapid pace at which she used to run when playing at tag, ran through the ballroom to the anteroom and downstairs into the yard.

The servants gathered round Natásha, but could not believe the strange order she brought them until the count himself, in his wife's name, confirmed the order to give up all the carts to the wounded and take the trunks to the storerooms. When they understood that order the servants set to work at this new task with pleasure and zeal. It no longer seemed strange to them but on the contrary it seemed the only thing that could be done, just as a quarter of an hour before it had not seemed strange to anyone that the wounded should be left behind and the goods carted away but that had seemed the only thing to do.

The whole household, as if to atone for not having done it sooner, set eagerly to work at the new task of placing the wounded in the carts. The wounded dragged themselves out of their rooms and stood with pale but happy faces round the carts. The news that carts were to be had spread to the neighboring houses, from which wounded men began to come into the Rostóvs' yard. Many of the wounded asked them not to unload the carts but only to let them sit on the top of the things. But the work of unloading, once started, could not be arrested. It seemed not to matter whether all or only half the things were left behind. Cases full of china, bronzes, pictures, and mirrors that had been so carefully packed the night before now lay about the yard, and still they went on searching for and finding possibilities of unloading this or that and letting the wounded have another and yet another cart.

"We can take four more men," said the steward. "They can have my trap, or else what is to become of them?"

"Let them have my wardrobe cart," said the countess. "Dunyásha can go with me in the carriage."

They unloaded the wardrobe cart and sent it to take wounded men from a house two doors off. The whole household, servants included, was bright and animated. Natásha was in a state of rapturous excitement such as she had not known for a long time.

"What could we fasten this onto?" asked the servants, trying to fix a trunk on the narrow footboard behind a carriage. "We must keep at least one cart."

"What's in it?" asked Natásha.

"The count's books."

"Leave it, Vasílich will put it away. It's not wanted."

The phaeton was full of people and there was a doubt as to where Count Peter could sit.

"On the box. You'll sit on the box, won't you, Pétya?" cried Natásha.

Sónya too was busy all this time, but the aim of her efforts was quite different from Natásha's. She was putting away the things that had to be left behind and making a list of them as the countess wished, and she tried to get as much taken away with them as possible.

# XVII

B efore two o'clock in the afternoon the Rostóvs' four carriages, packed full and with the horses harnessed, stood at the front door. One by one the carts with the wounded had moved out of the yard.

The calèche in which Prince Andrew was being taken attracted Sónya's attention as it passed the front porch. With the help of a maid she was arranging a seat for the countess in the huge high coach that stood at the entrance.

"Whose calèche is that?" she inquired, leaning out of the carriage window.

"Why, didn't you know, Miss?" replied the maid. "The wounded prince: he spent the night in our house and is going with us."

"But who is it? What's his name?"

"It's our intended that was—Prince Bolkónski himself! They say he is dying," replied the maid with a sigh.

Sónya jumped out of the coach and ran to the countess. The countess, tired out and already dressed in shawl and bonnet for her journey, was pacing up and down the drawing room, waiting for the household to assemble for the usual silent prayer with closed doors before starting. Natásha was not in the room.

"Mamma," said Sónya, "Prince Andrew is here, mortally wounded. He is going with us."

The countess opened her eyes in dismay and, seizing Sónya's arm, glanced around.

"Natásha?" she murmured.

At that moment this news had only one significance for both of them. They knew their Natásha, and alarm as to what would happen if she heard this news stifled all sympathy for the man they both liked.

"Natásha does not know yet, but he is going with us," said Sónya.

"You say he is dying?"

Sónya nodded.

The countess put her arms around Sónya and began to cry.

"The ways of God are past finding out!" she thought, feeling that the Almighty Hand, hitherto unseen, was becoming manifest in all that was now taking place.

"Well, Mamma? Everything is ready. What's the matter?" asked Natásha, as with animated face she ran into the room.

"Nothing," answered the countess. "If everything is ready let us start."

And the countess bent over her reticule to hide her agitated face. Sónya embraced Natásha and kissed her.

Natásha looked at her inquiringly.

"What is it? What has happened?"

"Nothing. . . No. . ."

"Is it something very bad for me? What is it?" persisted Natásha with her quick intuition.

Sónya sighed and made no reply. The count, Pétya, Madame Schoss, Mávra Kuzmínichna, and Vasílich came into the drawing room and, having closed the doors, they all sat down and remained for some moments silently seated without looking at one another.

The count was the first to rise, and with a loud sigh crossed himself before the icon. All the others did the same. Then the count embraced Mávra Kuzmínichna and Vasílich, who were to remain in Moscow, and while they caught at his hand and kissed his shoulder he patted their backs lightly with some vaguely affectionate and comforting words. The countess went into the oratory and there Sónya found her on her knees before the icons that had been left here and there hanging on the wall. (The most precious ones, with which some family tradition was connected, were being taken with them.)

In the porch and in the yard the men whom Pétya had armed with swords and daggers, with trousers tucked inside their high boots and with belts and girdles tightened, were taking leave of those remaining behind.

As is always the case at a departure, much had been forgotten or put in the wrong place, and for a long time two menservants stood one on each side of the open door and the carriage steps waiting to help the countess in, while maids rushed with cushions and bundles from the house to the carriages, the calèche, the phaeton, and back again.

"They always will forget everything!" said the countess. "Don't you know I can't sit like that?"

And Dunyásha, with clenched teeth, without replying but with an aggrieved look on her face, hastily got into the coach to rearrange the seat.

"Oh, those servants!" said the count, swaying his head.

Efím, the old coachman, who was the only one the countess trusted to drive her, sat perched up high on the box and did not so much as glance round at what was going on behind him. From thirty years' experience he knew it would be some time yet before the order, "Be off, in God's name!" would be given him: and he knew that even when it was said he would be stopped once or twice more while they sent back to fetch something that had been forgotten, and even after that he would again be stopped and the countess herself would lean out of the window and beg him for the love of heaven to drive carefully down the hill. He knew all this and therefore waited calmly for what would happen, with more patience than the horses, especially the near one, the chestnut Falcon, who was pawing the ground and champing his bit. At last all were seated, the carriage steps were folded and pulled up, the door was shut, somebody was sent for a traveling case, and the countess leaned out and said what she had to say. Then Efím deliberately doffed his hat and began crossing himself. The postilion and all the other servants did the same. "Off, in God's name!" said Efím, putting on his hat. "Start!" The postilion started the horses, the off pole horse tugged at his collar, the high springs creaked, and the body of the coach swayed. The footman sprang onto the box of the moving coach which jolted as it passed out of the yard onto the uneven roadway; the other vehicles jolted in their turn, and the procession of carriages moved up the street. In the carriages, the calèche, and the phaeton, all crossed themselves as they passed the church opposite the house. Those who were to remain in Moscow walked on either side of the vehicles seeing the travelers off.

Rarely had Natásha experienced so joyful a feeling as now, sitting in the carriage beside the countess and gazing at the slowly receding walls of forsaken, agitated Moscow. Occasionally she leaned out of the carriage window and looked back and then forward at the long train of wounded in front of them. Almost at the head of the line she could see the raised hood of Prince Andrew's calèche. She did not know who was in it, but each time she looked at the procession her eyes sought that calèche. She knew it was right in front.

In Kúdrino, from the Nikítski, Présnya, and Podnovínsk Streets came several other trains of vehicles similar to the Rostóvs', and as they passed along the Sadóvaya Street the carriages and carts formed two rows abreast.

As they were going round the Súkharev water tower Natásha, who was inquisitively and alertly scrutinizing the people driving or walking past, suddenly cried out in joyful surprise:

"Dear me! Mamma, Sónya, look, it's he!"

"Who? Who?"

"Look! Yes, on my word, it's Bezúkhov!" said Natásha, putting her head out of the carriage and staring at a tall, stout man in a coachman's long coat, who from his manner of walking and moving was evidently a gentleman in disguise, and who was passing under the arch of the Súkharev tower accompanied by a small, sallow-faced, beardless old man in a frieze coat.

"Yes, it really is Bezúkhov in a coachman's coat, with a queer-looking old boy. Really," said Natásha, "look, look!"

"No, it's not he. How can you talk such nonsense?"

"Mamma," screamed Natásha, "I'll stake my head it's he! I assure you! Stop, stop!" she cried to the coachman.

But the coachman could not stop, for from the Meshchánski Street came more carts and carriages, and the Rostóvs were being shouted at to move on and not block the way.

In fact, however, though now much farther off than before, the Rostóvs all saw Pierre—or someone extraordinarily like him—in a coachman's coat, going down the street with head bent and a serious face beside a small, beardless old man who looked like a footman. That old man noticed a face thrust out of the carriage window gazing at them, and respectfully touching Pierre's elbow said something to him and pointed to the carriage. Pierre, evidently engrossed in thought, could not at first understand him. At length when he had understood and looked in the direction the old man indicated, he recognized Natásha, and following his first impulse stepped instantly and rapidly toward the coach. But having taken a dozen steps he seemed to remember something and stopped.

Natásha's face, leaning out of the window, beamed with quizzical kindliness.

"Peter Kirílovich, come here! We have recognized you! This is wonderful!" she cried, holding out her hand to him. "What are you doing? Why are you like this?"

Pierre took her outstretched hand and kissed it awkwardly as he walked along beside her while the coach still moved on.

"What is the matter, Count?" asked the countess in a surprised and commiserating tone.

"What? What? Why? Don't ask me," said Pierre, and looked round at Natásha whose radiant, happy expression—of which he was conscious without looking at her—filled him with enchantment.

"Are you remaining in Moscow, then?"

Pierre hesitated.

"In Moscow?" he said in a questioning tone. "Yes, in Moscow. Good-by!"

"Ah, if only I were a man! I'd certainly stay with you. How splendid!" said Natásha. "Mamma, if you'll let me, I'll stay!"

Pierre glanced absently at Natásha and was about to say something, but the countess interrupted him.

"You were at the battle, we heard."

"Yes, I was," Pierre answered. "There will be another battle tomorrow. . ." he began, but Natásha interrupted him.

"But what is the matter with you, Count? You are not like yourself. . ."

"Oh, don't ask me, don't ask me! I don't know myself. Tomorrow. . . But no! Good-by, good-by!" he muttered. "It's an awful time!" and dropping behind the carriage he stepped onto the pavement.

Natásha continued to lean out of the window for a long time, beaming at him with her kindly, slightly quizzical, happy smile.

# XVIII

For the last two days, ever since leaving home, Pierre had been living in the empty house of his deceased benefactor, Bazdéev. This is how it happened.

When he woke up on the morning after his return to Moscow and his interview with Count Rostopchín, he could not for some time make out where he was and what was expected of him. When he was informed that among others awaiting him in his reception room there was a Frenchman who had brought a letter from his wife, the Countess Hélène, he felt suddenly overcome by that sense of confusion and hopelessness to which he was apt to succumb. He felt that everything was now at an end, all was in confusion and crumbling to pieces, that nobody was right or wrong, the future held nothing, and there was no escape from this position. Smiling unnaturally and muttering to himself, he first sat down on the sofa in an attitude of despair, then rose, went to the door of the reception room and peeped through the crack, returned flourishing his arms, and took up a book. His major-domo came in a second time to say that the Frenchman who had brought the letter from the countess was very anxious to see him if only for a minute, and that someone from Bazdéev's widow had called to ask Pierre to take charge of her husband's books, as she herself was leaving for the country.

"Oh, yes, in a minute; wait. . . or no! No, of course. . . go and say I will come directly," Pierre replied to the major-domo.

But as soon as the man had left the room Pierre took up his hat which was lying on the table and went out of his study by the other door. There was no one in the passage. He went along the whole length of this passage to the stairs and, frowning and rubbing his forehead with both hands, went down as far as the first landing. The hall porter was standing at the front door. From the landing where Pierre stood there was a second staircase leading to the back entrance. He went down that staircase and out into the yard. No one had seen him. But there were some carriages waiting, and as soon as Pierre stepped out of the gate the coachmen and the yard porter noticed him and raised their caps to him. When he felt he was being looked at he behaved like an ostrich which hides its head in a bush in order not to be seen: he hung his head and quickening his pace went down the street.

Of all the affairs awaiting Pierre that day the sorting of Joseph Bazdéev's books and papers appeared to him the most necessary.

He hired the first cab he met and told the driver to go to the Patriarch's Ponds, where the widow Bazdéev's house was.

Continually turning round to look at the rows of loaded carts that were making their way from all sides out of Moscow, and balancing his bulky body so as not to slip out of the ramshackle old vehicle, Pierre, experiencing the joyful feeling of a boy escaping from school, began to talk to his driver.

The man told him that arms were being distributed today at the Krémlin and that tomorrow everyone would be sent out beyond the Three Hills gates and a great battle would be fought there.

Having reached the Patriarch's Ponds Pierre found the Bazdéevs' house, where he had not been for a long time past. He went up to the gate. Gerásim, that sallow beardless old man Pierre had seen at Torzhók five years before with Joseph Bazdéev, came out in answer to his knock.

"At home?" asked Pierre.

"Owing to the present state of things Sophia Danílovna has gone to the Torzhók estate with the children, your excellency."

"I will come in all the same, I have to look through the books," said Pierre.

"Be so good as to step in. Makár Alexéevich, the brother of my late master—may the kingdom of heaven be his—has remained here, but he is in a weak state as you know," said the old servant.

Pierre knew that Makár Alexéevich was Joseph Bazdéev's half-insane brother and a hard drinker.

"Yes, yes, I know. Let us go in. . ." said Pierre and entered the house. A tall, bald-headed old man with a red nose, wearing a dressing gown and with galoshes on his bare feet, stood in the anteroom. On seeing Pierre he muttered something angrily and went away along the passage.

"He was a very clever man but has now grown quite feeble, as your honor sees," said Gerásim. "Will you step into the study?" Pierre nodded. "As it was sealed up so it has remained, but Sophia Danílovna gave orders that if anyone should come from you they were to have the books."

Pierre went into that gloomy study which he had entered with such trepidation in his benefactor's lifetime. The room, dusty and untouched since the death of Joseph Bazdéev was now even gloomier.

Gerásim opened one of the shutters and left the room on tiptoe. Pierre went round the study, approached the cupboard in which the manuscripts were kept, and took out what had once been one of the most important, the holy of holies of the order. This was the authentic Scotch Acts with Bazdéev's notes and explanations. He sat down at the dusty writing table, and, having laid the manuscripts before him, opened them out, closed them, finally pushed them away, and resting his head on his hand sank into meditation.

Gerásim looked cautiously into the study several times and saw Pierre always sitting in the same attitude.

More than two hours passed and Gerásim took the liberty of making a slight noise at the door to attract his attention, but Pierre did not hear him.

"Is the cabman to be discharged, your honor?"

"Oh yes!" said Pierre, rousing himself and rising hurriedly. "Look here," he added, taking Gerásim by a button of his coat and looking down at the old man with moist, shining, and ecstatic eyes, "I say, do you know that there is going to be a battle tomorrow?"

"We heard so," replied the man.

"I beg you not to tell anyone who I am, and to do what I ask you."

"Yes, your excellency," replied Gerásim. "Will you have something to eat?"

"No, but I want something else. I want peasant clothes and a pistol," said Pierre, unexpectedly blushing.

"Yes, your excellency," said Gerásim after thinking for a moment.

All the rest of that day Pierre spent alone in his benefactor's study, and Gerásim heard him pacing restlessly from one corner to another and talking to himself. And he spent the night on a bed made up for him there.

Gerásim, being a servant who in his time had seen many strange things, accepted Pierre's taking up his residence in the house without surprise, and seemed pleased to have someone to wait on. That same evening—without even asking himself what they were wanted for—he procured a coachman's coat and cap for Pierre, and promised to get him the pistol next day. Makár Alexéevich came twice that evening shuffling along in his galoshes as far as the door and stopped and looked ingratiatingly at Pierre. But as soon as Pierre turned toward him he wrapped his dressing gown around him with a shamefaced and angry look and hurried away. It was when Pierre (wearing the coachman's coat which Gerásim had procured for him and had disinfected by steam) was on his way with the old man to buy the pistol at the Súkharev market that he met the Rostóvs.

# XIX

Kutúzov's order to retreat through Moscow to the Ryazán road was issued at night on the first of September.

The first troops started at once, and during the night they marched slowly and steadily without hurry. At daybreak, however, those nearing the town at the Dorogomílov bridge saw ahead of them masses of soldiers crowding and hurrying across the bridge, ascending on the opposite side and blocking the streets and alleys, while endless masses of troops were bearing down on them from behind, and an unreasoning hurry and alarm overcame them. They all rushed forward to the bridge, onto it, and to the fords and the boats. Kutúzov himself had driven round by side streets to the other side of Moscow.

By ten o'clock in the morning of the second of September, only the rear guard remained in the Dorogomílov suburb, where they had ample room. The main army was on the other side of Moscow or beyond it.

At that very time, at ten in the morning of the second of September, Napoleon was standing among his troops on the Poklónny Hill looking at the panorama spread out before him. From the twenty-sixth of August to the second of September, that is from the battle of Borodinó to the entry of the French into Moscow, during the whole of that agitating, memorable week, there had been the extraordinary autumn weather that always comes as a surprise, when the sun hangs low and gives more heat than in spring, when everything shines so brightly in the rare clear atmosphere that the eyes smart, when the lungs are strengthened and refreshed by inhaling the aromatic autumn air, when even the nights are warm, and when in those dark warm nights, golden stars startle and delight us continually by falling from the sky.

At ten in the morning of the second of September this weather still held.

The brightness of the morning was magical. Moscow seen from the Poklónny Hill lay spaciously spread out with her river, her gardens, and her churches, and she seemed to be living her usual life, her cupolas glittering like stars in the sunlight.

The view of the strange city with its peculiar architecture, such as he had never seen before, filled Napoleon with the rather envious and uneasy curiosity men feel when they see an alien form of life that has no knowledge of them. This city was evidently living with the full force of its own life. By the indefinite signs which, even at a distance, distinguish a living body from a dead one, Napoleon from the Poklónny Hill perceived the throb of life in the town and felt, as it were, the breathing of that great and beautiful body.

Every Russian looking at Moscow feels her to be a mother; every foreigner who sees her, even if ignorant of her significance as the mother city, must feel her feminine character, and Napoleon felt it.

"Cette ville asiatique aux innombrables églises, Moscou la sainte. La voilà donc enfin, cette fameuse ville! Il était temps,"* said he, and dismounting he ordered a plan of Moscow to be spread out before him, and summoned Lelorgne d'Ideville, the interpreter.

"A town captured by the enemy is like a maid who has lost her honor," thought he (he had said so to Túchkov at Smolénsk). From that point of view he gazed at the Oriental beauty he had not seen before. It seemed strange to him that his long-felt wish, which had seemed unattainable, had at last been realized. In the clear morning light he gazed now at the city and now at the plan, considering its details, and the assurance of possessing it agitated and awed him.

"But could it be otherwise?" he thought. "Here is this capital at my feet. Where is Alexander now, and of what is he thinking? A strange, beautiful, and majestic city; and a strange and majestic moment! In what light must I appear to them!" thought he, thinking of his troops. "Here she is, the reward for all those fainthearted men," he reflected, glancing at those near him and at the troops who were approaching and forming up. "One word from me, one movement of my hand, and that ancient capital of the Tsars would perish. But my clemency is always ready to descend upon the vanquished. I must be magnanimous and truly great. But no, it can't be true that I am in Moscow," he suddenly thought. "Yet here she is lying at my feet, with her golden domes and crosses scintillating and twinkling in the sunshine. But I shall spare her. On the ancient monuments of barbarism and despotism I will inscribe great words of justice and mercy. . . It is just this which Alexander will feel most painfully, I know him." (It seemed to Napoleon that the chief import of what was taking place lay in the personal struggle between himself and Alexander.) "From the height of the Krémlin—yes, there is the Krémlin, yes—I will give them just laws; I will teach them the

---

* "That Asiatic city of the innumerable churches, holy Moscow! Here it is then at last, that famous city. It was high time."

LEO TOLSTOY

meaning of true civilization, I will make generations of boyars remember their conqueror with love. I will tell the deputation that I did not, and do not, desire war, that I have waged war only against the false policy of their court; that I love and respect Alexander and that in Moscow I will accept terms of peace worthy of myself and of my people. I do not wish to utilize the fortunes of war to humiliate an honored monarch. 'Boyars,' I will say to them, 'I do not desire war, I desire the peace and welfare of all my subjects.' However, I know their presence will inspire me, and I shall speak to them as I always do: clearly, impressively, and majestically. But can it be true that I am in Moscow? Yes, there she lies."

"Qu'on m'amène les boyars,"* said he to his suite.

A general with a brilliant suite galloped off at once to fetch the boyars.

Two hours passed. Napoleon had lunched and was again standing in the same place on the Poklónny Hill awaiting the deputation. His speech to the boyars had already taken definite shape in his imagination. That speech was full of dignity and greatness as Napoleon understood it.

He was himself carried away by the tone of magnanimity he intended to adopt toward Moscow. In his imagination he appointed days for assemblies at the palace of the Tsars, at which Russian notables and his own would mingle. He mentally appointed a governor, one who would win the hearts of the people. Having learned that there were many charitable institutions in Moscow he mentally decided that he would shower favors on them all. He thought that, as in Africa he had to put on a burnoose and sit in a mosque, so in Moscow he must be beneficent like the Tsars. And in order finally to touch the hearts of the Russians— and being like all Frenchmen unable to imagine anything sentimental without a reference to ma chère, ma tendre, ma pauvre mère†—he decided that he would place an inscription on all these establishments in large letters: "This establishment is dedicated to my dear mother." Or no, it should be simply: Maison de ma Mère,‡ he concluded. "But am I really in Moscow? Yes, here it lies before me, but why is the deputation from the city so long in appearing?" he wondered.

Meanwhile an agitated consultation was being carried on in whispers among his generals and marshals at the rear of his suite. Those sent to

---

* "Bring the boyars to me."
† "My dear, my tender, my poor mother."
‡ "House of my Mother."

fetch the deputation had returned with the news that Moscow was empty, that everyone had left it. The faces of those who were not conferring together were pale and perturbed. They were not alarmed by the fact that Moscow had been abandoned by its inhabitants (grave as that fact seemed), but by the question how to tell the Emperor—without putting him in the terrible position of appearing ridiculous—that he had been awaiting the boyars so long in vain: that there were drunken mobs left in Moscow but no one else. Some said that a deputation of some sort must be scraped together, others disputed that opinion and maintained that the Emperor should first be carefully and skillfully prepared, and then told the truth.

"He will have to be told, all the same," said some gentlemen of the suite. "But, gentlemen. . ."

The position was the more awkward because the Emperor, meditating upon his magnanimous plans, was pacing patiently up and down before the outspread map, occasionally glancing along the road to Moscow from under his lifted hand with a bright and proud smile.

"But it's impossible. . ." declared the gentlemen of the suite, shrugging their shoulders but not venturing to utter the implied word— le ridicule. . .

At last the Emperor, tired of futile expectation, his actor's instinct suggesting to him that the sublime moment having been too long drawn out was beginning to lose its sublimity, gave a sign with his hand. A single report of a signaling gun followed, and the troops, who were already spread out on different sides of Moscow, moved into the city through the Tver, Kalúga, and Dorogomílov gates. Faster and faster, vying with one another, they moved at the double or at a trot, vanishing amid the clouds of dust they raised and making the air ring with a deafening roar of mingling shouts.

Drawn on by the movement of his troops Napoleon rode with them as far as the Dorogomílov gate, but there again stopped and, dismounting from his horse, paced for a long time by the Kámmer-Kollézski rampart, awaiting the deputation.

# XX

Meanwhile Moscow was empty. There were still people in it, perhaps a fiftieth part of its former inhabitants had remained, but it was empty. It was empty in the sense that a dying queenless hive is empty.

In a queenless hive no life is left though to a superficial glance it seems as much alive as other hives.

The bees circle round a queenless hive in the hot beams of the midday sun as gaily as around the living hives; from a distance it smells of honey like the others, and bees fly in and out in the same way. But one has only to observe that hive to realize that there is no longer any life in it. The bees do not fly in the same way, the smell and the sound that meet the beekeeper are not the same. To the beekeeper's tap on the wall of the sick hive, instead of the former instant unanimous humming of tens of thousands of bees with their abdomens threateningly compressed, and producing by the rapid vibration of their wings an aerial living sound, the only reply is a disconnected buzzing from different parts of the deserted hive. From the alighting board, instead of the former spirituous fragrant smell of honey and venom, and the warm whiffs of crowded life, comes an odor of emptiness and decay mingling with the smell of honey. There are no longer sentinels sounding the alarm with their abdomens raised, and ready to die in defense of the hive. There is no longer the measured quiet sound of throbbing activity, like the sound of boiling water, but diverse discordant sounds of disorder. In and out of the hive long black robber bees smeared with honey fly timidly and shiftily. They do not sting, but crawl away from danger. Formerly only bees laden with honey flew into the hive, and they flew out empty; now they fly out laden. The beekeeper opens the lower part of the hive and peers in. Instead of black, glossy bees—tamed by toil, clinging to one another's legs and drawing out the wax, with a ceaseless hum of labor—that used to hang in long clusters down to the floor of the hive, drowsy shriveled bees crawl about separately in various directions on the floor and walls of the hive. Instead of a neatly glued floor, swept by the bees with the fanning of their wings, there is a floor littered with bits of wax, excrement, dying bees scarcely moving their legs, and dead ones that have not been cleared away.

The beekeeper opens the upper part of the hive and examines the super. Instead of serried rows of bees sealing up every gap in the combs and keeping the brood warm, he sees the skillful complex structures of the combs, but no longer in their former state of purity. All is neglected and foul. Black robber bees are swiftly and stealthily prowling about the combs, and the short home bees, shriveled and listless as if they were old, creep slowly about without trying to hinder the robbers, having lost all motive and all sense of life. Drones, bumblebees, wasps, and butterflies knock awkwardly against the walls of the hive in their flight. Here and there among the cells containing dead brood and honey an angry buzzing can sometimes be heard. Here and there a couple of bees, by force of habit and custom cleaning out the brood cells, with efforts beyond their strength laboriously drag away a dead bee or bumblebee without knowing why they do it. In another corner two old bees are languidly fighting, or cleaning themselves, or feeding one another, without themselves knowing whether they do it with friendly or hostile intent. In a third place a crowd of bees, crushing one another, attack some victim and fight and smother it, and the victim, enfeebled or killed, drops from above slowly and lightly as a feather, among the heap of corpses. The keeper opens the two center partitions to examine the brood cells. In place of the former close dark circles formed by thousands of bees sitting back to back and guarding the high mystery of generation, he sees hundreds of dull, listless, and sleepy shells of bees. They have almost all died unawares, sitting in the sanctuary they had guarded and which is now no more. They reek of decay and death. Only a few of them still move, rise, and feebly fly to settle on the enemy's hand, lacking the spirit to die stinging him; the rest are dead and fall as lightly as fish scales. The beekeeper closes the hive, chalks a mark on it, and when he has time tears out its contents and burns it clean.

So in the same way Moscow was empty when Napoleon, weary, uneasy, and morose, paced up and down in front of the Kámmer-Kollézski rampart, awaiting what to his mind was a necessary, if but formal, observance of the proprieties—a deputation.

In various corners of Moscow there still remained a few people aimlessly moving about, following their old habits and hardly aware of what they were doing.

When with due circumspection Napoleon was informed that Moscow was empty, he looked angrily at his informant, turned away, and silently continued to walk to and fro.

"My carriage!" he said.

He took his seat beside the aide-de-camp on duty and drove into the suburb. "Moscow deserted!" he said to himself. "What an incredible event!"

He did not drive into the town, but put up at an inn in the Dorogomílov suburb.

The coup de théâtre had not come off.

# XXI

The Russian troops were passing through Moscow from two o'clock at night till two in the afternoon and bore away with them the wounded and the last of the inhabitants who were leaving.

The greatest crush during the movement of the troops took place at the Stone, Moskvá, and Yaúza bridges.

While the troops, dividing into two parts when passing around the Krémlin, were thronging the Moskvá and the Stone bridges, a great many soldiers, taking advantage of the stoppage and congestion, turned back from the bridges and slipped stealthily and silently past the church of Vasíli the Beatified and under the Borovítski gate, back up the hill to the Red Square where some instinct told them they could easily take things not belonging to them. Crowds of the kind seen at cheap sales filled all the passages and alleys of the Bazaar. But there were no dealers with voices of ingratiating affability inviting customers to enter; there were no hawkers, nor the usual motley crowd of female purchasers—but only soldiers, in uniforms and overcoats though without muskets, entering the Bazaar empty-handed and silently making their way out through its passages with bundles. Tradesmen and their assistants (of whom there were but few) moved about among the soldiers quite bewildered. They unlocked their shops and locked them up again, and themselves carried goods away with the help of their assistants. On the square in front of the Bazaar were drummers beating the muster call. But the roll of the drums did not make the looting soldiers run in the direction of the drum as formerly, but made them, on the contrary, run farther away. Among the soldiers in the shops and passages some men were to be seen in gray coats, with closely shaven heads. Two officers, one with a scarf over his uniform and mounted on a lean, dark-gray horse, the other in an overcoat and on foot, stood at the corner of Ilyínka Street, talking. A third officer galloped up to them.

"The general orders them all to be driven out at once, without fail. This is outrageous! Half the men have dispersed."

"Where are you off to? . . . Where? . . ." he shouted to three infantrymen without muskets who, holding up the skirts of their overcoats, were slipping past him into the Bazaar passage. "Stop, you rascals!"

"But how are you going to stop them?" replied another officer. "There is no getting them together. The army should push on before the rest bolt, that's all!"

"How can one push on? They are stuck there, wedged on the bridge, and don't move. Shouldn't we put a cordon round to prevent the rest from running away?"

"Come, go in there and drive them out!" shouted the senior officer.

The officer in the scarf dismounted, called up a drummer, and went with him into the arcade. Some soldiers started running away in a group. A shopkeeper with red pimples on his cheeks near the nose, and a calm, persistent, calculating expression on his plump face, hurriedly and ostentatiously approached the officer, swinging his arms.

"Your honor!" said he. "Be so good as to protect us! We won't grudge trifles, you are welcome to anything—we shall be delighted! Pray! . . . I'll fetch a piece of cloth at once for such an honorable gentleman, or even two pieces with pleasure. For we feel how it is; but what's all this— sheer robbery! If you please, could not guards be placed if only to let us close the shop. . ."

Several shopkeepers crowded round the officer.

"Eh, what twaddle!" said one of them, a thin, stern-looking man. "When one's head is gone one doesn't weep for one's hair! Take what any of you like!" And flourishing his arm energetically he turned sideways to the officer.

"It's all very well for you, Iván Sidórych, to talk," said the first tradesman angrily. "Please step inside, your honor!"

"Talk indeed!" cried the thin one. "In my three shops here I have a hundred thousand rubles' worth of goods. Can they be saved when the army has gone? Eh, what people! 'Against God's might our hands can't fight.'"

"Come inside, your honor!" repeated the tradesman, bowing.

The officer stood perplexed and his face showed indecision.

"It's not my business!" he exclaimed, and strode on quickly down one of the passages.

From one open shop came the sound of blows and vituperation, and just as the officer came up to it a man in a gray coat with a shaven head was flung out violently.

This man, bent double, rushed past the tradesman and the officer. The officer pounced on the soldiers who were in the shops, but at that moment fearful screams reached them from the huge crowd on the Moskvá bridge and the officer ran out into the square.

"What is it? What is it?" he asked, but his comrade was already galloping off past Vasíli the Beatified in the direction from which the screams came.

The officer mounted his horse and rode after him. When he reached the bridge he saw two unlimbered guns, the infantry crossing the bridge, several overturned carts, and frightened and laughing faces among the troops. Beside the cannon a cart was standing to which two horses were harnessed. Four borzois with collars were pressing close to the wheels. The cart was loaded high, and at the very top, beside a child's chair with its legs in the air, sat a peasant woman uttering piercing and desperate shrieks. He was told by his fellow officers that the screams of the crowd and the shrieks of the woman were due to the fact that General Ermólov, coming up to the crowd and learning that soldiers were dispersing among the shops while crowds of civilians blocked the bridge, had ordered two guns to be unlimbered and made a show of firing at the bridge. The crowd, crushing one another, upsetting carts, and shouting and squeezing desperately, had cleared off the bridge and the troops were now moving forward.

# XXII

Meanwhile, the city itself was deserted. There was hardly anyone in the streets. The gates and shops were all closed, only here and there round the taverns solitary shouts or drunken songs could be heard. Nobody drove through the streets and footsteps were rarely heard. The Povarskáya was quite still and deserted. The huge courtyard of the Rostóvs' house was littered with wisps of hay and with dung from the horses, and not a soul was to be seen there. In the great drawing room of the house, which had been left with all it contained, were two people. They were the yard porter Ignát, and the page boy Míshka, Vasílich's grandson who had stayed in Moscow with his grandfather. Míshka had opened the clavichord and was strumming on it with one finger. The yard porter, his arms akimbo, stood smiling with satisfaction before the large mirror.

"Isn't it fine, eh, Uncle Ignát?" said the boy, suddenly beginning to strike the keyboard with both hands.

"Only fancy!" answered Ignát, surprised at the broadening grin on his face in the mirror.

"Impudence! Impudence!" they heard behind them the voice of Mávra Kuzmínichna who had entered silently. "How he's grinning, the fat mug! Is that what you're here for? Nothing's cleared away down there and Vasílich is worn out. Just you wait a bit!"

Ignát left off smiling, adjusted his belt, and went out of the room with meekly downcast eyes.

"Aunt, I did it gently," said the boy.

"I'll give you something gently, you monkey you!" cried Mávra Kuzmínichna, raising her arm threateningly. "Go and get the samovar to boil for your grandfather."

Mávra Kuzmínichna flicked the dust off the clavichord and closed it, and with a deep sigh left the drawing room and locked its main door.

Going out into the yard she paused to consider where she should go next—to drink tea in the servants' wing with Vasílich, or into the storeroom to put away what still lay about.

She heard the sound of quick footsteps in the quiet street. Someone stopped at the gate, and the latch rattled as someone tried to open it. Mávra Kuzmínichna went to the gate.

"Who do you want?"

"The count—Count Ilyá Andréevich Rostóv."

"And who are you?"

"An officer, I have to see him," came the reply in a pleasant, well-bred Russian voice.

Mávra Kuzmínichna opened the gate and an officer of eighteen, with the round face of a Rostóv, entered the yard.

"They have gone away, sir. Went away yesterday at vespertime," said Mávra Kuzmínichna cordially.

The young officer standing in the gateway, as if hesitating whether to enter or not, clicked his tongue.

"Ah, how annoying!" he muttered. "I should have come yesterday. . . Ah, what a pity."

Meanwhile, Mávra Kuzmínichna was attentively and sympathetically examining the familiar Rostóv features of the young man's face, his tattered coat and trodden-down boots.

"What did you want to see the count for?" she asked.

"Oh well. . . it can't be helped!" said he in a tone of vexation and placed his hand on the gate as if to leave.

He again paused in indecision.

"You see," he suddenly said, "I am a kinsman of the count's and he has been very kind to me. As you see" (he glanced with an amused air and good-natured smile at his coat and boots) "my things are worn out and I have no money, so I was going to ask the count. . ."

Mávra Kuzmínichna did not let him finish.

"Just wait a minute, sir. One little moment," said she.

And as soon as the officer let go of the gate handle she turned and, hurrying away on her old legs, went through the back yard to the servants' quarters.

While Mávra Kuzmínichna was running to her room the officer walked about the yard gazing at his worn-out boots with lowered head and a faint smile on his lips. "What a pity I've missed Uncle! What a nice old woman! Where has she run off to? And how am I to find the nearest way to overtake my regiment, which must by now be getting near the Rogózhski gate?" thought he. Just then Mávra Kuzmínichna appeared from behind the corner of the house with a frightened yet resolute look, carrying a rolled-up check kerchief in her hand. While still a few steps from the officer she unfolded the kerchief and took out of it a white twenty-five-ruble assignat and hastily handed it to him.

"If his excellency had been at home, as a kinsman he would of course. . . but as it is. . ."

Mávra Kuzmínichna grew abashed and confused. The officer did not decline, but took the note quietly and thanked her.

"If the count had been at home. . ." Mávra Kuzmínichna went on apologetically. "Christ be with you, sir! May God preserve you!" said she, bowing as she saw him out.

Swaying his head and smiling as if amused at himself, the officer ran almost at a trot through the deserted streets toward the Yaúza bridge to overtake his regiment.

But Mávra Kuzmínichna stood at the closed gate for some time with moist eyes, pensively swaying her head and feeling an unexpected flow of motherly tenderness and pity for the unknown young officer.

# XXIII

From an unfinished house on the Varvárka, the ground floor of which was a dramshop, came drunken shouts and songs. On benches round the tables in a dirty little room sat some ten factory hands. Tipsy and perspiring, with dim eyes and wide-open mouths, they were all laboriously singing some song or other. They were singing discordantly, arduously, and with great effort, evidently not because they wished to sing, but because they wanted to show they were drunk and on a spree. One, a tall, fair-haired lad in a clean blue coat, was standing over the others. His face with its fine straight nose would have been handsome had it not been for his thin, compressed, twitching lips and dull, gloomy, fixed eyes. Evidently possessed by some idea, he stood over those who were singing, and solemnly and jerkily flourished above their heads his white arm with the sleeve turned up to the elbow, trying unnaturally to spread out his dirty fingers. The sleeve of his coat kept slipping down and he always carefully rolled it up again with his left hand, as if it were most important that the sinewy white arm he was flourishing should be bare. In the midst of the song cries were heard, and fighting and blows in the passage and porch. The tall lad waved his arm.

"Stop it!" he exclaimed peremptorily. "There's a fight, lads!" And, still rolling up his sleeve, he went out to the porch.

The factory hands followed him. These men, who under the leadership of the tall lad were drinking in the dramshop that morning, had brought the publican some skins from the factory and for this had had drink served them. The blacksmiths from a neighboring smithy, hearing the sounds of revelry in the tavern and supposing it to have been broken into, wished to force their way in too and a fight in the porch had resulted.

The publican was fighting one of the smiths at the door, and when the workmen came out the smith, wrenching himself free from the tavern keeper, fell face downward on the pavement.

Another smith tried to enter the doorway, pressing against the publican with his chest.

The lad with the turned-up sleeve gave the smith a blow in the face and cried wildly: "They're fighting us, lads!"

At that moment the first smith got up and, scratching his bruised face to make it bleed, shouted in a tearful voice: "Police! Murder! . . . They've killed a man, lads!"

"Oh, gracious me, a man beaten to death—killed! . . ." screamed a woman coming out of a gate close by.

A crowd gathered round the bloodstained smith.

"Haven't you robbed people enough—taking their last shirts?" said a voice addressing the publican. "What have you killed a man for, you thief?"

The tall lad, standing in the porch, turned his bleared eyes from the publican to the smith and back again as if considering whom he ought to fight now.

"Murderer!" he shouted suddenly to the publican. "Bind him, lads!"

"I daresay you would like to bind me!" shouted the publican, pushing away the men advancing on him, and snatching his cap from his head he flung it on the ground.

As if this action had some mysterious and menacing significance, the workmen surrounding the publican paused in indecision.

"I know the law very well, mates! I'll take the matter to the captain of police. You think I won't get to him? Robbery is not permitted to anybody nowadays!" shouted the publican, picking up his cap.

"Come along then! Come along then!" the publican and the tall young fellow repeated one after the other, and they moved up the street together.

The bloodstained smith went beside them. The factory hands and others followed behind, talking and shouting.

At the corner of the Moroséyka, opposite a large house with closed shutters and bearing a bootmaker's signboard, stood a score of thin, worn-out, gloomy-faced bootmakers, wearing overalls and long tattered coats.

"He should pay folks off properly," a thin workingman, with frowning brows and a straggly beard, was saying.

"But he's sucked our blood and now he thinks he's quit of us. He's been misleading us all the week and now that he's brought us to this pass he's made off."

On seeing the crowd and the bloodstained man the workman ceased speaking, and with eager curiosity all the bootmakers joined the moving crowd.

"Where are all the folks going?"

"Why, to the police, of course!"

"I say, is it true that we have been beaten?" "And what did you think? Look what folks are saying."

Questions and answers were heard. The publican, taking advantage of the increased crowd, dropped behind and returned to his tavern.

The tall youth, not noticing the disappearance of his foe, waved his bare arm and went on talking incessantly, attracting general attention to himself. It was around him that the people chiefly crowded, expecting answers from him to the questions that occupied all their minds.

"He must keep order, keep the law, that's what the government is there for. Am I not right, good Christians?" said the tall youth, with a scarcely perceptible smile. "He thinks there's no government! How can one do without government? Or else there would be plenty who'd rob us."

"Why talk nonsense?" rejoined voices in the crowd. "Will they give up Moscow like this? They told you that for fun, and you believed it! Aren't there plenty of troops on the march? Let him in, indeed! That's what the government is for. You'd better listen to what people are saying," said some of the mob pointing to the tall youth.

By the wall of China-Town a smaller group of people were gathered round a man in a frieze coat who held a paper in his hand.

"An ukáse, they are reading an ukáse! Reading an ukáse!" cried voices in the crowd, and the people rushed toward the reader.

The man in the frieze coat was reading the broadsheet of August 31. When the crowd collected round him he seemed confused, but at the demand of the tall lad who had pushed his way up to him, he began in a rather tremulous voice to read the sheet from the beginning.

"Early tomorrow I shall go to his Serene Highness," he read ("Sirin Highness," said the tall fellow with a triumphant smile on his lips and a frown on his brow), "to consult with him to act, and to aid the army to exterminate these scoundrels. We too will take part. . ." the reader went on, and then paused ("Do you see," shouted the youth victoriously, "he's going to clear up the whole affair for you. . ."), "in destroying them, and will send these visitors to the devil. I will come back to dinner, and we'll set to work. We will do, completely do, and undo these scoundrels."

The last words were read out in the midst of complete silence. The tall lad hung his head gloomily. It was evident that no one had understood the last part. In particular, the words "I will come back to dinner," evidently displeased both reader and audience. The people's minds were tuned to a high pitch and this was too simple and needlessly comprehensible—it was what any one of them might have said and therefore was what an ukáse emanating from the highest authority should not say.

LEO TOLSTOY

They all stood despondent and silent. The tall youth moved his lips and swayed from side to side.

"We should ask him. . . that's he himself?" . . . "Yes, ask him indeed! . . . Why not? He'll explain" . . . voices in the rear of the crowd were suddenly heard saying, and the general attention turned to the police superintendent's trap which drove into the square attended by two mounted dragoons.

The superintendent of police, who had gone that morning by Count Rostopchín's orders to burn the barges and had in connection with that matter acquired a large sum of money which was at that moment in his pocket, on seeing a crowd bearing down upon him told his coachman to stop.

"What people are these?" he shouted to the men, who were moving singly and timidly in the direction of his trap.

"What people are these?" he shouted again, receiving no answer.

"Your honor. . ." replied the shopman in the frieze coat, "your honor, in accord with the proclamation of his highest excellency the count, they desire to serve, not sparing their lives, and it is not any kind of riot, but as his highest excellence said. . ."

"The count has not left, he is here, and an order will be issued concerning you," said the superintendent of police. "Go on!" he ordered his coachman.

The crowd halted, pressing around those who had heard what the superintendent had said, and looking at the departing trap.

The superintendent of police turned round at that moment with a scared look, said something to his coachman, and his horses increased their speed.

"It's a fraud, lads! Lead the way to him, himself!" shouted the tall youth. "Don't let him go, lads! Let him answer us! Keep him!" shouted different people and the people dashed in pursuit of the trap.

Following the superintendent of police and talking loudly the crowd went in the direction of the Lubyánka Street.

"There now, the gentry and merchants have gone away and left us to perish. Do they think we're dogs?" voices in the crowd were heard saying more and more frequently.

# XXIV

On the evening of the first of September, after his interview with Kutúzov, Count Rostopchín had returned to Moscow mortified and offended because he had not been invited to attend the council of war, and because Kutúzov had paid no attention to his offer to take part in the defense of the city; amazed also at the novel outlook revealed to him at the camp, which treated the tranquillity of the capital and its patriotic fervor as not merely secondary but quite irrelevant and unimportant matters. Distressed, offended, and surprised by all this, Rostopchín had returned to Moscow. After supper he lay down on a sofa without undressing, and was awakened soon after midnight by a courier bringing him a letter from Kutúzov. This letter requested the count to send police officers to guide the troops through the town, as the army was retreating to the Ryazán road beyond Moscow. This was not news to Rostopchín. He had known that Moscow would be abandoned not merely since his interview the previous day with Kutúzov on the Poklónny Hill but ever since the battle of Borodinó, for all the generals who came to Moscow after that battle had said unanimously that it was impossible to fight another battle, and since then the government property had been removed every night, and half the inhabitants had left the city with Rostopchín's own permission. Yet all the same this information astonished and irritated the count, coming as it did in the form of a simple note with an order from Kutúzov, and received at night, breaking in on his beauty sleep.

When later on in his memoirs Count Rostopchín explained his actions at this time, he repeatedly says that he was then actuated by two important considerations: to maintain tranquillity in Moscow and expedite the departure of the inhabitants. If one accepts this twofold aim all Rostopchín's actions appear irreproachable. "Why were the holy relics, the arms, ammunition, gunpowder, and stores of corn not removed? Why were thousands of inhabitants deceived into believing that Moscow would not be given up—and thereby ruined?" "To preserve the tranquillity of the city," explains Count Rostopchín. "Why were bundles of useless papers from the government offices, and Leppich's balloon and other articles removed?" "To leave the town empty," explains Count Rostopchín. One need only admit that public tranquillity is in danger and any action finds a justification.

All the horrors of the reign of terror were based only on solicitude for public tranquillity.

On what, then, was Count Rostopchín's fear for the tranquillity of Moscow based in 1812? What reason was there for assuming any probability of an uprising in the city? The inhabitants were leaving it and the retreating troops were filling it. Why should that cause the masses to riot?

Neither in Moscow nor anywhere in Russia did anything resembling an insurrection ever occur when the enemy entered a town. More than ten thousand people were still in Moscow on the first and second of September, and except for a mob in the governor's courtyard, assembled there at his bidding, nothing happened. It is obvious that there would have been even less reason to expect a disturbance among the people if after the battle of Borodinó, when the surrender of Moscow became certain or at least probable, Rostopchín instead of exciting the people by distributing arms and broadsheets had taken steps to remove all the holy relics, the gunpowder, munitions, and money, and had told the population plainly that the town would be abandoned.

Rostopchín, though he had patriotic sentiments, was a sanguine and impulsive man who had always moved in the highest administrative circles and had no understanding at all of the people he supposed himself to be guiding. Ever since the enemy's entry into Smolénsk he had in imagination been playing the role of director of the popular feeling of "the heart of Russia." Not only did it seem to him (as to all administrators) that he controlled the external actions of Moscow's inhabitants, but he also thought he controlled their mental attitude by means of his broadsheets and posters, written in a coarse tone which the people despise in their own class and do not understand from those in authority. Rostopchín was so pleased with the fine role of leader of popular feeling, and had grown so used to it, that the necessity of relinquishing that role and abandoning Moscow without any heroic display took him unawares and he suddenly felt the ground slip away from under his feet, so that he positively did not know what to do. Though he knew it was coming, he did not till the last moment wholeheartedly believe that Moscow would be abandoned, and did not prepare for it. The inhabitants left against his wishes. If the government offices were removed, this was only done on the demand of officials to whom the count yielded reluctantly. He was absorbed in the role he had created for himself. As is often the case with those gifted with an ardent imagination, though he had long known that Moscow would be abandoned he knew it only with his intellect, he did not believe it in his heart and did not adapt himself mentally to this new position of affairs.

All his painstaking and energetic activity (in how far it was useful and had any effect on the people is another question) had been simply directed toward arousing in the masses his own feeling of patriotic hatred of the French.

But when events assumed their true historical character, when expressing hatred for the French in words proved insufficient, when it was not even possible to express that hatred by fighting a battle, when self-confidence was of no avail in relation to the one question before Moscow, when the whole population streamed out of Moscow as one man, abandoning their belongings and proving by that negative action all the depth of their national feeling, then the role chosen by Rostopchín suddenly appeared senseless. He unexpectedly felt himself ridiculous, weak, and alone, with no ground to stand on.

When, awakened from his sleep, he received that cold, peremptory note from Kutúzov, he felt the more irritated the more he felt himself to blame. All that he had been specially put in charge of, the state property which he should have removed, was still in Moscow and it was no longer possible to take the whole of it away.

"Who is to blame for it? Who has let things come to such a pass?" he ruminated. "Not I, of course. I had everything ready. I had Moscow firmly in hand. And this is what they have let it come to! Villains! Traitors!" he thought, without clearly defining who the villains and traitors were, but feeling it necessary to hate those traitors whoever they might be who were to blame for the false and ridiculous position in which he found himself.

All that night Count Rostopchín issued orders, for which people came to him from all parts of Moscow. Those about him had never seen the count so morose and irritable.

"Your excellency, the Director of the Registrar's Department has sent for instructions. . . From the Consistory, from the Senate, from the University, from the Foundling Hospital, the Suffragan has sent. . . asking for information. . . What are your orders about the Fire Brigade? From the governor of the prison. . . from the superintendent of the lunatic asylum. . ." All night long such announcements were continually being received by the count.

To all these inquiries he gave brief and angry replies indicating that orders from him were not now needed, that the whole affair, carefully prepared by him, had now been ruined by somebody, and that that somebody would have to bear the whole responsibility for all that might happen.

"Oh, tell that blockhead," he said in reply to the question from the Registrar's Department, "that he should remain to guard his documents. Now why are you asking silly questions about the Fire Brigade? They have horses, let them be off to Vladímir, and not leave them to the French."

"Your excellency, the superintendent of the lunatic asylum has come: what are your commands?"

"My commands? Let them go away, that's all. . . And let the lunatics out into the town. When lunatics command our armies God evidently means these other madmen to be free."

In reply to an inquiry about the convicts in the prison, Count Rostopchín shouted angrily at the governor:

"Do you expect me to give you two battalions—which we have not got—for a convoy? Release them, that's all about it!"

"Your excellency, there are some political prisoners, Meshkóv, Vereshchágin. . ."

"Vereshchágin! Hasn't he been hanged yet?" shouted Rostopchín. "Bring him to me!"

# XXV

Toward nine o'clock in the morning, when the troops were already moving through Moscow, nobody came to the count any more for instructions. Those who were able to get away were going of their own accord, those who remained behind decided for themselves what they must do.

The count ordered his carriage that he might drive to Sokólniki, and sat in his study with folded hands, morose, sallow, and taciturn.

In quiet and untroubled times it seems to every administrator that it is only by his efforts that the whole population under his rule is kept going, and in this consciousness of being indispensable every administrator finds the chief reward of his labor and efforts. While the sea of history remains calm the ruler-administrator in his frail bark, holding on with a boat hook to the ship of the people and himself moving, naturally imagines that his efforts move the ship he is holding on to. But as soon as a storm arises and the sea begins to heave and the ship to move, such a delusion is no longer possible. The ship moves independently with its own enormous motion, the boat hook no longer reaches the moving vessel, and suddenly the administrator, instead of appearing a ruler and a source of power, becomes an insignificant, useless, feeble man.

Rostopchín felt this, and it was this which exasperated him.

The superintendent of police, whom the crowd had stopped, went in to see him at the same time as an adjutant who informed the count that the horses were harnessed. They were both pale, and the superintendent of police, after reporting that he had executed the instructions he had received, informed the count that an immense crowd had collected in the courtyard and wished to see him.

Without saying a word Rostopchín rose and walked hastily to his light, luxurious drawing room, went to the balcony door, took hold of the handle, let it go again, and went to the window from which he had a better view of the whole crowd. The tall lad was standing in front, flourishing his arm and saying something with a stern look. The blood-stained smith stood beside him with a gloomy face. A drone of voices was audible through the closed window.

"Is my carriage ready?" asked Rostopchín, stepping back from the window.

"It is, your excellency," replied the adjutant.

Rostopchín went again to the balcony door.

"But what do they want?" he asked the superintendent of police.

"Your excellency, they say they have got ready, according to your orders, to go against the French, and they shouted something about treachery. But it is a turbulent crowd, your excellency—I hardly managed to get away from it. Your excellency, I venture to suggest. . ."

"You may go. I don't need you to tell me what to do!" exclaimed Rostopchín angrily.

He stood by the balcony door looking at the crowd.

"This is what they have done with Russia! This is what they have done with me!" thought he, full of an irrepressible fury that welled up within him against the someone to whom what was happening might be attributed. As often happens with passionate people, he was mastered by anger but was still seeking an object on which to vent it. "Here is that mob, the dregs of the people," he thought as he gazed at the crowd: "this rabble they have roused by their folly! They want a victim," he thought as he looked at the tall lad flourishing his arm. And this thought occurred to him just because he himself desired a victim, something on which to vent his rage.

"Is the carriage ready?" he asked again.

"Yes, your excellency. What are your orders about Vereshchágin? He is waiting at the porch," said the adjutant.

"Ah!" exclaimed Rostopchín, as if struck by an unexpected recollection.

And rapidly opening the door he went resolutely out onto the balcony. The talking instantly ceased, hats and caps were doffed, and all eyes were raised to the count.

"Good morning, lads!" said the count briskly and loudly. "Thank you for coming. I'll come out to you in a moment, but we must first settle with the villain. We must punish the villain who has caused the ruin of Moscow. Wait for me!"

And the count stepped as briskly back into the room and slammed the door behind him.

A murmur of approbation and satisfaction ran through the crowd. "He'll settle with all the villains, you'll see! And you said the French. . . He'll show you what law is!" the mob were saying as if reproving one another for their lack of confidence.

A few minutes later an officer came hurriedly out of the front door, gave an order, and the dragoons formed up in line. The crowd moved eagerly from the balcony toward the porch. Rostopchín, coming out there with quick angry steps, looked hastily around as if seeking someone.

"Where is he?" he inquired. And as he spoke he saw a young man coming round the corner of the house between two dragoons. He had a long thin neck, and his head, that had been half shaved, was again covered by short hair. This young man was dressed in a threadbare blue cloth coat lined with fox fur, that had once been smart, and dirty hempen convict trousers, over which were pulled his thin, dirty, trodden-down boots. On his thin, weak legs were heavy chains which hampered his irresolute movements.

"Ah!" said Rostopchín, hurriedly turning away his eyes from the young man in the fur-lined coat and pointing to the bottom step of the porch. "Put him there."

The young man in his clattering chains stepped clumsily to the spot indicated, holding away with one finger the coat collar which chafed his neck, turned his long neck twice this way and that, sighed, and submissively folded before him his thin hands, unused to work.

For several seconds while the young man was taking his place on the step the silence continued. Only among the back rows of the people, who were all pressing toward the one spot, could sighs, groans, and the shuffling of feet be heard.

While waiting for the young man to take his place on the step Rostopchín stood frowning and rubbing his face with his hand.

"Lads!" said he, with a metallic ring in his voice. "This man, Vereshchágin, is the scoundrel by whose doing Moscow is perishing."

The young man in the fur-lined coat, stooping a little, stood in a submissive attitude, his fingers clasped before him. His emaciated young face, disfigured by the half-shaven head, hung down hopelessly. At the count's first words he raised it slowly and looked up at him as if wishing to say something or at least to meet his eye. But Rostopchín did not look at him. A vein in the young man's long thin neck swelled like a cord and went blue behind the ear, and suddenly his face flushed.

All eyes were fixed on him. He looked at the crowd, and rendered more hopeful by the expression he read on the faces there, he smiled sadly and timidly, and lowering his head shifted his feet on the step.

"He has betrayed his Tsar and his country, he has gone over to Bonaparte. He alone of all the Russians has disgraced the Russian name, he has caused Moscow to perish," said Rostopchín in a sharp, even voice, but suddenly he glanced down at Vereshchágin who continued to stand in the same submissive attitude. As if inflamed by the sight, he raised his arm and addressed the people, almost shouting:

"Deal with him as you think fit! I hand him over to you."

The crowd remained silent and only pressed closer and closer to one another. To keep one another back, to breathe in that stifling atmosphere, to be unable to stir, and to await something unknown, uncomprehended, and terrible, was becoming unbearable. Those standing in front, who had seen and heard what had taken place before them, all stood with wide-open eyes and mouths, straining with all their strength, and held back the crowd that was pushing behind them.

"Beat him! . . . Let the traitor perish and not disgrace the Russian name!" shouted Rostopchín. "Cut him down. I command it."

Hearing not so much the words as the angry tone of Rostopchín's voice, the crowd moaned and heaved forward, but again paused.

"Count!" exclaimed the timid yet theatrical voice of Vereshchágin in the midst of the momentary silence that ensued, "Count! One God is above us both. . ." He lifted his head and again the thick vein in his thin neck filled with blood and the color rapidly came and went in his face.

He did not finish what he wished to say.

"Cut him down! I command it. . ." shouted Rostopchín, suddenly growing pale like Vereshchágin.

"Draw sabers!" cried the dragoon officer, drawing his own.

Another still stronger wave flowed through the crowd and reaching the front ranks carried it swaying to the very steps of the porch. The tall youth, with a stony look on his face, and rigid and uplifted arm, stood beside Vereshchágin.

"Saber him!" the dragoon officer almost whispered.

And one of the soldiers, his face all at once distorted with fury, struck Vereshchágin on the head with the blunt side of his saber.

"Ah!" cried Vereshchágin in meek surprise, looking round with a frightened glance as if not understanding why this was done to him. A similar moan of surprise and horror ran through the crowd. "O Lord!" exclaimed a sorrowful voice.

But after the exclamation of surprise that had escaped from Vereshchágin he uttered a plaintive cry of pain, and that cry was fatal. The barrier of human feeling, strained to the utmost, that had held the crowd in check suddenly broke. The crime had begun and must now be completed. The plaintive moan of reproach was drowned by the threatening and angry roar of the crowd. Like the seventh and last wave that shatters a ship, that last irresistible wave burst from the rear and reached the front ranks, carrying them off their feet and engulfing them all. The dragoon was about to repeat his blow. Vereshchágin with a cry of horror, covering his head with his hands, rushed toward the crowd. The tall youth, against whom he stumbled, seized his thin neck with his hands and, yelling wildly, fell with him under the feet of the pressing, struggling crowd.

Some beat and tore at Vereshchágin, others at the tall youth. And the screams of those that were being trampled on and of those who tried to rescue the tall lad only increased the fury of the crowd. It was a long time before the dragoons could extricate the bleeding youth, beaten almost to death. And for a long time, despite the feverish haste with which the mob tried to end the work that had been begun, those who were hitting, throttling, and tearing at Vereshchágin were unable to kill him, for the crowd pressed from all sides, swaying as one mass with them in the center and rendering it impossible for them either to kill him or let him go.

"Hit him with an ax, eh! . . . Crushed? . . . Traitor, he sold Christ. . . Still alive. . . tenacious. . . serves him right! Torture serves a thief right. Use the hatchet! . . . What—still alive?"

Only when the victim ceased to struggle and his cries changed to a long-drawn, measured death rattle did the crowd around his prostrate, bleeding corpse begin rapidly to change places. Each one came up, glanced at what had been done, and with horror, reproach, and astonishment pushed back again.

"O Lord! The people are like wild beasts! How could he be alive?" voices in the crowd could be heard saying. "Quite a young fellow too. . . must have been a merchant's son. What men! . . . and they say he's not the right one. . . How not the right one? . . . O Lord! And there's another has been beaten too—they say he's nearly done for. . . Oh, the people. . . Aren't they afraid of sinning? . . ." said the same mob now, looking with pained distress at the dead body with its long, thin, half-severed neck and its livid face stained with blood and dust.

A painstaking police officer, considering the presence of a corpse in his excellency's courtyard unseemly, told the dragoons to take it away. Two dragoons took it by its distorted legs and dragged it along the ground. The gory, dust-stained, half-shaven head with its long neck trailed twisting along the ground. The crowd shrank back from it.

At the moment when Vereshchágin fell and the crowd closed in with savage yells and swayed about him, Rostopchín suddenly turned pale and, instead of going to the back entrance where his carriage awaited him, went with hurried steps and bent head, not knowing where and why, along the passage leading to the rooms on the ground floor. The count's face was white and he could not control the feverish twitching of his lower jaw.

"This way, your excellency. . . Where are you going? . . . This way, please. . ." said a trembling, frightened voice behind him.

Count Rostopchín was unable to reply and, turning obediently, went in the direction indicated. At the back entrance stood his calèche. The distant roar of the yelling crowd was audible even there. He hastily took his seat and told the coachman to drive him to his country house in Sokólniki.

When they reached the Myasnítski Street and could no longer hear the shouts of the mob, the count began to repent. He remembered with dissatisfaction the agitation and fear he had betrayed before his subordinates. "The mob is terrible—disgusting," he said to himself in French. "They are like wolves whom nothing but flesh can appease." "Count! One God is above us both!"—Vereshchágin's words suddenly recurred to him, and a disagreeable shiver ran down his back. But this was only a momentary feeling and Count Rostopchín smiled disdainfully at himself. "I had other duties," thought he. "The people had to be appeased. Many other victims have perished and are perishing for the public good"—and he began thinking of his social duties to his family and to the city entrusted to him, and of himself—not himself as Theodore Vasílyevich Rostopchín (he fancied that Theodore Vasílyevich Rostopchín was sacrificing himself for the public good) but himself as governor, the representative of authority and of the Tsar. "Had I been simply Theodore Vasílyevich my course of action would have been quite different, but it was my duty to safeguard my life and dignity as commander in chief."

Lightly swaying on the flexible springs of his carriage and no longer hearing the terrible sounds of the crowd, Rostopchín grew physically calm and, as always happens, as soon as he became physically tranquil his mind devised reasons why he should be mentally tranquil too. The thought which tranquillized Rostopchín was not a new one. Since the world began and men have killed one another no one has ever committed such a crime against his fellow man without comforting himself with this same idea. This idea is le bien public, the hypothetical welfare of other people.

To a man not swayed by passion that welfare is never certain, but he who commits such a crime always knows just where that welfare lies. And Rostopchín now knew it.

Not only did his reason not reproach him for what he had done, but he even found cause for self-satisfaction in having so successfully contrived to avail himself of a convenient opportunity to punish a criminal and at the same time pacify the mob.

"Vereshchágin was tried and condemned to death," thought Rostopchín (though the Senate had only condemned Vereshchágin to hard labor), "he was a traitor and a spy. I could not let him go unpunished and so I have killed two birds with one stone: to appease the mob I gave them a victim and at the same time punished a miscreant."

Having reached his country house and begun to give orders about domestic arrangements, the count grew quite tranquil.

Half an hour later he was driving with his fast horses across the Sokólniki field, no longer thinking of what had occurred but considering what was to come. He was driving to the Yaúza bridge where he had heard that Kutúzov was. Count Rostopchín was mentally preparing the angry and stinging reproaches he meant to address to Kutúzov for his deception. He would make that foxy old courtier feel that the responsibility for all the calamities that would follow the abandonment of the city and the ruin of Russia (as Rostopchín regarded it) would fall upon his doting old head. Planning beforehand what he would say to Kutúzov, Rostopchín turned angrily in his calèche and gazed sternly from side to side.

The Sokólniki field was deserted. Only at the end of it, in front of the almshouse and the lunatic asylum, could be seen some people in white and others like them walking singly across the field shouting and gesticulating.

One of these was running to cross the path of Count Rostopchín's carriage, and the count himself, his coachman, and his dragoons looked with vague horror and curiosity at these released lunatics and especially at the one running toward them.

Swaying from side to side on his long, thin legs in his fluttering dressing gown, this lunatic was running impetuously, his gaze fixed on Rostopchín, shouting something in a hoarse voice and making signs to him to stop. The lunatic's solemn, gloomy face was thin and yellow, with its beard growing in uneven tufts. His black, agate pupils with saffron-yellow whites moved restlessly near the lower eyelids.

"Stop! Pull up, I tell you!" he cried in a piercing voice, and again shouted something breathlessly with emphatic intonations and gestures.

Coming abreast of the calèche he ran beside it.

"Thrice have they slain me, thrice have I risen from the dead. They stoned me, crucified me. . . I shall rise. . . shall rise. . . shall rise. They have torn my body. The kingdom of God will be overthrown. . . Thrice will I overthrow it and thrice re-establish it!" he cried, raising his voice higher and higher.

Count Rostopchín suddenly grew pale as he had done when the crowd closed in on Vereshchágin. He turned away. "Go fas. . . faster!" he cried in a trembling voice to his coachman. The calèche flew over the ground as fast as the horses could draw it, but for a long time Count Rostopchín still heard the insane despairing screams growing fainter in the distance, while his eyes saw nothing but the astonished, frightened, bloodstained face of "the traitor" in the fur-lined coat.

Recent as that mental picture was, Rostopchín already felt that it had cut deep into his heart and drawn blood. Even now he felt clearly that the gory trace of that recollection would not pass with time, but that the terrible memory would, on the contrary, dwell in his heart ever more cruelly and painfully to the end of his life. He seemed still to hear the sound of his own words: "Cut him down! I command it. . ."

"Why did I utter those words? It was by some accident I said them. . . I need not have said them," he thought. "And then nothing would have happened." He saw the frightened and then infuriated face of the dragoon who dealt the blow, the look of silent, timid reproach that boy in the fur-lined coat had turned upon him. "But I did not do it for my own sake. I was bound to act that way. . . The mob, the traitor. . . the public welfare," thought he.

Troops were still crowding at the Yaúza bridge. It was hot. Kutúzov, dejected and frowning, sat on a bench by the bridge toying with his whip in the sand when a calèche dashed up noisily. A man in a general's uniform with plumes in his hat went up to Kutúzov and said something in French. It was Count Rostopchín. He told Kutúzov that he had come because Moscow, the capital, was no more and only the army remained.

"Things would have been different if your Serene Highness had not told me that you would not abandon Moscow without another battle; all this would not have happened," he said.

Kutúzov looked at Rostopchín as if, not grasping what was said to him, he was trying to read something peculiar written at that moment on the face of the man addressing him. Rostopchín grew confused and became silent. Kutúzov slightly shook his head and not taking his penetrating gaze from Rostopchín's face muttered softly:

"No! I shall not give up Moscow without a battle!"

Whether Kutúzov was thinking of something entirely different when he spoke those words, or uttered them purposely, knowing them to be meaningless, at any rate Rostopchín made no reply and hastily left him. And strange to say, the Governor of Moscow, the proud Count Rostopchín, took up a Cossack whip and went to the bridge where he began with shouts to drive on the carts that blocked the way.

# XXVI

Toward four o'clock in the afternoon Murat's troops were entering Moscow. In front rode a detachment of Württemberg hussars and behind them rode the King of Naples himself accompanied by a numerous suite.

About the middle of the Arbát Street, near the Church of the Miraculous Icon of St. Nicholas, Murat halted to await news from the advanced detachment as to the condition in which they had found the citadel, le Kremlin.

Around Murat gathered a group of those who had remained in Moscow. They all stared in timid bewilderment at the strange, long-haired commander dressed up in feathers and gold.

"Is that their Tsar himself? He's not bad!" low voices could be heard saying.

An interpreter rode up to the group.

"Take off your cap... your caps!" These words went from one to another in the crowd. The interpreter addressed an old porter and asked if it was far to the Krémlin. The porter, listening in perplexity to the unfamiliar Polish accent and not realizing that the interpreter was speaking Russian, did not understand what was being said to him and slipped behind the others.

Murat approached the interpreter and told him to ask where the Russian army was. One of the Russians understood what was asked and several voices at once began answering the interpreter. A French officer, returning from the advanced detachment, rode up to Murat and reported that the gates of the citadel had been barricaded and that there was probably an ambuscade there.

"Good!" said Murat and, turning to one of the gentlemen in his suite, ordered four light guns to be moved forward to fire at the gates.

The guns emerged at a trot from the column following Murat and advanced up the Arbát. When they reached the end of the Vozdvízhenka Street they halted and drew in the Square. Several French officers superintended the placing of the guns and looked at the Krémlin through field glasses.

The bells in the Krémlin were ringing for vespers, and this sound troubled the French. They imagined it to be a call to arms. A few infantrymen ran to the Kutáfyev Gate. Beams and wooden screens had been put there, and two musket shots rang out from under the gate as soon as an officer and men began to run toward it. A general who was standing by the guns shouted some words of command to the officer, and the latter ran back again with his men.

The sound of three more shots came from the gate.

One shot struck a French soldier's foot, and from behind the screens came the strange sound of a few voices shouting. Instantly as at a word of command the expression of cheerful serenity on the faces of the French general, officers, and men changed to one of determined concentrated readiness for strife and suffering. To all of them from the marshal to the least soldier, that place was not the Vozdvízhenka, Mokhaváya, or Kutáfyev Street, nor the Tróitsa Gate (places familiar in Moscow), but a new battlefield which would probably prove sanguinary. And all made ready for that battle. The cries from the gates ceased. The guns were advanced, the artillerymen blew the ash off their linstocks, and an officer gave the word "Fire!" This was followed by two whistling sounds of canister shot, one after another. The shot rattled against the stone of the gate and upon the wooden beams and screens, and two wavering clouds of smoke rose over the Square.

A few instants after the echo of the reports resounding over the stone-built Krémlin had died away the French heard a strange sound above their head. Thousands of crows rose above the walls and circled in the air, cawing and noisily flapping their wings. Together with that sound came a solitary human cry from the gateway and amid the smoke appeared the figure of a bareheaded man in a peasant's coat. He grasped a musket and took aim at the French. "Fire!" repeated the officer once more, and the reports of a musket and of two cannon shots were heard simultaneously. The gate was again hidden by smoke.

Nothing more stirred behind the screens and the French infantry soldiers and officers advanced to the gate. In the gateway lay three wounded and four dead. Two men in peasant coats ran away at the foot of the wall, toward the Známenka.

"Clear that away!" said the officer, pointing to the beams and the corpses, and the French soldiers, after dispatching the wounded, threw the corpses over the parapet.

Who these men were nobody knew. "Clear that away!" was all that was said of them, and they were thrown over the parapet and removed later on that they might not stink. Thiers alone dedicates a few eloquent lines to their memory: "These wretches had occupied the sacred citadel, having supplied themselves with guns from the arsenal, and fired" (the wretches) "at the French. Some of them were sabered and the Krémlin was purged of their presence."

Murat was informed that the way had been cleared. The French entered the gates and began pitching their camp in the Senate Square. Out of the windows of the Senate House the soldiers threw chairs into the Square for fuel and kindled fires there.

Other detachments passed through the Krémlin and encamped along the Moroséyka, the Lubyánka, and Pokróvka Streets. Others quartered themselves along the Vozdvízhenka, the Nikólski, and the Tverskóy Streets. No masters of the houses being found anywhere, the French were not billeted on the inhabitants as is usual in towns but lived in it as in a camp.

Though tattered, hungry, worn out, and reduced to a third of their original number, the French entered Moscow in good marching order. It was a weary and famished, but still a fighting and menacing army. But it remained an army only until its soldiers had dispersed into their different lodgings. As soon as the men of the various regiments began to disperse among the wealthy and deserted houses, the army was lost forever and there came into being something nondescript, neither citizens nor soldiers but what are known as marauders. When five weeks later these same men left Moscow, they no longer formed an army. They were a mob of marauders, each carrying a quantity of articles which seemed to him valuable or useful. The aim of each man when he left Moscow was no longer, as it had been, to conquer, but merely to keep what he had acquired. Like a monkey which puts its paw into the narrow neck of a jug, and having seized a handful of nuts will not open its fist for fear of losing what it holds, and therefore perishes, the French when they left Moscow had inevitably to perish because they carried their loot with them, yet to abandon what they had stolen was as impossible for them as it is for the monkey to open its paw and let go of its nuts. Ten minutes after each regiment had entered a Moscow district, not a soldier or officer was left. Men in military uniforms and Hessian boots could be seen through the windows, laughing and walking through the rooms. In cellars and storerooms similar men were busy among the provisions, and in the yards unlocking or breaking open coach house and stable doors, lighting fires in kitchens and kneading and baking bread with rolled-up sleeves, and cooking; or frightening, amusing, or caressing women and children. There were many such men both in the shops and houses—but there was no army.

Order after order was issued by the French commanders that day forbidding the men to disperse about the town, sternly forbidding any violence to the inhabitants or any looting, and announcing a roll call for that very evening. But despite all these measures the men, who had till then constituted an army, flowed all over the wealthy, deserted city with its comforts and plentiful supplies. As a hungry herd of cattle keeps well together when crossing a barren field, but gets out of hand and at once disperses uncontrollably as soon as it reaches rich pastures, so did the army disperse all over the wealthy city.

No residents were left in Moscow, and the soldiers—like water percolating through sand—spread irresistibly through the city in all directions from the Krémlin into which they had first marched. The cavalry, on entering a merchant's house that had been abandoned and finding there stabling more than sufficient for their horses, went on, all the same, to the next house which seemed to them better. Many of them appropriated several houses, chalked their names on them, and quarreled and even fought with other companies for them. Before they had had time to secure quarters the soldiers ran out into the streets to see the city and, hearing that everything had been abandoned, rushed to places where valuables were to be had for the taking. The officers followed to check the soldiers and were involuntarily drawn into doing the same. In Carriage Row carriages had been left in the shops, and generals flocked there to select calèches and coaches for themselves. The few inhabitants who had remained invited commanding officers to their houses, hoping thereby to secure themselves from being plundered. There were masses of wealth and there seemed no end to it. All around the quarters occupied by the French were other regions still unexplored and unoccupied where, they thought, yet greater riches might be found. And Moscow engulfed the army ever deeper and deeper. When water is spilled on dry ground both the dry ground and the water disappear and mud results; and in the same way the entry of the famished army into the rich and deserted city resulted in fires and looting and the destruction of both the army and the wealthy city.

THE FRENCH ATTRIBUTED THE FIRE of Moscow au patriotisme féroce de Rostopchíne,* the Russians to the barbarity of the French. In

---

* To Rostopchín's ferocious patriotism.

reality, however, it was not, and could not be, possible to explain the burning of Moscow by making any individual, or any group of people, responsible for it. Moscow was burned because it found itself in a position in which any town built of wood was bound to burn, quite apart from whether it had, or had not, a hundred and thirty inferior fire engines. Deserted Moscow had to burn as inevitably as a heap of shavings has to burn on which sparks continually fall for several days. A town built of wood, where scarcely a day passes without conflagrations when the house owners are in residence and a police force is present, cannot help burning when its inhabitants have left it and it is occupied by soldiers who smoke pipes, make campfires of the Senate chairs in the Senate Square, and cook themselves meals twice a day. In peacetime it is only necessary to billet troops in the villages of any district and the number of fires in that district immediately increases. How much then must the probability of fire be increased in an abandoned, wooden town where foreign troops are quartered. "Le patriotisme féroce de Rostopchine" and the barbarity of the French were not to blame in the matter. Moscow was set on fire by the soldiers' pipes, kitchens, and campfires, and by the carelessness of enemy soldiers occupying houses they did not own. Even if there was any arson (which is very doubtful, for no one had any reason to burn the houses—in any case a troublesome and dangerous thing to do), arson cannot be regarded as the cause, for the same thing would have happened without any incendiarism.

However tempting it might be for the French to blame Rostopchin's ferocity and for Russians to blame the scoundrel Bonaparte, or later on to place an heroic torch in the hands of their own people, it is impossible not to see that there could be no such direct cause of the fire, for Moscow had to burn as every village, factory, or house must burn which is left by its owners and in which strangers are allowed to live and cook their porridge. Moscow was burned by its inhabitants, it is true, but by those who had abandoned it and not by those who remained in it. Moscow when occupied by the enemy did not remain intact like Berlin, Vienna, and other towns, simply because its inhabitants abandoned it and did not welcome the French with bread and salt, nor bring them the keys of the city.

# XXVII

The absorption of the French by Moscow, radiating starwise as it did, only reached the quarter where Pierre was staying by the evening of the second of September.

After the last two days spent in solitude and unusual circumstances, Pierre was in a state bordering on insanity. He was completely obsessed by one persistent thought. He did not know how or when this thought had taken such possession of him, but he remembered nothing of the past, understood nothing of the present, and all he saw and heard appeared to him like a dream.

He had left home only to escape the intricate tangle of life's demands that enmeshed him, and which in his present condition he was unable to unravel. He had gone to Joseph Alexéevich's house, on the plea of sorting the deceased's books and papers, only in search of rest from life's turmoil, for in his mind the memory of Joseph Alexéevich was connected with a world of eternal, solemn, and calm thoughts, quite contrary to the restless confusion into which he felt himself being drawn. He sought a quiet refuge, and in Joseph Alexéevich's study he really found it. When he sat with his elbows on the dusty writing table in the deathlike stillness of the study, calm and significant memories of the last few days rose one after another in his imagination, particularly of the battle of Borodinó and of that vague sense of his own insignificance and insincerity compared with the truth, simplicity, and strength of the class of men he mentally classed as they. When Gerásim roused him from his reverie the idea occurred to him of taking part in the popular defense of Moscow which he knew was projected. And with that object he had asked Gerásim to get him a peasant's coat and a pistol, confiding to him his intentions of remaining in Joseph Alexéevich's house and keeping his name secret. Then during the first day spent in inaction and solitude (he tried several times to fix his attention on the Masonic manuscripts, but was unable to do so) the idea that had previously occurred to him of the cabalistic significance of his name in connection with Bonaparte's more than once vaguely presented itself. But the idea that he, L'russe Besuhof, was destined to set a limit to the power of the Beast was as yet only one of the fancies that often passed through his mind and left no trace behind.

When, having bought the coat merely with the object of taking part among the people in the defense of Moscow, Pierre had met the Rostóvs and Natásha had said to him: "Are you remaining in Moscow? . . . How splendid!" the thought flashed into his mind that it really would be a good thing, even if Moscow were taken, for him to remain there and do what he was predestined to do.

Next day, with the sole idea of not sparing himself and not lagging in any way behind them, Pierre went to the Three Hills gate. But when he returned to the house convinced that Moscow would not be defended, he suddenly felt that what before had seemed to him merely a possibility had now become absolutely necessary and inevitable. He must remain in Moscow, concealing his name, and must meet Napoleon and kill him, and either perish or put an end to the misery of all Europe—which it seemed to him was solely due to Napoleon.

Pierre knew all the details of the attempt on Bonaparte's life in 1809 by a German student in Vienna, and knew that the student had been shot. And the risk to which he would expose his life by carrying out his design excited him still more.

Two equally strong feelings drew Pierre irresistibly to this purpose. The first was a feeling of the necessity of sacrifice and suffering in view of the common calamity, the same feeling that had caused him to go to Mozháysk on the twenty-fifth and to make his way to the very thick of the battle and had now caused him to run away from his home and, in place of the luxury and comfort to which he was accustomed, to sleep on a hard sofa without undressing and eat the same food as Gerásim. The other was that vague and quite Russian feeling of contempt for everything conventional, artificial, and human—for everything the majority of men regard as the greatest good in the world. Pierre had first experienced this strange and fascinating feeling at the Slobóda Palace, when he had suddenly felt that wealth, power, and life—all that men so painstakingly acquire and guard—if it has any worth has so only by reason of the joy with which it can all be renounced.

It was the feeling that induces a volunteer recruit to spend his last penny on drink, and a drunken man to smash mirrors or glasses for no apparent reason and knowing that it will cost him all the money he possesses: the feeling which causes a man to perform actions which from an ordinary point of view are insane, to test, as it were, his personal power and strength, affirming the existence of a higher, nonhuman criterion of life.

From the very day Pierre had experienced this feeling for the first time at the Slobóda Palace he had been continuously under its influence, but only now found full satisfaction for it. Moreover, at this moment Pierre was supported in his design and prevented from renouncing it by what he had already done in that direction. If he were now to leave Moscow like everyone else, his flight from home, the peasant coat, the pistol, and his announcement to the Rostóvs that he would remain in Moscow would all become not merely meaningless but contemptible and ridiculous, and to this Pierre was very sensitive.

Pierre's physical condition, as is always the case, corresponded to his mental state. The unaccustomed coarse food, the vodka he drank during those days, the absence of wine and cigars, his dirty unchanged linen, two almost sleepless nights passed on a short sofa without bedding—all this kept him in a state of excitement bordering on insanity.

It was two o'clock in the afternoon. The French had already entered Moscow. Pierre knew this, but instead of acting he only thought about his undertaking, going over its minutest details in his mind. In his fancy he did not clearly picture to himself either the striking of the blow or the death of Napoleon, but with extraordinary vividness and melancholy enjoyment imagined his own destruction and heroic endurance.

"Yes, alone, for the sake of all, I must do it or perish!" he thought. "Yes, I will approach. . . and then suddenly. . . with pistol or dagger? But that is all the same! 'It is not I but the hand of Providence that punishes thee,' I shall say," thought he, imagining what he would say when killing Napoleon. "Well then, take me and execute me!" he went on, speaking to himself and bowing his head with a sad but firm expression.

While Pierre, standing in the middle of the room, was talking to himself in this way, the study door opened and on the threshold appeared the figure of Makár Alexéevich, always so timid before but now quite transformed.

His dressing gown was unfastened, his face red and distorted. He was obviously drunk. On seeing Pierre he grew confused at first, but noticing embarrassment on Pierre's face immediately grew bold and, staggering on his thin legs, advanced into the middle of the room.

"They're frightened," he said confidentially in a hoarse voice. "I say I won't surrender, I say. . . Am I not right, sir?"

He paused and then suddenly seeing the pistol on the table seized it with unexpected rapidity and ran out into the corridor.

Gerásim and the porter, who had followed Makár Alexéevich, stopped him in the vestibule and tried to take the pistol from him.

Pierre, coming out into the corridor, looked with pity and repulsion at the half-crazy old man. Makár Alexéevich, frowning with exertion, held on to the pistol and screamed hoarsely, evidently with some heroic fancy in his head.

"To arms! Board them! No, you shan't get it," he yelled.

"That will do, please, that will do. Have the goodness—please, sir, to let go! Please, sir. . ." pleaded Gerásim, trying carefully to steer Makár Alexéevich by the elbows back to the door.

"Who are you? Bonaparte! . . ." shouted Makár Alexéevich.

"That's not right, sir. Come to your room, please, and rest. Allow me to have the pistol."

"Be off, thou base slave! Touch me not! See this?" shouted Makár Alexéevich, brandishing the pistol. "Board them!"

"Catch hold!" whispered Gerásim to the porter.

They seized Makár Alexéevich by the arms and dragged him to the door.

The vestibule was filled with the discordant sounds of a struggle and of a tipsy, hoarse voice.

Suddenly a fresh sound, a piercing feminine scream, reverberated from the porch and the cook came running into the vestibule.

"It's them! Gracious heavens! O Lord, four of them, horsemen!" she cried.

Gerásim and the porter let Makár Alexéevich go, and in the now silent corridor the sound of several hands knocking at the front door could be heard.

# XXVIII

Pierre, having decided that until he had carried out his design he would disclose neither his identity nor his knowledge of French, stood at the half-open door of the corridor, intending to conceal himself as soon as the French entered. But the French entered and still Pierre did not retire—an irresistible curiosity kept him there.

There were two of them. One was an officer—a tall, soldierly, handsome man—the other evidently a private or an orderly, sunburned, short, and thin, with sunken cheeks and a dull expression. The officer walked in front, leaning on a stick and slightly limping. When he had advanced a few steps he stopped, having apparently decided that these were good quarters, turned round to the soldiers standing at the entrance, and in a loud voice of command ordered them to put up the horses. Having done that, the officer, lifting his elbow with a smart gesture, stroked his mustache and lightly touched his hat.

"Bonjour, la compagnie!"* said he gaily, smiling and looking about him.

No one gave any reply.

"Vous êtes le bourgeois?"† the officer asked Gerásim.

Gerásim gazed at the officer with an alarmed and inquiring look.

"Quartier, quartier, logement!" said the officer, looking down at the little man with a condescending and good-natured smile. "Les français sont de bons enfants. Que diable! Voyons! Ne nous fâchons pas, mon vieux!"‡ added he, clapping the scared and silent Gerásim on the shoulder. "Well, does no one speak French in this establishment?" he asked again in French, looking around and meeting Pierre's eyes. Pierre moved away from the door.

Again the officer turned to Gerásim and asked him to show him the rooms in the house.

"Master, not here—don't understand. . . me, you. . ." said Gerásim, trying to render his words more comprehensible by contorting them.

Still smiling, the French officer spread out his hands before Gerásim's nose, intimating that he did not understand him either,

---

* "Good day, everybody!"
† "Are you the master here?"
‡ "Quarters, quarters, lodgings! The French are good fellows. What the devil! There, don't let us be cross, old fellow!"

and moved, limping, to the door at which Pierre was standing. Pierre wished to go away and conceal himself, but at that moment he saw Makár Alexéevich appearing at the open kitchen door with the pistol in his hand. With a madman's cunning, Makár Alexéevich eyed the Frenchman, raised his pistol, and took aim.

"Board them!" yelled the tipsy man, trying to press the trigger. Hearing the yell the officer turned round, and at the same moment Pierre threw himself on the drunkard. Just when Pierre snatched at and struck up the pistol Makár Alexéevich at last got his fingers on the trigger, there was a deafening report, and all were enveloped in a cloud of smoke. The Frenchman turned pale and rushed to the door.

Forgetting his intention of concealing his knowledge of French, Pierre, snatching away the pistol and throwing it down, ran up to the officer and addressed him in French.

"You are not wounded?" he asked.

"I think not," answered the Frenchman, feeling himself over. "But I have had a lucky escape this time," he added, pointing to the damaged plaster of the wall. "Who is that man?" said he, looking sternly at Pierre.

"Oh, I am really in despair at what has occurred," said Pierre rapidly, quite forgetting the part he had intended to play. "He is an unfortunate madman who did not know what he was doing."

The officer went up to Makár Alexéevich and took him by the collar.

Makár Alexéevich was standing with parted lips, swaying, as if about to fall asleep, as he leaned against the wall.

"Brigand! You shall pay for this," said the Frenchman, letting go of him. "We French are merciful after victory, but we do not pardon traitors," he added, with a look of gloomy dignity and a fine energetic gesture.

Pierre continued, in French, to persuade the officer not to hold that drunken imbecile to account. The Frenchman listened in silence with the same gloomy expression, but suddenly turned to Pierre with a smile. For a few seconds he looked at him in silence. His handsome face assumed a melodramatically gentle expression and he held out his hand.

"You have saved my life. You are French," said he.

For a Frenchman that deduction was indubitable. Only a Frenchman could perform a great deed, and to save his life—the life of M. Ramballe, captain of the 13th Light Regiment—was undoubtedly a very great deed.

But however indubitable that conclusion and the officer's conviction based upon it, Pierre felt it necessary to disillusion him.

"I am Russian," he said quickly.

"Tut, tut, tut! Tell that to others," said the officer, waving his finger before his nose and smiling. "You shall tell me all about that presently. I am delighted to meet a compatriot. Well, and what are we to do with this man?" he added, addressing himself to Pierre as to a brother.

Even if Pierre were not a Frenchman, having once received that loftiest of human appellations he could not renounce it, said the officer's look and tone. In reply to his last question Pierre again explained who Makár Alexéevich was and how just before their arrival that drunken imbecile had seized the loaded pistol which they had not had time to recover from him, and begged the officer to let the deed go unpunished.

The Frenchman expanded his chest and made a majestic gesture with his arm.

"You have saved my life! You are French. You ask his pardon? I grant it you. Lead that man away!" said he quickly and energetically, and taking the arm of Pierre whom he had promoted to be a Frenchman for saving his life, he went with him into the room.

The soldiers in the yard, hearing the shot, came into the passage asking what had happened, and expressed their readiness to punish the culprits, but the officer sternly checked them.

"You will be called in when you are wanted," he said.

The soldiers went out again, and the orderly, who had meanwhile had time to visit the kitchen, came up to his officer.

"Captain, there is soup and a leg of mutton in the kitchen," said he. "Shall I serve them up?"

"Yes, and some wine," answered the captain.

# XXIX

When the French officer went into the room with Pierre the latter again thought it his duty to assure him that he was not French and wished to go away, but the officer would not hear of it. He was so very polite, amiable, good-natured, and genuinely grateful to Pierre for saving his life that Pierre had not the heart to refuse, and sat down with him in the parlor—the first room they entered. To Pierre's assurances that he was not a Frenchman, the captain, evidently not understanding how anyone could decline so flattering an appellation, shrugged his shoulders and said that if Pierre absolutely insisted on passing for a Russian let it be so, but for all that he would be forever bound to Pierre by gratitude for saving his life.

Had this man been endowed with the slightest capacity for perceiving the feelings of others, and had he at all understood what Pierre's feelings were, the latter would probably have left him, but the man's animated obtuseness to everything other than himself disarmed Pierre.

"A Frenchman or a Russian prince incognito," said the officer, looking at Pierre's fine though dirty linen and at the ring on his finger. "I owe my life to you and offer you my friendship. A Frenchman never forgets either an insult or a service. I offer you my friendship. That is all I can say."

There was so much good nature and nobility (in the French sense of the word) in the officer's voice, in the expression of his face and in his gestures, that Pierre, unconsciously smiling in response to the Frenchman's smile, pressed the hand held out to him.

"Captain Ramballe, of the 13th Light Regiment, Chevalier of the Legion of Honor for the affair on the seventh of September," he introduced himself, a self-satisfied irrepressible smile puckering his lips under his mustache. "Will you now be so good as to tell me with whom I have the honor of conversing so pleasantly, instead of being in the ambulance with that maniac's bullet in my body?"

Pierre replied that he could not tell him his name and, blushing, began to try to invent a name and to say something about his reason for concealing it, but the Frenchman hastily interrupted him.

"Oh, please!" said he. "I understand your reasons. You are an officer. . . a superior officer perhaps. You have borne arms against us. That's not my business. I owe you my life. That is enough for me. I am quite at your service. You belong to the gentry?" he concluded with a shade of inquiry in his tone. Pierre bent his head. "Your baptismal name, if you please. That is all I ask. Monsieur Pierre, you say. . . That's all I want to know."

When the mutton and an omelet had been served and a samovar and vodka brought, with some wine which the French had taken from a Russian cellar and brought with them, Ramballe invited Pierre to share his dinner, and himself began to eat greedily and quickly like a healthy and hungry man, munching his food rapidly with his strong teeth, continually smacking his lips, and repeating—"Excellent! Delicious!" His face grew red and was covered with perspiration. Pierre was hungry and shared the dinner with pleasure. Morel, the orderly, brought some hot water in a saucepan and placed a bottle of claret in it. He also brought a bottle of kvass, taken from the kitchen for them to try. That beverage was already known to the French and had been given a special name. They called it limonade de cochon (pig's lemonade), and Morel spoke well of the limonade de cochon he had found in the kitchen. But as the captain had the wine they had taken while passing through Moscow, he left the kvass to Morel and applied himself to the bottle of Bordeaux. He wrapped the bottle up to its neck in a table napkin and poured out wine for himself and for Pierre. The satisfaction of his hunger and the wine rendered the captain still more lively and he chatted incessantly all through dinner.

"Yes, my dear Monsieur Pierre, I owe you a fine votive candle for saving me from that maniac. . . You see, I have bullets enough in my body already. Here is one I got at Wagram" (he touched his side) "and a second at Smolénsk"—he showed a scar on his cheek—"and this leg which as you see does not want to march, I got that on the seventh at the great battle of la Moskowa. Sacré Dieu! It was splendid! That deluge of fire was worth seeing. It was a tough job you set us there, my word! You may be proud of it! And on my honor, in spite of the cough I caught there, I should be ready to begin again. I pity those who did not see it."

"I was there," said Pierre.

"Bah, really? So much the better! You are certainly brave foes. The great redoubt held out well, by my pipe!" continued the Frenchman. "And you made us pay dear for it. I was at it three times—sure as I sit here. Three times we reached the guns and three times we were thrown back like cardboard figures. Oh, it was beautiful, Monsieur Pierre! Your grenadiers were splendid, by heaven! I saw them close up their ranks six times in succession and march as if on parade. Fine fellows! Our King of Naples, who knows what's what, cried 'Bravo!' Ha, ha! So you are one of us soldiers!" he added, smiling, after a momentary pause. "So much the better, so much the better, Monsieur Pierre! Terrible in battle. . . gallant. . . with the fair" (he winked and smiled), "that's what the French are, Monsieur Pierre, aren't they?"

The captain was so naïvely and good-humoredly gay, so real, and so pleased with himself that Pierre almost winked back as he looked merrily at him. Probably the word "gallant" turned the captain's thoughts to the state of Moscow.

"Apropos, tell me please, is it true that the women have all left Moscow? What a queer idea! What had they to be afraid of?"

"Would not the French ladies leave Paris if the Russians entered it?" asked Pierre.

"Ha, ha, ha!" The Frenchman emitted a merry, sanguine chuckle, patting Pierre on the shoulder. "What a thing to say!" he exclaimed. "Paris? . . . But Paris, Paris. . ."

"Paris—the capital of the world," Pierre finished his remark for him.

The captain looked at Pierre. He had a habit of stopping short in the middle of his talk and gazing intently with his laughing, kindly eyes.

"Well, if you hadn't told me you were Russian, I should have wagered that you were Parisian! You have that. . . I don't know what, that. . ." and having uttered this compliment, he again gazed at him in silence.

"I have been in Paris. I spent years there," said Pierre.

"Oh yes, one sees that plainly. Paris! . . . A man who doesn't know Paris is a savage. You can tell a Parisian two leagues off. Paris is Talma, la Duchénois, Potier, the Sorbonne, the boulevards," and noticing that his conclusion was weaker than what had gone before, he added quickly: "There is only one Paris in the world. You have been to Paris and have remained Russian. Well, I don't esteem you the less for it."

Under the influence of the wine he had drunk, and after the days he had spent alone with his depressing thoughts, Pierre involuntarily enjoyed talking with this cheerful and good-natured man.

"To return to your ladies—I hear they are lovely. What a wretched idea to go and bury themselves in the steppes when the French army is in Moscow. What a chance those girls have missed! Your peasants, now—that's another thing; but you civilized people, you ought to know us better than that. We took Vienna, Berlin, Madrid, Naples, Rome, Warsaw, all the world's capitals. . . We are feared, but we are loved. We are nice to know. And then the Emperor. . ." he began, but Pierre interrupted him.

"The Emperor," Pierre repeated, and his face suddenly became sad and embarrassed, "is the Emperor. . . ?"

"The Emperor? He is generosity, mercy, justice, order, genius—that's what the Emperor is! It is I, Ramballe, who tell you so. . . I assure you I was his enemy eight years ago. My father was an emigrant count. . . But that man has vanquished me. He has taken hold of me. I could not resist the sight of the grandeur and glory with which he has covered France. When I understood what he wanted—when I saw that he was preparing a bed of laurels for us, you know, I said to myself: 'That is a monarch,' and I devoted myself to him! So there! Oh yes, mon cher, he is the greatest man of the ages past or future."

"Is he in Moscow?" Pierre stammered with a guilty look.

The Frenchman looked at his guilty face and smiled.

"No, he will make his entry tomorrow," he replied, and continued his talk.

Their conversation was interrupted by the cries of several voices at the gate and by Morel, who came to say that some Württemberg hussars had come and wanted to put up their horses in the yard where the captain's horses were. This difficulty had arisen chiefly because the hussars did not understand what was said to them in French.

The captain had their senior sergeant called in, and in a stern voice asked him to what regiment he belonged, who was his commanding officer, and by what right he allowed himself to claim quarters that were already occupied. The German who knew little French, answered the two first questions by giving the names of his regiment and of his commanding officer, but in reply to the third question which he did not understand said, introducing broken French into his own German, that he was the quartermaster of the regiment and his commander had ordered him to occupy all the houses one after another. Pierre, who knew German, translated what the German said to the captain and gave the captain's reply to the Württemberg hussar in German. When he had understood what was said to him, the German submitted and took his men elsewhere. The captain went out into the porch and gave some orders in a loud voice.

When he returned to the room Pierre was sitting in the same place as before, with his head in his hands. His face expressed suffering. He really was suffering at that moment. When the captain went out and he was left alone, suddenly he came to himself and realized the position he was in. It was not that Moscow had been taken or that the happy conquerors were masters in it and were patronizing him. Painful as that was it was not that which tormented Pierre at the moment. He was tormented by the consciousness of his own weakness. The few glasses of wine he had drunk and the conversation with this good-natured man had destroyed the mood of concentrated gloom in which he had spent the last few days and which was essential for the execution of his design. The pistol, dagger, and peasant coat were ready. Napoleon was to enter the town next day. Pierre still considered that it would be a useful and worthy action to slay the evildoer, but now he felt that he would not do it. He did not know why, but he felt a foreboding that he would not carry out his intention. He struggled against the confession of his weakness but dimly felt that he could not overcome it and that his former gloomy frame of mind, concerning vengeance, killing, and self-sacrifice, had been dispersed like dust by contact with the first man he met.

The captain returned to the room, limping slightly and whistling a tune.

The Frenchman's chatter which had previously amused Pierre now repelled him. The tune he was whistling, his gait, and the gesture with which he twirled his mustache, all now seemed offensive. "I will go away immediately. I won't say another word to him," thought Pierre. He thought this, but still sat in the same place. A strange feeling of weakness tied him to the spot; he wished to get up and go away, but could not do so.

The captain, on the other hand, seemed very cheerful. He paced up and down the room twice. His eyes shone and his mustache twitched as if he were smiling to himself at some amusing thought.

"The colonel of those Württembergers is delightful," he suddenly said. "He's a German, but a nice fellow all the same. . . But he's a German." He sat down facing Pierre. "By the way, you know German, then?"

Pierre looked at him in silence.

"What is the German for 'shelter'?"

"Shelter?" Pierre repeated. "The German for shelter is Unterkunft."

"How do you say it?" the captain asked quickly and doubtfully.

"Unterkunft," Pierre repeated.

"Onterkoff," said the captain and looked at Pierre for some seconds with laughing eyes. "These Germans are first-rate fools, don't you think so, Monsieur Pierre?" he concluded.

"Well, let's have another bottle of this Moscow Bordeaux, shall we? Morel will warm us up another little bottle. Morel!" he called out gaily.

Morel brought candles and a bottle of wine. The captain looked at Pierre by the candlelight and was evidently struck by the troubled expression on his companion's face. Ramballe, with genuine distress and sympathy in his face, went up to Pierre and bent over him.

"There now, we're sad," said he, touching Pierre's hand. "Have I upset you? No, really, have you anything against me?" he asked Pierre. "Perhaps it's the state of affairs?"

Pierre did not answer, but looked cordially into the Frenchman's eyes whose expression of sympathy was pleasing to him.

"Honestly, without speaking of what I owe you, I feel friendship for you. Can I do anything for you? Dispose of me. It is for life and death. I say it with my hand on my heart!" said he, striking his chest.

"Thank you," said Pierre.

The captain gazed intently at him as he had done when he learned that "shelter" was Unterkunft in German, and his face suddenly brightened.

"Well, in that case, I drink to our friendship!" he cried gaily, filling two glasses with wine.

Pierre took one of the glasses and emptied it. Ramballe emptied his too, again pressed Pierre's hand, and leaned his elbows on the table in a pensive attitude.

"Yes, my dear friend," he began, "such is fortune's caprice. Who would have said that I should be a soldier and a captain of dragoons in the service of Bonaparte, as we used to call him? Yet here I am in Moscow with him. I must tell you, mon cher," he continued in the sad and measured tones of a man who intends to tell a long story, "that our name is one of the most ancient in France."

And with a Frenchman's easy and naïve frankness the captain told Pierre the story of his ancestors, his childhood, youth, and manhood, and all about his relations and his financial and family affairs, "ma pauvre mère" playing of course an important part in the story.

"But all that is only life's setting, the real thing is love—love! Am I not right, Monsieur Pierre?" said he, growing animated. "Another glass?"

Pierre again emptied his glass and poured himself out a third.

"Oh, women, women!" and the captain, looking with glistening eyes at Pierre, began talking of love and of his love affairs.

There were very many of these, as one could easily believe, looking at the officer's handsome, self-satisfied face, and noting the eager enthusiasm with which he spoke of women. Though all Ramballe's love stories had the sensual character which Frenchmen regard as the special charm and poetry of love, yet he told his story with such sincere conviction that he alone had experienced and known all the charm of love and he described women so alluringly that Pierre listened to him with curiosity.

It was plain that l'amour which the Frenchman was so fond of was not that low and simple kind that Pierre had once felt for his wife, nor was it the romantic love stimulated by himself that he experienced for Natásha. (Ramballe despised both these kinds of love equally: the one he considered the "love of clodhoppers" and the other the "love of simpletons.") L'amour which the Frenchman worshiped consisted principally in the unnaturalness of his relation to the woman and in a combination of incongruities giving the chief charm to the feeling.

Thus the captain touchingly recounted the story of his love for a fascinating marquise of thirty-five and at the same time for a charming, innocent child of seventeen, daughter of the bewitching marquise. The conflict of magnanimity between the mother and the daughter, ending in the mother's sacrificing herself and offering her daughter in marriage to her lover, even now agitated the captain, though it was the memory of a distant past. Then he recounted an episode in which the husband played the part of the lover, and he—the lover—assumed the role of the husband, as well as several droll incidents from his recollections of Germany, where "shelter" is called Unterkunft and where the husbands eat sauerkraut and the young girls are "too blonde."

Finally, the latest episode in Poland still fresh in the captain's memory, and which he narrated with rapid gestures and glowing face, was of how he had saved the life of a Pole (in general, the saving of life continually occurred in the captain's stories) and the Pole had entrusted to him his enchanting wife (parisienne de cœur) while himself entering the French service. The captain was happy, the enchanting Polish lady wished to elope with him, but, prompted by magnanimity, the captain restored the wife to the husband, saying as he did so: "I have saved your life, and I save your honor!" Having repeated these words the captain wiped his eyes and gave himself a shake, as if driving away the weakness which assailed him at this touching recollection.

Listening to the captain's tales, Pierre—as often happens late in the evening and under the influence of wine—followed all that was told him, understood it all, and at the same time followed a train of personal memories which, he knew not why, suddenly arose in his mind. While listening to these love stories his own love for Natásha unexpectedly rose to his mind, and going over the pictures of that love in his imagination he mentally compared them with Ramballe's tales. Listening to the story of the struggle between love and duty, Pierre saw before his eyes every minutest detail of his last meeting with the object of his love at the Súkharev water tower. At the time of that meeting it had not produced an effect upon him—he had not even once recalled it. But now it seemed to him that that meeting had had in it something very important and poetic.

"Peter Kirílovich, come here! We have recognized you," he now seemed to hear the words she had uttered and to see before him her eyes, her smile, her traveling hood, and a stray lock of her hair. . . and there seemed to him something pathetic and touching in all this.

Having finished his tale about the enchanting Polish lady, the captain asked Pierre if he had ever experienced a similar impulse to sacrifice himself for love and a feeling of envy of the legitimate husband.

Challenged by this question Pierre raised his head and felt a need to express the thoughts that filled his mind. He began to explain that he understood love for a woman somewhat differently. He said that in all his life he had loved and still loved only one woman, and that she could never be his.

"Tiens!" said the captain.

Pierre then explained that he had loved this woman from his earliest years, but that he had not dared to think of her because she was too young, and because he had been an illegitimate son without a name. Afterwards when he had received a name and wealth he dared not think of her because he loved her too well, placing her far above everything in the world, and especially therefore above himself.

When he had reached this point, Pierre asked the captain whether he understood that.

The captain made a gesture signifying that even if he did not understand it he begged Pierre to continue.

"Platónic love, clouds. . ." he muttered.

Whether it was the wine he had drunk, or an impulse of frankness, or the thought that this man did not, and never would, know any of those who played a part in his story, or whether it was all these things together, something loosened Pierre's tongue. Speaking thickly and with a faraway look in his shining eyes, he told the whole story of his life: his marriage, Natásha's love for his best friend, her betrayal of him, and all his own simple relations with her. Urged on by Ramballe's questions he also told what he had at first concealed—his own position and even his name.

More than anything else in Pierre's story the captain was impressed by the fact that Pierre was very rich, had two mansions in Moscow, and that he had abandoned everything and not left the city, but remained there concealing his name and station.

When it was late at night they went out together into the street. The night was warm and light. To the left of the house on the Pokróvka a fire glowed—the first of those that were beginning in Moscow. To the right and high up in the sky was the sickle of the waning moon and opposite to it hung that bright comet which was connected in Pierre's heart with his love. At the gate stood Gerásim, the cook, and two Frenchmen. Their laughter and their mutually incomprehensible remarks in two languages could be heard. They were looking at the glow seen in the town.

There was nothing terrible in the one small, distant fire in the immense city.

Gazing at the high starry sky, at the moon, at the comet, and at the glow from the fire, Pierre experienced a joyful emotion. "There now, how good it is, what more does one need?" thought he. And suddenly remembering his intention he grew dizzy and felt so faint that he leaned against the fence to save himself from falling.

Without taking leave of his new friend, Pierre left the gate with unsteady steps and returning to his room lay down on the sofa and immediately fell asleep.

# XXX

The glow of the first fire that began on the second of September was watched from the various roads by the fugitive Muscovites and by the retreating troops, with many different feelings.

The Rostóv party spent the night at Mytíshchi, fourteen miles from Moscow. They had started so late on the first of September, the road had been so blocked by vehicles and troops, so many things had been forgotten for which servants were sent back, that they had decided to spend that night at a place three miles out of Moscow. The next morning they woke late and were again delayed so often that they only got as far as Great Mytíshchi. At ten o'clock that evening the Rostóv family and the wounded traveling with them were all distributed in the yards and huts of that large village. The Rostóvs' servants and coachmen and the orderlies of the wounded officers, after attending to their masters, had supper, fed the horses, and came out into the porches.

In a neighboring hut lay Raévski's adjutant with a fractured wrist. The awful pain he suffered made him moan incessantly and piteously, and his moaning sounded terrible in the darkness of the autumn night. He had spent the first night in the same yard as the Rostóvs. The countess said she had been unable to close her eyes on account of his moaning, and at Mytíshchi she moved into a worse hut simply to be farther away from the wounded man.

In the darkness of the night one of the servants noticed, above the high body of a coach standing before the porch, the small glow of another fire. One glow had long been visible and everybody knew that it was Little Mytíshchi burning—set on fire by Mamónov's Cossacks.

"But look here, brothers, there's another fire!" remarked an orderly.

All turned their attention to the glow.

"But they told us Little Mytíshchi had been set on fire by Mamónov's Cossacks."

"But that's not Mytíshchi, it's farther away."

"Look, it must be in Moscow!"

Two of the gazers went round to the other side of the coach and sat down on its steps.

"It's more to the left, why, Little Mytíshchi is over there, and this is right on the other side."

Several men joined the first two.

"See how it's flaring," said one. "That's a fire in Moscow: either in the Sushchévski or the Rogózhski quarter."

No one replied to this remark and for some time they all gazed silently at the spreading flames of the second fire in the distance.

Old Daniel Teréntich, the count's valet (as he was called), came up to the group and shouted at Míshka.

"What are you staring at, you good-for-nothing? . . . The count will be calling and there's nobody there; go and gather the clothes together."

"I only ran out to get some water," said Míshka.

"But what do you think, Daniel Teréntich? Doesn't it look as if that glow were in Moscow?" remarked one of the footmen.

Daniel Teréntich made no reply, and again for a long time they were all silent. The glow spread, rising and falling, farther and farther still.

"God have mercy. . . It's windy and dry. . ." said another voice.

"Just look! See what it's doing now. O Lord! You can even see the crows flying. Lord have mercy on us sinners!"

"They'll put it out, no fear!"

"Who's to put it out?" Daniel Teréntich, who had hitherto been silent, was heard to say. His voice was calm and deliberate. "Moscow it is, brothers," said he. "Mother Moscow, the white. . ." his voice faltered, and he gave way to an old man's sob.

And it was as if they had all only waited for this to realize the significance for them of the glow they were watching. Sighs were heard, words of prayer, and the sobbing of the count's old valet.

# XXXI

The valet, returning to the cottage, informed the count that Moscow was burning. The count donned his dressing gown and went out to look. Sónya and Madame Schoss, who had not yet undressed, went out with him. Only Natásha and the countess remained in the room. Pétya was no longer with the family, he had gone on with his regiment which was making for Tróitsa.

The countess, on hearing that Moscow was on fire, began to cry. Natásha, pale, with a fixed look, was sitting on the bench under the icons just where she had sat down on arriving and paid no attention to her father's words. She was listening to the ceaseless moaning of the adjutant, three houses off.

"Oh, how terrible," said Sónya returning from the yard chilled and frightened. "I believe the whole of Moscow will burn, there's an awful glow! Natásha, do look! You can see it from the window," she said to her cousin, evidently wishing to distract her mind.

But Natásha looked at her as if not understanding what was said to her and again fixed her eyes on the corner of the stove. She had been in this condition of stupor since the morning, when Sónya, to the surprise and annoyance of the countess, had for some unaccountable reason found it necessary to tell Natásha of Prince Andrew's wound and of his being with their party. The countess had seldom been so angry with anyone as she was with Sónya. Sónya had cried and begged to be forgiven and now, as if trying to atone for her fault, paid unceasing attention to her cousin.

"Look, Natásha, how dreadfully it is burning!" said she.

"What's burning?" asked Natásha. "Oh, yes, Moscow."

And as if in order not to offend Sónya and to get rid of her, she turned her face to the window, looked out in such a way that it was evident that she could not see anything, and again settled down in her former attitude.

"But you didn't see it!"

"Yes, really I did," Natásha replied in a voice that pleaded to be left in peace.

Both the countess and Sónya understood that, naturally, neither Moscow nor the burning of Moscow nor anything else could seem of importance to Natásha.

The count returned and lay down behind the partition. The countess went up to her daughter and touched her head with the back of her hand as she was wont to do when Natásha was ill, then touched her forehead with her lips as if to feel whether she was feverish, and finally kissed her.

"You are cold. You are trembling all over. You'd better lie down," said the countess.

"Lie down? All right, I will. I'll lie down at once," said Natásha.

When Natásha had been told that morning that Prince Andrew was seriously wounded and was traveling with their party, she had at first asked many questions: Where was he going? How was he wounded? Was it serious? And could she see him? But after she had been told that she could not see him, that he was seriously wounded but that his life was not in danger, she ceased to ask questions or to speak at all, evidently disbelieving what they told her, and convinced that say what she might she would still be told the same. All the way she had sat motionless in a corner of the coach with wide open eyes, and the expression in them which the countess knew so well and feared so much, and now she sat in the same way on the bench where she had seated herself on arriving. She was planning something and either deciding or had already decided something in her mind. The countess knew this, but what it might be she did not know, and this alarmed and tormented her.

"Natásha, undress, darling; lie down on my bed."

A bed had been made on a bedstead for the countess only. Madame Schoss and the two girls were to sleep on some hay on the floor.

"No, Mamma, I will lie down here on the floor," Natásha replied irritably and she went to the window and opened it. Through the open window the moans of the adjutant could be heard more distinctly. She put her head out into the damp night air, and the countess saw her slim neck shaking with sobs and throbbing against the window frame. Natásha knew it was not Prince Andrew who was moaning. She knew Prince Andrew was in the same yard as themselves and in a part of the hut across the passage; but this dreadful incessant moaning made her sob. The countess exchanged a look with Sónya.

"Lie down, darling; lie down, my pet," said the countess, softly touching Natásha's shoulders. "Come, lie down."

"Oh, yes. . . I'll lie down at once," said Natásha, and began hurriedly undressing, tugging at the tapes of her petticoat.

When she had thrown off her dress and put on a dressing jacket, she sat down with her foot under her on the bed that had been made up on the floor, jerked her thin and rather short plait of hair to the front, and began replaiting it. Her long, thin, practiced fingers rapidly unplaited, replaited, and tied up her plait. Her head moved from side to side from habit, but her eyes, feverishly wide, looked fixedly before her. When her toilet for the night was finished she sank gently onto the sheet spread over the hay on the side nearest the door.

"Natásha, you'd better lie in the middle," said Sónya.

"I'll stay here," muttered Natásha. "Do lie down," she added crossly, and buried her face in the pillow.

The countess, Madame Schoss, and Sónya undressed hastily and lay down. The small lamp in front of the icons was the only light left in the room. But in the yard there was a light from the fire at Little Mytíshchi a mile and a half away, and through the night came the noise of people shouting at a tavern Mamónov's Cossacks had set up across the street, and the adjutant's unceasing moans could still be heard.

For a long time Natásha listened attentively to the sounds that reached her from inside and outside the room and did not move. First she heard her mother praying and sighing and the creaking of her bed under her, then Madame Schoss' familiar whistling snore and Sónya's gentle breathing. Then the countess called to Natásha. Natásha did not answer.

"I think she's asleep, Mamma," said Sónya softly.

After a short silence the countess spoke again but this time no one replied.

Soon after that Natásha heard her mother's even breathing. Natásha did not move, though her little bare foot, thrust out from under the quilt, was growing cold on the bare floor.

As if to celebrate a victory over everybody, a cricket chirped in a crack in the wall. A cock crowed far off and another replied near by. The shouting in the tavern had died down; only the moaning of the adjutant was heard. Natásha sat up.

"Sónya, are you asleep? Mamma?" she whispered.

No one replied. Natásha rose slowly and carefully, crossed herself, and stepped cautiously on the cold and dirty floor with her slim, supple, bare feet. The boards of the floor creaked. Stepping cautiously from one foot to the other she ran like a kitten the few steps to the door and grasped the cold door handle.

It seemed to her that something heavy was beating rhythmically against all the walls of the room: it was her own heart, sinking with alarm and terror and overflowing with love.

She opened the door and stepped across the threshold and onto the cold, damp earthen floor of the passage. The cold she felt refreshed her. With her bare feet she touched a sleeping man, stepped over him, and opened the door into the part of the hut where Prince Andrew lay. It was dark in there. In the farthest corner, on a bench beside a bed on which something was lying, stood a tallow candle with a long, thick, and smoldering wick.

From the moment she had been told that morning of Prince Andrew's wound and his presence there, Natásha had resolved to see him. She did not know why she had to, she knew the meeting would be painful, but felt the more convinced that it was necessary.

All day she had lived only in hope of seeing him that night. But now that the moment had come she was filled with dread of what she might see. How was he maimed? What was left of him? Was he like that incessant moaning of the adjutant's? Yes, he was altogether like that. In her imagination he was that terrible moaning personified. When she saw an indistinct shape in the corner, and mistook his knees raised under the quilt for his shoulders, she imagined a horrible body there, and stood still in terror. But an irresistible impulse drew her forward. She cautiously took one step and then another, and found herself in the middle of a small room containing baggage. Another man—Timókhin—was lying in a corner on the benches beneath the icons, and two others—the doctor and a valet—lay on the floor.

The valet sat up and whispered something. Timókhin, kept awake by the pain in his wounded leg, gazed with wide-open eyes at this strange apparition of a girl in a white chemise, dressing jacket, and nightcap. The valet's sleepy, frightened exclamation, "What do you want? What's the matter?" made Natásha approach more swiftly to what was lying in the corner. Horribly unlike a man as that body looked, she must see him. She passed the valet, the snuff fell from the candle wick, and she saw Prince Andrew clearly with his arms outside the quilt, and such as she had always seen him.

He was the same as ever, but the feverish color of his face, his glittering eyes rapturously turned toward her, and especially his neck, delicate as a child's, revealed by the turn-down collar of his shirt, gave him a peculiarly innocent, childlike look, such as she had never seen on him before. She went up to him and with a swift, flexible, youthful movement dropped on her knees.

He smiled and held out his hand to her.

# XXXII

Seven days had passed since Prince Andrew found himself in the ambulance station on the field of Borodinó. His feverish state and the inflammation of his bowels, which were injured, were in the doctor's opinion sure to carry him off. But on the seventh day he ate with pleasure a piece of bread with some tea, and the doctor noticed that his temperature was lower. He had regained consciousness that morning. The first night after they left Moscow had been fairly warm and he had remained in the calèche, but at Mytíshchi the wounded man himself asked to be taken out and given some tea. The pain caused by his removal into the hut had made him groan aloud and again lose consciousness. When he had been placed on his camp bed he lay for a long time motionless with closed eyes. Then he opened them and whispered softly: "And the tea?" His remembering such a small detail of everyday life astonished the doctor. He felt Prince Andrew's pulse, and to his surprise and dissatisfaction found it had improved. He was dissatisfied because he knew by experience that if his patient did not die now, he would do so a little later with greater suffering. Timókhin, the red-nosed major of Prince Andrew's regiment, had joined him in Moscow and was being taken along with him, having been wounded in the leg at the battle of Borodinó. They were accompanied by a doctor, Prince Andrew's valet, his coachman, and two orderlies.

They gave Prince Andrew some tea. He drank it eagerly, looking with feverish eyes at the door in front of him as if trying to understand and remember something.

"I don't want any more. Is Timókhin here?" he asked.

Timókhin crept along the bench to him.

"I am here, your excellency."

"How's your wound?"

"Mine, sir? All right. But how about you?"

Prince Andrew again pondered as if trying to remember something.

"Couldn't one get a book?" he asked.

"What book?"

"The Gospels. I haven't one."

The doctor promised to procure it for him and began to ask how he was feeling. Prince Andrew answered all his questions reluctantly but reasonably, and then said he wanted a bolster placed under him as he was uncomfortable and in great pain. The doctor and valet lifted the cloak with which he was covered and, making wry faces at the noisome smell of mortifying flesh that came from the wound, began examining that dreadful place. The doctor was very much displeased about something and made a change in the dressings, turning the wounded man over so that he groaned again and grew unconscious and delirious from the agony. He kept asking them to get him the book and put it under him.

"What trouble would it be to you?" he said. "I have not got one. Please get it for me and put it under for a moment," he pleaded in a piteous voice.

The doctor went into the passage to wash his hands.

"You fellows have no conscience," said he to the valet who was pouring water over his hands. "For just one moment I didn't look after you. . . It's such pain, you know, that I wonder how he can bear it."

"By the Lord Jesus Christ, I thought we had put something under him!" said the valet.

The first time Prince Andrew understood where he was and what was the matter with him and remembered being wounded and how was when he asked to be carried into the hut after his calèche had stopped at Mytíshchi. After growing confused from pain while being carried into the hut he again regained consciousness, and while drinking tea once more recalled all that had happened to him, and above all vividly remembered the moment at the ambulance station when, at the sight of the sufferings of a man he disliked, those new thoughts had come to him which promised him happiness. And those thoughts, though now vague and indefinite, again possessed his soul. He remembered that he had now a new source of happiness and that this happiness had something to do with the Gospels. That was why he asked for a copy of them. The uncomfortable position in which they had put him and turned him over again confused his thoughts, and when he came to himself a third time it was in the complete stillness of the night. Everybody near him was sleeping. A cricket chirped from across the passage; someone was shouting and singing in the street; cockroaches rustled on the table, on the icons, and on the walls, and a big fly flopped at the head of the bed and around the candle beside him, the wick of which was charred and had shaped itself like a mushroom.

His mind was not in a normal state. A healthy man usually thinks of, feels, and remembers innumerable things simultaneously, but has the power and will to select one sequence of thoughts or events on

　　　　　　　　　　　　　　　　　　LEO TOLSTOY

which to fix his whole attention. A healthy man can tear himself away from the deepest reflections to say a civil word to someone who comes in and can then return again to his own thoughts. But Prince Andrew's mind was not in a normal state in that respect. All the powers of his mind were more active and clearer than ever, but they acted apart from his will. Most diverse thoughts and images occupied him simultaneously. At times his brain suddenly began to work with a vigor, clearness, and depth it had never reached when he was in health, but suddenly in the midst of its work it would turn to some unexpected idea and he had not the strength to turn it back again.

"Yes, a new happiness was revealed to me of which man cannot be deprived," he thought as he lay in the semidarkness of the quiet hut, gazing fixedly before him with feverish wide open eyes. "A happiness lying beyond material forces, outside the material influences that act on man—a happiness of the soul alone, the happiness of loving. Every man can understand it, but to conceive it and enjoin it was possible only for God. But how did God enjoin that law? And why was the Son. . . ?"

And suddenly the sequence of these thoughts broke off, and Prince Andrew heard (without knowing whether it was a delusion or reality) a soft whispering voice incessantly and rhythmically repeating "piti-piti-piti," and then "titi," and then again "piti-piti-piti," and "ti-ti" once more. At the same time he felt that above his face, above the very middle of it, some strange airy structure was being erected out of slender needles or splinters, to the sound of this whispered music. He felt that he had to balance carefully (though it was difficult) so that this airy structure should not collapse; but nevertheless it kept collapsing and again slowly rising to the sound of whispered rhythmic music—"it stretches, stretches, spreading out and stretching," said Prince Andrew to himself. While listening to this whispering and feeling the sensation of this drawing out and the construction of this edifice of needles, he also saw by glimpses a red halo round the candle, and heard the rustle of the cockroaches and the buzzing of the fly that flopped against his pillow and his face. Each time the fly touched his face it gave him a burning sensation and yet to his surprise it did not destroy the structure, though it knocked against the very region of his face where it was rising. But besides this there was something else of importance. It was something white by the door—the statue of a sphinx, which also oppressed him.

"But perhaps that's my shirt on the table," he thought, "and that's my legs, and that is the door, but why is it always stretching and drawing itself out, and 'piti-piti-piti' and 'ti-ti' and 'piti-piti-piti' . . . ? That's enough, please leave off!" Prince Andrew painfully entreated someone. And suddenly thoughts and feelings again swam to the surface of his mind with peculiar clearness and force.

"Yes—love," he thought again quite clearly. "But not love which loves for something, for some quality, for some purpose, or for some reason, but the love which I—while dying—first experienced when I saw my enemy and yet loved him. I experienced that feeling of love which is the very essence of the soul and does not require an object. Now again I feel that bliss. To love one's neighbors, to love one's enemies, to love everything, to love God in all His manifestations. It is possible to love someone dear to you with human love, but an enemy can only be loved by divine love. That is why I experienced such joy when I felt that I loved that man. What has become of him? Is he alive? . . .

"When loving with human love one may pass from love to hatred, but divine love cannot change. No, neither death nor anything else can destroy it. It is the very essence of the soul. Yet how many people have I hated in my life? And of them all, I loved and hated none as I did her." And he vividly pictured to himself Natásha, not as he had done in the past with nothing but her charms which gave him delight, but for the first time picturing to himself her soul. And he understood her feelings, her sufferings, shame, and remorse. He now understood for the first time all the cruelty of his rejection of her, the cruelty of his rupture with her. "If only it were possible for me to see her once more! Just once, looking into those eyes to say. . ."

"Piti-piti-piti and ti-ti and piti-piti-piti boom!" flopped the fly. . . And his attention was suddenly carried into another world, a world of reality and delirium in which something particular was happening. In that world some structure was still being erected and did not fall, something was still stretching out, and the candle with its red halo was still burning, and the same shirtlike sphinx lay near the door; but besides all this something creaked, there was a whiff of fresh air, and a new white sphinx appeared, standing at the door. And that sphinx had the pale face and shining eyes of the very Natásha of whom he had just been thinking.

"Oh, how oppressive this continual delirium is," thought Prince Andrew, trying to drive that face from his imagination. But the face remained before him with the force of reality and drew nearer. Prince Andrew wished to return to that former world of pure thought, but he could not,

LEO TOLSTOY

and delirium drew him back into its domain. The soft whispering voice continued its rhythmic murmur, something oppressed him and stretched out, and the strange face was before him. Prince Andrew collected all his strength in an effort to recover his senses, he moved a little, and suddenly there was a ringing in his ears, a dimness in his eyes, and like a man plunged into water he lost consciousness. When he came to himself, Natásha, that same living Natásha whom of all people he most longed to love with this new pure divine love that had been revealed to him, was kneeling before him. He realized that it was the real living Natásha, and he was not surprised but quietly happy. Natásha, motionless on her knees (she was unable to stir), with frightened eyes riveted on him, was restraining her sobs. Her face was pale and rigid. Only in the lower part of it something quivered.

Prince Andrew sighed with relief, smiled, and held out his hand.

"You?" he said. "How fortunate!"

With a rapid but careful movement Natásha drew nearer to him on her knees and, taking his hand carefully, bent her face over it and began kissing it, just touching it lightly with her lips.

"Forgive me!" she whispered, raising her head and glancing at him. "Forgive me!"

"I love you," said Prince Andrew.

"Forgive. . . !"

"Forgive what?" he asked.

"Forgive me for what I ha-ve do-ne!" faltered Natásha in a scarcely audible, broken whisper, and began kissing his hand more rapidly, just touching it with her lips.

"I love you more, better than before," said Prince Andrew, lifting her face with his hand so as to look into her eyes.

Those eyes, filled with happy tears, gazed at him timidly, compassionately, and with joyous love. Natásha's thin pale face, with its swollen lips, was more than plain—it was dreadful. But Prince Andrew did not see that, he saw her shining eyes which were beautiful. They heard the sound of voices behind them.

Peter the valet, who was now wide awake, had roused the doctor. Timókhin, who had not slept at all because of the pain in his leg, had long been watching all that was going on, carefully covering his bare body with the sheet as he huddled up on his bench.

"What's this?" said the doctor, rising from his bed. "Please go away, madam!"

At that moment a maid sent by the countess, who had noticed her daughter's absence, knocked at the door.

Like a somnambulist aroused from her sleep Natásha went out of the room and, returning to her hut, fell sobbing on her bed.

From that time, during all the rest of the Rostóvs' journey, at every halting place and wherever they spent a night, Natásha never left the wounded Bolkónski, and the doctor had to admit that he had not expected from a young girl either such firmness or such skill in nursing a wounded man.

Dreadful as the countess imagined it would be should Prince Andrew die in her daughter's arms during the journey—as, judging by what the doctor said, it seemed might easily happen—she could not oppose Natásha. Though with the intimacy now established between the wounded man and Natásha the thought occurred that should he recover their former engagement would be renewed, no one—least of all Natásha and Prince Andrew—spoke of this: the unsettled question of life and death, which hung not only over Bolkónski but over all Russia, shut out all other considerations.

# XXXIII

On the third of September Pierre awoke late. His head was aching, the clothes in which he had slept without undressing felt uncomfortable on his body, and his mind had a dim consciousness of something shameful he had done the day before. That something shameful was his yesterday's conversation with Captain Ramballe.

It was eleven by the clock, but it seemed peculiarly dark out of doors. Pierre rose, rubbed his eyes, and seeing the pistol with an engraved stock which Gerásim had replaced on the writing table, he remembered where he was and what lay before him that very day.

"Am I not too late?" he thought. "No, probably he won't make his entry into Moscow before noon."

Pierre did not allow himself to reflect on what lay before him, but hastened to act.

After arranging his clothes, he took the pistol and was about to go out. But it then occurred to him for the first time that he certainly could not carry the weapon in his hand through the streets. It was difficult to hide such a big pistol even under his wide coat. He could not carry it unnoticed in his belt or under his arm. Besides, it had been discharged, and he had not had time to reload it. "No matter, the dagger will do," he said to himself, though when planning his design he had more than once come to the conclusion that the chief mistake made by the student in 1809 had been to try to kill Napoleon with a dagger. But as his chief aim consisted not in carrying out his design, but in proving to himself that he would not abandon his intention and was doing all he could to achieve it, Pierre hastily took the blunt jagged dagger in a green sheath which he had bought at the Súkharev market with the pistol, and hid it under his waistcoat.

Having tied a girdle over his coat and pulled his cap low on his head, Pierre went down the corridor, trying to avoid making a noise or meeting the captain, and passed out into the street.

The conflagration, at which he had looked with so much indifference the evening before, had greatly increased during the night. Moscow was on fire in several places. The buildings in Carriage Row, across the river, in the Bazaar and the Povarskóy, as well as the barges on the Moskvá River and the timber yards by the Dorogomílov Bridge, were all ablaze.

Pierre's way led through side streets to the Povarskóy and from there to the church of St. Nicholas on the Arbát, where he had long before decided that the deed should be done. The gates of most of the houses were locked and the shutters up. The streets and lanes were deserted. The air was full of smoke and the smell of burning. Now and then he met Russians with anxious and timid faces, and Frenchmen with an air not of the city but of the camp, walking in the middle of the streets. Both the Russians and the French looked at Pierre with surprise. Besides his height and stoutness, and the strange morose look of suffering in his face and whole figure, the Russians stared at Pierre because they could not make out to what class he could belong. The French followed him with astonishment in their eyes chiefly because Pierre, unlike all the other Russians who gazed at the French with fear and curiosity, paid no attention to them. At the gate of one house three Frenchmen, who were explaining something to some Russians who did not understand them, stopped Pierre asking if he did not know French.

Pierre shook his head and went on. In another side street a sentinel standing beside a green caisson shouted at him, but only when the shout was threateningly repeated and he heard the click of the man's musket as he raised it did Pierre understand that he had to pass on the other side of the street. He heard nothing and saw nothing of what went on around him. He carried his resolution within himself in terror and haste, like something dreadful and alien to him, for, after the previous night's experience, he was afraid of losing it. But he was not destined to bring his mood safely to his destination. And even had he not been hindered by anything on the way, his intention could not now have been carried out, for Napoleon had passed the Arbát more than four hours previously on his way from the Dorogomílov suburb to the Krémlin, and was now sitting in a very gloomy frame of mind in a royal study in the Krémlin, giving detailed and exact orders as to measures to be taken immediately to extinguish the fire, to prevent looting, and to reassure the inhabitants. But Pierre did not know this; he was entirely absorbed in what lay before him, and was tortured—as those are who obstinately undertake a task that is impossible for them not because of its difficulty but because of its incompatibility with their natures—by the fear of weakening at the decisive moment and so losing his self-esteem.

Though he heard and saw nothing around him he found his way by instinct and did not go wrong in the side streets that led to the Povarskóy.

As Pierre approached that street the smoke became denser and denser—he even felt the heat of the fire. Occasionally curly tongues of flame rose from under the roofs of the houses. He met more people in the streets and they were more excited. But Pierre, though he felt that something unusual was happening around him, did not realize that he was approaching the fire. As he was going along a footpath across a wide-open space adjoining the Povarskóy on one side and the gardens of Prince Gruzínski's house on the other, Pierre suddenly heard the desperate weeping of a woman close to him. He stopped as if awakening from a dream and lifted his head.

By the side of the path, on the dusty dry grass, all sorts of household goods lay in a heap: featherbeds, a samovar, icons, and trunks. On the ground, beside the trunks, sat a thin woman no longer young, with long, prominent upper teeth, and wearing a black cloak and cap. This woman, swaying to and fro and muttering something, was choking with sobs. Two girls of about ten and twelve, dressed in dirty short frocks and cloaks, were staring at their mother with a look of stupefaction on their pale frightened faces. The youngest child, a boy of about seven, who wore an overcoat and an immense cap evidently not his own, was crying in his old nurse's arms. A dirty, barefooted maid was sitting on a trunk, and, having undone her pale-colored plait, was pulling it straight and sniffing at her singed hair. The woman's husband, a short, round-shouldered man in the undress uniform of a civilian official, with sausage-shaped whiskers and showing under his square-set cap the hair smoothly brushed forward over his temples, with expressionless face was moving the trunks, which were placed one on another, and was dragging some garments from under them.

As soon as she saw Pierre, the woman almost threw herself at his feet.

"Dear people, good Christians, save me, help me, dear friends. . . help us, somebody," she muttered between her sobs. "My girl. . . My daughter! My youngest daughter is left behind. She's burned! Ooh! Was it for this I nursed you. . . Ooh!"

"Don't, Mary Nikoláevna!" said her husband to her in a low voice, evidently only to justify himself before the stranger. "Sister must have taken her, or else where can she be?" he added.

"Monster! Villain!" shouted the woman angrily, suddenly ceasing to weep. "You have no heart, you don't feel for your own child! Another man would have rescued her from the fire. But this is a monster and neither a man nor a father! You, honored sir, are a noble man," she went on, addressing Pierre rapidly between her sobs. "The fire broke out alongside, and blew our way, the maid called out 'Fire!' and we rushed to collect our things. We ran out just as we were. . . This is what we have brought away. . . The icons, and my dowry bed, all the rest is lost. We seized the children. But not Katie! Ooh! O Lord! . . ." and again she began to sob. "My child, my dear one! Burned, burned!"

"But where was she left?" asked Pierre.

From the expression of his animated face the woman saw that this man might help her.

"Oh, dear sir!" she cried, seizing him by the legs. "My benefactor, set my heart at ease. . . Aníska, go, you horrid girl, show him the way!" she cried to the maid, angrily opening her mouth and still farther exposing her long teeth.

"Show me the way, show me, I. . . I'll do it," gasped Pierre rapidly.

The dirty maidservant stepped from behind the trunk, put up her plait, sighed, and went on her short, bare feet along the path. Pierre felt as if he had come back to life after a heavy swoon. He held his head higher, his eyes shone with the light of life, and with swift steps he followed the maid, overtook her, and came out on the Povarskóy. The whole street was full of clouds of black smoke. Tongues of flame here and there broke through that cloud. A great number of people crowded in front of the conflagration. In the middle of the street stood a French general saying something to those around him. Pierre, accompanied by the maid, was advancing to the spot where the general stood, but the French soldiers stopped him.

"On ne passe pas!"* cried a voice.

"This way, uncle," cried the girl. "We'll pass through the side street, by the Nikúlins'!"

Pierre turned back, giving a spring now and then to keep up with her. She ran across the street, turned down a side street to the left, and, passing three houses, turned into a yard on the right.

"It's here, close by," said she and, running across the yard, opened a gate in a wooden fence and, stopping, pointed out to him a small wooden wing of the house, which was burning brightly and fiercely. One of its sides had fallen in, another was on fire, and bright flames issued from the openings of the windows and from under the roof.

As Pierre passed through the fence gate, he was enveloped by hot air and involuntarily stopped.

---

* "You can't pass!"

"Which is it? Which is your house?" he asked.

"Ooh!" wailed the girl, pointing to the wing. "That's it, that was our lodging. You've burned to death, our treasure, Katie, my precious little missy! Ooh!" lamented Aníska, who at the sight of the fire felt that she too must give expression to her feelings.

Pierre rushed to the wing, but the heat was so great that he involuntarily passed round in a curve and came upon the large house that was as yet burning only at one end, just below the roof, and around which swarmed a crowd of Frenchmen. At first Pierre did not realize what these men, who were dragging something out, were about; but seeing before him a Frenchman hitting a peasant with a blunt saber and trying to take from him a fox-fur coat, he vaguely understood that looting was going on there, but he had no time to dwell on that idea.

The sounds of crackling and the din of falling walls and ceilings, the whistle and hiss of the flames, the excited shouts of the people, and the sight of the swaying smoke, now gathering into thick black clouds and now soaring up with glittering sparks, with here and there dense sheaves of flame (now red and now like golden fish scales creeping along the walls), and the heat and smoke and rapidity of motion, produced on Pierre the usual animating effects of a conflagration. It had a peculiarly strong effect on him because at the sight of the fire he felt himself suddenly freed from the ideas that had weighed him down. He felt young, bright, adroit, and resolute. He ran round to the other side of the lodge and was about to dash into that part of it which was still standing, when just above his head he heard several voices shouting and then a cracking sound and the ring of something heavy falling close beside him.

Pierre looked up and saw at a window of the large house some Frenchmen who had just thrown out the drawer of a chest, filled with metal articles. Other French soldiers standing below went up to the drawer.

"What does this fellow want?" shouted one of them referring to Pierre.

"There's a child in that house. Haven't you seen a child?" cried Pierre.

"What's he talking about? Get along!" said several voices, and one of the soldiers, evidently afraid that Pierre might want to take from them some of the plate and bronzes that were in the drawer, moved threateningly toward him.

"A child?" shouted a Frenchman from above. "I did hear something squealing in the garden. Perhaps it's his brat that the fellow is looking for. After all, one must be human, you know. . ."

"Where is it? Where?" said Pierre.

"There! There!" shouted the Frenchman at the window, pointing to the garden at the back of the house. "Wait a bit—I'm coming down."

And a minute or two later the Frenchman, a black-eyed fellow with a spot on his cheek, in shirt sleeves, really did jump out of a window on the ground floor, and clapping Pierre on the shoulder ran with him into the garden.

"Hurry up, you others!" he called out to his comrades. "It's getting hot."

When they reached a gravel path behind the house the Frenchman pulled Pierre by the arm and pointed to a round, graveled space where a three-year-old girl in a pink dress was lying under a seat.

"There is your child! Oh, a girl, so much the better!" said the Frenchman. "Good-by, Fatty. We must be human, we are all mortal you know!" and the Frenchman with the spot on his cheek ran back to his comrades.

Breathless with joy, Pierre ran to the little girl and was going to take her in his arms. But seeing a stranger the sickly, scrofulous-looking child, unattractively like her mother, began to yell and run away. Pierre, however, seized her and lifted her in his arms. She screamed desperately and angrily and tried with her little hands to pull Pierre's hands away and to bite them with her slobbering mouth. Pierre was seized by a sense of horror and repulsion such as he had experienced when touching some nasty little animal. But he made an effort not to throw the child down and ran with her to the large house. It was now, however, impossible to get back the way he had come; the maid, Aníska, was no longer there, and Pierre with a feeling of pity and disgust pressed the wet, painfully sobbing child to himself as tenderly as he could and ran with her through the garden seeking another way out.

# XXXIV

Having run through different yards and side streets, Pierre got back with his little burden to the Gruzínski garden at the corner of the Povarskóy. He did not at first recognize the place from which he had set out to look for the child, so crowded was it now with people and goods that had been dragged out of the houses. Besides Russian families who had taken refuge here from the fire with their belongings, there were several French soldiers in a variety of clothing. Pierre took no notice of them. He hurried to find the family of that civil servant in order to restore the daughter to her mother and go to save someone else. Pierre felt that he had still much to do and to do quickly. Glowing with the heat and from running, he felt at that moment more strongly than ever the sense of youth, animation, and determination that had come on him when he ran to save the child. She had now become quiet and, clinging with her little hands to Pierre's coat, sat on his arm gazing about her like some little wild animal. He glanced at her occasionally with a slight smile. He fancied he saw something pathetically innocent in that frightened, sickly little face.

He did not find the civil servant or his wife where he had left them. He walked among the crowd with rapid steps, scanning the various faces he met. Involuntarily he noticed a Georgian or Armenian family consisting of a very handsome old man of Oriental type, wearing a new, cloth-covered, sheepskin coat and new boots, an old woman of similar type, and a young woman. That very young woman seemed to Pierre the perfection of Oriental beauty, with her sharply outlined, arched, black eyebrows and the extraordinarily soft, bright color of her long, beautiful, expressionless face. Amid the scattered property and the crowd on the open space, she, in her rich satin cloak with a bright lilac shawl on her head, suggested a delicate exotic plant thrown out onto the snow. She was sitting on some bundles a little behind the old woman, and looked from under her long lashes with motionless, large, almond-shaped eyes at the ground before her. Evidently she was aware of her beauty and fearful because of it. Her face struck Pierre and, hurrying along by the fence, he turned several times to look at her. When he had reached the fence, still without finding those he sought, he stopped and looked about him.

With the child in his arms his figure was now more conspicuous than before, and a group of Russians, both men and women, gathered about him.

"Have you lost anyone, my dear fellow? You're of the gentry yourself, aren't you? Whose child is it?" they asked him.

Pierre replied that the child belonged to a woman in a black coat who had been sitting there with her other children, and he asked whether anyone knew where she had gone.

"Why, that must be the Anférovs," said an old deacon, addressing a pockmarked peasant woman. "Lord have mercy, Lord have mercy!" he added in his customary bass.

"The Anférovs? No," said the woman. "They left in the morning. That must be either Mary Nikoláevna's or the Ivánovs'!"

"He says 'a woman,' and Mary Nikoláevna is a lady," remarked a house serf.

"Do you know her? She's thin, with long teeth," said Pierre.

"That's Mary Nikoláevna! They went inside the garden when these wolves swooped down," said the woman, pointing to the French soldiers.

"O Lord, have mercy!" added the deacon.

"Go over that way, they're there. It's she! She kept on lamenting and crying," continued the woman. "It's she. Here, this way!"

But Pierre was not listening to the woman. He had for some seconds been intently watching what was going on a few steps away. He was looking at the Armenian family and at two French soldiers who had gone up to them. One of these, a nimble little man, was wearing a blue coat tied round the waist with a rope. He had a nightcap on his head and his feet were bare. The other, whose appearance particularly struck Pierre, was a long, lank, round-shouldered, fair-haired man, slow in his movements and with an idiotic expression of face. He wore a woman's loose gown of frieze, blue trousers, and large torn Hessian boots. The little barefooted Frenchman in the blue coat went up to the Armenians and, saying something, immediately seized the old man by his legs and the old man at once began pulling off his boots. The other in the frieze gown stopped in front of the beautiful Armenian girl and with his hands in his pockets stood staring at her, motionless and silent.

"Here, take the child!" said Pierre peremptorily and hurriedly to the woman, handing the little girl to her. "Give her back to them, give her back!" he almost shouted, putting the child, who began screaming, on the ground, and again looking at the Frenchman and the Armenian family.

The old man was already sitting barefoot. The little Frenchman had secured his second boot and was slapping one boot against the other. The old man was saying something in a voice broken by sobs, but Pierre caught but a glimpse of this, his whole attention was directed to the Frenchman in the frieze gown who meanwhile, swaying slowly from side to side, had drawn nearer to the young woman and taking his hands from his pockets had seized her by the neck.

The beautiful Armenian still sat motionless and in the same attitude, with her long lashes drooping as if she did not see or feel what the soldier was doing to her.

While Pierre was running the few steps that separated him from the Frenchman, the tall marauder in the frieze gown was already tearing from her neck the necklace the young Armenian was wearing, and the young woman, clutching at her neck, screamed piercingly.

"Let that woman alone!" exclaimed Pierre hoarsely in a furious voice, seizing the soldier by his round shoulders and throwing him aside.

The soldier fell, got up, and ran away. But his comrade, throwing down the boots and drawing his sword, moved threateningly toward Pierre.

"Voyons, pas de bêtises!"* he cried.

Pierre was in such a transport of rage that he remembered nothing and his strength increased tenfold. He rushed at the barefooted Frenchman and, before the latter had time to draw his sword, knocked him off his feet and hammered him with his fists. Shouts of approval were heard from the crowd around, and at the same moment a mounted patrol of French Uhlans appeared from round the corner. The Uhlans came up at a trot to Pierre and the Frenchman and surrounded them. Pierre remembered nothing of what happened after that. He only remembered beating someone and being beaten and finally feeling that his hands were bound and that a crowd of French soldiers stood around him and were searching him.

"Lieutenant, he has a dagger," were the first words Pierre understood.

"Ah, a weapon?" said the officer and turned to the barefooted soldier who had been arrested with Pierre. "All right, you can tell all about it at the court-martial." Then he turned to Pierre. "Do you speak French?"

---

* "Look here, no nonsense!"

Pierre looked around him with bloodshot eyes and did not reply. His face probably looked very terrible, for the officer said something in a whisper and four more Uhlans left the ranks and placed themselves on both sides of Pierre.

"Do you speak French?" the officer asked again, keeping at a distance from Pierre. "Call the interpreter."

A little man in Russian civilian clothes rode out from the ranks, and by his clothes and manner of speaking Pierre at once knew him to be a French salesman from one of the Moscow shops.

"He does not look like a common man," said the interpreter, after a searching look at Pierre.

"Ah, he looks very much like an incendiary," remarked the officer. "And ask him who he is," he added.

"Who are you?" asked the interpreter in poor Russian. "You must answer the chief."

"I will not tell you who I am. I am your prisoner—take me!" Pierre suddenly replied in French.

"Ah, ah!" muttered the officer with a frown. "Well then, march!"

A crowd had collected round the Uhlans. Nearest to Pierre stood the pockmarked peasant woman with the little girl, and when the patrol started she moved forward.

"Where are they taking you to, you poor dear?" said she. "And the little girl, the little girl, what am I to do with her if she's not theirs?" said the woman.

"What does that woman want?" asked the officer.

Pierre was as if intoxicated. His elation increased at the sight of the little girl he had saved.

"What does she want?" he murmured. "She is bringing me my daughter whom I have just saved from the flames," said he. "Goodby!" And without knowing how this aimless lie had escaped him, he went along with resolute and triumphant steps between the French soldiers.

The French patrol was one of those sent out through the various streets of Moscow by Durosnel's order to put a stop to the pillage, and especially to catch the incendiaries who, according to the general opinion which had that day originated among the higher French officers, were the cause of the conflagrations. After marching through a number of streets the patrol arrested five more Russian suspects: a small shopkeeper, two seminary students, a peasant, and a house serf, besides several looters. But of all these various suspected characters, Pierre was considered to be the most suspicious of all. When they had all been brought for the night to a large house on the Zúbov Rampart that was being used as a guardhouse, Pierre was placed apart under strict guard.

# I

In Petersburg at that time a complicated struggle was being carried on with greater heat than ever in the highest circles, between the parties of Rumyántsev, the French, Márya Fëdorovna, the Tsarévich, and others, drowned as usual by the buzzing of the court drones. But the calm, luxurious life of Petersburg, concerned only about phantoms and reflections of real life, went on in its old way and made it hard, except by a great effort, to realize the danger and the difficult position of the Russian people. There were the same receptions and balls, the same French theater, the same court interests and service interests and intrigues as usual. Only in the very highest circles were attempts made to keep in mind the difficulties of the actual position. Stories were whispered of how differently the two Empresses behaved in these difficult circumstances. The Empress Márya, concerned for the welfare of the charitable and educational institutions under her patronage, had given directions that they should all be removed to Kazán, and the things belonging to these institutions had already been packed up. The Empress Elisabeth, however, when asked what instructions she would be pleased to give—with her characteristic Russian patriotism had replied that she could give no directions about state institutions for that was the affair of the sovereign, but as far as she personally was concerned she would be the last to quit Petersburg.

At Anna Pávlovna's on the twenty-sixth of August, the very day of the battle of Borodinó, there was a soiree, the chief feature of which was to be the reading of a letter from His Lordship the Bishop when sending the Emperor an icon of the Venerable Sergius. It was regarded as a model of ecclesiastical, patriotic eloquence. Prince Vasíli himself, famed for his elocution, was to read it. (He used to read at the Empress'.) The art of his reading was supposed to lie in rolling out the words, quite independently of their meaning, in a loud and singsong voice alternating between a despairing wail and a tender murmur, so that the wail fell quite at random on one word and the murmur on another. This reading, as was always the case at Anna Pávlovna's soirees, had a political significance. That evening she expected several important personages who had to be made ashamed of their visits to the French theater and aroused to a patriotic temper. A good many people had already arrived, but Anna Pávlovna, not yet seeing all those whom she wanted in her drawing room, did not let the reading begin but wound up the springs of a general conversation.

The news of the day in Petersburg was the illness of Countess Bezúkhova. She had fallen ill unexpectedly a few days previously, had missed several gatherings of which she was usually the ornament, and was said to be receiving no one, and instead of the celebrated Petersburg doctors who usually attended her had entrusted herself to some Italian doctor who was treating her in some new and unusual way.

They all knew very well that the enchanting countess' illness arose from an inconvenience resulting from marrying two husbands at the same time, and that the Italian's cure consisted in removing such inconvenience; but in Anna Pávlovna's presence no one dared to think of this or even appear to know it.

"They say the poor countess is very ill. The doctor says it is angina pectoris."

"Angina? Oh, that's a terrible illness!"

"They say that the rivals are reconciled, thanks to the angina. . ." and the word angina was repeated with great satisfaction.

"The count is pathetic, they say. He cried like a child when the doctor told him the case was dangerous."

"Oh, it would be a terrible loss, she is an enchanting woman."

"You are speaking of the poor countess?" said Anna Pávlovna, coming up just then. "I sent to ask for news, and hear that she is a little better. Oh, she is certainly the most charming woman in the world," she went on, with a smile at her own enthusiasm. "We belong to different camps, but that does not prevent my esteeming her as she deserves. She is very unfortunate!" added Anna Pávlovna.

Supposing that by these words Anna Pávlovna was somewhat lifting the veil from the secret of the countess' malady, an unwary young man ventured to express surprise that well-known doctors had not been called in and that the countess was being attended by a charlatan who might employ dangerous remedies.

"Your information may be better than mine," Anna Pávlovna suddenly and venomously retorted on the inexperienced young man, "but I know on good authority that this doctor is a very learned and able man. He is private physician to the Queen of Spain."

And having thus demolished the young man, Anna Pávlovna turned to another group where Bilíbin was talking about the Austrians: having

LEO TOLSTOY

wrinkled up his face he was evidently preparing to smooth it out again and utter one of his mots.

"I think it is delightful," he said, referring to a diplomatic note that had been sent to Vienna with some Austrian banners captured from the French by Wittgenstein, "the hero of Petropol" as he was then called in Petersburg.

"What? What's that?" asked Anna Pávlovna, securing silence for the mot, which she had heard before.

And Bilíbin repeated the actual words of the diplomatic dispatch, which he had himself composed.

"The Emperor returns these Austrian banners," said Bilíbin, "friendly banners gone astray and found on a wrong path," and his brow became smooth again.

"Charming, charming!" observed Prince Vasíli.

"The path to Warsaw, perhaps," Prince Hippolyte remarked loudly and unexpectedly. Everybody looked at him, understanding what he meant. Prince Hippolyte himself glanced around with amused surprise. He knew no more than the others what his words meant. During his diplomatic career he had more than once noticed that such utterances were received as very witty, and at every opportunity he uttered in that way the first words that entered his head. "It may turn out very well," he thought, "but if not, they'll know how to arrange matters." And really, during the awkward silence that ensued, that insufficiently patriotic person entered whom Anna Pávlovna had been waiting for and wished to convert, and she, smiling and shaking a finger at Hippolyte, invited Prince Vasíli to the table and bringing him two candles and the manuscript begged him to begin. Everyone became silent.

"Most Gracious Sovereign and Emperor!" Prince Vasíli sternly declaimed, looking round at his audience as if to inquire whether anyone had anything to say to the contrary. But no one said anything. "Moscow, our ancient capital, the New Jerusalem, receives her Christ"—he placed a sudden emphasis on the word her—"as a mother receives her zealous sons into her arms, and through the gathering mists, foreseeing the brilliant glory of thy rule, sings in exultation, 'Hosanna, blessed is he that cometh!'"

Prince Vasíli pronounced these last words in a tearful voice.

Bilíbin attentively examined his nails, and many of those present appeared intimidated, as if asking in what they were to blame. Anna Pávlovna whispered the next words in advance, like an old woman muttering the prayer at Communion: "Let the bold and insolent Goliath. . ." she whispered.

Prince Vasíli continued.

"Let the bold and insolent Goliath from the borders of France encompass the realms of Russia with death-bearing terrors; humble Faith, the sling of the Russian David, shall suddenly smite his head in his bloodthirsty pride. This icon of the Venerable Sergius, the servant of God and zealous champion of old of our country's weal, is offered to Your Imperial Majesty. I grieve that my waning strength prevents rejoicing in the sight of your most gracious presence. I raise fervent prayers to Heaven that the Almighty may exalt the race of the just, and mercifully fulfill the desires of Your Majesty."

"What force! What a style!" was uttered in approval both of reader and of author.

Animated by that address Anna Pávlovna's guests talked for a long time of the state of the fatherland and offered various conjectures as to the result of the battle to be fought in a few days.

"You will see," said Anna Pávlovna, "that tomorrow, on the Emperor's birthday, we shall receive news. I have a favorable presentiment!"

# II

Anna Pávlovna's presentiment was in fact fulfilled. Next day during the service at the palace church in honor of the Emperor's birthday, Prince Volkónski was called out of the church and received a dispatch from Prince Kutúzov. It was Kutúzov's report, written from Tatárinova on the day of the battle. Kutúzov wrote that the Russians had not retreated a step, that the French losses were much heavier than ours, and that he was writing in haste from the field of battle before collecting full information. It followed that there must have been a victory. And at once, without leaving the church, thanks were rendered to the Creator for His help and for the victory.

Anna Pávlovna's presentiment was justified, and all that morning a joyously festive mood reigned in the city. Everyone believed the victory to have been complete, and some even spoke of Napoleon's having been captured, of his deposition, and of the choice of a new ruler for France.

It is very difficult for events to be reflected in their real strength and completeness amid the conditions of court life and far from the scene of action. General events involuntarily group themselves around some particular incident. So now the courtiers' pleasure was based as much on the fact that the news had arrived on the Emperor's birthday as on the fact of the victory itself. It was like a successfully arranged surprise. Mention was made in Kutúzov's report of the Russian losses, among which figured the names of Túchkov, Bagratión, and Kutáysov. In the Petersburg world this sad side of the affair again involuntarily centered round a single incident: Kutáysov's death. Everybody knew him, the Emperor liked him, and he was young and interesting. That day everyone met with the words:

"What a wonderful coincidence! Just during the service. But what a loss Kutáysov is! How sorry I am!"

"What did I tell about Kutúzov?" Prince Vasíli now said with a prophet's pride. "I always said he was the only man capable of defeating Napoleon."

But next day no news arrived from the army and the public mood grew anxious. The courtiers suffered because of the suffering the suspense occasioned the Emperor.

"Fancy the Emperor's position!" said they, and instead of extolling Kutúzov as they had done the day before, they condemned him as the cause of the Emperor's anxiety. That day Prince Vasíli no longer boasted of his protégé Kutúzov, but remained silent when the commander in chief was mentioned. Moreover, toward evening, as if everything conspired to make Petersburg society anxious and uneasy, a terrible piece of news was added. Countess Hélène Bezúkhova had suddenly died of that terrible malady it had been so agreeable to mention. Officially, at large gatherings, everyone said that Countess Bezúkhova had died of a terrible attack of angina pectoris, but in intimate circles details were mentioned of how the private physician of the Queen of Spain had prescribed small doses of a certain drug to produce a certain effect; but Hélène, tortured by the fact that the old count suspected her and that her husband to whom she had written (that wretched, profligate Pierre) had not replied, had suddenly taken a very large dose of the drug, and had died in agony before assistance could be rendered her. It was said that Prince Vasíli and the old count had turned upon the Italian, but the latter had produced such letters from the unfortunate deceased that they had immediately let the matter drop.

Talk in general centered round three melancholy facts: the Emperor's lack of news, the loss of Kutáysov, and the death of Hélène.

On the third day after Kutúzov's report a country gentleman arrived from Moscow, and news of the surrender of Moscow to the French spread through the whole town. This was terrible! What a position for the Emperor to be in! Kutúzov was a traitor, and Prince Vasíli during the visits of condolence paid to him on the occasion of his daughter's death said of Kutúzov, whom he had formerly praised (it was excusable for him in his grief to forget what he had said), that it was impossible to expect anything else from a blind and depraved old man.

"I only wonder that the fate of Russia could have been entrusted to such a man."

As long as this news remained unofficial it was possible to doubt it, but the next day the following communication was received from Count Rostopchín:

Prince Kutúzov's adjutant has brought me a letter in which he demands police officers to guide the army to the Ryazán road. He writes that he is regretfully abandoning Moscow. Sire! Kutúzov's action decides the fate of the capital and of your empire! Russia will shudder to learn of the abandonment of the city in which her greatness is centered and in which lie the ashes of your ancestors! I shall follow the army. I have had everything removed, and it only remains for me to weep over the fate of my fatherland.

On receiving this dispatch the Emperor sent Prince Volkónski to Kutúzov with the following rescript:

Prince Michael Ilariónovich! Since the twenty-ninth of August I have received no communication from you, yet on the first of September I received from the commander in chief of Moscow, via Yaroslávl, the sad news that you, with the army, have decided to abandon Moscow. You can yourself imagine the effect this news has had on me, and your silence increases my astonishment. I am sending this by Adjutant-General Prince Volkónski, to hear from you the situation of the army and the reasons that have induced you to take this melancholy decision.

# III

Nine days after the abandonment of Moscow, a messenger from Kutúzov reached Petersburg with the official announcement of that event. This messenger was Michaud, a Frenchman who did not know Russian, but who was quoique étranger, russe de cœur et d'âme,[*] as he said of himself.

The Emperor at once received this messenger in his study at the palace on Stone Island. Michaud, who had never seen Moscow before the campaign and who did not know Russian, yet felt deeply moved (as he wrote) when he appeared before notre très gracieux souverain[†] with the news of the burning of Moscow, dont les flammes éclairaient sa route.[‡]

Though the source of M. Michaud's chagrin must have been different from that which caused Russians to grieve, he had such a sad face when shown into the Emperor's study that the latter at once asked:

"Have you brought me sad news, Colonel?"

"Very sad, sire," replied Michaud, lowering his eyes with a sigh. "The abandonment of Moscow."

"Have they surrendered my ancient capital without a battle?" asked the Emperor quickly, his face suddenly flushing.

Michaud respectfully delivered the message Kutúzov had entrusted to him, which was that it had been impossible to fight before Moscow, and that as the only remaining choice was between losing the army as well as Moscow, or losing Moscow alone, the field marshal had to choose the latter.

The Emperor listened in silence, not looking at Michaud.

"Has the enemy entered the city?" he asked.

"Yes, sire, and Moscow is now in ashes. I left it all in flames," replied Michaud in a decided tone, but glancing at the Emperor he was frightened by what he had done.

The Emperor began to breathe heavily and rapidly, his lower lip trembled, and tears instantly appeared in his fine blue eyes.

But this lasted only a moment. He suddenly frowned, as if blaming himself for his weakness, and raising his head addressed Michaud in a firm voice:

---

[*] Though a foreigner, Russian in heart and soul.

[†] Our most gracious sovereign.

[‡] Whose flames illumined his route.

"I see, Colonel, from all that is happening, that Providence requires great sacrifices of us. . . I am ready to submit myself in all things to His will; but tell me, Michaud, how did you leave the army when it saw my ancient capital abandoned without a battle? Did you not notice discouragement? . . ."

Seeing that his most gracious ruler was calm once more, Michaud also grew calm, but was not immediately ready to reply to the Emperor's direct and relevant question which required a direct answer.

"Sire, will you allow me to speak frankly as befits a loyal soldier?" he asked to gain time.

"Colonel, I always require it," replied the Emperor. "Conceal nothing from me, I wish to know absolutely how things are."

"Sire!" said Michaud with a subtle, scarcely perceptible smile on his lips, having now prepared a well-phrased reply, "sire, I left the whole army, from its chiefs to the lowest soldier, without exception in desperate and agonized terror. . ."

"How is that?" the Emperor interrupted him, frowning sternly. "Would misfortune make my Russians lose heart? . . . Never!"

Michaud had only waited for this to bring out the phrase he had prepared.

"Sire," he said, with respectful playfulness, "they are only afraid lest Your Majesty, in the goodness of your heart, should allow yourself to be persuaded to make peace. They are burning for the combat," declared this representative of the Russian nation, "and to prove to Your Majesty by the sacrifice of their lives how devoted they are. . ."

"Ah!" said the Emperor reassured, and with a kindly gleam in his eyes, he patted Michaud on the shoulder. "You set me at ease, Colonel."

He bent his head and was silent for some time.

"Well, then, go back to the army," he said, drawing himself up to his full height and addressing Michaud with a gracious and majestic gesture, "and tell our brave men and all my good subjects wherever you go that when I have not a soldier left I shall put myself at the head of my beloved nobility and my good peasants and so use the last resources of my empire. It still offers me more than my enemies suppose," said the Emperor growing more and more animated; "but should it ever be ordained by Divine Providence," he continued, raising to heaven his fine eyes shining with emotion, "that my dynasty should cease to reign on the throne of my ancestors, then after exhausting all the means at my command, I shall let my beard grow to here" (he pointed halfway down his chest) "and go and eat potatoes with the meanest of my peasants, rather than sign the disgrace of my country and of my beloved people whose sacrifices I know how to appreciate."

Having uttered these words in an agitated voice the Emperor suddenly turned away as if to hide from Michaud the tears that rose to his eyes, and went to the further end of his study. Having stood there a few moments, he strode back to Michaud and pressed his arm below the elbow with a vigorous movement. The Emperor's mild and handsome face was flushed and his eyes gleamed with resolution and anger.

"Colonel Michaud, do not forget what I say to you here, perhaps we may recall it with pleasure someday. . . Napoleon or I," said the Emperor, touching his breast. "We can no longer both reign together. I have learned to know him, and he will not deceive me any more. . ."

And the Emperor paused, with a frown.

When he heard these words and saw the expression of firm resolution in the Emperor's eyes, Michaud—quoique étranger, russe de cœur et d'âme,—at that solemn moment felt himself enraptured by all that he had heard (as he used afterwards to say), and gave expression to his own feelings and those of the Russian people whose representative he considered himself to be, in the following words:

"Sire!" said he, "Your Majesty is at this moment signing the glory of the nation and the salvation of Europe!"

With an inclination of the head the Emperor dismissed him.

# IV

It is natural for us who were not living in those days to imagine that when half Russia had been conquered and the inhabitants were fleeing to distant provinces, and one levy after another was being raised for the defense of the fatherland, all Russians from the greatest to the least were solely engaged in sacrificing themselves, saving their fatherland, or weeping over its downfall. The tales and descriptions of that time without exception speak only of the self-sacrifice, patriotic devotion, despair, grief, and the heroism of the Russians. But it was not really so. It appears so to us because we see only the general historic interest of that time and do not see all the personal human interests that people had. Yet in reality those personal interests of the moment so much transcend the general interests that they always prevent the public interest from being felt or even noticed. Most of the people at that time paid no attention to the general progress of events but were guided only by their private interests, and they were the very people whose activities at that period were most useful.

Those who tried to understand the general course of events and to take part in it by self-sacrifice and heroism were the most useless members of society, they saw everything upside down, and all they did for the common good turned out to be useless and foolish—like Pierre's and Mamónov's regiments which looted Russian villages, and the lint the young ladies prepared and that never reached the wounded, and so on. Even those, fond of intellectual talk and of expressing their feelings, who discussed Russia's position at the time involuntarily introduced into their conversation either a shade of pretense and falsehood or useless condemnation and anger directed against people accused of actions no one could possibly be guilty of. In historic events the rule forbidding us to eat of the fruit of the Tree of Knowledge is specially applicable. Only unconscious action bears fruit, and he who plays a part in an historic event never understands its significance. If he tries to realize it his efforts are fruitless.

The more closely a man was engaged in the events then taking place in Russia the less did he realize their significance. In Petersburg and in the provinces at a distance from Moscow, ladies, and gentlemen in militia uniforms, wept for Russia and its ancient capital and talked of self-sacrifice and so on; but in the army which retired beyond Moscow there was little talk or thought of Moscow, and when they caught sight of its burned ruins no one swore to be avenged on the French, but they thought about their next pay, their next quarters, of Matrëshka the vivandière, and like matters.

As the war had caught him in the service, Nicholas Rostóv took a close and prolonged part in the defense of his country, but did so casually, without any aim at self-sacrifice, and he therefore looked at what was going on in Russia without despair and without dismally racking his brains over it. Had he been asked what he thought of the state of Russia, he would have said that it was not his business to think about it, that Kutúzov and others were there for that purpose, but that he had heard that the regiments were to be made up to their full strength, that fighting would probably go on for a long time yet, and that things being so it was quite likely he might be in command of a regiment in a couple of years' time.

As he looked at the matter in this way, he learned that he was being sent to Vorónezh to buy remounts for his division, not only without regret at being prevented from taking part in the coming battle, but with the greatest pleasure—which he did not conceal and which his comrades fully understood.

A few days before the battle of Borodinó, Nicholas received the necessary money and warrants, and having sent some hussars on in advance, he set out with post horses for Vorónezh.

Only a man who has experienced it—that is, has passed some months continuously in an atmosphere of campaigning and war—can understand the delight Nicholas felt when he escaped from the region covered by the army's foraging operations, provision trains, and hospitals. When—free from soldiers, wagons, and the filthy traces of a camp—he saw villages with peasants and peasant women, gentlemen's country houses, fields where cattle were grazing, posthouses with stationmasters asleep in them, he rejoiced as though seeing all this for the first time. What for a long while specially surprised and delighted him were the women, young and healthy, without a dozen officers making up to each of them; women, too, who were pleased and flattered that a passing officer should joke with them.

In the highest spirits Nicholas arrived at night at a hotel in Vorónezh, ordered things he had long been deprived of in camp, and next day, very clean-shaven and in a full-dress uniform he had not worn for a long time, went to present himself to the authorities.

The commander of the militia was a civilian general, an old man who was evidently pleased with his military designation and rank. He received Nicholas brusquely (imagining this to be characteristically military) and questioned him with an important air, as if considering the general progress of affairs and approving and disapproving with full right to do so. Nicholas was in such good spirits that this merely amused him.

From the commander of the militia he drove to the governor. The governor was a brisk little man, very simple and affable. He indicated the stud farms at which Nicholas might procure horses, recommended to him a horse dealer in the town and a landowner fourteen miles out of town who had the best horses, and promised to assist him in every way.

"You are Count Ilyá Rostóv's son? My wife was a great friend of your mother's. We are at home on Thursdays—today is Thursday, so please come and see us quite informally," said the governor, taking leave of him.

Immediately on leaving the governor's, Nicholas hired post horses and, taking his squadron quartermaster with him, drove at a gallop to the landowner, fourteen miles away, who had the stud. Everything seemed to him pleasant and easy during that first part of his stay in Vorónezh and, as usually happens when a man is in a pleasant state of mind, everything went well and easily.

The landowner to whom Nicholas went was a bachelor, an old cavalryman, a horse fancier, a sportsman, the possessor of some century-old brandy and some old Hungarian wine, who had a snuggery where he smoked, and who owned some splendid horses.

In very few words Nicholas bought seventeen picked stallions for six thousand rubles—to serve, as he said, as samples of his remounts. After dining and taking rather too much of the Hungarian wine, Nicholas—having exchanged kisses with the landowner, with whom he was already on the friendliest terms—galloped back over abominable roads, in the brightest frame of mind, continually urging on the driver so as to be in time for the governor's party.

When he had changed, poured water over his head, and scented himself, Nicholas arrived at the governor's rather late, but with the phrase "better late than never" on his lips.

It was not a ball, nor had dancing been announced, but everyone knew that Catherine Petróvna would play valses and the écossaise on the clavichord and that there would be dancing, and so everyone had come as to a ball.

Provincial life in 1812 went on very much as usual, but with this difference, that it was livelier in the towns in consequence of the arrival of many wealthy families from Moscow, and as in everything that went on in Russia at that time a special recklessness was noticeable, an "in for a penny, in for a pound—who cares?" spirit, and the inevitable small talk, instead of turning on the weather and mutual acquaintances, now turned on Moscow, the army, and Napoleon.

The society gathered together at the governor's was the best in Vorónezh.

There were a great many ladies and some of Nicholas' Moscow acquaintances, but there were no men who could at all vie with the cavalier of St. George, the hussar remount officer, the good-natured and well-bred Count Rostóv. Among the men was an Italian prisoner, an officer of the French army; and Nicholas felt that the presence of that prisoner enhanced his own importance as a Russian hero. The Italian was, as it were, a war trophy. Nicholas felt this, it seemed to him that everyone regarded the Italian in the same light, and he treated him cordially though with dignity and restraint.

As soon as Nicholas entered in his hussar uniform, diffusing around him a fragrance of perfume and wine, and had uttered the words "better late than never" and heard them repeated several times by others, people clustered around him; all eyes turned on him, and he felt at once that he had entered into his proper position in the province—that of a universal favorite: a very pleasant position, and intoxicatingly so after his long privations. At posting stations, at inns, and in the landowner's snuggery, maidservants had been flattered by his notice, and here too at the governor's party there were (as it seemed to Nicholas) an inexhaustible number of pretty young women, married and unmarried, impatiently awaiting his notice. The women and girls flirted with him and, from the first day, the people concerned themselves to get this fine young daredevil of an hussar married and settled down. Among these was the governor's wife herself, who welcomed Rostóv as a near relative and called him "Nicholas."

Catherine Petróvna did actually play valses and the écossaise, and dancing began in which Nicholas still further captivated the provincial society by his agility. His particularly free manner of dancing even surprised them all. Nicholas was himself rather surprised at the way he danced that evening. He had never danced like that in Moscow and would even have considered such a very free and easy manner improper and in bad form, but here he felt it incumbent on him to astonish them all by something unusual, something they would have to accept as the regular thing in the capital though new to them in the provinces.

All the evening Nicholas paid attention to a blue-eyed, plump and pleasing little blonde, the wife of one of the provincial officials. With the naïve conviction of young men in a merry mood that other men's wives were created for them, Rostóv did not leave the lady's side and treated her husband in a friendly and conspiratorial style, as if, without speaking of it, they knew how capitally Nicholas and the lady would get on together. The husband, however, did not seem to share that conviction and tried to behave morosely with Rostóv. But the latter's good-natured naïveté was so boundless that sometimes even he involuntarily yielded to Nicholas' good humor. Toward the end of the evening, however, as the wife's face grew more flushed and animated, the husband's became more and more melancholy and solemn, as though there were but a given amount of animation between them and as the wife's share increased the husband's diminished.

# V

Nicholas sat leaning slightly forward in an armchair, bending closely over the blonde lady and paying her mythological compliments with a smile that never left his face. Jauntily shifting the position of his legs in their tight riding breeches, diffusing an odor of perfume, and admiring his partner, himself, and the fine outlines of his legs in their well-fitting Hessian boots, Nicholas told the blonde lady that he wished to run away with a certain lady here in Vorónezh.

"Which lady?"

"A charming lady, a divine one. Her eyes" (Nicholas looked at his partner) "are blue, her mouth coral and ivory; her figure" (he glanced at her shoulders) "like Diana's. . ."

The husband came up and sullenly asked his wife what she was talking about.

"Ah, Nikíta Iványch!" cried Nicholas, rising politely, and as if wishing Nikíta Iványch to share his joke, he began to tell him of his intention to elope with a blonde lady.

The husband smiled gloomily, the wife gaily. The governor's good-natured wife came up with a look of disapproval.

"Anna Ignátyevna wants to see you, Nicholas," said she, pronouncing the name so that Nicholas at once understood that Anna Ignátyevna was a very important person. "Come, Nicholas! You know you let me call you so?"

"Oh, yes, Aunt. Who is she?"

"Anna Ignátyevna Malvíntseva. She has heard from her niece how you rescued her. . . Can you guess?"

"I rescued such a lot of them!" said Nicholas.

"Her niece, Princess Bolkónskaya. She is here in Vorónezh with her aunt. Oho! How you blush. Why, are. . . ?"

"Not a bit! Please don't, Aunt!"

"Very well, very well! . . . Oh, what a fellow you are!"

The governor's wife led him up to a tall and very stout old lady with a blue headdress, who had just finished her game of cards with the most important personages of the town. This was Malvíntseva, Princess Mary's aunt on her mother's side, a rich, childless widow who always lived in Vorónezh. When Rostóv approached her she was standing settling up for the game. She looked at him and, screwing up her eyes sternly, continued to upbraid the general who had won from her.

"Very pleased, mon cher," she then said, holding out her hand to Nicholas. "Pray come and see me."

After a few words about Princess Mary and her late father, whom Malvíntseva had evidently not liked, and having asked what Nicholas knew of Prince Andrew, who also was evidently no favorite of hers, the important old lady dismissed Nicholas after repeating her invitation to come to see her.

Nicholas promised to come and blushed again as he bowed. At the mention of Princess Mary he experienced a feeling of shyness and even of fear, which he himself did not understand.

When he had parted from Malvíntseva Nicholas wished to return to the dancing, but the governor's little wife placed her plump hand on his sleeve and, saying that she wanted to have a talk with him, led him to her sitting room, from which those who were there immediately withdrew so as not to be in her way.

"Do you know, dear boy," began the governor's wife with a serious expression on her kind little face, "that really would be the match for you: would you like me to arrange it?"

"Whom do you mean, Aunt?" asked Nicholas.

"I will make a match for you with the princess. Catherine Petróvna speaks of Lily, but I say, no—the princess! Do you want me to do it? I am sure your mother will be grateful to me. What a charming girl she is, really! And she is not at all so plain, either."

"Not at all," replied Nicholas as if offended at the idea. "As befits a soldier, Aunt, I don't force myself on anyone or refuse anything," he said before he had time to consider what he was saying.

"Well then, remember, this is not a joke!"

"Of course not!"

"Yes, yes," the governor's wife said as if talking to herself. "But, my dear boy, among other things you are too attentive to the other, the blonde. One is sorry for the husband, really. . ."

"Oh no, we are good friends with him," said Nicholas in the simplicity of his heart; it did not enter his head that a pastime so pleasant to himself might not be pleasant to someone else.

"But what nonsense I have been saying to the governor's wife!" thought Nicholas suddenly at supper. "She will really begin to arrange a match. . . and Sónya. . . ?" And on taking leave of the governor's wife, when she again smilingly said to him, "Well then, remember!" he drew her aside.

"But see here, to tell the truth, Aunt. . ."

"What is it, my dear? Come, let's sit down here," said she.

Nicholas suddenly felt a desire and need to tell his most intimate thoughts (which he would not have told to his mother, his sister, or his friend) to this woman who was almost a stranger. When he afterwards recalled that impulse to unsolicited and inexplicable frankness which had very important results for him, it seemed to him—as it seems to everyone in such cases—that it was merely some silly whim that seized him: yet that burst of frankness, together with other trifling events, had immense consequences for him and for all his family.

"You see, Aunt, Mamma has long wanted me to marry an heiress, but the very idea of marrying for money is repugnant to me."

"Oh yes, I understand," said the governor's wife.

"But Princess Bolkónskaya—that's another matter. I will tell you the truth. In the first place I like her very much, I feel drawn to her; and then, after I met her under such circumstances—so strangely, the idea often occurred to me: 'This is fate.' Especially if you remember that Mamma had long been thinking of it; but I had never happened to meet her before, somehow it had always happened that we did not meet. And as long as my sister Natásha was engaged to her brother it was of course out of the question for me to think of marrying her. And it must needs happen that I should meet her just when Natásha's engagement had been broken off. . . and then everything. . . So you see. . . I never told this to anyone and never will, only to you."

The governor's wife pressed his elbow gratefully.

"You know Sónya, my cousin? I love her, and promised to marry her, and will do so. . . So you see there can be no question about—" said Nicholas incoherently and blushing.

"My dear boy, what a way to look at it! You know Sónya has nothing and you yourself say your Papa's affairs are in a very bad way. And what about your mother? It would kill her, that's one thing. And what sort of life would it be for Sónya—if she's a girl with a heart? Your mother in despair, and you all ruined. . . No, my dear, you and Sónya ought to understand that."

Nicholas remained silent. It comforted him to hear these arguments.

"All the same, Aunt, it is impossible," he rejoined with a sigh, after a short pause. "Besides, would the princess have me? And besides, she is now in mourning. How can one think of it!"

"But you don't suppose I'm going to get you married at once? There is always a right way of doing things," replied the governor's wife.

"What a matchmaker you are, Aunt. . ." said Nicholas, kissing her plump little hand.

# VI

On reaching Moscow after her meeting with Rostóv, Princess Mary had found her nephew there with his tutor, and a letter from Prince Andrew giving her instructions how to get to her Aunt Malvíntseva at Vorónezh. That feeling akin to temptation which had tormented her during her father's illness, since his death, and especially since her meeting with Rostóv was smothered by arrangements for the journey, anxiety about her brother, settling in a new house, meeting new people, and attending to her nephew's education. She was sad. Now, after a month passed in quiet surroundings, she felt more and more deeply the loss of her father which was associated in her mind with the ruin of Russia. She was agitated and incessantly tortured by the thought of the dangers to which her brother, the only intimate person now remaining to her, was exposed. She was worried too about her nephew's education for which she had always felt herself incompetent, but in the depths of her soul she felt at peace—a peace arising from consciousness of having stifled those personal dreams and hopes that had been on the point of awakening within her and were related to her meeting with Rostóv.

The day after her party the governor's wife came to see Malvíntseva and, after discussing her plan with the aunt, remarked that though under present circumstances a formal betrothal was, of course, not to be thought of, all the same the young people might be brought together and could get to know one another. Malvíntseva expressed approval, and the governor's wife began to speak of Rostóv in Mary's presence, praising him and telling how he had blushed when Princess Mary's name was mentioned. But Princess Mary experienced a painful rather than a joyful feeling—her mental tranquillity was destroyed, and desires, doubts, self-reproach, and hopes reawoke.

During the two days that elapsed before Rostóv called, Princess Mary continually thought of how she ought to behave to him. First she decided not to come to the drawing room when he called to see her aunt—that it would not be proper for her, in her deep mourning, to receive visitors; then she thought this would be rude after what he had done for her; then it occurred to her that her aunt and the governor's wife had intentions concerning herself and Rostóv—their looks and words at times seemed to confirm this supposition—then she told herself that only she, with her sinful nature, could think this of them: they could not forget that situated as she was, while still wearing deep mourning, such matchmaking would be an insult to her and to her father's memory. Assuming that she did go down to see him, Princess Mary imagined the words he would say to her and what she would say to him, and these words sometimes seemed undeservedly cold and then to mean too much. More than anything she feared lest the confusion she felt might overwhelm her and betray her as soon as she saw him.

But when on Sunday after church the footman announced in the drawing room that Count Rostóv had called, the princess showed no confusion, only a slight blush suffused her cheeks and her eyes lit up with a new and radiant light.

"You have met him, Aunt?" said she in a calm voice, unable herself to understand that she could be outwardly so calm and natural.

When Rostóv entered the room, the princess dropped her eyes for an instant, as if to give the visitor time to greet her aunt, and then just as Nicholas turned to her she raised her head and met his look with shining eyes. With a movement full of dignity and grace she half rose with a smile of pleasure, held out her slender, delicate hand to him, and began to speak in a voice in which for the first time new deep womanly notes vibrated. Mademoiselle Bourienne, who was in the drawing room, looked at Princess Mary in bewildered surprise. Herself a consummate coquette, she could not have maneuvered better on meeting a man she wished to attract.

"Either black is particularly becoming to her or she really has greatly improved without my having noticed it. And above all, what tact and grace!" thought Mademoiselle Bourienne.

Had Princess Mary been capable of reflection at that moment, she would have been more surprised than Mademoiselle Bourienne at the change that had taken place in herself. From the moment she recognized that dear, loved face, a new life force took possession of her and compelled her to speak and act apart from her own will. From the time Rostóv entered, her face became suddenly transformed. It was as if a light had been kindled in a carved and painted lantern and the intricate, skillful, artistic work on its sides, that previously seemed dark, coarse, and meaningless, was suddenly shown up in unexpected and striking beauty. For the first time all that pure, spiritual, inward travail through which she had lived appeared on the surface. All her inward labor, her dissatisfaction with herself, her sufferings, her strivings after goodness, her meekness, love, and self-sacrifice—all this now shone in those radiant eyes, in her delicate smile, and in every trait of her gentle face.

Rostóv saw all this as clearly as if he had known her whole life. He felt that the being before him was quite different from, and better than, anyone he had met before, and above all better than himself.

Their conversation was very simple and unimportant. They spoke of the war, and like everyone else unconsciously exaggerated their sorrow about it; they spoke of their last meeting—Nicholas trying to change the subject—they talked of the governor's kind wife, of Nicholas' relations, and of Princess Mary's.

She did not talk about her brother, diverting the conversation as soon as her aunt mentioned Andrew. Evidently she could speak of Russia's misfortunes with a certain artificiality, but her brother was too near her heart and she neither could nor would speak lightly of him. Nicholas noticed this, as he noticed every shade of Princess Mary's character with an observation unusual to him, and everything confirmed his conviction that she was a quite unusual and extraordinary being. Nicholas blushed and was confused when people spoke to him about the princess (as she did when he was mentioned) and even when he thought of her, but in her presence he felt quite at ease, and said not at all what he had prepared, but what, quite appropriately, occurred to him at the moment.

When a pause occurred during his short visit, Nicholas, as is usual when there are children, turned to Prince Andrew's little son, caressing him and asking whether he would like to be an hussar. He took the boy on his knee, played with him, and looked round at Princess Mary. With a softened, happy, timid look she watched the boy she loved in the arms of the man she loved. Nicholas also noticed that look and, as if understanding it, flushed with pleasure and began to kiss the boy with good natured playfulness.

As she was in mourning Princess Mary did not go out into society, and Nicholas did not think it the proper thing to visit her again; but all the same the governor's wife went on with her matchmaking, passing on to Nicholas the flattering things Princess Mary said of him and vice versa, and insisting on his declaring himself to Princess Mary. For this purpose she arranged a meeting between the young people at the bishop's house before Mass.

Though Rostóv told the governor's wife that he would not make any declaration to Princess Mary, he promised to go.

As at Tilsit Rostóv had not allowed himself to doubt that what everybody considered right was right, so now, after a short but sincere struggle between his effort to arrange his life by his own sense of justice, and in obedient submission to circumstances, he chose the latter and yielded to the power he felt irresistibly carrying him he knew not where. He knew that after his promise to Sónya it would be what he deemed base to declare his feelings to Princess Mary. And he knew that he would never act basely. But he also knew (or rather felt at the bottom of his heart) that by resigning himself now to the force of circumstances and to those who were guiding him, he was not only doing nothing wrong, but was doing something very important—more important than anything he had ever done in his life.

After meeting Princess Mary, though the course of his life went on externally as before, all his former amusements lost their charm for him and he often thought about her. But he never thought about her as he had thought of all the young ladies without exception whom he had met in society, nor as he had for a long time, and at one time rapturously, thought about Sónya. He had pictured each of those young ladies as almost all honest-hearted young men do, that is, as a possible wife, adapting her in his imagination to all the conditions of married life: a white dressing gown, his wife at the tea table, his wife's carriage, little ones, Mamma and Papa, their relations to her, and so on—and these pictures of the future had given him pleasure. But with Princess Mary, to whom they were trying to get him engaged, he could never picture anything of future married life. If he tried, his pictures seemed incongruous and false. It made him afraid.

# VII

The dreadful news of the battle of Borodinó, of our losses in killed and wounded, and the still more terrible news of the loss of Moscow reached Vorónezh in the middle of September. Princess Mary, having learned of her brother's wound only from the Gazette and having no definite news of him, prepared (so Nicholas heard, he had not seen her again himself) to set off in search of Prince Andrew.

When he received the news of the battle of Borodinó and the abandonment of Moscow, Rostóv was not seized with despair, anger, the desire for vengeance, or any feeling of that kind, but everything in Vorónezh suddenly seemed to him dull and tiresome, and he experienced an indefinite feeling of shame and awkwardness. The conversations he heard seemed to him insincere; he did not know how to judge all these affairs and felt that only in the regiment would everything again become clear to him. He made haste to finish buying the horses, and often became unreasonably angry with his servant and squadron quartermaster.

A few days before his departure a special thanksgiving, at which Nicholas was present, was held in the cathedral for the Russian victory. He stood a little behind the governor and held himself with military decorum through the service, meditating on a great variety of subjects. When the service was over the governor's wife beckoned him to her.

"Have you seen the princess?" she asked, indicating with a movement of her head a lady standing on the opposite side, beyond the choir.

Nicholas immediately recognized Princess Mary not so much by the profile he saw under her bonnet as by the feeling of solicitude, timidity, and pity that immediately overcame him. Princess Mary, evidently engrossed by her thoughts, was crossing herself for the last time before leaving the church.

Nicholas looked at her face with surprise. It was the same face he had seen before, there was the same general expression of refined, inner, spiritual labor, but now it was quite differently lit up. There was a pathetic expression of sorrow, prayer, and hope in it. As had occurred before when she was present, Nicholas went up to her without waiting to be prompted by the governor's wife and not asking himself whether or not it was right and proper to address her here in church, and told her he had heard of her trouble and sympathized with his whole soul. As soon as she heard his voice a vivid glow kindled in her face, lighting up both her sorrow and her joy.

"There is one thing I wanted to tell you, Princess," said Rostóv. "It is that if your brother, Prince Andrew Nikoláevich, were not living, it would have been at once announced in the Gazette, as he is a colonel."

The princess looked at him, not grasping what he was saying, but cheered by the expression of regretful sympathy on his face.

"And I have known so many cases of a splinter wound" (the Gazette said it was a shell) "either proving fatal at once or being very slight," continued Nicholas. "We must hope for the best, and I am sure. . ."

Princess Mary interrupted him.

"Oh, that would be so dread. . ." she began and, prevented by agitation from finishing, she bent her head with a movement as graceful as everything she did in his presence and, looking up at him gratefully, went out, following her aunt.

That evening Nicholas did not go out, but stayed at home to settle some accounts with the horse dealers. When he had finished that business it was already too late to go anywhere but still too early to go to bed, and for a long time he paced up and down the room, reflecting on his life, a thing he rarely did.

Princess Mary had made an agreeable impression on him when he had met her in Smolénsk province. His having encountered her in such exceptional circumstances, and his mother having at one time mentioned her to him as a good match, had drawn his particular attention to her. When he met her again in Vorónezh the impression she made on him was not merely pleasing but powerful. Nicholas had been struck by the peculiar moral beauty he observed in her at this time. He was, however, preparing to go away and it had not entered his head to regret that he was thus depriving himself of chances of meeting her. But that day's encounter in church had, he felt, sunk deeper than was desirable for his peace of mind. That pale, sad, refined face, that radiant look, those gentle graceful gestures, and especially the deep and tender sorrow expressed in all her features agitated him and evoked his sympathy. In men Rostóv could not bear to see the expression of a higher spiritual life (that was why he did not like

Prince Andrew) and he referred to it contemptuously as philosophy and dreaminess, but in Princess Mary that very sorrow which revealed the depth of a whole spiritual world foreign to him was an irresistible attraction.

"She must be a wonderful woman. A real angel!" he said to himself. "Why am I not free? Why was I in such a hurry with Sónya?" And he involuntarily compared the two: the lack of spirituality in the one and the abundance of it in the other—a spirituality he himself lacked and therefore valued most highly. He tried to picture what would happen were he free. How he would propose to her and how she would become his wife. But no, he could not imagine that. He felt awed, and no clear picture presented itself to his mind. He had long ago pictured to himself a future with Sónya, and that was all clear and simple just because it had all been thought out and he knew all there was in Sónya, but it was impossible to picture a future with Princess Mary, because he did not understand her but simply loved her.

Reveries about Sónya had had something merry and playful in them, but to dream of Princess Mary was always difficult and a little frightening.

"How she prayed!" he thought. "It was plain that her whole soul was in her prayer. Yes, that was the prayer that moves mountains, and I am sure her prayer will be answered. Why don't I pray for what I want?" he suddenly thought. "What do I want? To be free, released from Sónya. . . She was right," he thought, remembering what the governor's wife had said: "Nothing but misfortune can come of marrying Sónya. Muddles, grief for Mamma. . . business difficulties. . . muddles, terrible muddles! Besides, I don't love her—not as I should. O, God! release me from this dreadful, inextricable position!" he suddenly began to pray. "Yes, prayer can move mountains, but one must have faith and not pray as Natásha and I used to as children, that the snow might turn into sugar—and then run out into the yard to see whether it had done so. No, but I am not praying for trifles now," he thought as he put his pipe down in a corner, and folding his hands placed himself before the icon. Softened by memories of Princess Mary he began to pray as he had not done for a long time. Tears were in his eyes and in his throat when the door opened and Lavrúshka came in with some papers.

"Blockhead! Why do you come in without being called?" cried Nicholas, quickly changing his attitude.

"From the governor," said Lavrúshka in a sleepy voice. "A courier has arrived and there's a letter for you."

"Well, all right, thanks. You can go!"

Nicholas took the two letters, one of which was from his mother and the other from Sónya. He recognized them by the handwriting and opened Sónya's first. He had read only a few lines when he turned pale and his eyes opened wide with fear and joy.

"No, it's not possible!" he cried aloud.

Unable to sit still he paced up and down the room holding the letter and reading it. He glanced through it, then read it again, and then again, and standing still in the middle of the room he raised his shoulders, stretching out his hands, with his mouth wide open and his eyes fixed. What he had just been praying for with confidence that God would hear him had come to pass; but Nicholas was as much astonished as if it were something extraordinary and unexpected, and as if the very fact that it had happened so quickly proved that it had not come from God to whom he had prayed, but by some ordinary coincidence.

This unexpected and, as it seemed to Nicholas, quite voluntary letter from Sónya freed him from the knot that fettered him and from which there had seemed no escape. She wrote that the last unfortunate events—the loss of almost the whole of the Rostóvs' Moscow property—and the countess' repeatedly expressed wish that Nicholas should marry Princess Bolkónskaya, together with his silence and coldness of late, had all combined to make her decide to release him from his promise and set him completely free.

> It would be too painful to me to think that I might be a cause of sorrow or discord in the family that has been so good to me (she wrote), and my love has no aim but the happiness of those I love; so, Nicholas, I beg you to consider yourself free, and to be assured that, in spite of everything, no one can love you more than does
>
> Your Sónya

Both letters were written from Tróitsa. The other, from the countess, described their last days in Moscow, their departure, the fire, and the destruction of all their property. In this letter the countess also mentioned that Prince Andrew was among the wounded traveling with them; his state was very critical, but the doctor said there was now more hope. Sónya and Natásha were nursing him.

Next day Nicholas took his mother's letter and went to see Princess Mary. Neither he nor she said a word about what "Natásha nursing him" might mean, but thanks to this letter Nicholas suddenly became almost as intimate with the princess as if they were relations.

The following day he saw Princess Mary off on her journey to Yaroslávl, and a few days later left to rejoin his regiment.

# VIII

Sónya's letter written from Tróitsa, which had come as an answer to Nicholas' prayer, was prompted by this: the thought of getting Nicholas married to an heiress occupied the old countess' mind more and more. She knew that Sónya was the chief obstacle to this happening, and Sónya's life in the countess' house had grown harder and harder, especially after they had received a letter from Nicholas telling of his meeting with Princess Mary in Boguchárovo. The countess let no occasion slip of making humiliating or cruel allusions to Sónya.

But a few days before they left Moscow, moved and excited by all that was going on, she called Sónya to her and, instead of reproaching and making demands on her, tearfully implored her to sacrifice herself and repay all that the family had done for her by breaking off her engagement with Nicholas.

"I shall not be at peace till you promise me this."

Sónya burst into hysterical tears and replied through her sobs that she would do anything and was prepared for anything, but gave no actual promise and could not bring herself to decide to do what was demanded of her. She must sacrifice herself for the family that had reared and brought her up. To sacrifice herself for others was Sónya's habit. Her position in the house was such that only by sacrifice could she show her worth, and she was accustomed to this and loved doing it. But in all her former acts of self-sacrifice she had been happily conscious that they raised her in her own esteem and in that of others, and so made her more worthy of Nicholas whom she loved more than anything in the world. But now they wanted her to sacrifice the very thing that constituted the whole reward for her self-sacrifice and the whole meaning of her life. And for the first time she felt bitterness against those who had been her benefactors only to torture her the more painfully; she felt jealous of Natásha who had never experienced anything of this sort, had never needed to sacrifice herself, but made others sacrifice themselves for her and yet was beloved by everybody. And for the first time Sónya felt that out of her pure, quiet love for Nicholas a passionate feeling was beginning to grow up which was stronger than principle, virtue, or religion. Under the influence of this feeling Sónya, whose life of dependence had taught her involuntarily to be secretive, having answered the countess in vague general terms, avoided talking with her and resolved to wait till she should see Nicholas, not in order to set him free but on the contrary at that meeting to bind him to her forever.

The bustle and terror of the Rostóvs' last days in Moscow stifled the gloomy thoughts that oppressed Sónya. She was glad to find escape from them in practical activity. But when she heard of Prince Andrew's presence in their house, despite her sincere pity for him and for Natásha, she was seized by a joyful and superstitious feeling that God did not intend her to be separated from Nicholas. She knew that Natásha loved no one but Prince Andrew and had never ceased to love him. She knew that being thrown together again under such terrible circumstances they would again fall in love with one another, and that Nicholas would then not be able to marry Princess Mary as they would be within the prohibited degrees of affinity. Despite all the terror of what had happened during those last days and during the first days of their journey, this feeling that Providence was intervening in her personal affairs cheered Sónya.

At the Tróitsa monastery the Rostóvs first broke their journey for a whole day.

Three large rooms were assigned to them in the monastery hostelry, one of which was occupied by Prince Andrew. The wounded man was much better that day and Natásha was sitting with him. In the next room sat the count and countess respectfully conversing with the prior, who was calling on them as old acquaintances and benefactors of the monastery. Sónya was there too, tormented by curiosity as to what Prince Andrew and Natásha were talking about. She heard the sound of their voices through the door. That door opened and Natásha came out, looking excited. Not noticing the monk, who had risen to greet her and was drawing back the wide sleeve on his right arm, she went up to Sónya and took her hand.

"Natásha, what are you about? Come here!" said the countess.

Natásha went up to the monk for his blessing, and he advised her to pray for aid to God and His saint.

As soon as the prior withdrew, Natásha took her friend by the hand and went with her into the unoccupied room.

"Sónya, will he live?" she asked. "Sónya, how happy I am, and how unhappy! . . . Sónya, dovey, everything is as it used to be. If only he lives! He cannot. . . because. . . because. . . of. . ." and Natásha burst into tears.

"Yes! I knew it! Thank God!" murmured Sónya. "He will live."

Sónya was not less agitated than her friend by the latter's fear and grief and by her own personal feelings which she shared with no one. Sobbing, she kissed and comforted Natásha. "If only he lives!" she thought. Having wept, talked, and wiped away their tears, the two friends went together to Prince Andrew's door. Natásha opened it cautiously and glanced into the room, Sónya standing beside her at the half-open door.

Prince Andrew was lying raised high on three pillows. His pale face was calm, his eyes closed, and they could see his regular breathing.

"O, Natásha!" Sónya suddenly almost screamed, catching her companion's arm and stepping back from the door.

"What? What is it?" asked Natásha.

"It's that, that. . ." said Sónya, with a white face and trembling lips.

Natásha softly closed the door and went with Sónya to the window, not yet understanding what the latter was telling her.

"You remember," said Sónya with a solemn and frightened expression. "You remember when I looked in the mirror for you. . . at Otrádnoe at Christmas? Do you remember what I saw?"

"Yes, yes!" cried Natásha opening her eyes wide, and vaguely recalling that Sónya had told her something about Prince Andrew whom she had seen lying down.

"You remember?" Sónya went on. "I saw it then and told everybody, you and Dunyásha. I saw him lying on a bed," said she, making a gesture with her hand and a lifted finger at each detail, "and that he had his eyes closed and was covered just with a pink quilt, and that his hands were folded," she concluded, convincing herself that the details she had just seen were exactly what she had seen in the mirror.

She had in fact seen nothing then but had mentioned the first thing that came into her head, but what she had invented then seemed to her now as real as any other recollection. She not only remembered what she had then said—that he turned to look at her and smiled and was covered with something red—but was firmly convinced that she had then seen and said that he was covered with a pink quilt and that his eyes were closed.

"Yes, yes, it really was pink!" cried Natásha, who now thought she too remembered the word pink being used, and saw in this the most extraordinary and mysterious part of the prediction.

"But what does it mean?" she added meditatively.

"Oh, I don't know, it is all so strange," replied Sónya, clutching at her head.

A few minutes later Prince Andrew rang and Natásha went to him, but Sónya, feeling unusually excited and touched, remained at the window thinking about the strangeness of what had occurred.

They had an opportunity that day to send letters to the army, and the countess was writing to her son.

"Sónya!" said the countess, raising her eyes from her letter as her niece passed, "Sónya, won't you write to Nicholas?" She spoke in a soft, tremulous voice, and in the weary eyes that looked over her spectacles Sónya read all that the countess meant to convey with these words. Those eyes expressed entreaty, shame at having to ask, fear of a refusal, and readiness for relentless hatred in case of such refusal.

Sónya went up to the countess and, kneeling down, kissed her hand.

"Yes, Mamma, I will write," said she.

Sónya was softened, excited, and touched by all that had occurred that day, especially by the mysterious fulfillment she had just seen of her vision. Now that she knew that the renewal of Natásha's relations with Prince Andrew would prevent Nicholas from marrying Princess Mary, she was joyfully conscious of a return of that self-sacrificing spirit in which she was accustomed to live and loved to live. So with a joyful consciousness of performing a magnanimous deed—interrupted several times by the tears that dimmed her velvety black eyes—she wrote that touching letter the arrival of which had so amazed Nicholas.

# IX

The officer and soldiers who had arrested Pierre treated him with hostility but yet with respect, in the guardhouse to which he was taken. In their attitude toward him could still be felt both uncertainty as to who he might be—perhaps a very important person—and hostility as a result of their recent personal conflict with him.

But when the guard was relieved next morning, Pierre felt that for the new guard—both officers and men—he was not as interesting as he had been to his captors; and in fact the guard of the second day did not recognize in this big, stout man in a peasant coat the vigorous person who had fought so desperately with the marauder and the convoy and had uttered those solemn words about saving a child; they saw in him only No. 17 of the captured Russians, arrested and detained for some reason by order of the Higher Command. If they noticed anything remarkable about Pierre, it was only his unabashed, meditative concentration and thoughtfulness, and the way he spoke French, which struck them as surprisingly good. In spite of this he was placed that day with the other arrested suspects, as the separate room he had occupied was required by an officer.

All the Russians confined with Pierre were men of the lowest class and, recognizing him as a gentleman, they all avoided him, more especially as he spoke French. Pierre felt sad at hearing them making fun of him.

That evening he learned that all these prisoners (he, probably, among them) were to be tried for incendiarism. On the third day he was taken with the others to a house where a French general with a white mustache sat with two colonels and other Frenchmen with scarves on their arms. With the precision and definiteness customary in addressing prisoners, and which is supposed to preclude human frailty, Pierre like the others was questioned as to who he was, where he had been, with what object, and so on.

These questions, like questions put at trials generally, left the essence of the matter aside, shut out the possibility of that essence's being revealed, and were designed only to form a channel through which the judges wished the answers of the accused to flow so as to lead to the desired result, namely a conviction. As soon as Pierre began to say anything that did not fit in with that aim, the channel was removed and the water could flow to waste. Pierre felt, moreover, what the accused always feel at their trial, perplexity as to why these questions were put to him. He had a feeling that it was only out of condescension or a kind of civility that this device of placing a channel was employed. He knew he was in these men's power, that only by force had they brought him there, that force alone gave them the right to demand answers to their questions, and that the sole object of that assembly was to inculpate him. And so, as they had the power and wish to inculpate him, this expedient of an inquiry and trial seemed unnecessary. It was evident that any answer would lead to conviction. When asked what he was doing when he was arrested, Pierre replied in a rather tragic manner that he was restoring to its parents a child he had saved from the flames. Why had he fought the marauder? Pierre answered that he "was protecting a woman," and that "to protect a woman who was being insulted was the duty of every man; that. . ." They interrupted him, for this was not to the point. Why was he in the yard of a burning house where witnesses had seen him? He replied that he had gone out to see what was happening in Moscow. Again they interrupted him: they had not asked where he was going, but why he was found near the fire? Who was he? they asked, repeating their first question, which he had declined to answer. Again he replied that he could not answer it.

"Put that down, that's bad. . . very bad," sternly remarked the general with the white mustache and red flushed face.

On the fourth day fires broke out on the Zúbovski rampart.

Pierre and thirteen others were moved to the coach house of a merchant's house near the Crimean bridge. On his way through the streets Pierre felt stifled by the smoke which seemed to hang over the whole city. Fires were visible on all sides. He did not then realize the significance of the burning of Moscow, and looked at the fires with horror.

He passed four days in the coach house near the Crimean bridge and during that time learned, from the talk of the French soldiers, that all those confined there were awaiting a decision which might come any day from the marshal. What marshal this was, Pierre could not learn from the soldiers. Evidently for them "the marshal" represented a very high and rather mysterious power.

These first days, before the eighth of September when the prisoners were had up for a second examination, were the hardest of all for Pierre.

# X

O n the eighth of September an officer—a very important one judging by the respect the guards showed him—entered the coach house where the prisoners were. This officer, probably someone on the staff, was holding a paper in his hand, and called over all the Russians there, naming Pierre as "the man who does not give his name." Glancing indolently and indifferently at all the prisoners, he ordered the officer in charge to have them decently dressed and tidied up before taking them to the marshal. An hour later a squad of soldiers arrived and Pierre with thirteen others was led to the Virgin's Field. It was a fine day, sunny after rain, and the air was unusually pure. The smoke did not hang low as on the day when Pierre had been taken from the guardhouse on the Zúbovski rampart, but rose through the pure air in columns. No flames were seen, but columns of smoke rose on all sides, and all Moscow as far as Pierre could see was one vast charred ruin. On all sides there were waste spaces with only stoves and chimney stacks still standing, and here and there the blackened walls of some brick houses. Pierre gazed at the ruins and did not recognize districts he had known well. Here and there he could see churches that had not been burned. The Krémlin, which was not destroyed, gleamed white in the distance with its towers and the belfry of Iván the Great. The domes of the New Convent of the Virgin glittered brightly and its bells were ringing particularly clearly. These bells reminded Pierre that it was Sunday and the feast of the Nativity of the Virgin. But there seemed to be no one to celebrate this holiday: everywhere were blackened ruins, and the few Russians to be seen were tattered and frightened people who tried to hide when they saw the French.

It was plain that the Russian nest was ruined and destroyed, but in place of the Russian order of life that had been destroyed, Pierre unconsciously felt that a quite different, firm, French order had been established over this ruined nest. He felt this in the looks of the soldiers who, marching in regular ranks briskly and gaily, were escorting him and the other criminals; he felt it in the looks of an important French official in a carriage and pair driven by a soldier, whom they met on the way. He felt it in the merry sounds of regimental music he heard from the left side of the field, and felt and realized it especially from the list of prisoners the French officer had read out when he came that morning. Pierre had been taken by one set of soldiers and led first to one and then to another place with dozens of other men, and it seemed that they might have forgotten him, or confused him with the others. But no: the answers he had given when questioned had come back to him in his designation as "the man who does not give his name," and under that appellation, which to Pierre seemed terrible, they were now leading him somewhere with unhesitating assurance on their faces that he and all the other prisoners were exactly the ones they wanted and that they were being taken to the proper place. Pierre felt himself to be an insignificant chip fallen among the wheels of a machine whose action he did not understand but which was working well.

He and the other prisoners were taken to the right side of the Virgin's Field, to a large white house with an immense garden not far from the convent. This was Prince Shcherbátov's house, where Pierre had often been in other days, and which, as he learned from the talk of the soldiers, was now occupied by the marshal, the Duke of Eckmühl (Davout).

They were taken to the entrance and led into the house one by one. Pierre was the sixth to enter. He was conducted through a glass gallery, an anteroom, and a hall, which were familiar to him, into a long low study at the door of which stood an adjutant.

Davout, spectacles on nose, sat bent over a table at the further end of the room. Pierre went close up to him, but Davout, evidently consulting a paper that lay before him, did not look up. Without raising his eyes, he said in a low voice:

"Who are you?"

Pierre was silent because he was incapable of uttering a word. To him Davout was not merely a French general, but a man notorious for his cruelty. Looking at his cold face, as he sat like a stern schoolmaster who was prepared to wait awhile for an answer, Pierre felt that every instant of delay might cost him his life; but he did not know what to say. He did not venture to repeat what he had said at his first examination, yet to disclose his rank and position was dangerous and embarrassing. So he was silent. But before he had decided what to do, Davout raised his head, pushed his spectacles back on his forehead, screwed up his eyes, and looked intently at him.

"I know that man," he said in a cold, measured tone, evidently calculated to frighten Pierre.

The chill that had been running down Pierre's back now seized his head as in a vise.

"You cannot know me, General, I have never seen you. . ."

"He is a Russian spy," Davout interrupted, addressing another general who was present, but whom Pierre had not noticed.

Davout turned away. With an unexpected reverberation in his voice Pierre rapidly began:

"No, monseigneur," he said, suddenly remembering that Davout was a duke. "No, monseigneur, you cannot have known me. I am a militia officer and have not quitted Moscow."

"Your name?" asked Davout.

"Bezúkhov."

"What proof have I that you are not lying?"

"Monseigneur!" exclaimed Pierre, not in an offended but in a pleading voice.

Davout looked up and gazed intently at him. For some seconds they looked at one another, and that look saved Pierre. Apart from conditions of war and law, that look established human relations between the two men. At that moment an immense number of things passed dimly through both their minds, and they realized that they were both children of humanity and were brothers.

At the first glance, when Davout had only raised his head from the papers where human affairs and lives were indicated by numbers, Pierre was merely a circumstance, and Davout could have shot him without burdening his conscience with an evil deed, but now he saw in him a human being. He reflected for a moment.

"How can you show me that you are telling the truth?" said Davout coldly.

Pierre remembered Ramballe, and named him and his regiment and the street where the house was.

"You are not what you say," returned Davout.

In a trembling, faltering voice Pierre began adducing proofs of the truth of his statements.

But at that moment an adjutant entered and reported something to Davout.

Davout brightened up at the news the adjutant brought, and began buttoning up his uniform. It seemed that he had quite forgotten Pierre.

When the adjutant reminded him of the prisoner, he jerked his head in Pierre's direction with a frown and ordered him to be led away. But where they were to take him Pierre did not know: back to the coach house or to the place of execution his companions had pointed out to him as they crossed the Virgin's Field.

He turned his head and saw that the adjutant was putting another question to Davout.

"Yes, of course!" replied Davout, but what this "yes" meant, Pierre did not know.

Pierre could not afterwards remember how he went, whether it was far, or in which direction. His faculties were quite numbed, he was stupefied, and noticing nothing around him went on moving his legs as the others did till they all stopped and he stopped too. The only thought in his mind at that time was: who was it that had really sentenced him to death? Not the men on the commission that had first examined him—not one of them wished to or, evidently, could have done it. It was not Davout, who had looked at him in so human a way. In another moment Davout would have realized that he was doing wrong, but just then the adjutant had come in and interrupted him. The adjutant, also, had evidently had no evil intent though he might have refrained from coming in. Then who was executing him, killing him, depriving him of life—him, Pierre, with all his memories, aspirations, hopes, and thoughts? Who was doing this? And Pierre felt that it was no one.

It was a system—a concurrence of circumstances.

A system of some sort was killing him—Pierre—depriving him of life, of everything, annihilating him.

# XI

From Prince Shcherbátov's house the prisoners were led straight down the Virgin's Field, to the left of the nunnery, as far as a kitchen garden in which a post had been set up. Beyond that post a fresh pit had been dug in the ground, and near the post and the pit a large crowd stood in a semicircle. The crowd consisted of a few Russians and many of Napoleon's soldiers who were not on duty—Germans, Italians, and Frenchmen, in a variety of uniforms. To the right and left of the post stood rows of French troops in blue uniforms with red epaulets and high boots and shakos.

The prisoners were placed in a certain order, according to the list (Pierre was sixth), and were led to the post. Several drums suddenly began to beat on both sides of them, and at that sound Pierre felt as if part of his soul had been torn away. He lost the power of thinking or understanding. He could only hear and see. And he had only one wish—that the frightful thing that had to happen should happen quickly. Pierre looked round at his fellow prisoners and scrutinized them.

The two first were convicts with shaven heads. One was tall and thin, the other dark, shaggy, and sinewy, with a flat nose. The third was a domestic serf, about forty-five years old, with grizzled hair and a plump, well-nourished body. The fourth was a peasant, a very handsome man with a broad, light-brown beard and black eyes. The fifth was a factory hand, a thin, sallow-faced lad of eighteen in a loose coat.

Pierre heard the French consulting whether to shoot them separately or two at a time. "In couples," replied the officer in command in a calm voice. There was a stir in the ranks of the soldiers and it was evident that they were all hurrying—not as men hurry to do something they understand, but as people hurry to finish a necessary but unpleasant and incomprehensible task.

A French official wearing a scarf came up to the right of the row of prisoners and read out the sentence in Russian and in French.

Then two pairs of Frenchmen approached the criminals and at the officer's command took the two convicts who stood first in the row. The convicts stopped when they reached the post and, while sacks were being brought, looked dumbly around as a wounded beast looks at an approaching huntsman. One crossed himself continually, the other scratched his back and made a movement of the lips resembling a smile. With hurried hands the soldiers blindfolded them, drawing the sacks over their heads, and bound them to the post.

Twelve sharpshooters with muskets stepped out of the ranks with a firm regular tread and halted eight paces from the post. Pierre turned away to avoid seeing what was going to happen. Suddenly a crackling, rolling noise was heard which seemed to him louder than the most terrific thunder, and he looked round. There was some smoke, and the Frenchmen were doing something near the pit, with pale faces and trembling hands. Two more prisoners were led up. In the same way and with similar looks, these two glanced vainly at the onlookers with only a silent appeal for protection in their eyes, evidently unable to understand or believe what was going to happen to them. They could not believe it because they alone knew what their life meant to them, and so they neither understood nor believed that it could be taken from them.

Again Pierre did not wish to look and again turned away; but again the sound as of a frightful explosion struck his ear, and at the same moment he saw smoke, blood, and the pale, scared faces of the Frenchmen who were again doing something by the post, their trembling hands impeding one another. Pierre, breathing heavily, looked around as if asking what it meant. The same question was expressed in all the looks that met his.

On the faces of all the Russians and of the French soldiers and officers without exception, he read the same dismay, horror, and conflict that were in his own heart. "But who, after all, is doing this? They are all suffering as I am. Who then is it? Who?" flashed for an instant through his mind.

"Sharpshooters of the 86th, forward!" shouted someone. The fifth prisoner, the one next to Pierre, was led away—alone. Pierre did not understand that he was saved, that he and the rest had been brought there only to witness the execution. With ever-growing horror, and no sense of joy or relief, he gazed at what was taking place. The fifth man was the factory lad in the loose cloak. The moment they laid hands on him he sprang aside in terror and clutched at Pierre. (Pierre shuddered and shook himself free.) The lad was unable to walk. They dragged him along, holding him up under the arms, and he screamed. When they got him to the post he grew quiet, as if he suddenly understood something. Whether he understood that screaming was useless or whether he thought it incredible that men should kill him, at any rate he took his stand at the post, waiting to be blindfolded like the others, and like a wounded animal looked around him with glittering eyes.

Pierre was no longer able to turn away and close his eyes. His curiosity and agitation, like that of the whole crowd, reached the highest pitch at this fifth murder. Like the others this fifth man seemed calm; he wrapped his loose cloak closer and rubbed one bare foot with the other.

When they began to blindfold him he himself adjusted the knot which hurt the back of his head; then when they propped him against the bloodstained post, he leaned back and, not being comfortable in that position, straightened himself, adjusted his feet, and leaned back again more comfortably. Pierre did not take his eyes from him and did not miss his slightest movement.

Probably a word of command was given and was followed by the reports of eight muskets; but try as he would Pierre could not afterwards remember having heard the slightest sound of the shots. He only saw how the workman suddenly sank down on the cords that held him, how blood showed itself in two places, how the ropes slackened under the weight of the hanging body, and how the workman sat down, his head hanging unnaturally and one leg bent under him. Pierre ran up to the post. No one hindered him. Pale, frightened people were doing something around the workman. The lower jaw of an old Frenchman with a thick mustache trembled as he untied the ropes. The body collapsed. The soldiers dragged it awkwardly from the post and began pushing it into the pit.

They all plainly and certainly knew that they were criminals who must hide the traces of their guilt as quickly as possible.

Pierre glanced into the pit and saw that the factory lad was lying with his knees close up to his head and one shoulder higher than the other. That shoulder rose and fell rhythmically and convulsively, but spadefuls of earth were already being thrown over the whole body. One of the soldiers, evidently suffering, shouted gruffly and angrily at Pierre to go back. But Pierre did not understand him and remained near the post, and no one drove him away.

When the pit had been filled up a command was given. Pierre was taken back to his place, and the rows of troops on both sides of the post made a half turn and went past it at a measured pace. The twenty-four sharpshooters with discharged muskets, standing in the center of the circle, ran back to their places as the companies passed by.

Pierre gazed now with dazed eyes at these sharpshooters who ran in couples out of the circle. All but one rejoined their companies. This one, a young soldier, his face deadly pale, his shako pushed back, and his musket resting on the ground, still stood near the pit at the spot from which he had fired. He swayed like a drunken man, taking some steps forward and back to save himself from falling. An old, noncommissioned officer ran out of the ranks and taking him by the elbow dragged him to his company. The crowd of Russians and Frenchmen began to disperse. They all went away silently and with drooping heads.

"That will teach them to start fires," said one of the Frenchmen.

Pierre glanced round at the speaker and saw that it was a soldier who was trying to find some relief after what had been done, but was not able to do so. Without finishing what he had begun to say he made a hopeless movement with his arm and went away.

# XII

After the execution Pierre was separated from the rest of the prisoners and placed alone in a small, ruined, and befouled church. Toward evening a noncommissioned officer entered with two soldiers and told him that he had been pardoned and would now go to the barracks for the prisoners of war. Without understanding what was said to him, Pierre got up and went with the soldiers. They took him to the upper end of the field, where there were some sheds built of charred planks, beams, and battens, and led him into one of them. In the darkness some twenty different men surrounded Pierre. He looked at them without understanding who they were, why they were there, or what they wanted of him. He heard what they said, but did not understand the meaning of the words and made no kind of deduction from or application of them. He replied to questions they put to him, but did not consider who was listening to his replies, nor how they would understand them. He looked at their faces and figures, but they all seemed to him equally meaningless.

From the moment Pierre had witnessed those terrible murders committed by men who did not wish to commit them, it was as if the mainspring of his life, on which everything depended and which made everything appear alive, had suddenly been wrenched out and everything had collapsed into a heap of meaningless rubbish. Though he did not acknowledge it to himself, his faith in the right ordering of the universe, in humanity, in his own soul, and in God, had been destroyed. He had experienced this before, but never so strongly as now. When similar doubts had assailed him before, they had been the result of his own wrongdoing, and at the bottom of his heart he had felt that relief from his despair and from those doubts was to be found within himself. But now he felt that the universe had crumbled before his eyes and only meaningless ruins remained, and this not by any fault of his own. He felt that it was not in his power to regain faith in the meaning of life.

Around him in the darkness men were standing and evidently something about him interested them greatly. They were telling him something and asking him something. Then they led him away somewhere, and at last he found himself in a corner of the shed among men who were laughing and talking on all sides.

"Well, then, mates. . . that very prince who. . ." some voice at the other end of the shed was saying, with a strong emphasis on the word who.

Sitting silent and motionless on a heap of straw against the wall, Pierre sometimes opened and sometimes closed his eyes. But as soon as he closed them he saw before him the dreadful face of the factory lad—especially dreadful because of its simplicity—and the faces of the murderers, even more dreadful because of their disquiet. And he opened his eyes again and stared vacantly into the darkness around him.

Beside him in a stooping position sat a small man of whose presence he was first made aware by a strong smell of perspiration which came from him every time he moved. This man was doing something to his legs in the darkness, and though Pierre could not see his face he felt that the man continually glanced at him. On growing used to the darkness Pierre saw that the man was taking off his leg bands, and the way he did it aroused Pierre's interest.

Having unwound the string that tied the band on one leg, he carefully coiled it up and immediately set to work on the other leg, glancing up at Pierre. While one hand hung up the first string the other was already unwinding the band on the second leg. In this way, having carefully removed the leg bands by deft circular motions of his arm following one another uninterruptedly, the man hung the leg bands up on some pegs fixed above his head. Then he took out a knife, cut something, closed the knife, placed it under the head of his bed, and, seating himself comfortably, clasped his arms round his lifted knees and fixed his eyes on Pierre. The latter was conscious of something pleasant, comforting, and well-rounded in these deft movements, in the man's well-ordered arrangements in his corner, and even in his very smell, and he looked at the man without taking his eyes from him.

"You've seen a lot of trouble, sir, eh?" the little man suddenly said.

And there was so much kindliness and simplicity in his singsong voice that Pierre tried to reply, but his jaw trembled and he felt tears rising to his eyes. The little fellow, giving Pierre no time to betray his confusion, instantly continued in the same pleasant tones:

"Eh, lad, don't fret!" said he, in the tender singsong caressing voice old Russian peasant women employ. "Don't fret, friend—'suffer an hour, live for an age!' that's how it is, my dear fellow. And here we live, thank heaven, without offense. Among these folk, too, there are good men as well as bad," said he, and still speaking, he turned on his knees with a supple movement, got up, coughed, and went off to another part of the shed.

"Eh, you rascal!" Pierre heard the same kind voice saying at the other end of the shed. "So you've come, you rascal? She remembers. . . Now, now, that'll do!"

And the soldier, pushing away a little dog that was jumping up at him, returned to his place and sat down. In his hands he had something wrapped in a rag.

"Here, eat a bit, sir," said he, resuming his former respectful tone as he unwrapped and offered Pierre some baked potatoes. "We had soup for dinner and the potatoes are grand!"

Pierre had not eaten all day and the smell of the potatoes seemed extremely pleasant to him. He thanked the soldier and began to eat.

"Well, are they all right?" said the soldier with a smile. "You should do like this."

He took a potato, drew out his clasp knife, cut the potato into two equal halves on the palm of his hand, sprinkled some salt on it from the rag, and handed it to Pierre.

"The potatoes are grand!" he said once more. "Eat some like that!"

Pierre thought he had never eaten anything that tasted better.

"Oh, I'm all right," said he, "but why did they shoot those poor fellows? The last one was hardly twenty."

"Tss, tt. . . !" said the little man. "Ah, what a sin. . . what a sin!" he added quickly, and as if his words were always waiting ready in his mouth and flew out involuntarily he went on: "How was it, sir, that you stayed in Moscow?"

"I didn't think they would come so soon. I stayed accidentally," replied Pierre.

"And how did they arrest you, dear lad? At your house?"

"No, I went to look at the fire, and they arrested me there, and tried me as an incendiary."

"Where there's law there's injustice," put in the little man.

"And have you been here long?" Pierre asked as he munched the last of the potato.

"I? It was last Sunday they took me, out of a hospital in Moscow."

"Why, are you a soldier then?"

"Yes, we are soldiers of the Ápsheron regiment. I was dying of fever. We weren't told anything. There were some twenty of us lying there. We had no idea, never guessed at all."

"And do you feel sad here?" Pierre inquired.

"How can one help it, lad? My name is Platón, and the surname is Karatáev," he added, evidently wishing to make it easier for Pierre to address him. "They call me 'little falcon' in the regiment. How is one to help feeling sad? Moscow—she's the mother of cities. How can one see all this and not feel sad? But 'the maggot gnaws the cabbage, yet dies first'; that's what the old folks used to tell us," he added rapidly.

"What? What did you say?" asked Pierre.

"Who? I?" said Karatáev. "I say things happen not as we plan but as God judges," he replied, thinking that he was repeating what he had said before, and immediately continued:

"Well, and you, have you a family estate, sir? And a house? So you have abundance, then? And a housewife? And your old parents, are they still living?" he asked.

And though it was too dark for Pierre to see, he felt that a suppressed smile of kindliness puckered the soldier's lips as he put these questions. He seemed grieved that Pierre had no parents, especially that he had no mother.

"A wife for counsel, a mother-in-law for welcome, but there's none as dear as one's own mother!" said he. "Well, and have you little ones?" he went on asking.

Again Pierre's negative answer seemed to distress him, and he hastened to add:

"Never mind! You're young folks yet, and please God may still have some. The great thing is to live in harmony. . ."

"But it's all the same now," Pierre could not help saying.

"Ah, my dear fellow!" rejoined Karatáev, "never decline a prison or a beggar's sack!"

He seated himself more comfortably and coughed, evidently preparing to tell a long story.

"Well, my dear fellow, I was still living at home," he began. "We had a well-to-do homestead, plenty of land, we peasants lived well and our house was one to thank God for. When Father and we went out mowing there were seven of us. We lived well. We were real peasants. It so happened. . ."

And Platón Karatáev told a long story of how he had gone into someone's copse to take wood, how he had been caught by the keeper, had been tried, flogged, and sent to serve as a soldier.

"Well, lad," and a smile changed the tone of his voice, "we thought it was a misfortune but it turned out a blessing! If it had not been for my sin, my brother would have had to go as a soldier. But he, my younger brother, had five little ones, while I, you see, only left a wife behind. We had a little girl, but God took her before I went as a soldier. I come home on leave and I'll tell you how it was, I look and see that they are living better than before. The yard full of cattle, the women at home, two brothers away earning wages, and only Michael the youngest, at home. Father, he says, 'All my children are the same to me: it hurts the same whichever finger gets bitten. But if Platón hadn't been shaved for a soldier, Michael would have had to go.' called us all to him and, will you believe it, placed us in front of the icons. 'Michael,' he says, 'come here and bow down to his feet; and you, young woman, you bow down too; and you, grandchildren, also bow down before him! Do you understand?' he says. That's how it is, dear fellow. Fate looks for a head. But we are always judging, 'that's not well—that's not right!' Our luck is like water in a dragnet: you pull at it and it bulges, but when you've drawn it out it's empty! That's how it is."

And Platón shifted his seat on the straw.

After a short silence he rose.

"Well, I think you must be sleepy," said he, and began rapidly crossing himself and repeating:

"Lord Jesus Christ, holy Saint Nicholas, Frola and Lavra! Lord Jesus Christ, holy Saint Nicholas, Frola and Lavra! Lord Jesus Christ, have mercy on us and save us!" he concluded, then bowed to the ground, got up, sighed, and sat down again on his heap of straw. "That's the way. Lay me down like a stone, O God, and raise me up like a loaf," he muttered as he lay down, pulling his coat over him.

"What prayer was that you were saying?" asked Pierre.

"Eh?" murmured Platón, who had almost fallen asleep. "What was I saying? I was praying. Don't you pray?"

"Yes, I do," said Pierre. "But what was that you said: Frola and Lavra?"

"Well, of course," replied Platón quickly, "the horses' saints. One must pity the animals too. Eh, the rascal! Now you've curled up and got warm, you daughter of a bitch!" said Karatáev, touching the dog that lay at his feet, and again turning over he fell asleep immediately.

Sounds of crying and screaming came from somewhere in the distance outside, and flames were visible through the cracks of the shed, but inside it was quiet and dark. For a long time Pierre did not sleep, but lay with eyes open in the darkness, listening to the regular snoring of Platón who lay beside him, and he felt that the world that had been shattered was once more stirring in his soul with a new beauty and on new and unshakable foundations.

# XIII

Twenty-three soldiers, three officers, and two officials were confined in the shed in which Pierre had been placed and where he remained for four weeks.

When Pierre remembered them afterwards they all seemed misty figures to him except Platón Karatáev, who always remained in his mind a most vivid and precious memory and the personification of everything Russian, kindly, and round. When Pierre saw his neighbor next morning at dawn the first impression of him, as of something round, was fully confirmed: Platón's whole figure—in a French overcoat girdled with a cord, a soldier's cap, and bast shoes—was round. His head was quite round, his back, chest, shoulders, and even his arms, which he held as if ever ready to embrace something, were rounded, his pleasant smile and his large, gentle brown eyes were also round.

Platón Karatáev must have been fifty, judging by his stories of campaigns he had been in, told as by an old soldier. He did not himself know his age and was quite unable to determine it. But his brilliantly white, strong teeth which showed in two unbroken semicircles when he laughed—as he often did—were all sound and good, there was not a gray hair in his beard or on his head, and his whole body gave an impression of suppleness and especially of firmness and endurance.

His face, despite its fine, rounded wrinkles, had an expression of innocence and youth, his voice was pleasant and musical. But the chief peculiarity of his speech was its directness and appositeness. It was evident that he never considered what he had said or was going to say, and consequently the rapidity and justice of his intonation had an irresistible persuasiveness.

His physical strength and agility during the first days of his imprisonment were such that he seemed not to know what fatigue and sickness meant. Every night before lying down, he said: "Lord, lay me down as a stone and raise me up as a loaf!" and every morning on getting up, he said: "I lay down and curled up, I get up and shake myself." And indeed he only had to lie down, to fall asleep like a stone, and he only had to shake himself, to be ready without a moment's delay for some work, just as children are ready to play directly they awake. He could do everything, not very well but not badly. He baked, cooked, sewed, planed, and mended boots. He was always busy, and only at night allowed himself conversation—of which he was fond—and songs. He did not sing like a trained singer who knows he is listened to, but like the birds, evidently giving vent to the sounds in the same way that one stretches oneself or walks about to get rid of stiffness, and the sounds were always high-pitched, mournful, delicate, and almost feminine, and his face at such times was very serious.

Having been taken prisoner and allowed his beard to grow, he seemed to have thrown off all that had been forced upon him—everything military and alien to himself—and had returned to his former peasant habits.

"A soldier on leave—a shirt outside breeches," he would say.

He did not like talking about his life as a soldier, though he did not complain, and often mentioned that he had not been flogged once during the whole of his army service. When he related anything it was generally some old and evidently precious memory of his "Christian" life, as he called his peasant existence. The proverbs, of which his talk was full, were for the most part not the coarse and indecent saws soldiers employ, but those folk sayings which taken without a context seem so insignificant, but when used appositely suddenly acquire a significance of profound wisdom.

He would often say the exact opposite of what he had said on a previous occasion, yet both would be right. He liked to talk and he talked well, adorning his speech with terms of endearment and with folk sayings which Pierre thought he invented himself, but the chief charm of his talk lay in the fact that the commonest events— sometimes just such as Pierre had witnessed without taking notice of them—assumed in Karatáev's a character of solemn fitness. He liked to hear the folk tales one of the soldiers used to tell of an evening (they were always the same), but most of all he liked to hear stories of real life. He would smile joyfully when listening to such stories, now and then putting in a word or asking a question to make the moral beauty of what he was told clear to himself. Karatáev had no attachments, friendships, or love, as Pierre understood them, but loved and lived affectionately with everything life brought him in contact with, particularly with man—not any particular man, but those with whom he happened to be. He loved his dog, his comrades, the French, and Pierre who was his neighbor, but Pierre felt that in spite of Karatáev's affectionate tenderness for him (by which he unconsciously gave Pierre's spiritual life its due) he would not have grieved for a moment at parting from him. And Pierre began to feel in the same way toward Karatáev.

To all the other prisoners Platón Karatáev seemed a most ordinary soldier. They called him "little falcon" or "Platósha," chaffed him good-naturedly, and sent him on errands. But to Pierre he always remained what he had seemed that first night: an unfathomable, rounded, eternal personification of the spirit of simplicity and truth.

Platón Karatáev knew nothing by heart except his prayers. When he began to speak he seemed not to know how he would conclude.

Sometimes Pierre, struck by the meaning of his words, would ask him to repeat them, but Platón could never recall what he had said a moment before, just as he never could repeat to Pierre the words of his favorite song: native and birch tree and my heart is sick occurred in it, but when spoken and not sung, no meaning could be got out of it. He did not, and could not, understand the meaning of words apart from their context. Every word and action of his was the manifestation of an activity unknown to him, which was his life. But his life, as he regarded it, had no meaning as a separate thing. It had meaning only as part of a whole of which he was always conscious. His words and actions flowed from him as evenly, inevitably, and spontaneously as fragrance exhales from a flower. He could not understand the value or significance of any word or deed taken separately.

# XIV

When Princess Mary heard from Nicholas that her brother was with the Rostóvs at Yaroslávl she at once prepared to go there, in spite of her aunt's efforts to dissuade her—and not merely to go herself but to take her nephew with her. Whether it were difficult or easy, possible or impossible, she did not ask and did not want to know: it was her duty, not only to herself, to be near her brother who was perhaps dying, but to do everything possible to take his son to him, and so she prepared to set off. That she had not heard from Prince Andrew himself, Princess Mary attributed to his being too weak to write or to his considering the long journey too hard and too dangerous for her and his son.

In a few days Princess Mary was ready to start. Her equipages were the huge family coach in which she had traveled to Vorónezh, a semiopen trap, and a baggage cart. With her traveled Mademoiselle Bourienne, little Nicholas and his tutor, her old nurse, three maids, Tíkhon, and a young footman and courier her aunt had sent to accompany her.

The usual route through Moscow could not be thought of, and the roundabout way Princess Mary was obliged to take through Lípetsk, Ryazán, Vladímir, and Shúya was very long and, as post horses were not everywhere obtainable, very difficult, and near Ryazán where the French were said to have shown themselves was even dangerous.

During this difficult journey Mademoiselle Bourienne, Dessalles, and Princess Mary's servants were astonished at her energy and firmness of spirit. She went to bed later and rose earlier than any of them, and no difficulties daunted her. Thanks to her activity and energy, which infected her fellow travelers, they approached Yaroslávl by the end of the second week.

The last days of her stay in Vorónezh had been the happiest of her life. Her love for Rostóv no longer tormented or agitated her. It filled her whole soul, had become an integral part of herself, and she no longer struggled against it. Latterly she had become convinced that she loved and was beloved, though she never said this definitely to herself in words. She had become convinced of it at her last interview with Nicholas, when he had come to tell her that her brother was with the Rostóvs. Not by a single word had Nicholas alluded to the fact that Prince Andrew's relations with Natásha might, if he recovered, be renewed, but Princess Mary saw by his face that he knew and thought of this.

Yet in spite of that, his relation to her—considerate, delicate, and loving—not only remained unchanged, but it sometimes seemed to Princess Mary that he was even glad that the family connection between them allowed him to express his friendship more freely. She knew that she loved for the first and only time in her life and felt that she was beloved, and was happy in regard to it.

But this happiness on one side of her spiritual nature did not prevent her feeling grief for her brother with full force; on the contrary, that spiritual tranquility on the one side made it the more possible for her to give full play to her feeling for her brother. That feeling was so strong at the moment of leaving Vorónezh that those who saw her off, as they looked at her careworn, despairing face, felt sure she would fall ill on the journey. But the very difficulties and preoccupations of the journey, which she took so actively in hand, saved her for a while from her grief and gave her strength.

As always happens when traveling, Princess Mary thought only of the journey itself, forgetting its object. But as she approached Yaroslávl the thought of what might await her there—not after many days, but that very evening—again presented itself to her and her agitation increased to its utmost limit.

The courier who had been sent on in advance to find out where the Rostóvs were staying in Yaroslávl, and in what condition Prince Andrew was, when he met the big coach just entering the town gates was appalled by the terrible pallor of the princess' face that looked out at him from the window.

"I have found out everything, your excellency: the Rostóvs are staying at the merchant Brónnikov's house, in the Square not far from here, right above the Vólga," said the courier.

Princess Mary looked at him with frightened inquiry, not understanding why he did not reply to what she chiefly wanted to know: how was her brother? Mademoiselle Bourienne put that question for her.

"How is the prince?" she asked.

"His excellency is staying in the same house with them."

"Then he is alive," thought Princess Mary, and asked in a low voice: "How is he?"

"The servants say he is still the same."

What "still the same" might mean Princess Mary did not ask, but with an unnoticed glance at little seven-year-old Nicholas, who was sitting in front of her looking with pleasure at the town, she bowed her head and did not raise it again till the heavy coach, rumbling, shaking and swaying, came to a stop. The carriage steps clattered as they were let down.

The carriage door was opened. On the left there was water—a great river—and on the right a porch. There were people at the entrance: servants, and a rosy girl with a large plait of black hair, smiling as it seemed to Princess Mary in an unpleasantly affected way. (This was Sónya.) Princess Mary ran up the steps. "This way, this way!" said the girl, with the same artificial smile, and the princess found herself in the hall facing an elderly woman of Oriental type, who came rapidly to meet her with a look of emotion. This was the countess. She embraced Princess Mary and kissed her.

"Mon enfant!" she muttered, "je vous aime et vous connais depuis longtemps."*

Despite her excitement, Princess Mary realized that this was the countess and that it was necessary to say something to her. Hardly knowing how she did it, she contrived to utter a few polite phrases in French in the same tone as those that had been addressed to her, and asked: "How is he?"

"The doctor says that he is not in danger," said the countess, but as she spoke she raised her eyes with a sigh, and her gesture conveyed a contradiction of her words.

"Where is he? Can I see him—can I?" asked the princess.

"One moment, Princess, one moment, my dear! Is this his son?" said the countess, turning to little Nicholas who was coming in with Dessalles. "There will be room for everybody, this is a big house. Oh, what a lovely boy!"

The countess took Princess Mary into the drawing room, where Sónya was talking to Mademoiselle Bourienne. The countess caressed the boy, and the old count came in and welcomed the princess. He had changed very much since Princess Mary had last seen him. Then he had been a brisk, cheerful, self-assured old man; now he seemed a pitiful, bewildered person. While talking to Princess Mary he continually looked round as if asking everyone whether he was doing the right thing. After the

---

* "My child! I love you and have known you a long time."

destruction of Moscow and of his property, thrown out of his accustomed groove he seemed to have lost the sense of his own significance and to feel that there was no longer a place for him in life.

In spite of her one desire to see her brother as soon as possible, and her vexation that at the moment when all she wanted was to see him they should be trying to entertain her and pretending to admire her nephew, the princess noticed all that was going on around her and felt the necessity of submitting, for a time, to this new order of things which she had entered. She knew it to be necessary, and though it was hard for her she was not vexed with these people.

"This is my niece," said the count, introducing Sónya—"You don't know her, Princess?"

Princess Mary turned to Sónya and, trying to stifle the hostile feeling that arose in her toward the girl, she kissed her. But she felt oppressed by the fact that the mood of everyone around her was so far from what was in her own heart.

"Where is he?" she asked again, addressing them all.

"He is downstairs. Natásha is with him," answered Sónya, flushing. "We have sent to ask. I think you must be tired, Princess."

Tears of vexation showed themselves in Princess Mary's eyes. She turned away and was about to ask the countess again how to go to him, when light, impetuous, and seemingly buoyant steps were heard at the door. The princess looked round and saw Natásha coming in, almost running—that Natásha whom she had liked so little at their meeting in Moscow long since.

But hardly had the princess looked at Natásha's face before she realized that here was a real comrade in her grief, and consequently a friend. She ran to meet her, embraced her, and began to cry on her shoulder.

As soon as Natásha, sitting at the head of Prince Andrew's bed, heard of Princess Mary's arrival, she softly left his room and hastened to her with those swift steps that had sounded buoyant to Princess Mary.

There was only one expression on her agitated face when she ran into the drawing room—that of love—boundless love for him, for her, and for all that was near to the man she loved; and of pity, suffering for others, and passionate desire to give herself entirely to helping them. It was plain that at that moment there was in Natásha's heart no thought of herself or of her own relations with Prince Andrew.

Princess Mary, with her acute sensibility, understood all this at the first glance at Natásha's face, and wept on her shoulder with sorrowful pleasure.

"Come, come to him, Mary," said Natásha, leading her into the other room.

Princess Mary raised her head, dried her eyes, and turned to Natásha. She felt that from her she would be able to understand and learn everything.

"How. . ." she began her question but stopped short.

She felt that it was impossible to ask, or to answer, in words. Natásha's face and eyes would have to tell her all more clearly and profoundly.

Natásha was gazing at her, but seemed afraid and in doubt whether to say all she knew or not; she seemed to feel that before those luminous eyes which penetrated into the very depths of her heart, it was impossible not to tell the whole truth which she saw. And suddenly, Natásha's lips twitched, ugly wrinkles gathered round her mouth, and covering her face with her hands she burst into sobs.

Princess Mary understood.

But she still hoped, and asked, in words she herself did not trust:

"But how is his wound? What is his general condition?"

"You, you. . . will see," was all Natásha could say.

They sat a little while downstairs near his room till they had left off crying and were able to go to him with calm faces.

"How has his whole illness gone? Is it long since he grew worse? When did this happen?" Princess Mary inquired.

Natásha told her that at first there had been danger from his feverish condition and the pain he suffered, but at Tróitsa that had passed and the doctor had only been afraid of gangrene. That danger had also passed. When they reached Yaroslávl the wound had begun to fester (Natásha knew all about such things as festering) and the doctor had said that the festering might take a normal course. Then fever set in, but the doctor had said the fever was not very serious.

"But two days ago this suddenly happened," said Natásha, struggling with her sobs. "I don't know why, but you will see what he is like."

"Is he weaker? Thinner?" asked the princess.

"No, it's not that, but worse. You will see. O, Mary, he is too good, he cannot, cannot live, because. . ."

# XV

When Natásha opened Prince Andrew's door with a familiar movement and let Princess Mary pass into the room before her, the princess felt the sobs in her throat. Hard as she had tried to prepare herself, and now tried to remain tranquil, she knew that she would be unable to look at him without tears.

The princess understood what Natásha had meant by the words: "two days ago this suddenly happened." She understood those words to mean that he had suddenly softened and that this softening and gentleness were signs of approaching death. As she stepped to the door she already saw in imagination Andrew's face as she remembered it in childhood, a gentle, mild, sympathetic face which he had rarely shown, and which therefore affected her very strongly. She was sure he would speak soft, tender words to her such as her father had uttered before his death, and that she would not be able to bear it and would burst into sobs in his presence. Yet sooner or later it had to be, and she went in. The sobs rose higher and higher in her throat as she more and more clearly distinguished his form and her shortsighted eyes tried to make out his features, and then she saw his face and met his gaze.

He was lying in a squirrel-fur dressing gown on a divan, surrounded by pillows. He was thin and pale. In one thin, translucently white hand he held a handkerchief, while with the other he stroked the delicate mustache he had grown, moving his fingers slowly. His eyes gazed at them as they entered.

On seeing his face and meeting his eyes Princess Mary's pace suddenly slackened, she felt her tears dry up and her sobs ceased. She suddenly felt guilty and grew timid on catching the expression of his face and eyes.

"But in what am I to blame?" she asked herself. And his cold, stern look replied: "Because you are alive and thinking of the living, while I. . ."

In the deep gaze that seemed to look not outwards but inwards there was an almost hostile expression as he slowly regarded his sister and Natásha.

He kissed his sister, holding her hand in his as was their wont.

"How are you, Mary? How did you manage to get here?" said he in a voice as calm and aloof as his look.

Had he screamed in agony, that scream would not have struck such horror into Princess Mary's heart as the tone of his voice.

"And have you brought little Nicholas?" he asked in the same slow, quiet manner and with an obvious effort to remember.

"How are you now?" said Princess Mary, herself surprised at what she was saying.

"That, my dear, you must ask the doctor," he replied, and again making an evident effort to be affectionate, he said with his lips only (his words clearly did not correspond to his thoughts):

"Merci, chère amie, d'être venue."*

Princess Mary pressed his hand. The pressure made him wince just perceptibly. He was silent, and she did not know what to say. She now understood what had happened to him two days before. In his words, his tone, and especially in that calm, almost antagonistic look could be felt an estrangement from everything belonging to this world, terrible in one who is alive. Evidently only with an effort did he understand anything living; but it was obvious that he failed to understand, not because he lacked the power to do so but because he understood something else—something the living did not and could not understand—and which wholly occupied his mind.

"There, you see how strangely fate has brought us together," said he, breaking the silence and pointing to Natásha. "She looks after me all the time."

Princess Mary heard him and did not understand how he could say such a thing. He, the sensitive, tender Prince Andrew, how could he say that, before her whom he loved and who loved him? Had he expected to live he could not have said those words in that offensively cold tone. If he had not known that he was dying, how could he have failed to pity her and how could he speak like that in her presence? The only explanation was that he was indifferent, because something else, much more important, had been revealed to him.

The conversation was cold and disconnected and continually broke off.

"Mary came by way of Ryazán," said Natásha.

Prince Andrew did not notice that she called his sister Mary, and only after calling her so in his presence did Natásha notice it herself.

"Really?" he asked.

---

* "Thank you for coming, my dear."

"They told her that all Moscow has been burned down, and that. . ."

Natásha stopped. It was impossible to talk. It was plain that he was making an effort to listen, but could not do so.

"Yes, they say it's burned," he said. "It's a great pity," and he gazed straight before him, absently stroking his mustache with his fingers.

"And so you have met Count Nicholas, Mary?" Prince Andrew suddenly said, evidently wishing to speak pleasantly to them. "He wrote here that he took a great liking to you," he went on simply and calmly, evidently unable to understand all the complex significance his words had for living people. "If you liked him too, it would be a good thing for you to get married," he added rather more quickly, as if pleased at having found words he had long been seeking.

Princess Mary heard his words but they had no meaning for her, except as a proof of how far away he now was from everything living.

"Why talk of me?" she said quietly and glanced at Natásha.

Natásha, who felt her glance, did not look at her. All three were again silent.

"Andrew, would you like. . ." Princess Mary suddenly said in a trembling voice, "would you like to see little Nicholas? He is always talking about you!"

Prince Andrew smiled just perceptibly and for the first time, but Princess Mary, who knew his face so well, saw with horror that he did not smile with pleasure or affection for his son, but with quiet, gentle irony because he thought she was trying what she believed to be the last means of arousing him.

"Yes, I shall be very glad to see him. Is he quite well?"

When little Nicholas was brought into Prince Andrew's room he looked at his father with frightened eyes, but did not cry, because no one else was crying. Prince Andrew kissed him and evidently did not know what to say to him.

When Nicholas had been led away, Princess Mary again went up to her brother, kissed him, and unable to restrain her tears any longer began to cry.

He looked at her attentively.

"Is it about Nicholas?" he asked.

Princess Mary nodded her head, weeping.

"Mary, you know the Gosp. . ." but he broke off.

"What did you say?"

"Nothing. You mustn't cry here," he said, looking at her with the same cold expression.

When Princess Mary began to cry, he understood that she was crying at the thought that little Nicholas would be left without a father. With a great effort he tried to return to life and to see things from their point of view.

"Yes, to them it must seem sad!" he thought. "But how simple it is.

"The fowls of the air sow not, neither do they reap, yet your Father feedeth them," he said to himself and wished to say to Princess Mary; "but no, they will take it their own way, they won't understand! They can't understand that all those feelings they prize so—all our feelings, all those ideas that seem so important to us, are unnecessary. We cannot understand one another," and he remained silent.

Prince Andrew's little son was seven. He could scarcely read, and knew nothing. After that day he lived through many things, gaining knowledge, observation, and experience, but had he possessed all the faculties he afterwards acquired, he could not have had a better or more profound understanding of the meaning of the scene he had witnessed between his father, Mary, and Natásha, than he had then. He understood it completely, and, leaving the room without crying, went silently up to Natásha who had come out with him and looked shyly at her with his beautiful, thoughtful eyes, then his uplifted, rosy upper lip trembled and leaning his head against her he began to cry.

After that he avoided Dessalles and the countess who caressed him and either sat alone or came timidly to Princess Mary, or to Natásha of whom he seemed even fonder than of his aunt, and clung to them quietly and shyly.

When Princess Mary had left Prince Andrew she fully understood what Natásha's face had told her. She did not speak any more to Natásha of hopes of saving his life. She took turns with her beside his sofa, and did not cry any more, but prayed continually, turning in soul to that Eternal and Unfathomable, whose presence above the dying man was now so evident.

# XVI

Not only did Prince Andrew know he would die, but he felt that he was dying and was already half dead. He was conscious of an aloofness from everything earthly and a strange and joyous lightness of existence. Without haste or agitation he awaited what was coming. That inexorable, eternal, distant, and unknown the presence of which he had felt continually all his life—was now near to him and, by the strange lightness he experienced, almost comprehensible and palpable. . .

Formerly he had feared the end. He had twice experienced that terribly tormenting fear of death—the end—but now he no longer understood that fear.

He had felt it for the first time when the shell spun like a top before him, and he looked at the fallow field, the bushes, and the sky, and knew that he was face to face with death. When he came to himself after being wounded and the flower of eternal, unfettered love had instantly unfolded itself in his soul as if freed from the bondage of life that had restrained it, he no longer feared death and ceased to think about it.

During the hours of solitude, suffering, and partial delirium he spent after he was wounded, the more deeply he penetrated into the new principle of eternal love revealed to him, the more he unconsciously detached himself from earthly life. To love everything and everybody and always to sacrifice oneself for love meant not to love anyone, not to live this earthly life. And the more imbued he became with that principle of love, the more he renounced life and the more completely he destroyed that dreadful barrier which—in the absence of such love—stands between life and death. When during those first days he remembered that he would have to die, he said to himself: "Well, what of it? So much the better!"

But after the night in Mytíshchi when, half delirious, he had seen her for whom he longed appear before him and, having pressed her hand to his lips, had shed gentle, happy tears, love for a particular woman again crept unobserved into his heart and once more bound him to life. And joyful and agitating thoughts began to occupy his mind. Recalling the moment at the ambulance station when he had seen Kurágin, he could not now regain the feeling he then had, but was tormented by the question whether Kurágin was alive. And he dared not inquire.

His illness pursued its normal physical course, but what Natásha referred to when she said: "This suddenly happened," had occurred two days before Princess Mary arrived. It was the last spiritual struggle between life and death, in which death gained the victory. It was the unexpected realization of the fact that he still valued life as presented to him in the form of his love for Natásha, and a last, though ultimately vanquished, attack of terror before the unknown.

It was evening. As usual after dinner he was slightly feverish, and his thoughts were preternaturally clear. Sónya was sitting by the table. He began to doze. Suddenly a feeling of happiness seized him.

"Ah, she has come!" thought he.

And so it was: in Sónya's place sat Natásha who had just come in noiselessly.

Since she had begun looking after him, he had always experienced this physical consciousness of her nearness. She was sitting in an armchair placed sideways, screening the light of the candle from him, and was knitting a stocking. She had learned to knit stockings since Prince Andrew had casually mentioned that no one nursed the sick so well as old nurses who knit stockings, and that there is something soothing in the knitting of stockings. The needles clicked lightly in her slender, rapidly moving hands, and he could clearly see the thoughtful profile of her drooping face. She moved, and the ball rolled off her knees. She started, glanced round at him, and screening the candle with her hand stooped carefully with a supple and exact movement, picked up the ball, and regained her former position.

He looked at her without moving and saw that she wanted to draw a deep breath after stooping, but refrained from doing so and breathed cautiously.

At the Tróitsa monastery they had spoken of the past, and he had told her that if he lived he would always thank God for his wound which had brought them together again, but after that they never spoke of the future.

"Can it or can it not be?" he now thought as he looked at her and listened to the light click of the steel needles. "Can fate have brought me to her so strangely only for me to die? . . . Is it possible that the truth of life has been revealed to me only to show me that I have spent my life in falsity? I love her more than anything in the world! But what am I to do if I love her?" he thought, and he involuntarily groaned, from a habit acquired during his sufferings.

On hearing that sound Natásha put down the stocking, leaned nearer to him, and suddenly, noticing his shining eyes, stepped lightly up to him and bent over him.

"You are not asleep?"

"No, I have been looking at you a long time. I felt you come in. No one else gives me that sense of soft tranquillity that you do. . . that light. I want to weep for joy."

Natásha drew closer to him. Her face shone with rapturous joy.

"Natásha, I love you too much! More than anything in the world."

"And I!"—She turned away for an instant. "Why too much?" she asked.

"Why too much? . . . Well, what do you, what do you feel in your soul, your whole soul—shall I live? What do you think?"

"I am sure of it, sure!" Natásha almost shouted, taking hold of both his hands with a passionate movement.

He remained silent awhile.

"How good it would be!" and taking her hand he kissed it.

Natásha felt happy and agitated, but at once remembered that this would not do and that he had to be quiet.

"But you have not slept," she said, repressing her joy. "Try to sleep. . . please!"

He pressed her hand and released it, and she went back to the candle and sat down again in her former position. Twice she turned and looked at him, and her eyes met his beaming at her. She set herself a task on her stocking and resolved not to turn round till it was finished.

Soon he really shut his eyes and fell asleep. He did not sleep long and suddenly awoke with a start and in a cold perspiration.

As he fell asleep he had still been thinking of the subject that now always occupied his mind—about life and death, and chiefly about death. He felt himself nearer to it.

"Love? What is love?" he thought.

"Love hinders death. Love is life. All, everything that I understand, I understand only because I love. Everything is, everything exists, only because I love. Everything is united by it alone. Love is God, and to die means that I, a particle of love, shall return to the general and eternal source." These thoughts seemed to him comforting. But they were only thoughts. Something was lacking in them, they were not clear, they were too one-sidedly personal and brain-spun. And there was the former agitation and obscurity. He fell asleep.

LEO TOLSTOY

He dreamed that he was lying in the room he really was in, but that he was quite well and unwounded. Many various, indifferent, and insignificant people appeared before him. He talked to them and discussed something trivial. They were preparing to go away somewhere. Prince Andrew dimly realized that all this was trivial and that he had more important cares, but he continued to speak, surprising them by empty witticisms. Gradually, unnoticed, all these persons began to disappear and a single question, that of the closed door, superseded all else. He rose and went to the door to bolt and lock it. Everything depended on whether he was, or was not, in time to lock it. He went, and tried to hurry, but his legs refused to move and he knew he would not be in time to lock the door though he painfully strained all his powers. He was seized by an agonizing fear. And that fear was the fear of death. It stood behind the door. But just when he was clumsily creeping toward the door, that dreadful something on the other side was already pressing against it and forcing its way in. Something not human—death—was breaking in through that door, and had to be kept out. He seized the door, making a final effort to hold it back—to lock it was no longer possible—but his efforts were weak and clumsy and the door, pushed from behind by that terror, opened and closed again.

Once again it pushed from outside. His last superhuman efforts were vain and both halves of the door noiselessly opened. It entered, and it was death, and Prince Andrew died.

But at the instant he died, Prince Andrew remembered that he was asleep, and at the very instant he died, having made an effort, he awoke.

"Yes, it was death! I died and woke up. Yes, death is an awakening!" And all at once it grew light in his soul and the veil that had till then concealed the unknown was lifted from his spiritual vision. He felt as if powers till then confined within him had been liberated, and that strange lightness did not again leave him.

When, waking in a cold perspiration, he moved on the divan, Natásha went up and asked him what was the matter. He did not answer and looked at her strangely, not understanding.

That was what had happened to him two days before Princess Mary's arrival. From that day, as the doctor expressed it, the wasting fever assumed a malignant character, but what the doctor said did not interest Natásha, she saw the terrible moral symptoms which to her were more convincing.

From that day an awakening from life came to Prince Andrew together with his awakening from sleep. And compared to the duration of life it did not seem to him slower than an awakening from sleep compared to the duration of a dream.

There was nothing terrible or violent in this comparatively slow awakening.

His last days and hours passed in an ordinary and simple way. Both Princess Mary and Natásha, who did not leave him, felt this. They did not weep or shudder and during these last days they themselves felt that they were not attending on him (he was no longer there, he had left them) but on what reminded them most closely of him—his body. Both felt this so strongly that the outward and terrible side of death did not affect them and they did not feel it necessary to foment their grief. Neither in his presence nor out of it did they weep, nor did they ever talk to one another about him. They felt that they could not express in words what they understood.

They both saw that he was sinking slowly and quietly, deeper and deeper, away from them, and they both knew that this had to be so and that it was right.

He confessed, and received communion: everyone came to take leave of him. When they brought his son to him, he pressed his lips to the boy's and turned away, not because he felt it hard and sad (Princess Mary and Natásha understood that) but simply because he thought it was all that was required of him, but when they told him to bless the boy, he did what was demanded and looked round as if asking whether there was anything else he should do.

When the last convulsions of the body, which the spirit was leaving, occurred, Princess Mary and Natásha were present.

"Is it over?" said Princess Mary when his body had for a few minutes lain motionless, growing cold before them. Natásha went up, looked at the dead eyes, and hastened to close them. She closed them but did not kiss them, but clung to that which reminded her most nearly of him—his body.

"Where has he gone? Where is he now? . . ."

When the body, washed and dressed, lay in the coffin on a table, everyone came to take leave of him and they all wept.

Little Nicholas cried because his heart was rent by painful perplexity. The countess and Sónya cried from pity for Natásha and because he was no more. The old count cried because he felt that before long, he, too, must take the same terrible step.

Natásha and Princess Mary also wept now, but not because of their own personal grief; they wept with a reverent and softening emotion which had taken possession of their souls at the consciousness of the simple and solemn mystery of death that had been accomplished in their presence.

BOOK THIRTEEN
1812

# I

M an's mind cannot grasp the causes of events in their completeness, but the desire to find those causes is implanted in man's soul. And without considering the multiplicity and complexity of the conditions any one of which taken separately may seem to be the cause, he snatches at the first approximation to a cause that seems to him intelligible and says: "This is the cause!" In historical events (where the actions of men are the subject of observation) the first and most primitive approximation to present itself was the will of the gods and, after that, the will of those who stood in the most prominent position—the heroes of history. But we need only penetrate to the essence of any historic event—which lies in the activity of the general mass of men who take part in it—to be convinced that the will of the historic hero does not control the actions of the mass but is itself continually controlled. It may seem to be a matter of indifference whether we understand the meaning of historical events this way or that; yet there is the same difference between a man who says that the people of the West moved on the East because Napoleon wished it and a man who says that this happened because it had to happen, as there is between those who declared that the earth was stationary and that the planets moved round it and those who admitted that they did not know what upheld the earth, but knew there were laws directing its movement and that of the other planets. There is, and can be, no cause of an historical event except the one cause of all causes. But there are laws directing events, and some of these laws are known to us while we are conscious of others we cannot comprehend. The discovery of these laws is only possible when we have quite abandoned the attempt to find the cause in the will of some one man, just as the discovery of the laws of the motion of the planets was possible only when men abandoned the conception of the fixity of the earth.

The historians consider that, next to the battle of Borodinó and the occupation of Moscow by the enemy and its destruction by fire, the most important episode of the war of 1812 was the movement of the Russian army from the Ryazána to the Kalúga road and to the Tarútino camp— the so-called flank march across the Krásnaya Pakhrá River. They ascribe the glory of that achievement of genius to different men and dispute as to whom the honor is due. Even foreign historians, including the French, acknowledge the genius of the Russian commanders when they speak of that flank march. But it is hard to understand why military writers, and following them others, consider this flank march to be the profound conception of some one man who saved Russia and destroyed Napoleon. In the first place it is hard to understand where the profundity and genius of this movement lay, for not much mental effort was needed to see that the best position for an army when it is not being attacked is where there are most provisions; and even a dull boy of thirteen could have guessed that the best position for an army after its retreat from Moscow in 1812 was on the Kalúga road. So it is impossible to understand by what reasoning the historians reach the conclusion that this maneuver was a profound one. And it is even more difficult to understand just why they think that this maneuver was calculated to save Russia and destroy the French; for this flank march, had it been preceded, accompanied, or followed by other circumstances, might have proved ruinous to the Russians and salutary for the French. If the position of the Russian army really began to improve from the time of that march, it does not at all follow that the march was the cause of it.

That flank march might not only have failed to give any advantage to the Russian army, but might in other circumstances have led to its destruction. What would have happened had Moscow not burned down? If Murat had not lost sight of the Russians? If Napoleon had not remained inactive? If the Russian army at Krásnaya Pakhrá had given battle as Bennigsen and Barclay advised? What would have happened had the French attacked the Russians while they were marching beyond the Pakhrá? What would have happened if on approaching Tarútino, Napoleon had attacked the Russians with but a tenth of the energy he had shown when he attacked them at Smolénsk? What would have happened had the French moved on Petersburg? . . . In any of these eventualities the flank march that brought salvation might have proved disastrous.

The third and most incomprehensible thing is that people studying history deliberately avoid seeing that this flank march cannot be attributed to any one man, that no one ever foresaw it, and that in reality, like the retreat from Filí, it did not suggest itself to anyone in its entirety, but resulted—moment by moment, step by step, event by event—from an endless number of most diverse circumstances and was only seen in its entirety when it had been accomplished and belonged to the past.

At the council at Filí the prevailing thought in the minds of the Russian commanders was the one naturally suggesting itself, namely, a direct retreat by the Nízhni road. In proof of this there is the fact that the majority of the council voted for such a retreat, and above all there is the well-known conversation after the council, between the commander in chief and Lanskóy, who was in charge of the commissariat department. Lanskóy informed the commander in chief that the army supplies were for the most part stored along the Oká in the Túla and Ryazán provinces, and that if they retreated on Nízhni the army would be separated from its supplies by the broad river Oká, which cannot be crossed early in winter. This was the first indication of the necessity of deviating from what had previously seemed the most natural course—a direct retreat on Nízhni-Nóvgorod. The army turned more to the south, along the Ryazán road and nearer to its supplies. Subsequently the inactivity of the French (who even lost sight of the Russian army), concern for the safety of the arsenal at Túla, and especially the advantages of drawing nearer to its supplies caused the army to turn still further south to the Túla road. Having crossed over, by a forced march, to the Túla road beyond the Pakhrá, the Russian commanders intended to remain at Podólsk and had no thought of the Tarútino position; but innumerable circumstances and the reappearance of French troops who had for a time lost touch with the Russians, and projects of giving battle, and above all the abundance of provisions in Kalúga province, obliged our army to turn still more to the south and to cross from the Túla to the Kalúga road and go to Tarútino, which was between the roads along which those supplies lay. Just as it is impossible to say when it was decided to abandon Moscow, so it is impossible to say precisely when, or by whom, it was decided to move to Tarútino. Only when the army had got there, as the result of innumerable and varying forces, did people begin to assure themselves that they had desired this movement and long ago foreseen its result.

# II

The famous flank movement merely consisted in this: after the advance of the French had ceased, the Russian army, which had been continually retreating straight back from the invaders, deviated from that direct course and, not finding itself pursued, was naturally drawn toward the district where supplies were abundant.

If instead of imagining to ourselves commanders of genius leading the Russian army, we picture that army without any leaders, it could not have done anything but make a return movement toward Moscow, describing an arc in the direction where most provisions were to be found and where the country was richest.

That movement from the Nízhni to the Ryazán, Túla, and Kalúga roads was so natural that even the Russian marauders moved in that direction, and demands were sent from Petersburg for Kutúzov to take his army that way. At Tarútino Kutúzov received what was almost a reprimand from the Emperor for having moved his army along the Ryazán road, and the Emperor's letter indicated to him the very position he had already occupied near Kalúga.

Having rolled like a ball in the direction of the impetus given by the whole campaign and by the battle of Borodinó, the Russian army—when the strength of that impetus was exhausted and no fresh push was received—assumed the position natural to it.

Kutúzov's merit lay, not in any strategic maneuver of genius, as it is called, but in the fact that he alone understood the significance of what had happened. He alone then understood the meaning of the French army's inactivity, he alone continued to assert that the battle of Borodinó had been a victory, he alone—who as commander in chief might have been expected to be eager to attack—employed his whole strength to restrain the Russian army from useless engagements.

The beast wounded at Borodinó was lying where the fleeing hunter had left him; but whether he was still alive, whether he was strong and merely lying low, the hunter did not know. Suddenly the beast was heard to moan.

The moan of that wounded beast (the French army) which betrayed its calamitous condition was the sending of Lauriston to Kutúzov's camp with overtures for peace.

Napoleon, with his usual assurance that whatever entered his head was right, wrote to Kutúzov the first words that occurred to him, though they were meaningless.

MONSIEUR LE PRINCE KOUTOUZOV:

I am sending one of my adjutants-general to discuss several interesting questions with you. I beg your Highness to credit what he says to you, especially when he expresses the sentiment of esteem and special regard I have long entertained for your person. This letter having no other object, I pray God, monsieur le prince Koutouzov, to keep you in His holy and gracious protection!

NAPOLEON
Moscow, October 30, 1812

Kutúzov replied: "I should be cursed by posterity were I looked on as the initiator of a settlement of any sort. Such is the present spirit of my nation." But he continued to exert all his powers to restrain his troops from attacking.

During the month that the French troops were pillaging in Moscow and the Russian troops were quietly encamped at Tarútino, a change had taken place in the relative strength of the two armies—both in spirit and in number—as a result of which the superiority had passed to the Russian side. Though the condition and numbers of the French army were unknown to the Russians, as soon as that change occurred the need of attacking at once showed itself by countless signs. These signs were: Lauriston's mission; the abundance of provisions at Tarútino; the reports coming in from all sides of the inactivity and disorder of the French; the flow of recruits to our regiments; the fine weather; the long rest the Russian soldiers had enjoyed, and the impatience to do what they had been assembled for, which usually shows itself in an army that has been resting; curiosity as to what the French army, so long lost sight of, was doing; the boldness with which our outposts now scouted close up to the French stationed at Tarútino; the news of easy successes gained by peasants and guerrilla troops over the French, the envy aroused by this; the desire for revenge that lay in the heart of every Russian as long as the French were in Moscow, and (above all) a dim consciousness in every soldier's mind that the relative strength of the armies had changed and that the advantage was now on our side. There was a substantial change in the relative strength, and an advance had become inevitable. And at once, as a clock begins to strike and chime as soon as the minute hand has completed a full circle, this change was shown by an increased activity, whirring, and chiming in the higher spheres.

# III

The Russian army was commanded by Kutúzov and his staff, and also by the Emperor from Petersburg. Before the news of the abandonment of Moscow had been received in Petersburg, a detailed plan of the whole campaign had been drawn up and sent to Kutúzov for his guidance. Though this plan had been drawn up on the supposition that Moscow was still in our hands, it was approved by the staff and accepted as a basis for action. Kutúzov only replied that movements arranged from a distance were always difficult to execute. So fresh instructions were sent for the solution of difficulties that might be encountered, as well as fresh people who were to watch Kutúzov's actions and report upon them.

Besides this, the whole staff of the Russian army was now reorganized. The posts left vacant by Bagratión, who had been killed, and by Barclay, who had gone away in dudgeon, had to be filled. Very serious consideration was given to the question whether it would be better to put A in B's place and B in D's, or on the contrary to put D in A's place, and so on—as if anything more than A's or B's satisfaction depended on this.

As a result of the hostility between Kutúzov and Bennigsen, his Chief of Staff, the presence of confidential representatives of the Emperor, and these transfers, a more than usually complicated play of parties was going on among the staff of the army. A was undermining B, D was undermining C, and so on in all possible combinations and permutations. In all these plottings the subject of intrigue was generally the conduct of the war, which all these men believed they were directing; but this affair of the war went on independently of them, as it had to go: that is, never in the way people devised, but flowing always from the essential attitude of the masses. Only in the highest spheres did all these schemes, crossings, and interminglings appear to be a true reflection of what had to happen.

PRINCE MICHAEL ILARIÓNOVICH! (WROTE THE Emperor on the second of October in a letter that reached Kutúzov after the battle at Tarútino) Since September 2 Moscow has been in the hands of the enemy. Your last reports were written on the twentieth, and during all this time not only has no action been taken against the enemy or for the relief of the ancient capital, but according to your last report you have even retreated farther. Sérpukhov is already occupied by an enemy detachment and Túla with its famous arsenal, so indispensable to the army, is in danger. From General Wintzingerode's reports, I see that an enemy corps of ten thousand men is moving on the Petersburg road. Another corps of several thousand men is moving on Dmítrov. A third has advanced along the Vladímir road, and a fourth, rather considerable detachment is stationed between Rúza and Mozháysk. Napoleon himself was in Moscow as late as the twenty-fifth. In view of all this information, when the enemy has scattered his forces in large detachments, and with Napoleon and his Guards in Moscow, is it possible that the enemy's forces confronting you are so considerable as not to allow of your taking the offensive? On the contrary, he is probably pursuing you with detachments, or at most with an army corps much weaker than the army entrusted to you. It would seem that, availing yourself of these circumstances, you might advantageously attack a weaker one and annihilate him, or at least oblige him to retreat, retaining in our hands an important part of the provinces now occupied by the enemy, and thereby averting danger from Túla and other towns in the interior. You will be responsible if the enemy is able to direct a force of any size against Petersburg to threaten this capital in which it has not been possible to retain many troops; for with the army entrusted to you, and acting with resolution and energy, you have ample means to avert this fresh calamity. Remember that you have still to answer to our offended country for the loss of Moscow. You have experienced my readiness to reward you. That readiness will not weaken in me, but I and Russia have a right to expect from you all the zeal, firmness, and success which your intellect, military talent, and the courage of the troops you command justify us in expecting.

BUT BY THE TIME THIS letter, which proved that the real relation of the forces had already made itself felt in Petersburg, was dispatched, Kutúzov had found himself unable any longer to restrain the army he commanded from attacking and a battle had taken place.

On the second of October a Cossack, Shapoválov, who was out scouting, killed one hare and wounded another. Following the wounded hare he made his way far into the forest and came upon the left flank of Murat's army, encamped there without any precautions. The Cossack laughingly told his comrades how he had almost fallen into the hands of the French. A cornet, hearing the story, informed his commander.

The Cossack was sent for and questioned. The Cossack officers wished to take advantage of this chance to capture some horses, but one of the superior officers, who was acquainted with the higher authorities, reported the incident to a general on the staff. The state of things on the staff had of late been exceedingly strained. Ermólov had been to see Bennigsen a few days previously and had entreated him to use his influence with the commander in chief to induce him to take the offensive.

"If I did not know you I should think you did not want what you are asking for. I need only advise anything and his Highness is sure to do the opposite," replied Bennigsen.

The Cossack's report, confirmed by horse patrols who were sent out, was the final proof that events had matured. The tightly coiled spring was released, the clock began to whirr and the chimes to play. Despite all his supposed power, his intellect, his experience, and his knowledge of men, Kutúzov—having taken into consideration the Cossack's report, a note from Bennigsen who sent personal reports to the Emperor, the wishes he supposed the Emperor to hold, and the fact that all the generals expressed the same wish—could no longer check the inevitable movement, and gave the order to do what he regarded as useless and harmful—gave his approval, that is, to the accomplished fact.

# IV

Bennigsen's note and the Cossack's information that the left flank of the French was unguarded were merely final indications that it was necessary to order an attack, and it was fixed for the fifth of October.

On the morning of the fourth of October Kutúzov signed the dispositions. Toll read them to Ermólov, asking him to attend to the further arrangements.

"All right—all right. I haven't time just now," replied Ermólov, and left the hut.

The dispositions drawn up by Toll were very good. As in the Austerlitz dispositions, it was written—though not in German this time:

"The First Column will march here and here," "the Second Column will march there and there," and so on; and on paper, all these columns arrived at their places at the appointed time and destroyed the enemy. Everything had been admirably thought out as is usual in dispositions, and as is always the case, not a single column reached its place at the appointed time.

When the necessary number of copies of the dispositions had been prepared, an officer was summoned and sent to deliver them to Ermólov to deal with. A young officer of the Horse Guards, Kutúzov's orderly, pleased at the importance of the mission entrusted to him, went to Ermólov's quarters.

"Gone away," said Ermólov's orderly.

The officer of the Horse Guards went to a general with whom Ermólov was often to be found.

"No, and the general's out too."

The officer, mounting his horse, rode off to someone else.

"No, he's gone out."

"If only they don't make me responsible for this delay! What a nuisance it is!" thought the officer, and he rode round the whole camp. One man said he had seen Ermólov ride past with some other generals, others said he must have returned home. The officer searched till six o'clock in the evening without even stopping to eat. Ermólov was nowhere to be found and no one knew where he was. The officer snatched a little food at a comrade's, and rode again to the vanguard to find Milorádovich. Milorádovich too was away, but here he was told that he had gone to a ball at General Kíkin's and that Ermólov was probably there too.

"But where is it?"

"Why, there, over at Échkino," said a Cossack officer, pointing to a country house in the far distance.

"What, outside our line?"

"They've put two regiments as outposts, and they're having such a spree there, it's awful! Two bands and three sets of singers!"

The officer rode out beyond our lines to Échkino. While still at a distance he heard as he rode the merry sounds of a soldier's dance song proceeding from the house.

"In the meadows. . . in the meadows!" he heard, accompanied by whistling and the sound of a torban, drowned every now and then by shouts. These sounds made his spirits rise, but at the same time he was afraid that he would be blamed for not having executed sooner the important order entrusted to him. It was already past eight o'clock. He dismounted and went up into the porch of a large country house which had remained intact between the Russian and French forces. In the refreshment room and the hall, footmen were bustling about with wine and viands. Groups of singers stood outside the windows. The officer was admitted and immediately saw all the chief generals of the army together, and among them Ermólov's big imposing figure. They all had their coats unbuttoned and were standing in a semicircle with flushed and animated faces, laughing loudly. In the middle of the room a short handsome general with a red face was dancing the trepák with much spirit and agility.

"Ha, ha, ha! Bravo, Nicholas Iványch! Ha, ha, ha!"

The officer felt that by arriving with important orders at such a moment he was doubly to blame, and he would have preferred to wait; but one of the generals espied him and, hearing what he had come about, informed Ermólov.

Ermólov came forward with a frown on his face and, hearing what the officer had to say, took the papers from him without a word.

"You think he went off just by chance?" said a comrade, who was on the staff that evening, to the officer of the Horse Guards, referring to Ermólov. "It was a trick. It was done on purpose to get Konovnítsyn into trouble. You'll see what a mess there'll be tomorrow."

# V

Next day the decrepit Kutúzov, having given orders to be called early, said his prayers, dressed, and, with an unpleasant consciousness of having to direct a battle he did not approve of, got into his calèche and drove from Letashóvka (a village three and a half miles from Tarútino) to the place where the attacking columns were to meet. He sat in the calèche, dozing and waking up by turns, and listening for any sound of firing on the right as an indication that the action had begun. But all was still quiet. A damp dull autumn morning was just dawning. On approaching Tarútino Kutúzov noticed cavalrymen leading their horses to water across the road along which he was driving. Kutúzov looked at them searchingly, stopped his carriage, and inquired what regiment they belonged to. They belonged to a column that should have been far in front and in ambush long before then. "It may be a mistake," thought the old commander in chief. But a little further on he saw infantry regiments with their arms piled and the soldiers, only partly dressed, eating their rye porridge and carrying fuel. He sent for an officer. The officer reported that no order to advance had been received.

"How! Not rec. . ." Kutúzov began, but checked himself immediately and sent for a senior officer. Getting out of his calèche, he waited with drooping head and breathing heavily, pacing silently up and down. When Eýkhen, the officer of the general staff whom he had summoned, appeared, Kutúzov went purple in the face, not because that officer was to blame for the mistake, but because he was an object of sufficient importance for him to vent his wrath on. Trembling and panting the old man fell into that state of fury in which he sometimes used to roll on the ground, and he fell upon Eýkhen, threatening him with his hands, shouting and loading him with gross abuse. Another man, Captain Brózin, who happened to turn up and who was not at all to blame, suffered the same fate.

"What sort of another blackguard are you? I'll have you shot! Scoundrels!" yelled Kutúzov in a hoarse voice, waving his arms and reeling.

He was suffering physically. He, the commander in chief, a Serene Highness who everybody said possessed powers such as no man had ever had in Russia, to be placed in this position—made the laughingstock of the whole army! "I needn't have been in such a hurry to pray about today, or have kept awake thinking everything over all night," thought he to himself. "When I was a chit of an officer no one would have dared to mock me so. . . and now!" He was in a state of physical suffering as if from corporal punishment, and could not avoid expressing it by cries of anger and distress. But his strength soon began to fail him, and looking about him, conscious of having said much that was amiss, he again got into his calèche and drove back in silence.

His wrath, once expended, did not return, and blinking feebly he listened to excuses and self-justifications (Ermólov did not come to see him till the next day) and to the insistence of Bennigsen, Konovnítsyn, and Toll that the movement that had miscarried should be executed next day. And once more Kutúzov had to consent.

# VI

Next day the troops assembled in their appointed places in the evening and advanced during the night. It was an autumn night with dark purple clouds, but no rain. The ground was damp but not muddy, and the troops advanced noiselessly, only occasionally a jingling of the artillery could be faintly heard. The men were forbidden to talk out loud, to smoke their pipes, or to strike a light, and they tried to prevent their horses neighing. The secrecy of the undertaking heightened its charm and they marched gaily. Some columns, supposing they had reached their destination, halted, piled arms, and settled down on the cold ground, but the majority marched all night and arrived at places where they evidently should not have been.

Only Count Orlóv-Denísov with his Cossacks (the least important detachment of all) got to his appointed place at the right time. This detachment halted at the outskirts of a forest, on the path leading from the village of Stromílova to Dmítrovsk.

Toward dawn, Count Orlóv-Denísov, who had dozed off, was awakened by a deserter from the French army being brought to him. This was a Polish sergeant of Poniatowski's corps, who explained in Polish that he had come over because he had been slighted in the service: that he ought long ago to have been made an officer, that he was braver than any of them, and so he had left them and wished to pay them out. He said that Murat was spending the night less than a mile from where they were, and that if they would let him have a convoy of a hundred men he would capture him alive. Count Orlóv-Denísov consulted his fellow officers.

The offer was too tempting to be refused. Everyone volunteered to go and everybody advised making the attempt. After much disputing and arguing, Major-General Grékov with two Cossack regiments decided to go with the Polish sergeant.

"Now, remember," said Count Orlóv-Denísov to the sergeant at parting, "if you have been lying I'll have you hanged like a dog; but if it's true you shall have a hundred gold pieces!"

Without replying, the sergeant, with a resolute air, mounted and rode away with Grékov whose men had quickly assembled. They disappeared into the forest, and Count Orlóv-Denísov, having seen Grékov off, returned, shivering from the freshness of the early dawn and excited by what he had undertaken on his own responsibility, and began looking at the enemy camp, now just visible in the deceptive light of dawn and the dying campfires. Our columns ought to have begun to appear on an open declivity to his right. He looked in that direction, but though the columns would have been visible quite far off, they were not to be seen. It seemed to the count that things were beginning to stir in the French camp, and his keen-sighted adjutant confirmed this.

"Oh, it is really too late," said Count Orlóv, looking at the camp.

As often happens when someone we have trusted is no longer before our eyes, it suddenly seemed quite clear and obvious to him that the sergeant was an impostor, that he had lied, and that the whole Russian attack would be ruined by the absence of those two regiments, which he would lead away heaven only knew where. How could one capture a commander in chief from among such a mass of troops!

"I am sure that rascal was lying," said the count.

"They can still be called back," said one of his suite, who like Count Orlóv felt distrustful of the adventure when he looked at the enemy's camp.

"Eh? Really. . . what do you think? Should we let them go on or not?"

"Will you have them fetched back?"

"Fetch them back, fetch them back!" said Count Orlóv with sudden determination, looking at his watch. "It will be too late. It is quite light."

And the adjutant galloped through the forest after Grékov. When Grékov returned, Count Orlóv-Denísov, excited both by the abandoned attempt and by vainly awaiting the infantry columns that still did not appear, as well as by the proximity of the enemy, resolved to advance. All his men felt the same excitement.

"Mount!" he commanded in a whisper. The men took their places and crossed themselves. . . "Forward, with God's aid!"

"Hurrah-ah-ah!" reverberated in the forest, and the Cossack companies, trailing their lances and advancing one after another as if poured out of a sack, dashed gaily across the brook toward the camp.

One desperate, frightened yell from the first French soldier who saw the Cossacks, and all who were in the camp, undressed and only just waking up, ran off in all directions, abandoning cannons, muskets, and horses.

Had the Cossacks pursued the French, without heeding what was behind and around them, they would have captured Murat and everything there. That was what the officers desired. But it was impossible to make the Cossacks budge when once they had got booty and prisoners. None of them listened to orders. Fifteen hundred prisoners and thirty-eight guns were taken on the spot, besides standards and (what seemed most important to the Cossacks) horses, saddles, horsecloths, and the like. All this had to be dealt with, the prisoners and guns secured, the booty divided—not without some shouting and even a little fighting among themselves—and it was on this that the Cossacks all busied themselves.

The French, not being farther pursued, began to recover themselves: they formed into detachments and began firing. Orlóv-Denísov, still waiting for the other columns to arrive, advanced no further.

Meantime, according to the dispositions which said that "the First Column will march" and so on, the infantry of the belated columns, commanded by Bennigsen and directed by Toll, had started in due order and, as always happens, had got somewhere, but not to their appointed places. As always happens the men, starting cheerfully, began to halt; murmurs were heard, there was a sense of confusion, and finally a backward movement. Adjutants and generals galloped about, shouted, grew angry, quarreled, said they had come quite wrong and were late, gave vent to a little abuse, and at last gave it all up and went forward, simply to get somewhere. "We shall get somewhere or other!" And they did indeed get somewhere, though not to their right places; a few eventually even got to their right place, but too late to be of any use and only in time to be fired at. Toll, who in this battle played the part of Weyrother at Austerlitz, galloped assiduously from place to place, finding everything upside down everywhere. Thus he stumbled on Bagovút's corps in a wood when it was already broad daylight, though the corps should long before have joined Orlóv-Denísov. Excited and vexed by the failure and supposing that someone must be responsible for it, Toll galloped up to the commander of the corps and began upbraiding him severely, saying that he ought to be shot. General Bagovút, a fighting old soldier of placid temperament, being also upset by all the delay, confusion, and cross-purposes, fell into a rage to everybody's surprise and quite contrary to his usual character and said disagreeable things to Toll.

"I prefer not to take lessons from anyone, but I can die with my men as well as anybody," he said, and advanced with a single division.

Coming out onto a field under the enemy's fire, this brave general went straight ahead, leading his men under fire, without considering in his agitation whether going into action now, with a single division, would be of any use or no. Danger, cannon balls, and bullets were just what he needed in his angry mood. One of the first bullets killed him, and other bullets killed many of his men. And his division remained under fire for some time quite uselessly.

# VII

Meanwhile another column was to have attacked the French from the front, but Kutúzov accompanied that column. He well knew that nothing but confusion would come of this battle undertaken against his will, and as far as was in his power held the troops back. He did not advance.

He rode silently on his small gray horse, indolently answering suggestions that they should attack.

"The word attack is always on your tongue, but you don't see that we are unable to execute complicated maneuvers," said he to Milorádovich who asked permission to advance.

"We couldn't take Murat prisoner this morning or get to the place in time, and nothing can be done now!" he replied to someone else.

When Kutúzov was informed that at the French rear—where according to the reports of the Cossacks there had previously been nobody—there were now two battalions of Poles, he gave a sidelong glance at Ermólov who was behind him and to whom he had not spoken since the previous day.

"You see! They are asking to attack and making plans of all kinds, but as soon as one gets to business nothing is ready, and the enemy, forewarned, takes measures accordingly."

Ermólov screwed up his eyes and smiled faintly on hearing these words. He understood that for him the storm had blown over, and that Kutúzov would content himself with that hint.

"He's having a little fun at my expense," said Ermólov softly, nudging with his knee Raévski who was at his side.

Soon after this, Ermólov moved up to Kutúzov and respectfully remarked:

"It is not too late yet, your Highness—the enemy has not gone away—if you were to order an attack! If not, the Guards will not so much as see a little smoke."

Kutúzov did not reply, but when they reported to him that Murat's troops were in retreat he ordered an advance, though at every hundred paces he halted for three quarters of an hour.

The whole battle consisted in what Orlóv-Denísov's Cossacks had done: the rest of the army merely lost some hundreds of men uselessly.

In consequence of this battle Kutúzov received a diamond decoration, and Bennigsen some diamonds and a hundred thousand rubles, others also received pleasant recognitions corresponding to their various grades, and following the battle fresh changes were made in the staff.

"That's how everything is done with us, all topsy-turvy!" said the Russian officers and generals after the Tarútino battle, letting it be understood that some fool there is doing things all wrong but that we ourselves should not have done so, just as people speak today. But people who talk like that either do not know what they are talking about or deliberately deceive themselves. No battle—Tarútino, Borodinó, or Austerlitz—takes place as those who planned it anticipated. That is an essential condition.

A countless number of free forces (for nowhere is man freer than during a battle, where it is a question of life and death) influence the course taken by the fight, and that course never can be known in advance and never coincides with the direction of any one force.

If many simultaneously and variously directed forces act on a given body, the direction of its motion cannot coincide with any one of those forces, but will always be a mean—what in mechanics is represented by the diagonal of a parallelogram of forces.

If in the descriptions given by historians, especially French ones, we find their wars and battles carried out in accordance with previously formed plans, the only conclusion to be drawn is that those descriptions are false.

The battle of Tarútino obviously did not attain the aim Toll had in view—to lead the troops into action in the order prescribed by the dispositions; nor that which Count Orlóv-Denísov may have had in view—to take Murat prisoner; nor the result of immediately destroying the whole corps, which Bennigsen and others may have had in view; nor the aim of the officer who wished to go into action to distinguish himself; nor that of the Cossack who wanted more booty than he got, and so on. But if the aim of the battle was what actually resulted and what all the Russians of that day desired—to drive the French out of Russia and destroy their army—it is quite clear that the battle of Tarútino, just because of its incongruities, was exactly what was wanted at that stage of the campaign. It would be difficult and even impossible to imagine any result more opportune than the actual outcome of this battle. With a minimum of effort and insignificant losses, despite the greatest confusion, the most important results of the whole campaign were attained: the transition from retreat to advance, an exposure of the weakness of the French, and the administration of that shock which Napoleon's army had only awaited to begin its flight.

.

# VIII

Napoleon enters Moscow after the brilliant victory de la Moskowa; there can be no doubt about the victory for the battlefield remains in the hands of the French. The Russians retreat and abandon their ancient capital. Moscow, abounding in provisions, arms, munitions, and incalculable wealth, is in Napoleon's hands. The Russian army, only half the strength of the French, does not make a single attempt to attack for a whole month. Napoleon's position is most brilliant. He can either fall on the Russian army with double its strength and destroy it; negotiate an advantageous peace, or in case of a refusal make a menacing move on Petersburg, or even, in the case of a reverse, return to Smolénsk or Vílna; or remain in Moscow; in short, no special genius would seem to be required to retain the brilliant position the French held at that time. For that, only very simple and easy steps were necessary: not to allow the troops to loot, to prepare winter clothing—of which there was sufficient in Moscow for the whole army—and methodically to collect the provisions, of which (according to the French historians) there were enough in Moscow to supply the whole army for six months. Yet Napoleon, that greatest of all geniuses, who the historians declare had control of the army, took none of these steps.

He not merely did nothing of the kind, but on the contrary he used his power to select the most foolish and ruinous of all the courses open to him. Of all that Napoleon might have done: wintering in Moscow, advancing on Petersburg or on Nízhni-Nóvgorod, or retiring by a more northerly or more southerly route (say by the road Kutúzov afterwards took), nothing more stupid or disastrous can be imagined than what he actually did. He remained in Moscow till October, letting the troops plunder the city; then, hesitating whether to leave a garrison behind him, he quitted Moscow, approached Kutúzov without joining battle, turned to the right and reached Málo-Yaroslávets, again without attempting to break through and take the road Kutúzov took, but retiring instead to Mozháysk along the devastated Smolénsk road. Nothing more stupid than that could have been devised, or more disastrous for the army, as the sequel showed. Had Napoleon's aim been to destroy his army, the most skillful strategist could hardly have devised any series of actions that would so completely have accomplished that purpose, independently of anything the Russian army might do.

Napoleon, the man of genius, did this! But to say that he destroyed his army because he wished to, or because he was very stupid, would be as unjust as to say that he had brought his troops to Moscow because he wished to and because he was very clever and a genius.

In both cases his personal activity, having no more force than the personal activity of any soldier, merely coincided with the laws that guided the event.

The historians quite falsely represent Napoleon's faculties as having weakened in Moscow, and do so only because the results did not justify his actions. He employed all his ability and strength to do the best he could for himself and his army, as he had done previously and as he did subsequently in 1813. His activity at that time was no less astounding than it was in Egypt, in Italy, in Austria, and in Prussia. We do not know for certain in how far his genius was genuine in Egypt—where forty centuries looked down upon his grandeur—for his great exploits there are all told us by Frenchmen. We cannot accurately estimate his genius in Austria or Prussia, for we have to draw our information from French or German sources, and the incomprehensible surrender of whole corps without fighting and of fortresses without a siege must incline Germans to recognize his genius as the only explanation of the war carried on in Germany. But we, thank God, have no need to recognize his genius in order to hide our shame. We have paid for the right to look at the matter plainly and simply, and we will not abandon that right.

His activity in Moscow was as amazing and as full of genius as elsewhere. Order after order and plan after plan were issued by him from the time he entered Moscow till the time he left it. The absence of citizens and of a deputation, and even the burning of Moscow, did not disconcert him. He did not lose sight either of the welfare of his army or of the doings of the enemy, or of the welfare of the people of Russia, or of the direction of affairs in Paris, or of diplomatic considerations concerning the terms of the anticipated peace.

# IX

With regard to military matters, Napoleon immediately on his entry into Moscow gave General Sabastiani strict orders to observe the movements of the Russian army, sent army corps out along the different roads, and charged Murat to find Kutúzov. Then he gave careful directions about the fortification of the Krémlin, and drew up a brilliant plan for a future campaign over the whole map of Russia.

With regard to diplomatic questions, Napoleon summoned Captain Yákovlev, who had been robbed and was in rags and did not know how to get out of Moscow, minutely explained to him his whole policy and his magnanimity, and having written a letter to the Emperor Alexander in which he considered it his duty to inform his Friend and Brother that Rostopchín had managed affairs badly in Moscow, he dispatched Yákovlev to Petersburg.

Having similarly explained his views and his magnanimity to Tutólmin, he dispatched that old man also to Petersburg to negotiate.

With regard to legal matters, immediately after the fires he gave orders to find and execute the incendiaries. And the scoundrel Rostopchín was punished by an order to burn down his houses.

With regard to administrative matters, Moscow was granted a constitution. A municipality was established and the following announcement issued:

## Inhabitants of Moscow!

Your misfortunes are cruel, but His Majesty the Emperor and King desires to arrest their course. Terrible examples have taught you how he punishes disobedience and crime. Strict measures have been taken to put an end to disorder and to re-establish public security. A paternal administration, chosen from among yourselves, will form your municipality or city government. It will take care of you, of your needs, and of your welfare. Its members will be distinguished by a red ribbon worn across the shoulder, and the mayor of the city will wear a white belt as well. But when not on duty they will only wear a red ribbon round the left arm.

The city police is established on its former footing, and better order already prevails in consequence of its activity. The government has appointed two commissaries general, or chiefs of police, and twenty commissaries or captains of wards have been appointed to the different wards of the city. You will recognize them by the white ribbon they will wear on the left arm. Several churches of different denominations are open, and divine service is performed in them unhindered. Your fellow citizens are returning every day to their homes and orders have been given that they should find in them the help and protection due to their misfortunes. These are the measures the government has adopted to re-establish order and relieve your condition. But to achieve this aim it is necessary that you should add your efforts and should, if possible, forget the misfortunes you have suffered, should entertain the hope of a less cruel fate, should be certain that inevitable and ignominious death awaits those who make any attempt on your persons or on what remains of your property, and finally that you should not doubt that these will be safeguarded, since such is the will of the greatest and most just of monarchs. Soldiers and citizens, of whatever nation you may be, re-establish public confidence, the source of the welfare of a state, live like brothers, render mutual aid and protection one to another, unite to defeat the intentions of the evil-minded, obey the military and civil authorities, and your tears will soon cease to flow!

With regard to supplies for the army, Napoleon decreed that all the troops in turn should enter Moscow à la maraude* to obtain provisions for themselves, so that the army might have its future provided for.

With regard to religion, Napoleon ordered the priests to be brought back and services to be again performed in the churches.

With regard to commerce and to provisioning the army, the following was placarded everywhere:

## PROCLAMATION

You, peaceful inhabitants of Moscow, artisans and workmen whom misfortune has driven from the city, and you scattered tillers of the soil, still kept out in the fields by groundless fear, listen! Tranquillity is returning to this capital and order is being

---

* As looters.

restored in it. Your fellow countrymen are emerging boldly from their hiding places on finding that they are respected. Any violence to them or to their property is promptly punished. His Majesty the Emperor and King protects them, and considers no one among you his enemy except those who disobey his orders. He desires to end your misfortunes and restore you to your homes and families. Respond, therefore, to his benevolent intentions and come to us without fear. Inhabitants, return with confidence to your abodes! You will soon find means of satisfying your needs. Craftsmen and industrious artisans, return to your work, your houses, your shops, where the protection of guards awaits you! You shall receive proper pay for your work. And lastly you too, peasants, come from the forests where you are hiding in terror, return to your huts without fear, in full assurance that you will find protection! Markets are established in the city where peasants can bring their surplus supplies and the products of the soil. The government has taken the following steps to ensure freedom of sale for them: (1) From today, peasants, husbandmen, and those living in the neighborhood of Moscow may without any danger bring their supplies of all kinds to two appointed markets, of which one is on the Mokhováya Street and the other at the Provision Market. (2) Such supplies will be bought from them at such prices as seller and buyer may agree on, and if a seller is unable to obtain a fair price he will be free to take his goods back to his village and no one may hinder him under any pretense. (3) Sunday and Wednesday of each week are appointed as the chief market days and to that end a sufficient number of troops will be stationed along the highroads on Tuesdays and Saturdays at such distances from the town as to protect the carts. (4) Similar measures will be taken that peasants with their carts and horses may meet with no hindrance on their return journey. (5) Steps will immediately be taken to re-establish ordinary trading.

Inhabitants of the city and villages, and you, workingmen and artisans, to whatever nation you belong, you are called on to carry out the paternal intentions of His Majesty the Emperor and King and to co-operate with him for the public welfare! Lay your respect and confidence at his feet and do not delay to unite with us!

With the object of raising the spirits of the troops and of the people, reviews were constantly held and rewards distributed. The Emperor rode through the streets to comfort the inhabitants, and, despite his preoccupation with state affairs, himself visited the theaters that were established by his order.

In regard to philanthropy, the greatest virtue of crowned heads, Napoleon also did all in his power. He caused the words Maison de ma Mère to be inscribed on the charitable institutions, thereby combining tender filial affection with the majestic benevolence of a monarch. He visited the Foundling Hospital and, allowing the orphans saved by him to kiss his white hands, graciously conversed with Tutólmin. Then, as Thiers eloquently recounts, he ordered his soldiers to be paid in forged Russian money which he had prepared: "Raising the use of these means by an act worthy of himself and of the French army, he let relief be distributed to those who had been burned out. But as food was too precious to be given to foreigners, who were for the most part enemies, Napoleon preferred to supply them with money with which to purchase food from outside, and had paper rubles distributed to them."

With reference to army discipline, orders were continually being issued to inflict severe punishment for the nonperformance of military duties and to suppress robbery.

# X

B ut strange to say, all these measures, efforts, and plans—which were not at all worse than others issued in similar circumstances—did not affect the essence of the matter but, like the hands of a clock detached from the mechanism, swung about in an arbitrary and aimless way without engaging the cogwheels.

With reference to the military side—the plan of campaign—that work of genius of which Thiers remarks that, "His genius never devised anything more profound, more skillful, or more admirable," and enters into a polemic with M. Fain to prove that this work of genius must be referred not to the fourth but to the fifteenth of October—that plan never was or could be executed, for it was quite out of touch with the facts of the case. The fortifying of the Krémlin, for which la Mosquée (as Napoleon termed the church of Basil the Beatified) was to have been razed to the ground, proved quite useless. The mining of the Krémlin only helped toward fulfilling Napoleon's wish that it should be blown up when he left Moscow—as a child wants the floor on which he has hurt himself to be beaten. The pursuit of the Russian army, about which Napoleon was so concerned, produced an unheard-of result. The French generals lost touch with the Russian army of sixty thousand men, and according to Thiers it was only eventually found, like a lost pin, by the skill—and apparently the genius—of Murat.

With reference to diplomacy, all Napoleon's arguments as to his magnanimity and justice, both to Tutólmin and to Yákovlev (whose chief concern was to obtain a greatcoat and a conveyance), proved useless; Alexander did not receive these envoys and did not reply to their embassage.

With regard to legal matters, after the execution of the supposed incendiaries the rest of Moscow burned down.

With regard to administrative matters, the establishment of a municipality did not stop the robberies and was only of use to certain people who formed part of that municipality and under pretext of preserving order looted Moscow or saved their own property from being looted.

With regard to religion, as to which in Egypt matters had so easily been settled by Napoleon's visit to a mosque, no results were achieved. Two or three priests who were found in Moscow did try to carry out

Napoleon's wish, but one of them was slapped in the face by a French soldier while conducting service, and a French official reported of another that: "The priest whom I found and invited to say Mass cleaned and locked up the church. That night the doors were again broken open, the padlocks smashed, the books mutilated, and other disorders perpetrated."

With reference to commerce, the proclamation to industrious workmen and to peasants evoked no response. There were no industrious workmen, and the peasants caught the commissaries who ventured too far out of town with the proclamation and killed them.

As to the theaters for the entertainment of the people and the troops, these did not meet with success either. The theaters set up in the Krémlin and in Posnyákov's house were closed again at once because the actors and actresses were robbed.

Even philanthropy did not have the desired effect. The genuine as well as the false paper money which flooded Moscow lost its value. The French, collecting booty, cared only for gold. Not only was the paper money valueless which Napoleon so graciously distributed to the unfortunate, but even silver lost its value in relation to gold.

But the most amazing example of the ineffectiveness of the orders given by the authorities at that time was Napoleon's attempt to stop the looting and re-establish discipline.

This is what the army authorities were reporting:

"Looting continues in the city despite the decrees against it. Order is not yet restored and not a single merchant is carrying on trade in a lawful manner. The sutlers alone venture to trade, and they sell stolen goods."

"The neighborhood of my ward continues to be pillaged by soldiers of the 3rd Corps who, not satisfied with taking from the unfortunate inhabitants hiding in the cellars the little they have left, even have the ferocity to wound them with their sabers, as I have repeatedly witnessed."

"Nothing new, except that the soldiers are robbing and pillaging— October 9."

"Robbery and pillaging continue. There is a band of thieves in our district who ought to be arrested by a strong force—October 11."

"The Emperor is extremely displeased that despite the strict orders to stop pillage, parties of marauding Guards are continually seen returning to the Krémlin. Among the Old Guard disorder and pillage were renewed more violently than ever yesterday evening, last night, and today. The Emperor sees with regret that the picked soldiers appointed to guard his person, who should set an example of discipline, carry disobedience to such a point that they break into the cellars and stores containing army supplies. Others have disgraced themselves to the extent of disobeying sentinels and officers, and have abused and beaten them."

"The Grand Marshal of the palace," wrote the governor, "complains bitterly that in spite of repeated orders, the soldiers continue to commit nuisances in all the courtyards and even under the very windows of the Emperor."

That army, like a herd of cattle run wild and trampling underfoot the provender which might have saved it from starvation, disintegrated and perished with each additional day it remained in Moscow. But it did not go away.

It began to run away only when suddenly seized by a panic caused by the capture of transport trains on the Smolénsk road, and by the battle of Tarútino. The news of that battle of Tarútino, unexpectedly received by Napoleon at a review, evoked in him a desire to punish the Russians (Thiers says), and he issued the order for departure which the whole army was demanding.

Fleeing from Moscow the soldiers took with them everything they had stolen. Napoleon, too, carried away his own personal trésor, but on seeing the baggage trains that impeded the army, he was (Thiers says) horror-struck. And yet with his experience of war he did not order all the superfluous vehicles to be burned, as he had done with those of a certain marshal when approaching Moscow. He gazed at the calèches and carriages in which soldiers were riding and remarked that it was a very good thing, as those vehicles could be used to carry provisions, the sick, and the wounded.

The plight of the whole army resembled that of a wounded animal which feels it is perishing and does not know what it is doing. To study the skillful tactics and aims of Napoleon and his army from the time it entered Moscow till it was destroyed is like studying the dying leaps and shudders of a mortally wounded animal. Very often a wounded animal, hearing a rustle, rushes straight at the hunter's gun, runs forward and back again, and hastens its own end. Napoleon, under pressure from his whole army, did the same thing. The rustle of the battle of Tarútino frightened the beast, and it rushed forward onto the hunter's gun, reached him, turned back, and finally—like any wild beast—ran back along the most disadvantageous and dangerous path, where the old scent was familiar.

During the whole of that period Napoleon, who seems to us to have been the leader of all these movements—as the figurehead of a ship may seem to a savage to guide the vessel—acted like a child who, holding a couple of strings inside a carriage, thinks he is driving it.

# XI

E arly in the morning of the sixth of October Pierre went out of the shed, and on returning stopped by the door to play with a little blue-gray dog, with a long body and short bandy legs, that jumped about him. This little dog lived in their shed, sleeping beside Karatáev at night; it sometimes made excursions into the town but always returned again. Probably it had never had an owner, and it still belonged to nobody and had no name. The French called it Azor; the soldier who told stories called it Femgálka; Karatáev and others called it Gray, or sometimes Flabby. Its lack of a master, a name, or even of a breed or any definite color did not seem to trouble the blue-gray dog in the least. Its furry tail stood up firm and round as a plume, its bandy legs served it so well that it would often gracefully lift a hind leg and run very easily and quickly on three legs, as if disdaining to use all four. Everything pleased it. Now it would roll on its back, yelping with delight, now bask in the sun with a thoughtful air of importance, and now frolic about playing with a chip of wood or a straw.

Pierre's attire by now consisted of a dirty torn shirt (the only remnant of his former clothing), a pair of soldier's trousers which by Karatáev's advice he tied with string round the ankles for warmth, and a peasant coat and cap. Physically he had changed much during this time. He no longer seemed stout, though he still had the appearance of solidity and strength hereditary in his family. A beard and mustache covered the lower part of his face, and a tangle of hair, infested with lice, curled round his head like a cap. The look of his eyes was resolute, calm, and animatedly alert, as never before. The former slackness which had shown itself even in his eyes was now replaced by an energetic readiness for action and resistance. His feet were bare.

Pierre first looked down the field across which vehicles and horsemen were passing that morning, then into the distance across the river, then at the dog who was pretending to be in earnest about biting him, and then at his bare feet which he placed with pleasure in various positions, moving his dirty thick big toes. Every time he looked at his bare feet a smile of animated self-satisfaction flitted across his face. The sight of them reminded him of all he had experienced and learned during these weeks and this recollection was pleasant to him.

For some days the weather had been calm and clear with slight frosts in the mornings—what is called an "old wives' summer."

In the sunshine the air was warm, and that warmth was particularly pleasant with the invigorating freshness of the morning frost still in the air.

On everything—far and near—lay the magic crystal glitter seen only at that time of autumn. The Sparrow Hills were visible in the distance, with the village, the church, and the large white house. The bare trees, the sand, the bricks and roofs of the houses, the green church spire, and the corners of the white house in the distance, all stood out in the transparent air in most delicate outline and with unnatural clearness. Near by could be seen the familiar ruins of a half-burned mansion occupied by the French, with lilac bushes still showing dark green beside the fence. And even that ruined and befouled house—which in dull weather was repulsively ugly—seemed quietly beautiful now, in the clear, motionless brilliance.

A French corporal, with coat unbuttoned in a homely way, a skullcap on his head, and a short pipe in his mouth, came from behind a corner of the shed and approached Pierre with a friendly wink.

"What sunshine, Monsieur Kiril!" (Their name for Pierre.) "Eh? Just like spring!"

And the corporal leaned against the door and offered Pierre his pipe, though whenever he offered it Pierre always declined it.

"To be on the march in such weather. . ." he began.

Pierre inquired what was being said about leaving, and the corporal told him that nearly all the troops were starting and there ought to be an order about the prisoners that day. Sokolóv, one of the soldiers in the shed with Pierre, was dying, and Pierre told the corporal that something should be done about him. The corporal replied that Pierre need not worry about that as they had an ambulance and a permanent hospital and arrangements would be made for the sick, and that in general everything that could happen had been foreseen by the authorities.

"Besides, Monsieur Kiril, you have only to say a word to the captain, you know. He is a man who never forgets anything. Speak to the captain when he makes his round, he will do anything for you."

(The captain of whom the corporal spoke often had long chats with Pierre and showed him all sorts of favors.)

"'You see, St. Thomas,' he said to me the other day. 'Monsieur Kiril is a man of education, who speaks French. He is a Russian seigneur who has had misfortunes, but he is a man. He knows what's what. . . If he wants anything and asks me, he won't get a refusal. When one has studied, you see, one likes education and well-bred people.' It is for your sake I mention it, Monsieur Kiril. The other day if it had not been for you that affair would have ended ill."

And after chatting a while longer, the corporal went away. (The affair he had alluded to had happened a few days before—a fight between the prisoners and the French soldiers, in which Pierre had succeeded in pacifying his comrades.) Some of the prisoners who had heard Pierre talking to the corporal immediately asked what the Frenchman had said. While Pierre was repeating what he had been told about the army leaving Moscow, a thin, sallow, tattered French soldier came up to the door of the shed. Rapidly and timidly raising his fingers to his forehead by way of greeting, he asked Pierre whether the soldier Platoche to whom he had given a shirt to sew was in that shed.

A week before the French had had boot leather and linen issued to them, which they had given out to the prisoners to make up into boots and shirts for them.

"Ready, ready, dear fellow!" said Karatáev, coming out with a neatly folded shirt.

Karatáev, on account of the warm weather and for convenience at work, was wearing only trousers and a tattered shirt as black as soot. His hair was bound round, workman fashion, with a wisp of lime-tree bast, and his round face seemed rounder and pleasanter than ever.

"A promise is own brother to performance! I said Friday and here it is, ready," said Platón, smiling and unfolding the shirt he had sewn.

The Frenchman glanced around uneasily and then, as if overcoming his hesitation, rapidly threw off his uniform and put on the shirt. He had a long, greasy, flowered silk waistcoat next to his sallow, thin bare body, but no shirt. He was evidently afraid the prisoners looking on would laugh at him, and thrust his head into the shirt hurriedly. None of the prisoners said a word.

"See, it fits well!" Platón kept repeating, pulling the shirt straight.

The Frenchman, having pushed his head and hands through, without raising his eyes, looked down at the shirt and examined the seams.

"You see, dear man, this is not a sewing shop, and I had no proper tools; and, as they say, one needs a tool even to kill a louse," said Platón with one of his round smiles, obviously pleased with his work.

"It's good, quite good, thank you," said the Frenchman, in French, "but there must be some linen left over."

"It will fit better still when it sets to your body," said Karatáev, still admiring his handiwork. "You'll be nice and comfortable. . ."

"Thanks, thanks, old fellow... But the bits left over?" said the Frenchman again and smiled. He took out an assignation ruble note and gave it to Karatáev. "But give me the pieces that are over."

Pierre saw that Platón did not want to understand what the Frenchman was saying, and he looked on without interfering. Karatáev thanked the Frenchman for the money and went on admiring his own work. The Frenchman insisted on having the pieces returned that were left over and asked Pierre to translate what he said.

"What does he want the bits for?" said Karatáev. "They'd make fine leg bands for us. Well, never mind."

And Karatáev, with a suddenly changed and saddened expression, took a small bundle of scraps from inside his shirt and gave it to the Frenchman without looking at him. "Oh dear!" muttered Karatáev and went away. The Frenchman looked at the linen, considered for a moment, then looked inquiringly at Pierre and, as if Pierre's look had told him something, suddenly blushed and shouted in a squeaky voice:

"Platoche! Eh, Platoche! Keep them yourself!" And handing back the odd bits he turned and went out.

"There, look at that," said Karatáev, swaying his head. "People said they were not Christians, but they too have souls. It's what the old folk used to say: 'A sweating hand's an open hand, a dry hand's close.' He's naked, but yet he's given it back."

Karatáev smiled thoughtfully and was silent awhile looking at the pieces.

"But they'll make grand leg bands, dear friend," he said, and went back into the shed.

# XII

Four weeks had passed since Pierre had been taken prisoner and though the French had offered to move him from the men's to the officers' shed, he had stayed in the shed where he was first put.

In burned and devastated Moscow Pierre experienced almost the extreme limits of privation a man can endure; but thanks to his physical strength and health, of which he had till then been unconscious, and thanks especially to the fact that the privations came so gradually that it was impossible to say when they began, he endured his position not only lightly but joyfully. And just at this time he obtained the tranquillity and ease of mind he had formerly striven in vain to reach. He had long sought in different ways that tranquillity of mind, that inner harmony which had so impressed him in the soldiers at the battle of Borodinó. He had sought it in philanthropy, in Freemasonry, in the dissipations of town life, in wine, in heroic feats of self-sacrifice, and in romantic love for Natásha; he had sought it by reasoning—and all these quests and experiments had failed him. And now without thinking about it he had found that peace and inner harmony only through the horror of death, through privation, and through what he recognized in Karatáev.

Those dreadful moments he had lived through at the executions had as it were forever washed away from his imagination and memory the agitating thoughts and feelings that had formerly seemed so important. It did not now occur to him to think of Russia, or the war, or politics, or Napoleon. It was plain to him that all these things were no business of his, and that he was not called on to judge concerning them and therefore could not do so. "Russia and summer weather are not bound together," he thought, repeating words of Karatáev's which he found strangely consoling. His intention of killing Napoleon and his calculations of the cabalistic number of the beast of the Apocalypse now seemed to him meaningless and even ridiculous. His anger with his wife and anxiety that his name should not be smirched now seemed not merely trivial but even amusing. What concern was it of his that somewhere or other that woman was leading the life she preferred? What did it matter to anybody, and especially to him, whether or not they found out that their prisoner's name was Count Bezúkhov?

He now often remembered his conversation with Prince Andrew and quite agreed with him, though he understood Prince Andrew's thoughts somewhat differently. Prince Andrew had thought and said that happiness could only be negative, but had said it with a shade of bitterness and irony as though he was really saying that all desire for positive happiness is implanted in us merely to torment us and never be satisfied. But Pierre believed it without any mental reservation. The absence of suffering, the satisfaction of one's needs and consequent freedom in the choice of one's occupation, that is, of one's way of life, now seemed to Pierre to be indubitably man's highest happiness. Here and now for the first time he fully appreciated the enjoyment of eating when he wanted to eat, drinking when he wanted to drink, sleeping when he wanted to sleep, of warmth when he was cold, of talking to a fellow man when he wished to talk and to hear a human voice. The satisfaction of one's needs—good food, cleanliness, and freedom— now that he was deprived of all this, seemed to Pierre to constitute perfect happiness; and the choice of occupation, that is, of his way of life—now that that was so restricted—seemed to him such an easy matter that he forgot that a superfluity of the comforts of life destroys all joy in satisfying one's needs, while great freedom in the choice of occupation—such freedom as his wealth, his education, and his social position had given him in his own life—is just what makes the choice of occupation insolubly difficult and destroys the desire and possibility of having an occupation.

All Pierre's daydreams now turned on the time when he would be free. Yet subsequently, and for the rest of his life, he thought and spoke with enthusiasm of that month of captivity, of those irrecoverable, strong, joyful sensations, and chiefly of the complete peace of mind and inner freedom which he experienced only during those weeks.

When on the first day he got up early, went out of the shed at dawn, and saw the cupolas and crosses of the New Convent of the Virgin still dark at first, the hoarfrost on the dusty grass, the Sparrow Hills, and the wooded banks above the winding river vanishing in the purple distance, when he felt the contact of the fresh air and heard the noise of the crows flying from Moscow across the field, and when afterwards light gleamed from the east and the sun's rim appeared solemnly from behind a cloud, and the cupolas and crosses, the hoarfrost, the distance and the river, all began to sparkle in the glad light—Pierre felt a new joy and strength in life such as he had never before known. And this not only stayed with him during the whole of his imprisonment, but even grew in strength as the hardships of his position increased.

That feeling of alertness and of readiness for anything was still further strengthened in him by the high opinion his fellow prisoners formed of him soon after his arrival at the shed. With his knowledge of languages, the respect shown him by the French, his simplicity, his readiness to give anything asked of him (he received the allowance of three rubles a week made to officers); with his strength, which he showed to the soldiers by pressing nails into the walls of the hut; his gentleness to his companions, and his capacity for sitting still and thinking without doing anything (which seemed to them incomprehensible), he appeared to them a rather mysterious and superior being. The very qualities that had been a hindrance, if not actually harmful, to him in the world he had lived in—his strength, his disdain for the comforts of life, his absent-mindedness and simplicity—here among these people gave him almost the status of a hero. And Pierre felt that their opinion placed responsibilities upon him.

# XIII

The French evacuation began on the night between the sixth and seventh of October: kitchens and sheds were dismantled, carts loaded, and troops and baggage trains started.

At seven in the morning a French convoy in marching trim, wearing shakos and carrying muskets, knapsacks, and enormous sacks, stood in front of the sheds, and animated French talk mingled with curses sounded all along the lines.

In the shed everyone was ready, dressed, belted, shod, and only awaited the order to start. The sick soldier, Sokolóv, pale and thin with dark shadows round his eyes, alone sat in his place barefoot and not dressed. His eyes, prominent from the emaciation of his face, gazed inquiringly at his comrades who were paying no attention to him, and he moaned regularly and quietly. It was evidently not so much his sufferings that caused him to moan (he had dysentery) as his fear and grief at being left alone.

Pierre, girt with a rope round his waist and wearing shoes Karatáev had made for him from some leather a French soldier had torn off a tea chest and brought to have his boots mended with, went up to the sick man and squatted down beside him.

"You know, Sokolóv, they are not all going away! They have a hospital here. You may be better off than we others," said Pierre.

"O Lord! Oh, it will be the death of me! O Lord!" moaned the man in a louder voice.

"I'll go and ask them again directly," said Pierre, rising and going to the door of the shed.

Just as Pierre reached the door, the corporal who had offered him a pipe the day before came up to it with two soldiers. The corporal and soldiers were in marching kit with knapsacks and shakos that had metal straps, and these changed their familiar faces.

The corporal came, according to orders, to shut the door. The prisoners had to be counted before being let out.

"Corporal, what will they do with the sick man? . . ." Pierre began.

But even as he spoke he began to doubt whether this was the corporal he knew or a stranger, so unlike himself did the corporal seem at that moment. Moreover, just as Pierre was speaking a sharp rattle of drums was suddenly heard from both sides. The corporal frowned at

Pierre's words and, uttering some meaningless oaths, slammed the door. The shed became semidark, and the sharp rattle of the drums on two sides drowned the sick man's groans.

"There it is!...It again!..." said Pierre to himself, and an involuntary shudder ran down his spine. In the corporal's changed face, in the sound of his voice, in the stirring and deafening noise of the drums, he recognized that mysterious, callous force which compelled people against their will to kill their fellow men—that force the effect of which he had witnessed during the executions. To fear or to try to escape that force, to address entreaties or exhortations to those who served as its tools, was useless. Pierre knew this now. One had to wait and endure. He did not again go to the sick man, nor turn to look at him, but stood frowning by the door of the hut.

When that door was opened and the prisoners, crowding against one another like a flock of sheep, squeezed into the exit, Pierre pushed his way forward and approached that very captain who as the corporal had assured him was ready to do anything for him. The captain was also in marching kit, and on his cold face appeared that same it which Pierre had recognized in the corporal's words and in the roll of the drums.

"Pass on, pass on!" the captain reiterated, frowning sternly, and looking at the prisoners who thronged past him.

Pierre went up to him, though he knew his attempt would be vain.

"What now?" the officer asked with a cold look as if not recognizing Pierre.

Pierre told him about the sick man.

"He'll manage to walk, devil take him!" said the captain. "Pass on, pass on!" he continued without looking at Pierre.

"But he is dying," Pierre again began.

"Be so good..." shouted the captain, frowning angrily.

"Dram-da-da-dam, dam-dam..." rattled the drums, and Pierre understood that this mysterious force completely controlled these men and that it was now useless to say any more.

The officer prisoners were separated from the soldiers and told to march in front. There were about thirty officers, with Pierre among them, and about three hundred men.

The officers, who had come from the other sheds, were all strangers to Pierre and much better dressed than he. They looked at him and at his shoes mistrustfully, as at an alien. Not far from him walked a fat major with a sallow, bloated, angry face, who was wearing a Kazán dressing gown tied round with a towel, and who evidently enjoyed the respect of his fellow prisoners. He kept one hand, in which he clasped his tobacco pouch, inside the bosom of his dressing gown and held the stem of his pipe firmly with the other. Panting and puffing, the major grumbled and growled at everybody because he thought he was being pushed and that they were all hurrying when they had nowhere to hurry to and were all surprised at something when there was nothing to be surprised at. Another, a thin little officer, was speaking to everyone, conjecturing where they were now being taken and how far they would get that day. An official in felt boots and wearing a commissariat uniform ran round from side to side and gazed at the ruins of Moscow, loudly announcing his observations as to what had been burned down and what this or that part of the city was that they could see. A third officer, who by his accent was a Pole, disputed with the commissariat officer, arguing that he was mistaken in his identification of the different wards of Moscow.

"What are you disputing about?" said the major angrily. "What does it matter whether it is St. Nicholas or St. Blasius? You see it's burned down, and there's an end of it. . . What are you pushing for? Isn't the road wide enough?" said he, turning to a man behind him who was not pushing him at all.

"Oh, oh, oh! What have they done?" the prisoners on one side and another were heard saying as they gazed on the charred ruins. "All beyond the river, and Zúbova, and in the Krémlin. . . Just look! There's not half of it left. Yes, I told you—the whole quarter beyond the river, and so it is."

"Well, you know it's burned, so what's the use of talking?" said the major.

As they passed near a church in the Khamóvniki (one of the few unburned quarters of Moscow) the whole mass of prisoners suddenly started to one side and exclamations of horror and disgust were heard.

"Ah, the villains! What heathens! Yes; dead, dead, so he is. . . And smeared with something!"

Pierre too drew near the church where the thing was that evoked these exclamations, and dimly made out something leaning against the palings surrounding the church. From the words of his comrades who saw better than he did, he found that this was the body of a man, set upright against the palings with its face smeared with soot.

"Go on! What the devil. . . Go on! Thirty thousand devils! . . ." the convoy guards began cursing and the French soldiers, with fresh virulence, drove away with their swords the crowd of prisoners who were gazing at the dead man.

# XIV

Through the cross streets of the Khamóvniki quarter the prisoners marched, followed only by their escort and the vehicles and wagons belonging to that escort, but when they reached the supply stores they came among a huge and closely packed train of artillery mingled with private vehicles.

At the bridge they all halted, waiting for those in front to get across. From the bridge they had a view of endless lines of moving baggage trains before and behind them. To the right, where the Kalúga road turns near Neskúchny, endless rows of troops and carts stretched away into the distance. These were troops of Beauharnais' corps which had started before any of the others. Behind, along the riverside and across the Stone Bridge, were Ney's troops and transport.

Davout's troops, in whose charge were the prisoners, were crossing the Crimean bridge and some were already debouching into the Kalúga road. But the baggage trains stretched out so that the last of Beauharnais' train had not yet got out of Moscow and reached the Kalúga road when the vanguard of Ney's army was already emerging from the Great Ordýnka Street.

When they had crossed the Crimean bridge the prisoners moved a few steps forward, halted, and again moved on, and from all sides vehicles and men crowded closer and closer together. They advanced the few hundred paces that separated the bridge from the Kalúga road, taking more than an hour to do so, and came out upon the square where the streets of the Transmoskvá ward and the Kalúga road converge, and the prisoners jammed close together had to stand for some hours at that crossway. From all sides, like the roar of the sea, were heard the rattle of wheels, the tramp of feet, and incessant shouts of anger and abuse. Pierre stood pressed against the wall of a charred house, listening to that noise which mingled in his imagination with the roll of the drums.

To get a better view, several officer prisoners climbed onto the wall of the half-burned house against which Pierre was leaning.

"What crowds! Just look at the crowds! . . . They've loaded goods even on the cannon! Look there, those are furs!" they exclaimed. "Just see what the blackguards have looted. . . There! See what that one has behind in the cart. . . Why, those are settings taken from some icons, by heaven! . . . Oh, the rascals! . . . See how that fellow has loaded himself up, he can hardly walk! Good lord, they've even grabbed those chaises! . . . See that fellow there sitting on the trunks. . . Heavens! They're fighting."

"That's right, hit him on the snout—on his snout! Like this, we shan't get away before evening. Look, look there. . . Why, that must be Napoleon's own. See what horses! And the monograms with a crown! It's like a portable house. . . That fellow's dropped his sack and doesn't see it. Fighting again. . . A woman with a baby, and not bad-looking either! Yes, I dare say, that's the way they'll let you pass. . . Just look, there's no end to it. Russian wenches, by heaven, so they are! In carriages—see how comfortably they've settled themselves!"

Again, as at the church in Khamóvniki, a wave of general curiosity bore all the prisoners forward onto the road, and Pierre, thanks to his stature, saw over the heads of the others what so attracted their curiosity. In three carriages involved among the munition carts, closely squeezed together, sat women with rouged faces, dressed in glaring colors, who were shouting something in shrill voices.

From the moment Pierre had recognized the appearance of the mysterious force nothing had seemed to him strange or dreadful: neither the corpse smeared with soot for fun nor these women hurrying away nor the burned ruins of Moscow. All that he now witnessed scarcely made an impression on him—as if his soul, making ready for a hard struggle, refused to receive impressions that might weaken it.

The women's vehicles drove by. Behind them came more carts, soldiers, wagons, soldiers, gun carriages, carriages, soldiers, ammunition carts, more soldiers, and now and then women.

Pierre did not see the people as individuals but saw their movement.

All these people and horses seemed driven forward by some invisible power. During the hour Pierre watched them they all came flowing from the different streets with one and the same desire to get on quickly; they all jostled one another, began to grow angry and to fight, white teeth gleamed, brows frowned, ever the same words of abuse flew from side to side, and all the faces bore the same swaggeringly resolute and coldly cruel expression that had struck Pierre that morning on the corporal's face when the drums were beating.

It was not till nearly evening that the officer commanding the escort collected his men and with shouts and quarrels forced his way in among the baggage trains, and the prisoners, hemmed in on all sides, emerged onto the Kalúga road.

They marched very quickly, without resting, and halted only when the sun began to set. The baggage carts drew up close together and the men began to prepare for their night's rest. They all appeared angry and dissatisfied. For a long time, oaths, angry shouts, and fighting could be heard from all sides. A carriage that followed the escort ran into one of the carts and knocked a hole in it with its pole. Several soldiers ran toward the cart from different sides: some beat the carriage horses on their heads, turning them aside, others fought among themselves, and Pierre saw that one German was badly wounded on the head by a sword.

It seemed that all these men, now that they had stopped amid fields in the chill dusk of the autumn evening, experienced one and the same feeling of unpleasant awakening from the hurry and eagerness to push on that had seized them at the start. Once at a standstill they all seemed to understand that they did not yet know where they were going, and that much that was painful and difficult awaited them on this journey.

During this halt the escort treated the prisoners even worse than they had done at the start. It was here that the prisoners for the first time received horseflesh for their meat ration.

From the officer down to the lowest soldier they showed what seemed like personal spite against each of the prisoners, in unexpected contrast to their former friendly relations.

This spite increased still more when, on calling over the roll of prisoners, it was found that in the bustle of leaving Moscow one Russian soldier, who had pretended to suffer from colic, had escaped. Pierre saw a Frenchman beat a Russian soldier cruelly for straying too far from the road, and heard his friend the captain reprimand and threaten to court-martial a noncommissioned officer on account of the escape of the Russian. To the noncommissioned officer's excuse that the prisoner was ill and could not walk, the officer replied that the order was to shoot those who lagged behind. Pierre felt that that fatal force which had crushed him during the executions, but which he had not felt during his imprisonment, now again controlled his existence. It was terrible, but he felt that in proportion to the efforts of that fatal force to crush him, there grew and strengthened in his soul a power of life independent of it.

He ate his supper of buckwheat soup with horseflesh and chatted with his comrades.

Neither Pierre nor any of the others spoke of what they had seen in Moscow, or of the roughness of their treatment by the French, or of the order to shoot them which had been announced to them. As if in reaction against the worsening of their position they were all particularly animated and gay. They spoke of personal reminiscences, of amusing scenes they had witnessed during the campaign, and avoided all talk of their present situation.

The sun had set long since. Bright stars shone out here and there in the sky. A red glow as of a conflagration spread above the horizon from the rising full moon, and that vast red ball swayed strangely in the gray haze. It grew light. The evening was ending, but the night had not yet come. Pierre got up and left his new companions, crossing between the campfires to the other side of the road where he had been told the common soldier prisoners were stationed. He wanted to talk to them. On the road he was stopped by a French sentinel who ordered him back.

Pierre turned back, not to his companions by the campfire, but to an unharnessed cart where there was nobody. Tucking his legs under him and dropping his head he sat down on the cold ground by the wheel of the cart and remained motionless a long while sunk in thought. Suddenly he burst out into a fit of his broad, good-natured laughter, so loud that men from various sides turned with surprise to see what this strange and evidently solitary laughter could mean.

"Ha-ha-ha!" laughed Pierre. And he said aloud to himself: "The soldier did not let me pass. They took me and shut me up. They hold me captive. What, me? Me? My immortal soul? Ha-ha-ha! Ha-ha-ha! . . ." and he laughed till tears started to his eyes.

A man got up and came to see what this queer big fellow was laughing at all by himself. Pierre stopped laughing, got up, went farther away from the inquisitive man, and looked around him.

The huge, endless bivouac that had previously resounded with the crackling of campfires and the voices of many men had grown quiet, the red campfires were growing paler and dying down. High up in the light sky hung the full moon. Forests and fields beyond the camp, unseen before, were now visible in the distance. And farther still, beyond those forests and fields, the bright, oscillating, limitless distance lured one to itself. Pierre glanced up at the sky and the twinkling stars in its faraway depths. "And all that is me, all that is within me, and it is all I!" thought Pierre. "And they caught all that and put it into a shed boarded up with planks!" He smiled, and went and lay down to sleep beside his companions.

# XV

In the early days of October another envoy came to Kutúzov with a letter from Napoleon proposing peace and falsely dated from Moscow, though Napoleon was already not far from Kutúzov on the old Kalúga road. Kutúzov replied to this letter as he had done to the one formerly brought by Lauriston, saying that there could be no question of peace.

Soon after that a report was received from Dórokhov's guerrilla detachment operating to the left of Tarútino that troops of Broussier's division had been seen at Formínsk and that being separated from the rest of the French army they might easily be destroyed. The soldiers and officers again demanded action. Generals on the staff, excited by the memory of the easy victory at Tarútino, urged Kutúzov to carry out Dórokhov's suggestion. Kutúzov did not consider any offensive necessary. The result was a compromise which was inevitable: a small detachment was sent to Formínsk to attack Broussier.

By a strange coincidence, this task, which turned out to be a most difficult and important one, was entrusted to Dokhtúrov—that same modest little Dokhtúrov whom no one had described to us as drawing up plans of battles, dashing about in front of regiments, showering crosses on batteries, and so on, and who was thought to be and was spoken of as undecided and undiscerning—but whom we find commanding wherever the position was most difficult all through the Russo-French wars from Austerlitz to the year 1813. At Austerlitz he remained last at the Augezd dam, rallying the regiments, saving what was possible when all were flying and perishing and not a single general was left in the rear guard. Ill with fever he went to Smolénsk with twenty thousand men to defend the town against Napoleon's whole army. In Smolénsk, at the Malákhov Gate, he had hardly dozed off in a paroxysm of fever before he was awakened by the bombardment of the town—and Smolénsk held out all day long. At the battle of Borodinó, when Bagratión was killed and nine tenths of the men of our left flank had fallen and the full force of the French artillery fire was directed against it, the man sent there was this same irresolute and undiscerning Dokhtúrov—Kutúzov hastening to rectify a mistake he had made by sending someone else there first. And the quiet little Dokhtúrov rode thither, and Borodinó became the greatest glory of the Russian army. Many heroes have been described to us in verse and prose, but of Dokhtúrov scarcely a word has been said.

It was Dokhtúrov again whom they sent to Formínsk and from there to Málo-Yaroslávets, the place where the last battle with the French was fought and where the obvious disintegration of the French army began; and we are told of many geniuses and heroes of that period of the campaign, but of Dokhtúrov nothing or very little is said and that dubiously. And this silence about Dokhtúrov is the clearest testimony to his merit.

It is natural for a man who does not understand the workings of a machine to imagine that a shaving that has fallen into it by chance and is interfering with its action and tossing about in it is its most important part. The man who does not understand the construction of the machine cannot conceive that the small connecting cogwheel which revolves quietly is one of the most essential parts of the machine, and not the shaving which merely harms and hinders the working.

On the tenth of October when Dokhtúrov had gone halfway to Formínsk and stopped at the village of Aristóvo, preparing faithfully to execute the orders he had received, the whole French army having, in its convulsive movement, reached Murat's position apparently in order to give battle—suddenly without any reason turned off to the left onto the new Kalúga road and began to enter Formínsk, where only Broussier had been till then. At that time Dokhtúrov had under his command, besides Dórokhov's detachment, the two small guerrilla detachments of Figner and Seslávin.

On the evening of October 11 Seslávin came to the Aristóvo headquarters with a French guardsman he had captured. The prisoner said that the troops that had entered Formínsk that day were the vanguard of the whole army, that Napoleon was there and the whole army had left Moscow four days previously. That same evening a house serf who had come from Bórovsk said he had seen an immense army entering the town. Some Cossacks of Dokhtúrov's detachment reported having sighted the French Guards marching along the road to Bórovsk. From all these reports it was evident that where they had expected to meet a single division there was now the whole French army marching from Moscow in an unexpected direction—along the Kalúga road. Dokhtúrov was unwilling to undertake any action, as it was not clear to him now what he ought to do. He had been ordered to attack Formínsk. But only Broussier had been there at that time and now the whole French army was there. Ermólov wished to act on his own judgment, but Dokhtúrov insisted that he must have Kutúzov's instructions. So it was decided to send a dispatch to the staff.

For this purpose a capable officer, Bolkhovítinov, was chosen, who was to explain the whole affair by word of mouth, besides delivering a written report. Toward midnight Bolkhovítinov, having received the dispatch and verbal instructions, galloped off to the General Staff accompanied by a Cossack with spare horses.

# XVI

It was a warm, dark, autumn night. It had been raining for four days. Having changed horses twice and galloped twenty miles in an hour and a half over a sticky, muddy road, Bolkhovítinov reached Litashëvka after one o'clock at night. Dismounting at a cottage on whose wattle fence hung a signboard, GENERAL STAFF, and throwing down his reins, he entered a dark passage.

"The general on duty, quick! It's very important!" said he to someone who had risen and was sniffing in the dark passage.

"He has been very unwell since the evening and this is the third night he has not slept," said the orderly pleadingly in a whisper. "You should wake the captain first."

"But this is very important, from General Dokhtúrov," said Bolkhovítinov, entering the open door which he had found by feeling in the dark.

The orderly had gone in before him and began waking somebody.

"Your honor, your honor! A courier."

"What? What's that? From whom?" came a sleepy voice.

"From Dokhtúrov and from Alexéy Petróvich. Napoleon is at Formínsk," said Bolkhovítinov, unable to see in the dark who was speaking but guessing by the voice that it was not Konovnítsyn.

The man who had wakened yawned and stretched himself.

"I don't like waking him," he said, fumbling for something. "He is very ill. Perhaps this is only a rumor."

"Here is the dispatch," said Bolkhovítinov. "My orders are to give it at once to the general on duty."

"Wait a moment, I'll light a candle. You damned rascal, where do you always hide it?" said the voice of the man who was stretching himself, to the orderly. (This was Shcherbínin, Konovnítsyn's adjutant.) "I've found it, I've found it!" he added.

The orderly was striking a light and Shcherbínin was fumbling for something on the candlestick.

"Oh, the nasty beasts!" said he with disgust.

By the light of the sparks Bolkhovítinov saw Shcherbínin's youthful face as he held the candle, and the face of another man who was still asleep. This was Konovnítsyn.

When the flame of the sulphur splinters kindled by the tinder burned up, first blue and then red, Shcherbínin lit the tallow candle, from the candlestick of which the cockroaches that had been gnawing it were running away, and looked at the messenger. Bolkhovítinov was bespattered all over with mud and had smeared his face by wiping it with his sleeve.

"Who gave the report?" inquired Shcherbínin, taking the envelope.

"The news is reliable," said Bolkhovítinov. "Prisoners, Cossacks, and the scouts all say the same thing."

"There's nothing to be done, we'll have to wake him," said Shcherbínin, rising and going up to the man in the nightcap who lay covered by a greatcoat. "Peter Petróvich!" said he. (Konovnítsyn did not stir.) "To the General Staff!" he said with a smile, knowing that those words would be sure to arouse him.

And in fact the head in the nightcap was lifted at once. On Konovnítsyn's handsome, resolute face with cheeks flushed by fever, there still remained for an instant a faraway dreamy expression remote from present affairs, but then he suddenly started and his face assumed its habitual calm and firm appearance.

"Well, what is it? From whom?" he asked immediately but without hurry, blinking at the light.

While listening to the officer's report Konovnítsyn broke the seal and read the dispatch. Hardly had he done so before he lowered his legs in their woolen stockings to the earthen floor and began putting on his boots. Then he took off his nightcap, combed his hair over his temples, and donned his cap.

"Did you get here quickly? Let us go to his Highness."

Konovnítsyn had understood at once that the news brought was of great importance and that no time must be lost. He did not consider or ask himself whether the news was good or bad. That did not interest him. He regarded the whole business of the war not with his intelligence or his reason but by something else. There was within him a deep unexpressed conviction that all would be well, but that one must not trust to this and still less speak about it, but must only attend to one's own work. And he did his work, giving his whole strength to the task.

Peter Petróvich Konovnítsyn, like Dokhtúrov, seems to have been included merely for propriety's sake in the list of the so-called heroes of 1812—the Barclays, Raévskis, Ermólovs, Plátovs, and Milorádoviches. Like Dokhtúrov he had the reputation of being a man of very limited capacity and information, and like Dokhtúrov he never made plans of battle but was always found where the situation was most difficult. Since his appointment as general on duty he had always slept with his door open, giving orders that every messenger should be allowed to wake him up. In battle he was always under fire, so that Kutúzov reproved him for it and feared to send him to the front, and like Dokhtúrov he was one of those unnoticed cogwheels that, without clatter or noise, constitute the most essential part of the machine.

Coming out of the hut into the damp, dark night Konovnítsyn frowned—partly from an increased pain in his head and partly at the unpleasant thought that occurred to him, of how all that nest of influential men on the staff would be stirred up by this news, especially Bennigsen, who ever since Tarútino had been at daggers drawn with Kutúzov; and how they would make suggestions, quarrel, issue orders, and rescind them. And this premonition was disagreeable to him though he knew it could not be helped.

And in fact Toll, to whom he went to communicate the news, immediately began to expound his plans to a general sharing his quarters, until Konovnítsyn, who listened in weary silence, reminded him that they must go to see his Highness.

# XVII

Kutúzov like all old people did not sleep much at night. He often fell asleep unexpectedly in the daytime, but at night, lying on his bed without undressing, he generally remained awake thinking.

So he lay now on his bed, supporting his large, heavy, scarred head on his plump hand, with his one eye open, meditating and peering into the darkness.

Since Bennigsen, who corresponded with the Emperor and had more influence than anyone else on the staff, had begun to avoid him, Kutúzov was more at ease as to the possibility of himself and his troops being obliged to take part in useless aggressive movements. The lesson of the Tarútino battle and of the day before it, which Kutúzov remembered with pain, must, he thought, have some effect on others too.

"They must understand that we can only lose by taking the offensive. Patience and time are my warriors, my champions," thought Kutúzov. He knew that an apple should not be plucked while it is green. It will fall of itself when ripe, but if picked unripe the apple is spoiled, the tree is harmed, and your teeth are set on edge. Like an experienced sportsman he knew that the beast was wounded, and wounded as only the whole strength of Russia could have wounded it, but whether it was mortally wounded or not was still an undecided question. Now by the fact of Lauriston and Barthélemi having been sent, and by the reports of the guerrillas, Kutúzov was almost sure that the wound was mortal. But he needed further proofs and it was necessary to wait.

"They want to run to see how they have wounded it. Wait and we shall see! Continual maneuvers, continual advances!" thought he. "What for? Only to distinguish themselves! As if fighting were fun. They are like children from whom one can't get any sensible account of what has happened because they all want to show how well they can fight. But that's not what is needed now.

"And what ingenious maneuvers they all propose to me! It seems to them that when they have thought of two or three contingencies" (he remembered the general plan sent him from Petersburg) "they have foreseen everything. But the contingencies are endless."

The undecided question as to whether the wound inflicted at Borodinó was mortal or not had hung over Kutúzov's head for a whole month. On the one hand the French had occupied Moscow. On the other Kutúzov felt assured with all his being that the terrible blow into which he and all the Russians had put their whole strength must have been mortal. But in any case proofs were needed; he had waited a whole month for them and grew more impatient the longer he waited. Lying on his bed during those sleepless nights he did just what he reproached those younger generals for doing. He imagined all sorts of possible contingencies, just like the younger men, but with this difference, that he saw thousands of contingencies instead of two or three and based nothing on them. The longer he thought the more contingencies presented themselves. He imagined all sorts of movements of the Napoleonic army as a whole or in sections—against Petersburg, or against him, or to outflank him. He thought too of the possibility (which he feared most of all) that Napoleon might fight him with his own weapon and remain in Moscow awaiting him. Kutúzov even imagined that Napoleon's army might turn back through Medýn and Yukhnóv, but the one thing he could not foresee was what happened—the insane, convulsive stampede of Napoleon's army during its first eleven days after leaving Moscow: a stampede which made possible what Kutúzov had not yet even dared to think of—the complete extermination of the French. Dórokhov's report about Broussier's division, the guerrillas' reports of distress in Napoleon's army, rumors of preparations for leaving Moscow, all confirmed the supposition that the French army was beaten and preparing for flight. But these were only suppositions, which seemed important to the younger men but not to Kutúzov. With his sixty years' experience he knew what value to attach to rumors, knew how apt people who desire anything are to group all news so that it appears to confirm what they desire, and he knew how readily in such cases they omit all that makes for the contrary. And the more he desired it the less he allowed himself to believe it. This question absorbed all his mental powers. All else was to him only life's customary routine. To such customary routine belonged his conversations with the staff, the letters he wrote from Tarútino to Madame de Staël, the reading of novels, the distribution of awards, his correspondence with Petersburg, and so on. But the destruction of the French, which he alone foresaw, was his heart's one desire.

On the night of the eleventh of October he lay leaning on his arm and thinking of that.

There was a stir in the next room and he heard the steps of Toll, Konovnítsyn, and Bolkhovítinov.

"Eh, who's there? Come in, come in! What news?" the field marshal called out to them.

While a footman was lighting a candle, Toll communicated the substance of the news.

"Who brought it?" asked Kutúzov with a look which, when the candle was lit, struck Toll by its cold severity.

"There can be no doubt about it, your Highness."

"Call him in, call him here."

Kutúzov sat up with one leg hanging down from the bed and his big paunch resting against the other which was doubled under him. He screwed up his seeing eye to scrutinize the messenger more carefully, as if wishing to read in his face what preoccupied his own mind.

"Tell me, tell me, friend," said he to Bolkhovítinov in his low, aged voice, as he pulled together the shirt which gaped open on his chest, "come nearer—nearer. What news have you brought me? Eh? That Napoleon has left Moscow? Are you sure? Eh?"

Bolkhovítinov gave a detailed account from the beginning of all he had been told to report.

"Speak quicker, quicker! Don't torture me!" Kutúzov interrupted him.

Bolkhovítinov told him everything and was then silent, awaiting instructions. Toll was beginning to say something but Kutúzov checked him. He tried to say something, but his face suddenly puckered and wrinkled; he waved his arm at Toll and turned to the opposite side of the room, to the corner darkened by the icons that hung there.

"O Lord, my Creator, Thou has heard our prayer. . ." said he in a tremulous voice with folded hands. "Russia is saved. I thank Thee, O Lord!" and he wept.

# XVIII

From the time he received this news to the end of the campaign all Kutúzov's activity was directed toward restraining his troops, by authority, by guile, and by entreaty, from useless attacks, maneuvers, or encounters with the perishing enemy. Dokhtúrov went to Málo-Yaroslávets, but Kutúzov lingered with the main army and gave orders for the evacuation of Kalúga—a retreat beyond which town seemed to him quite possible.

Everywhere Kutúzov retreated, but the enemy without waiting for his retreat fled in the opposite direction.

Napoleon's historians describe to us his skilled maneuvers at Tarútino and Málo-Yaroslávets, and make conjectures as to what would have happened had Napoleon been in time to penetrate into the rich southern provinces.

But not to speak of the fact that nothing prevented him from advancing into those southern provinces (for the Russian army did not bar his way), the historians forget that nothing could have saved his army, for then already it bore within itself the germs of inevitable ruin. How could that army—which had found abundant supplies in Moscow and had trampled them underfoot instead of keeping them, and on arriving at Smolénsk had looted provisions instead of storing them—how could that army recuperate in Kalúga province, which was inhabited by Russians such as those who lived in Moscow, and where fire had the same property of consuming what was set ablaze?

That army could not recover anywhere. Since the battle of Borodinó and the pillage of Moscow it had borne within itself, as it were, the chemical elements of dissolution.

The members of what had once been an army—Napoleon himself and all his soldiers—fled without knowing whither, each concerned only to make his escape as quickly as possible from this position, of the hopelessness of which they were all more or less vaguely conscious.

So it came about that at the council at Málo-Yaroslávets, when the generals pretending to confer together expressed various opinions, all mouths were closed by the opinion uttered by the simple-minded soldier Mouton who, speaking last, said what they all felt: that the one thing needful was to get away as quickly as possible; and no one, not even Napoleon, could say anything against that truth which they all recognized.

But though they all realized that it was necessary to get away, there still remained a feeling of shame at admitting that they must flee. An external shock was needed to overcome that shame, and this shock came in due time. It was what the French called "le hourra de l'Empereur."

The day after the council at Málo-Yaroslávets Napoleon rode out early in the morning amid the lines of his army with his suite of marshals and an escort, on the pretext of inspecting the army and the scene of the previous and of the impending battle. Some Cossacks on the prowl for booty fell in with the Emperor and very nearly captured him. If the Cossacks did not capture Napoleon then, what saved him was the very thing that was destroying the French army, the booty on which the Cossacks fell. Here as at Tarútino they went after plunder, leaving the men. Disregarding Napoleon they rushed after the plunder and Napoleon managed to escape.

When les enfants du Don might so easily have taken the Emperor himself in the midst of his army, it was clear that there was nothing for it but to fly as fast as possible along the nearest, familiar road. Napoleon with his forty-year-old stomach understood that hint, not feeling his former agility and boldness, and under the influence of the fright the Cossacks had given him he at once agreed with Mouton and issued orders—as the historians tell us—to retreat by the Smolénsk road.

That Napoleon agreed with Mouton, and that the army retreated, does not prove that Napoleon caused it to retreat, but that the forces which influenced the whole army and directed it along the Mozháysk (that is, the Smolénsk) road acted simultaneously on him also.

# XIX

A man in motion always devises an aim for that motion. To be able to go a thousand miles he must imagine that something good awaits him at the end of those thousand miles. One must have the prospect of a promised land to have the strength to move.

The promised land for the French during their advance had been Moscow, during their retreat it was their native land. But that native land was too far off, and for a man going a thousand miles it is absolutely necessary to set aside his final goal and to say to himself: "Today I shall get to a place twenty-five miles off where I shall rest and spend the night," and during the first day's journey that resting place eclipses his ultimate goal and attracts all his hopes and desires. And the impulses felt by a single person are always magnified in a crowd.

For the French retreating along the old Smolénsk road, the final goal—their native land—was too remote, and their immediate goal was Smolénsk, toward which all their desires and hopes, enormously intensified in the mass, urged them on. It was not that they knew that much food and fresh troops awaited them in Smolénsk, nor that they were told so (on the contrary their superior officers, and Napoleon himself, knew that provisions were scarce there), but because this alone could give them strength to move on and endure their present privations. So both those who knew and those who did not know deceived themselves, and pushed on to Smolénsk as to a promised land.

Coming out onto the highroad the French fled with surprising energy and unheard-of rapidity toward the goal they had fixed on. Besides the common impulse which bound the whole crowd of French into one mass and supplied them with a certain energy, there was another cause binding them together—their great numbers. As with the physical law of gravity, their enormous mass drew the individual human atoms to itself. In their hundreds of thousands they moved like a whole nation.

Each of them desired nothing more than to give himself up as a prisoner to escape from all this horror and misery; but on the one hand the force of this common attraction to Smolénsk, their goal, drew each of them in the same direction; on the other hand an army corps could not surrender to a company, and though the French availed themselves of every convenient opportunity to detach themselves and to surrender on the slightest decent pretext, such pretexts did not always occur. Their very numbers and their crowded and swift movement deprived them of that possibility and rendered it not only difficult but impossible for the Russians to stop this movement, to which the French were directing all their energies. Beyond a certain limit no mechanical disruption of the body could hasten the process of decomposition.

A lump of snow cannot be melted instantaneously. There is a certain limit of time in less than which no amount of heat can melt the snow. On the contrary the greater the heat the more solidified the remaining snow becomes.

Of the Russian commanders Kutúzov alone understood this. When the flight of the French army along the Smolénsk road became well defined, what Konovnítsyn had foreseen on the night of the eleventh of October began to occur. The superior officers all wanted to distinguish themselves, to cut off, to seize, to capture, and to overthrow the French, and all clamored for action.

Kutúzov alone used all his power (and such power is very limited in the case of any commander in chief) to prevent an attack.

He could not tell them what we say now: "Why fight, why block the road, losing our own men and inhumanly slaughtering unfortunate wretches? What is the use of that, when a third of their army has melted away on the road from Moscow to Vyázma without any battle?" But drawing from his aged wisdom what they could understand, he told them of the golden bridge, and they laughed at and slandered him, flinging themselves on, rending and exulting over the dying beast.

Ermólov, Milorádovich, Plátov, and others in proximity to the French near Vyázma could not resist their desire to cut off and break up two French corps, and by way of reporting their intention to Kutúzov they sent him a blank sheet of paper in an envelope.

And try as Kutúzov might to restrain the troops, our men attacked, trying to bar the road. Infantry regiments, we are told, advanced to the attack with music and with drums beating, and killed and lost thousands of men.

But they did not cut off or overthrow anybody and the French army, closing up more firmly at the danger, continued, while steadily melting away, to pursue its fatal path to Smolénsk.

BOOK FOURTEEN

1812

# I

The Battle of Borodinó, with the occupation of Moscow that followed it and the flight of the French without further conflicts, is one of the most instructive phenomena in history.

All historians agree that the external activity of states and nations in their conflicts with one another is expressed in wars, and that as a direct result of greater or less success in war the political strength of states and nations increases or decreases.

Strange as may be the historical account of how some king or emperor, having quarreled with another, collects an army, fights his enemy's army, gains a victory by killing three, five, or ten thousand men, and subjugates a kingdom and an entire nation of several millions, all the facts of history (as far as we know it) confirm the truth of the statement that the greater or lesser success of one army against another is the cause, or at least an essential indication, of an increase or decrease in the strength of the nation—even though it is unintelligible why the defeat of an army—a hundredth part of a nation—should oblige that whole nation to submit. An army gains a victory, and at once the rights of the conquering nation have increased to the detriment of the defeated. An army has suffered defeat, and at once a people loses its rights in proportion to the severity of the reverse, and if its army suffers a complete defeat the nation is quite subjugated.

So according to history it has been found from the most ancient times, and so it is to our own day. All Napoleon's wars serve to confirm this rule. In proportion to the defeat of the Austrian army Austria loses its rights, and the rights and the strength of France increase. The victories of the French at Jena and Auerstädt destroy the independent existence of Prussia.

But then, in 1812, the French gain a victory near Moscow. Moscow is taken and after that, with no further battles, it is not Russia that ceases to exist, but the French army of six hundred thousand, and then Napoleonic France itself. To strain the facts to fit the rules of history: to say that the field of battle at Borodinó remained in the hands of the Russians, or that after Moscow there were other battles that destroyed Napoleon's army, is impossible.

After the French victory at Borodinó there was no general engagement nor any that were at all serious, yet the French army ceased to exist. What does this mean? If it were an example taken from the history of China, we might say that it was not an historic phenomenon (which is the historians' usual expedient when anything does not fit their standards); if the matter concerned some brief conflict in which only a small number of troops took part, we might treat it as an exception; but this event occurred before our fathers' eyes, and for them it was a question of the life or death of their fatherland, and it happened in the greatest of all known wars.

The period of the campaign of 1812 from the battle of Borodinó to the expulsion of the French proved that the winning of a battle does not produce a conquest and is not even an invariable indication of conquest; it proved that the force which decides the fate of peoples lies not in the conquerors, nor even in armies and battles, but in something else.

The French historians, describing the condition of the French army before it left Moscow, affirm that all was in order in the Grand Army, except the cavalry, the artillery, and the transport—there was no forage for the horses or the cattle. That was a misfortune no one could remedy, for the peasants of the district burned their hay rather than let the French have it.

The victory gained did not bring the usual results because the peasants Karp and Vlas (who after the French had evacuated Moscow drove in their carts to pillage the town, and in general personally failed to manifest any heroic feelings), and the whole innumerable multitude of such peasants, did not bring their hay to Moscow for the high price offered them, but burned it instead.

Let us imagine two men who have come out to fight a duel with rapiers according to all the rules of the art of fencing. The fencing has gone on for some time; suddenly one of the combatants, feeling himself wounded and understanding that the matter is no joke but concerns his life, throws down his rapier, and seizing the first cudgel that comes to hand begins to brandish it. Then let us imagine that the combatant who so sensibly employed the best and simplest means to attain his end was at the same time influenced by traditions of chivalry and, desiring to conceal the facts of the case, insisted that he had gained his victory with the rapier according to all the rules of art. One can imagine what confusion and obscurity would result from such an account of the duel.

The fencer who demanded a contest according to the rules of fencing was the French army; his opponent who threw away the rapier and snatched up the cudgel was the Russian people; those who try to explain the matter according to the rules of fencing are the historians who have described the event.

After the burning of Smolénsk a war began which did not follow any previous traditions of war. The burning of towns and villages, the retreats after battles, the blow dealt at Borodinó and the renewed retreat, the burning of Moscow, the capture of marauders, the seizure of transports, and the guerrilla war were all departures from the rules.

Napoleon felt this, and from the time he took up the correct fencing attitude in Moscow and instead of his opponent's rapier saw a cudgel raised above his head, he did not cease to complain to Kutúzov and to the Emperor Alexander that the war was being carried on contrary to all the rules—as if there were any rules for killing people. In spite of the complaints of the French as to the nonobservance of the rules, in spite of the fact that to some highly placed Russians it seemed rather disgraceful to fight with a cudgel and they wanted to assume a pose en quarte or en tierce according to all the rules, and to make an adroit thrust en prime, and so on—the cudgel of the people's war was lifted with all its menacing and majestic strength, and without consulting anyone's tastes or rules and regardless of anything else, it rose and fell with stupid simplicity, but consistently, and belabored the French till the whole invasion had perished.

And it is well for a people who do not—as the French did in 1813—salute according to all the rules of art, and, presenting the hilt of their rapier gracefully and politely, hand it to their magnanimous conqueror, but at the moment of trial, without asking what rules others have adopted in similar cases, simply and easily pick up the first cudgel that comes to hand and strike with it till the feeling of resentment and revenge in their soul yields to a feeling of contempt and compassion.

O ne of the most obvious and advantageous departures from the so-called laws of war is the action of scattered groups against men pressed together in a mass. Such action always occurs in wars that take on a national character. In such actions, instead of two crowds opposing each other, the men disperse, attack singly, run away when attacked by stronger forces, but again attack when opportunity offers. This was done by the guerrillas in Spain, by the mountain tribes in the Caucasus, and by the Russians in 1812.

People have called this kind of war "guerrilla warfare" and assume that by so calling it they have explained its meaning. But such a war does not fit in under any rule and is directly opposed to a well-known rule of tactics which is accepted as infallible. That rule says that an attacker should concentrate his forces in order to be stronger than his opponent at the moment of conflict.

Guerrilla war (always successful, as history shows) directly infringes that rule.

This contradiction arises from the fact that military science assumes the strength of an army to be identical with its numbers. Military science says that the more troops the greater the strength. Les gros bataillons ont toujours raison.*

For military science to say this is like defining momentum in mechanics by reference to the mass only: stating that momenta are equal or unequal to each other simply because the masses involved are equal or unequal.

Momentum (quantity of motion) is the product of mass and velocity.

In military affairs the strength of an army is the product of its mass and some unknown x.

Military science, seeing in history innumerable instances of the fact that the size of any army does not coincide with its strength and that small detachments defeat larger ones, obscurely admits the existence of this unknown factor and tries to discover it—now in a geometric formation, now in the equipment employed, now, and most usually, in the genius of the commanders. But the assignment of these various

---

* Large battalions are always victorious.

meanings to the factor does not yield results which accord with the historic facts.

Yet it is only necessary to abandon the false view (adopted to gratify the "heroes") of the efficacy of the directions issued in wartime by commanders, in order to find this unknown quantity.

That unknown quantity is the spirit of the army, that is to say, the greater or lesser readiness to fight and face danger felt by all the men composing an army, quite independently of whether they are, or are not, fighting under the command of a genius, in two—or three-line formation, with cudgels or with rifles that repeat thirty times a minute. Men who want to fight will always put themselves in the most advantageous conditions for fighting.

The spirit of an army is the factor which multiplied by the mass gives the resulting force. To define and express the significance of this unknown factor—the spirit of an army—is a problem for science.

This problem is only solvable if we cease arbitrarily to substitute for the unknown x itself the conditions under which that force becomes apparent—such as the commands of the general, the equipment employed, and so on—mistaking these for the real significance of the factor, and if we recognize this unknown quantity in its entirety as being the greater or lesser desire to fight and to face danger. Only then, expressing known historic facts by equations and comparing the relative significance of this factor, can we hope to define the unknown.

Ten men, battalions, or divisions, fighting fifteen men, battalions, or divisions, conquer—that is, kill or take captive—all the others, while themselves losing four, so that on the one side four and on the other fifteen were lost. Consequently the four were equal to the fifteen, and therefore $4x = 15y$. Consequently $x/y = 15/4$. This equation does not give us the value of the unknown factor but gives us a ratio between two unknowns. And by bringing variously selected historic units (battles, campaigns, periods of war) into such equations, a series of numbers could be obtained in which certain laws should exist and might be discovered.

The tactical rule that an army should act in masses when attacking, and in smaller groups in retreat, unconsciously confirms the truth that the strength of an army depends on its spirit. To lead men forward under fire more discipline (obtainable only by movement in masses) is needed than is needed to resist attacks. But this rule which leaves out of account the spirit of the army continually proves incorrect and is in particularly striking contrast to the facts when some strong rise or fall in the spirit of the troops occurs, as in all national wars.

The French, retreating in 1812—though according to tactics they should have separated into detachments to defend themselves—congregated into a mass because the spirit of the army had so fallen that only the mass held the army together. The Russians, on the contrary, ought according to tactics to have attacked in mass, but in fact they split up into small units, because their spirit had so risen that separate individuals, without orders, dealt blows at the French without needing any compulsion to induce them to expose themselves to hardships and dangers.

# III

The so-called partisan war began with the entry of the French into Smolénsk.

Before partisan warfare had been officially recognized by the government, thousands of enemy stragglers, marauders, and foragers had been destroyed by the Cossacks and the peasants, who killed them off as instinctively as dogs worry a stray mad dog to death. Denís Davýdov, with his Russian instinct, was the first to recognize the value of this terrible cudgel which regardless of the rules of military science destroyed the French, and to him belongs the credit for taking the first step toward regularizing this method of warfare.

On August 24 Davýdov's first partisan detachment was formed and then others were recognized. The further the campaign progressed the more numerous these detachments became.

The irregulars destroyed the great army piecemeal. They gathered the fallen leaves that dropped of themselves from that withered tree—the French army—and sometimes shook that tree itself. By October, when the French were fleeing toward Smolénsk, there were hundreds of such companies, of various sizes and characters. There were some that adopted all the army methods and had infantry, artillery, staffs, and the comforts of life. Others consisted solely of Cossack cavalry. There were also small scratch groups of foot and horse, and groups of peasants and landowners that remained unknown. A sacristan commanded one party which captured several hundred prisoners in the course of a month; and there was Vasílisa, the wife of a village elder, who slew hundreds of the French.

The partisan warfare flamed up most fiercely in the latter days of October. Its first period had passed: when the partisans themselves, amazed at their own boldness, feared every minute to be surrounded and captured by the French, and hid in the forests without unsaddling, hardly daring to dismount and always expecting to be pursued. By the end of October this kind of warfare had taken definite shape: it had become clear to all what could be ventured against the French and what could not. Now only the commanders of detachments with staffs, and moving according to rules at a distance from the French, still regarded many things as impossible. The small bands that had started their activities long before and had already observed the French closely considered things possible which the commanders of the big detachments did not dare to contemplate. The Cossacks and peasants who crept in among the French now considered everything possible.

On October 22, Denísov (who was one of the irregulars) was with his group at the height of the guerrilla enthusiasm. Since early morning he and his party had been on the move. All day long he had been watching from the forest that skirted the highroad a large French convoy of cavalry baggage and Russian prisoners separated from the rest of the army, which—as was learned from spies and prisoners— was moving under a strong escort to Smolénsk. Besides Denísov and Dólokhov (who also led a small party and moved in Denísov's vicinity), the commanders of some large divisions with staffs also knew of this convoy and, as Denísov expressed it, were sharpening their teeth for it. Two of the commanders of large parties—one a Pole and the other a German—sent invitations to Denísov almost simultaneously, requesting him to join up with their divisions to attack the convoy.

"No, bwother, I have gwown mustaches myself," said Denísov on reading these documents, and he wrote to the German that, despite his heartfelt desire to serve under so valiant and renowned a general, he had to forgo that pleasure because he was already under the command of the Polish general. To the Polish general he replied to the same effect, informing him that he was already under the command of the German.

Having arranged matters thus, Denísov and Dólokhov intended, without reporting matters to the higher command, to attack and seize that convoy with their own small forces. On October 22 it was moving from the village of Mikúlino to that of Shámshevo. To the left of the road between Mikúlino and Shámshevo there were large forests, extending in some places up to the road itself though in others a mile or more back from it. Through these forests Denísov and his party rode all day, sometimes keeping well back in them and sometimes coming to the very edge, but never losing sight of the moving French. That morning, Cossacks of Denísov's party had seized and carried off into the forest two wagons loaded with cavalry saddles, which had stuck in the mud not far from Mikúlino where the forest ran close to the road. Since then, and until evening, the party had watched the movements of the French without attacking. It was necessary to let the French reach Shámshevo quietly without alarming them and then, after joining Dólokhov who was to come that evening to a consultation at a watchman's hut in the forest less than a mile from Shámshevo, to surprise the French at dawn, falling like an avalanche on their heads from two sides, and rout and capture them all at one blow.

In their rear, more than a mile from Mikúlino where the forest came right up to the road, six Cossacks were posted to report if any fresh columns of French should show themselves.

Beyond Shámshevo, Dólokhov was to observe the road in the same way, to find out at what distance there were other French troops. They reckoned that the convoy had fifteen hundred men. Denísov had two hundred, and Dólokhov might have as many more, but the disparity of numbers did not deter Denísov. All that he now wanted to know was what troops these were and to learn that he had to capture a "tongue"— that is, a man from the enemy column. That morning's attack on the wagons had been made so hastily that the Frenchmen with the wagons had all been killed; only a little drummer boy had been taken alive, and as he was a straggler he could tell them nothing definite about the troops in that column.

Denísov considered it dangerous to make a second attack for fear of putting the whole column on the alert, so he sent Tíkhon Shcherbáty, a peasant of his party, to Shámshevo to try and seize at least one of the French quartermasters who had been sent on in advance.

# IV

I t was a warm rainy autumn day. The sky and the horizon were both the color of muddy water. At times a sort of mist descended, and then suddenly heavy slanting rain came down.

Denísov in a felt cloak and a sheepskin cap from which the rain ran down was riding a thin thoroughbred horse with sunken sides. Like his horse, which turned its head and laid its ears back, he shrank from the driving rain and gazed anxiously before him. His thin face with its short, thick black beard looked angry.

Beside Denísov rode an esaul,* Denísov's fellow worker, also in felt cloak and sheepskin cap, and riding a large sleek Don horse.

Esaul Lováyski the Third was a tall man as straight as an arrow, pale-faced, fair-haired, with narrow light eyes and with calm self-satisfaction in his face and bearing. Though it was impossible to say in what the peculiarity of the horse and rider lay, yet at first glance at the esaul and Denísov one saw that the latter was wet and uncomfortable and was a man mounted on a horse, while looking at the esaul one saw that he was as comfortable and as much at ease as always and that he was not a man who had mounted a horse, but a man who was one with his horse, a being consequently possessed of twofold strength.

A little ahead of them walked a peasant guide, wet to the skin and wearing a gray peasant coat and a white knitted cap.

A little behind, on a poor, small, lean Kirghíz mount with an enormous tail and mane and a bleeding mouth, rode a young officer in a blue French overcoat.

Beside him rode an hussar, with a boy in a tattered French uniform and blue cap behind him on the crupper of his horse. The boy held on to the hussar with cold, red hands, and raising his eyebrows gazed about him with surprise. This was the French drummer boy captured that morning.

Behind them along the narrow, sodden, cut up forest road came hussars in threes and fours, and then Cossacks: some in felt cloaks, some in French greatcoats, and some with horsecloths over their heads. The horses, being drenched by the rain, all looked black whether chestnut or bay. Their necks, with their wet, close-clinging manes, looked strangely

---

* A captain of Cossacks.

thin. Steam rose from them. Clothes, saddles, reins, were all wet, slippery, and sodden, like the ground and the fallen leaves that strewed the road. The men sat huddled up trying not to stir, so as to warm the water that had trickled to their bodies and not admit the fresh cold water that was leaking in under their seats, their knees, and at the back of their necks. In the midst of the outspread line of Cossacks two wagons, drawn by French horses and by saddled Cossack horses that had been hitched on in front, rumbled over the tree stumps and branches and splashed through the water that lay in the ruts.

Denísov's horse swerved aside to avoid a pool in the track and bumped his rider's knee against a tree.

"Oh, the devil!" exclaimed Denísov angrily, and showing his teeth he struck his horse three times with his whip, splashing himself and his comrades with mud.

Denísov was out of sorts both because of the rain and also from hunger (none of them had eaten anything since morning), and yet more because he still had no news from Dólokhov and the man sent to capture a "tongue" had not returned.

"There'll hardly be another such chance to fall on a transport as today. It's too risky to attack them by oneself, and if we put it off till another day one of the big guerrilla detachments will snatch the prey from under our noses," thought Denísov, continually peering forward, hoping to see a messenger from Dólokhov.

On coming to a path in the forest along which he could see far to the right, Denísov stopped.

"There's someone coming," said he.

The esaul looked in the direction Denísov indicated.

"There are two, an officer and a Cossack. But it is not presupposable that it is the lieutenant colonel himself," said the esaul, who was fond of using words the Cossacks did not know.

The approaching riders having descended a decline were no longer visible, but they reappeared a few minutes later. In front, at a weary gallop and using his leather whip, rode an officer, disheveled and drenched, whose trousers had worked up to above his knees. Behind him, standing in the stirrups, trotted a Cossack. The officer, a very young lad with a broad rosy face and keen merry eyes, galloped up to Denísov and handed him a sodden envelope.

"From the general," said the officer. "Please excuse its not being quite dry."

Denísov, frowning, took the envelope and opened it.

"There, they kept telling us: 'It's dangerous, it's dangerous,'" said the officer, addressing the esaul while Denísov was reading the dispatch. "But Komaróv and I"—he pointed to the Cossack—"were prepared. We have each of us two pistols. . . But what's this?" he asked, noticing the French drummer boy. "A prisoner? You've already been in action? May I speak to him?"

"Wostóv! Pétya!" exclaimed Denísov, having run through the dispatch. "Why didn't you say who you were?" and turning with a smile he held out his hand to the lad.

The officer was Pétya Rostóv.

All the way Pétya had been preparing himself to behave with Denísov as befitted a grown-up man and an officer—without hinting at their previous acquaintance. But as soon as Denísov smiled at him Pétya brightened up, blushed with pleasure, forgot the official manner he had been rehearsing, and began telling him how he had already been in a battle near Vyázma and how a certain hussar had distinguished himself there.

"Well, I am glad to see you," Denísov interrupted him, and his face again assumed its anxious expression.

"Michael Feoklítych," said he to the esaul, "this is again fwom that German, you know. He"—he indicated Pétya—"is serving under him."

And Denísov told the esaul that the dispatch just delivered was a repetition of the German general's demand that he should join forces with him for an attack on the transport.

"If we don't take it tomowwow, he'll snatch it fwom under our noses," he added.

While Denísov was talking to the esaul, Pétya—abashed by Denísov's cold tone and supposing that it was due to the condition of his trousers—furtively tried to pull them down under his greatcoat so that no one should notice it, while maintaining as martial an air as possible.

"Will there be any orders, your honor?" he asked Denísov, holding his hand at the salute and resuming the game of adjutant and general for which he had prepared himself, "or shall I remain with your honor?"

"Orders?" Denísov repeated thoughtfully. "But can you stay till tomowwow?"

"Oh, please. . . May I stay with you?" cried Pétya.

"But, just what did the genewal tell you? To weturn at once?" asked Denísov.

Pétya blushed.

"He gave me no instructions. I think I could?" he returned, inquiringly.

"Well, all wight," said Denísov.

And turning to his men he directed a party to go on to the halting place arranged near the watchman's hut in the forest, and told the officer on the Kirghíz horse (who performed the duties of an adjutant) to go and find out where Dólokhov was and whether he would come that evening. Denísov himself intended going with the esaul and Pétya to the edge of the forest where it reached out to Shámshevo, to have a look at the part of the French bivouac they were to attack next day.

"Well, old fellow," said he to the peasant guide, "lead us to Shámshevo."

Denísov, Pétya, and the esaul, accompanied by some Cossacks and the hussar who had the prisoner, rode to the left across a ravine to the edge of the forest.

# V

The rain had stopped, and only the mist was falling and drops from the trees. Denísov, the esaul, and Pétya rode silently, following the peasant in the knitted cap who, stepping lightly with outturned toes and moving noiselessly in his bast shoes over the roots and wet leaves, silently led them to the edge of the forest.

He ascended an incline, stopped, looked about him, and advanced to where the screen of trees was less dense. On reaching a large oak tree that had not yet shed its leaves, he stopped and beckoned mysteriously to them with his hand.

Denísov and Pétya rode up to him. From the spot where the peasant was standing they could see the French. Immediately beyond the forest, on a downward slope, lay a field of spring rye. To the right, beyond a steep ravine, was a small village and a landowner's house with a broken roof. In the village, in the house, in the garden, by the well, by the pond, over all the rising ground, and all along the road uphill from the bridge leading to the village, not more than five hundred yards away, crowds of men could be seen through the shimmering mist. Their un-Russian shouting at their horses which were straining uphill with the carts, and their calls to one another, could be clearly heard.

"Bwing the prisoner here," said Denísov in a low voice, not taking his eyes off the French.

A Cossack dismounted, lifted the boy down, and took him to Denísov. Pointing to the French troops, Denísov asked him what these and those of them were. The boy, thrusting his cold hands into his pockets and lifting his eyebrows, looked at Denísov in affright, but in spite of an evident desire to say all he knew gave confused answers, merely assenting to everything Denísov asked him. Denísov turned away from him frowning and addressed the esaul, conveying his own conjectures to him.

Pétya, rapidly turning his head, looked now at the drummer boy, now at Denísov, now at the esaul, and now at the French in the village and along the road, trying not to miss anything of importance.

"Whether Dólokhov comes or not, we must seize it, eh?" said Denísov with a merry sparkle in his eyes.

"It is a very suitable spot," said the esaul.

"We'll send the infantwy down by the swamps," Denísov continued. "They'll cweep up to the garden; you'll wide up fwom there with the

Cossacks"—he pointed to a spot in the forest beyond the village—"and I with my hussars fwom here. And at the signal shot. . ."

"The hollow is impassable—there's a swamp there," said the esaul. "The horses would sink. We must ride round more to the left. . ."

While they were talking in undertones the crack of a shot sounded from the low ground by the pond, a puff of white smoke appeared, then another, and the sound of hundreds of seemingly merry French voices shouting together came up from the slope. For a moment Denísov and the esaul drew back. They were so near that they thought they were the cause of the firing and shouting. But the firing and shouting did not relate to them. Down below, a man wearing something red was running through the marsh. The French were evidently firing and shouting at him.

"Why, that's our Tíkhon," said the esaul.

"So it is! It is!"

"The wascal!" said Denísov.

"He'll get away!" said the esaul, screwing up his eyes.

The man whom they called Tíkhon, having run to the stream, plunged in so that the water splashed in the air, and, having disappeared for an instant, scrambled out on all fours, all black with the wet, and ran on. The French who had been pursuing him stopped.

"Smart, that!" said the esaul.

"What a beast!" said Denísov with his former look of vexation. "What has he been doing all this time?"

"Who is he?" asked Pétya.

"He's our plastún. I sent him to capture a 'tongue.'"

"Oh, yes," said Pétya, nodding at the first words Denísov uttered as if he understood it all, though he really did not understand anything of it.

Tíkhon Shcherbáty was one of the most indispensable men in their band. He was a peasant from Pokróvsk, near the river Gzhat. When Denísov had come to Pokróvsk at the beginning of his operations and had as usual summoned the village elder and asked him what he knew about the French, the elder, as though shielding himself, had replied, as all village elders did, that he had neither seen nor heard anything of them. But when Denísov explained that his purpose was to kill the French, and asked if no French had strayed that way, the elder replied that some "more-orderers" had really been at their village, but that Tíkhon Shcherbáty was the only man who dealt with such matters. Denísov had Tíkhon called and, having praised him for his activity, said a few words in the elder's presence about loyalty to the Tsar and the country and the hatred of the French that all sons of the fatherland should cherish.

"We don't do the French any harm," said Tíkhon, evidently frightened by Denísov's words. "We only fooled about with the lads for fun, you know! We killed a score or so of 'more-orderers,' but we did no harm else. . ."

Next day when Denísov had left Pokróvsk, having quite forgotten about this peasant, it was reported to him that Tíkhon had attached himself to their party and asked to be allowed to remain with it. Denísov gave orders to let him do so.

Tíkhon, who at first did rough work, laying campfires, fetching water, flaying dead horses, and so on, soon showed a great liking and aptitude for partisan warfare. At night he would go out for booty and always brought back French clothing and weapons, and when told to would bring in French captives also. Denísov then relieved him from drudgery and began taking him with him when he went out on expeditions and had him enrolled among the Cossacks.

Tíkhon did not like riding, and always went on foot, never lagging behind the cavalry. He was armed with a musketoon (which he carried rather as a joke), a pike and an ax, which latter he used as a wolf uses its teeth, with equal ease picking fleas out of its fur or crunching thick bones. Tíkhon with equal accuracy would split logs with blows at arm's length, or holding the head of the ax would cut thin little pegs or carve spoons. In Denísov's party he held a peculiar and exceptional position. When anything particularly difficult or nasty had to be done—to push a cart out of the mud with one's shoulders, pull a horse out of a swamp by its tail, skin it, slink in among the French, or walk more than thirty miles in a day—everybody pointed laughingly at Tíkhon.

"It won't hurt that devil—he's as strong as a horse!" they said of him.

Once a Frenchman Tíkhon was trying to capture fired a pistol at him and shot him in the fleshy part of the back. That wound (which Tíkhon treated only with internal and external applications of vodka) was the subject of the liveliest jokes by the whole detachment—jokes in which Tíkhon readily joined.

"Hallo, mate! Never again? Gave you a twist?" the Cossacks would banter him. And Tíkhon, purposely writhing and making faces, pretended to be angry and swore at the French with the funniest curses.

The only effect of this incident on Tíkhon was that after being wounded he seldom brought in prisoners.

He was the bravest and most useful man in the party. No one found more opportunities for attacking, no one captured or killed more Frenchmen, and consequently he was made the buffoon of all the Cossacks and hussars and willingly accepted that role. Now he had been sent by Denísov overnight to Shámshevo to capture a "tongue." But whether because he had not been content to take only one Frenchman or because he had slept through the night, he had crept by day into some bushes right among the French and, as Denísov had witnessed from above, had been detected by them.

# VI

After talking for some time with the esaul about next day's attack, which now, seeing how near they were to the French, he seemed to have definitely decided on, Denísov turned his horse and rode back.

"Now, my lad, we'll go and get dwy," he said to Pétya.

As they approached the watchhouse Denísov stopped, peering into the forest. Among the trees a man with long legs and long, swinging arms, wearing a short jacket, bast shoes, and a Kazán hat, was approaching with long, light steps. He had a musketoon over his shoulder and an ax stuck in his girdle. When he espied Denísov he hastily threw something into the bushes, removed his sodden hat by its floppy brim, and approached his commander. It was Tíkhon. His wrinkled and pockmarked face and narrow little eyes beamed with self-satisfied merriment. He lifted his head high and gazed at Denísov as if repressing a laugh.

"Well, where did you disappear to?" inquired Denísov.

"Where did I disappear to? I went to get Frenchmen," answered Tíkhon boldly and hurriedly, in a husky but melodious bass voice.

"Why did you push yourself in there by daylight? You ass! Well, why haven't you taken one?"

"Oh, I took one all right," said Tíkhon.

"Where is he?"

"You see, I took him first thing at dawn," Tíkhon continued, spreading out his flat feet with outturned toes in their bast shoes. "I took him into the forest. Then I see he's no good and think I'll go and fetch a likelier one."

"You see? . . . What a wogue—it's just as I thought," said Denísov to the esaul. "Why didn't you bwing that one?"

"What was the good of bringing him?" Tíkhon interrupted hastily and angrily—"that one wouldn't have done for you. As if I don't know what sort you want!"

"What a bwute you are! . . . Well?"

"I went for another one," Tíkhon continued, "and I crept like this through the wood and lay down." (He suddenly lay down on his stomach with a supple movement to show how he had done it.) "One turned up and I grabbed him, like this." (He jumped up quickly and lightly.) "'Come along to the colonel,' I said. He starts yelling, and suddenly there were four of them. They rushed at me with their little swords. So I went for them with my ax, this way: 'What are you up to?' says I. 'Christ be with you!'" shouted Tíkhon, waving his arms with an angry scowl and throwing out his chest.

"Yes, we saw from the hill how you took to your heels through the puddles!" said the esaul, screwing up his glittering eyes.

Pétya badly wanted to laugh, but noticed that they all refrained from laughing. He turned his eyes rapidly from Tíkhon's face to the esaul's and Denísov's, unable to make out what it all meant.

"Don't play the fool!" said Denísov, coughing angrily. "Why didn't you bwing the first one?"

Tíkhon scratched his back with one hand and his head with the other, then suddenly his whole face expanded into a beaming, foolish grin, disclosing a gap where he had lost a tooth (that was why he was called Shcherbáty—the gap-toothed). Denísov smiled, and Pétya burst into a peal of merry laughter in which Tíkhon himself joined.

"Oh, but he was a regular good-for-nothing," said Tíkhon. "The clothes on him—poor stuff! How could I bring him? And so rude, your honor! Why, he says: 'I'm a general's son myself, I won't go!' he says."

"You are a bwute!" said Denísov. "I wanted to question. . ."

"But I questioned him," said Tíkhon. "He said he didn't know much. 'There are a lot of us,' he says, 'but all poor stuff—only soldiers in name,' he says. 'Shout loud at them,' he says, 'and you'll take them all,'" Tíkhon concluded, looking cheerfully and resolutely into Denísov's eyes.

"I'll give you a hundwed sharp lashes—that'll teach you to play the fool!" said Denísov severely.

"But why are you angry?" remonstrated Tíkhon, "just as if I'd never seen your Frenchmen! Only wait till it gets dark and I'll fetch you any of them you want—three if you like."

"Well, let's go," said Denísov, and rode all the way to the watchhouse in silence and frowning angrily.

Tíkhon followed behind and Pétya heard the Cossacks laughing with him and at him, about some pair of boots he had thrown into the bushes.

When the fit of laughter that had seized him at Tíkhon's words and smile had passed and Pétya realized for a moment that this Tíkhon had killed a man, he felt uneasy. He looked round at the captive drummer boy and felt a pang in his heart. But this uneasiness lasted only a moment. He felt it necessary to hold his head higher, to brace himself, and to question the esaul with an air of importance about tomorrow's undertaking, that he might not be unworthy of the company in which he found himself.

The officer who had been sent to inquire met Denísov on the way with the news that Dólokhov was soon coming and that all was well with him.

Denísov at once cheered up and, calling Pétya to him, said: "Well, tell me about yourself."

# VII

Pétya, having left his people after their departure from Moscow, joined his regiment and was soon taken as orderly by a general commanding a large guerrilla detachment. From the time he received his commission, and especially since he had joined the active army and taken part in the battle of Vyázma, Pétya had been in a constant state of blissful excitement at being grown-up and in a perpetual ecstatic hurry not to miss any chance to do something really heroic. He was highly delighted with what he saw and experienced in the army, but at the same time it always seemed to him that the really heroic exploits were being performed just where he did not happen to be. And he was always in a hurry to get where he was not.

When on the twenty-first of October his general expressed a wish to send somebody to Denísov's detachment, Pétya begged so piteously to be sent that the general could not refuse. But when dispatching him he recalled Pétya's mad action at the battle of Vyázma, where instead of riding by the road to the place to which he had been sent, he had galloped to the advanced line under the fire of the French and had there twice fired his pistol. So now the general explicitly forbade his taking part in any action whatever of Denísov's. That was why Pétya had blushed and grown confused when Denísov asked him whether he could stay. Before they had ridden to the outskirts of the forest Pétya had considered he must carry out his instructions strictly and return at once. But when he saw the French and saw Tíkhon and learned that there would certainly be an attack that night, he decided, with the rapidity with which young people change their views, that the general, whom he had greatly respected till then, was a rubbishy German, that Denísov was a hero, the esaul a hero, and Tíkhon a hero too, and that it would be shameful for him to leave them at a moment of difficulty.

It was already growing dusk when Denísov, Pétya, and the esaul rode up to the watchhouse. In the twilight saddled horses could be seen, and Cossacks and hussars who had rigged up rough shelters in the glade and were kindling glowing fires in a hollow of the forest where the French could not see the smoke. In the passage of the small watchhouse a Cossack with sleeves rolled up was chopping some mutton. In the room three officers of Denísov's band were converting a door into a tabletop. Pétya took off his wet clothes, gave them to be dried, and at once began helping the officers to fix up the dinner table.

In ten minutes the table was ready and a napkin spread on it. On the table were vodka, a flask of rum, white bread, roast mutton, and salt.

Sitting at table with the officers and tearing the fat savory mutton with his hands, down which the grease trickled, Pétya was in an ecstatic childish state of love for all men, and consequently of confidence that others loved him in the same way.

"So then what do you think, Vasíli Dmítrich?" said he to Denísov. "It's all right my staying a day with you?" And not waiting for a reply he answered his own question: "You see I was told to find out—well, I am finding out. . . Only do let me into the very. . . into the chief. . . I don't want a reward. . . But I want. . ."

Pétya clenched his teeth and looked around, throwing back his head and flourishing his arms.

"Into the vewy chief. . ." Denísov repeated with a smile.

"Only, please let me command something, so that I may really command. . ." Pétya went on. "What would it be to you? . . . Oh, you want a knife?" he said, turning to an officer who wished to cut himself a piece of mutton.

And he handed him his clasp knife. The officer admired it.

"Please keep it. I have several like it," said Pétya, blushing. "Heavens! I was quite forgetting!" he suddenly cried. "I have some raisins, fine ones; you know, seedless ones. We have a new sutler and he has such capital things. I bought ten pounds. I am used to something sweet. Would you like some? . . ." and Pétya ran out into the passage to his Cossack and brought back some bags which contained about five pounds of raisins. "Have some, gentlemen, have some!"

"You want a coffeepot, don't you?" he asked the esaul. "I bought a capital one from our sutler! He has splendid things. And he's very honest, that's the chief thing. I'll be sure to send it to you. Or perhaps your flints are giving out, or are worn out—that happens sometimes, you know. I have brought some with me, here they are"—and he showed a bag—"a hundred flints. I bought them very cheap. Please take as many as you want, or all if you like. . ."

Then suddenly, dismayed lest he had said too much, Pétya stopped and blushed.

He tried to remember whether he had not done anything else that was foolish. And running over the events of the day he remembered the French drummer boy. "It's capital for us here, but what of him? Where have they put him? Have they fed him? Haven't they hurt his feelings?" he thought. But having caught himself saying too much about the flints, he was now afraid to speak out.

"I might ask," he thought, "but they'll say: 'He's a boy himself and so he pities the boy.' I'll show them tomorrow whether I'm a boy. Will it seem odd if I ask?" Pétya thought. "Well, never mind!" and immediately, blushing and looking anxiously at the officers to see if they appeared ironical, he said:

"May I call in that boy who was taken prisoner and give him something to eat? . . . Perhaps. . ."

"Yes, he's a poor little fellow," said Denísov, who evidently saw nothing shameful in this reminder. "Call him in. His name is Vincent Bosse. Have him fetched."

"I'll call him," said Pétya.

"Yes, yes, call him. A poor little fellow," Denísov repeated.

Pétya was standing at the door when Denísov said this. He slipped in between the officers, came close to Denísov, and said:

"Let me kiss you, dear old fellow! Oh, how fine, how splendid!"

And having kissed Denísov he ran out of the hut.

"Bosse! Vincent!" Pétya cried, stopping outside the door.

"Who do you want, sir?" asked a voice in the darkness.

Pétya replied that he wanted the French lad who had been captured that day.

"Ah, Vesénny?" said a Cossack.

Vincent, the boy's name, had already been changed by the Cossacks into Vesénny (vernal) and into Vesénya by the peasants and soldiers. In both these adaptations the reference to spring (vesná) matched the impression made by the young lad.

"He is warming himself there by the bonfire. Ho, Vesénya! Vesénya!—Vesénny!" laughing voices were heard calling to one another in the darkness.

"He's a smart lad," said an hussar standing near Pétya. "We gave him something to eat a while ago. He was awfully hungry!"

The sound of bare feet splashing through the mud was heard in the darkness, and the drummer boy came to the door.

"Ah, c'est vous!" said Pétya. "Voulez-vous manger? N'ayez pas peur, on ne vous fera pas de mal,"* he added shyly and affectionately, touching the boy's hand. "Entrez, entrez."†

---

* "Ah, it's you! Do you want something to eat? Don't be afraid, they won't hurt you."
† "Come in, come in."

"Merci, monsieur,"* said the drummer boy in a trembling almost childish voice, and he began scraping his dirty feet on the threshold.

There were many things Pétya wanted to say to the drummer boy, but did not dare to. He stood irresolutely beside him in the passage. Then in the darkness he took the boy's hand and pressed it.

"Come in, come in!" he repeated in a gentle whisper. "Oh, what can I do for him?" he thought, and opening the door he let the boy pass in first.

When the boy had entered the hut, Pétya sat down at a distance from him, considering it beneath his dignity to pay attention to him. But he fingered the money in his pocket and wondered whether it would seem ridiculous to give some to the drummer boy.

---

* "Thank you, sir."

# VIII

The arrival of Dólokhov diverted Pétya's attention from the drummer boy, to whom Denísov had had some mutton and vodka given, and whom he had had dressed in a Russian coat so that he might be kept with their band and not sent away with the other prisoners. Pétya had heard in the army many stories of Dólokhov's extraordinary bravery and of his cruelty to the French, so from the moment he entered the hut Pétya did not take his eyes from him, but braced himself up more and more and held his head high, that he might not be unworthy even of such company.

Dólokhov's appearance amazed Pétya by its simplicity.

Denísov wore a Cossack coat, had a beard, had an icon of Nicholas the Wonder-Worker on his breast, and his way of speaking and everything he did indicated his unusual position. But Dólokhov, who in Moscow had worn a Persian costume, had now the appearance of a most correct officer of the Guards. He was clean-shaven and wore a Guardsman's padded coat with an Order of St. George at his buttonhole and a plain forage cap set straight on his head. He took off his wet felt cloak in a corner of the room, and without greeting anyone went up to Denísov and began questioning him about the matter in hand. Denísov told him of the designs the large detachments had on the transport, of the message Pétya had brought, and his own replies to both generals. Then he told him all he knew of the French detachment.

"That's so. But we must know what troops they are and their numbers," said Dólokhov. "It will be necessary to go there. We can't start the affair without knowing for certain how many there are. I like to work accurately. Here now—wouldn't one of these gentlemen like to ride over to the French camp with me? I have brought a spare uniform."

"I, I. . . I'll go with you!" cried Pétya.

"There's no need for you to go at all," said Denísov, addressing Dólokhov, "and as for him, I won't let him go on any account."

"I like that!" exclaimed Pétya. "Why shouldn't I go?"

"Because it's useless."

"Well, you must excuse me, because. . . because. . . I shall go, and that's all. You'll take me, won't you?" he said, turning to Dólokhov.

"Why not?" Dólokhov answered absently, scrutinizing the face of the French drummer boy. "Have you had that youngster with you long?" he asked Denísov.

"He was taken today but he knows nothing. I'm keeping him with me."

"Yes, and where do you put the others?" inquired Dólokhov.

"Where? I send them away and take a weceipt for them," shouted Denísov, suddenly flushing. "And I say boldly that I have not a single man's life on my conscience. Would it be difficult for you to send thirty or thwee hundwed men to town under escort, instead of staining—I speak bluntly—staining the honor of a soldier?"

"That kind of amiable talk would be suitable from this young count of sixteen," said Dólokhov with cold irony, "but it's time for you to drop it."

"Why, I've not said anything! I only say that I'll certainly go with you," said Pétya shyly.

"But for you and me, old fellow, it's time to drop these amenities," continued Dólokhov, as if he found particular pleasure in speaking of this subject which irritated Denísov. "Now, why have you kept this lad?" he went on, swaying his head. "Because you are sorry for him! Don't we know those 'receipts' of yours? You send a hundred men away, and thirty get there. The rest either starve or get killed. So isn't it all the same not to send them?"

The esaul, screwing up his light-colored eyes, nodded approvingly.

"That's not the point. I'm not going to discuss the matter. I do not wish to take it on my conscience. You say they'll die. All wight. Only not by my fault!"

Dólokhov began laughing.

"Who has told them not to capture me these twenty times over? But if they did catch me they'd string me up to an aspen tree, and with all your chivalry just the same." He paused. "However, we must get to work. Tell the Cossack to fetch my kit. I have two French uniforms in it. Well, are you coming with me?" he asked Pétya.

"I? Yes, yes, certainly!" cried Pétya, blushing almost to tears and glancing at Denísov.

While Dólokhov had been disputing with Denísov what should be done with prisoners, Pétya had once more felt awkward and restless; but again he had no time to grasp fully what they were talking about. "If grown-up, distinguished men think so, it must be necessary and right," thought he. "But above all Denísov must not dare to imagine that I'll obey him and that he can order me about. I will certainly go to the French camp with Dólokhov. If he can, so can I!"

And to all Denísov's persuasions, Pétya replied that he too was accustomed to do everything accurately and not just anyhow, and that he never considered personal danger.

"For you'll admit that if we don't know for sure how many of them there are. . . hundreds of lives may depend on it, while there are only two of us. Besides, I want to go very much and certainly will go, so don't hinder me," said he. "It will only make things worse. . ."

# IX

Having put on French greatcoats and shakos, Pétya and Dólokhov rode to the clearing from which Denísov had reconnoitered the French camp, and emerging from the forest in pitch darkness they descended into the hollow. On reaching the bottom, Dólokhov told the Cossacks accompanying him to await him there and rode on at a quick trot along the road to the bridge. Pétya, his heart in his mouth with excitement, rode by his side.

"If we're caught, I won't be taken alive! I have a pistol," whispered he.

"Don't talk Russian," said Dólokhov in a hurried whisper, and at that very moment they heard through the darkness the challenge: "Qui vive?"* and the click of a musket.

The blood rushed to Pétya's face and he grasped his pistol.

"Lanciers du 6-me,"† replied Dólokhov, neither hastening nor slackening his horse's pace.

The black figure of a sentinel stood on the bridge.

"Mot d'ordre."‡

Dólokhov reined in his horse and advanced at a walk.

"Dites donc, le colonel Gérard est ici?"§ he asked.

"Mot d'ordre," repeated the sentinel, barring the way and not replying.

"Quand un officier fait sa ronde, les sentinelles ne demandent pas le mot d'ordre. . ." cried Dólokhov suddenly flaring up and riding straight at the sentinel. "Je vous demande si le colonel est ici."¶

And without waiting for an answer from the sentinel, who had stepped aside, Dólokhov rode up the incline at a walk.

Noticing the black outline of a man crossing the road, Dólokhov stopped him and inquired where the commander and officers were. The man, a soldier with a sack over his shoulder, stopped, came close up to Dólokhov's horse, touched it with his hand, and explained simply and in a friendly way that the commander and the officers were higher

---

\* "Who goes there?"

† "Lancers of the 6th Regiment."

‡ "Password."

§ "Tell me, is Colonel Gérard here?"

¶ "When an officer is making his round, sentinels don't ask him for the password. . . I am asking you if the colonel is here."

up the hill to the right in the courtyard of the farm, as he called the landowner's house.

Having ridden up the road, on both sides of which French talk could be heard around the campfires, Dólokhov turned into the courtyard of the landowner's house. Having ridden in, he dismounted and approached a big blazing campfire, around which sat several men talking noisily. Something was boiling in a small cauldron at the edge of the fire and a soldier in a peaked cap and blue overcoat, lit up by the fire, was kneeling beside it stirring its contents with a ramrod.

"Oh, he's a hard nut to crack," said one of the officers who was sitting in the shadow at the other side of the fire.

"He'll make them get a move on, those fellows!" said another, laughing.

Both fell silent, peering out through the darkness at the sound of Dólokhov's and Pétya's steps as they advanced to the fire leading their horses.

"Bonjour, messieurs!"* said Dólokhov loudly and clearly.

There was a stir among the officers in the shadow beyond the fire, and one tall, long-necked officer, walking round the fire, came up to Dólokhov.

"Is that you, Clément?" he asked. "Where the devil. . . ?" But, noticing his mistake, he broke off short and, with a frown, greeted Dólokhov as a stranger, asking what he could do for him.

Dólokhov said that he and his companion were trying to overtake their regiment, and addressing the company in general asked whether they knew anything of the 6th Regiment. None of them knew anything, and Pétya thought the officers were beginning to look at him and Dólokhov with hostility and suspicion. For some seconds all were silent.

"If you were counting on the evening soup, you have come too late," said a voice from behind the fire with a repressed laugh.

Dólokhov replied that they were not hungry and must push on farther that night.

He handed the horses over to the soldier who was stirring the pot and squatted down on his heels by the fire beside the officer with the long neck. That officer did not take his eyes from Dólokhov and again asked to what regiment he belonged. Dólokhov, as if he had not heard the question, did not reply, but lighting a short French pipe which he

---

* "Good day, gentlemen."

took from his pocket began asking the officer in how far the road before them was safe from Cossacks.

"Those brigands are everywhere," replied an officer from behind the fire.

Dólokhov remarked that the Cossacks were a danger only to stragglers such as his companion and himself, "but probably they would not dare to attack large detachments?" he added inquiringly. No one replied.

"Well, now he'll come away," Pétya thought every moment as he stood by the campfire listening to the talk.

But Dólokhov restarted the conversation which had dropped and began putting direct questions as to how many men there were in the battalion, how many battalions, and how many prisoners. Asking about the Russian prisoners with that detachment, Dólokhov said:

"A horrid business dragging these corpses about with one! It would be better to shoot such rabble," and burst into loud laughter, so strange that Pétya thought the French would immediately detect their disguise, and involuntarily took a step back from the campfire.

No one replied a word to Dólokhov's laughter, and a French officer whom they could not see (he lay wrapped in a greatcoat) rose and whispered something to a companion. Dólokhov got up and called to the soldier who was holding their horses.

"Will they bring our horses or not?" thought Pétya, instinctively drawing nearer to Dólokhov.

The horses were brought.

"Good evening, gentlemen," said Dólokhov.

Pétya wished to say "Good night" but could not utter a word. The officers were whispering together. Dólokhov was a long time mounting his horse which would not stand still, then he rode out of the yard at a footpace. Pétya rode beside him, longing to look round to see whether or not the French were running after them, but not daring to.

Coming out onto the road Dólokhov did not ride back across the open country, but through the village. At one spot he stopped and listened. "Do you hear?" he asked. Pétya recognized the sound of Russian voices and saw the dark figures of Russian prisoners round their campfires. When they had descended to the bridge Pétya and Dólokhov rode past the sentinel, who without saying a word paced morosely up and down it, then they descended into the hollow where the Cossacks awaited them.

"Well now, good-by. Tell Denísov, 'at the first shot at daybreak,'" said Dólokhov and was about to ride away, but Pétya seized hold of him.

"Really!" he cried, "you are such a hero! Oh, how fine, how splendid! How I love you!"

"All right, all right!" said Dólokhov. But Pétya did not let go of him and Dólokhov saw through the gloom that Pétya was bending toward him and wanted to kiss him. Dólokhov kissed him, laughed, turned his horse, and vanished into the darkness.

# X

Having returned to the watchman's hut, Pétya found Denísov in the passage. He was awaiting Pétya's return in a state of agitation, anxiety, and self-reproach for having let him go.

"Thank God!" he exclaimed. "Yes, thank God!" he repeated, listening to Pétya's rapturous account. "But, devil take you, I haven't slept because of you! Well, thank God. Now lie down. We can still get a nap before morning."

"But. . . no," said Pétya, "I don't want to sleep yet. Besides I know myself, if I fall asleep it's finished. And then I am used to not sleeping before a battle."

He sat awhile in the hut joyfully recalling the details of his expedition and vividly picturing to himself what would happen next day.

Then, noticing that Denísov was asleep, he rose and went out of doors.

It was still quite dark outside. The rain was over, but drops were still falling from the trees. Near the watchman's hut the black shapes of the Cossacks' shanties and of horses tethered together could be seen. Behind the hut the dark shapes of the two wagons with their horses beside them were discernible, and in the hollow the dying campfire gleamed red. Not all the Cossacks and hussars were asleep; here and there, amid the sounds of falling drops and the munching of the horses near by, could be heard low voices which seemed to be whispering.

Pétya came out, peered into the darkness, and went up to the wagons. Someone was snoring under them, and around them stood saddled horses munching their oats. In the dark Pétya recognized his own horse, which he called "Karabákh" though it was of Ukranian breed, and went up to it.

"Well, Karabákh! We'll do some service tomorrow," said he, sniffing its nostrils and kissing it.

"Why aren't you asleep, sir?" said a Cossack who was sitting under a wagon.

"No, ah. . . Likhachëv—isn't that your name? Do you know I have only just come back! We've been into the French camp."

And Pétya gave the Cossack a detailed account not only of his ride but also of his object, and why he considered it better to risk his life than to act "just anyhow."

"Well, you should get some sleep now," said the Cossack.

"No, I am used to this," said Pétya. "I say, aren't the flints in your pistols worn out? I brought some with me. Don't you want any? You can have some."

The Cossack bent forward from under the wagon to get a closer look at Pétya.

"Because I am accustomed to doing everything accurately," said Pétya. "Some fellows do things just anyhow, without preparation, and then they're sorry for it afterwards. I don't like that."

"Just so," said the Cossack.

"Oh yes, another thing! Please, my dear fellow, will you sharpen my saber for me? It's got bl. . ." (Pétya feared to tell a lie, and the saber never had been sharpened.) "Can you do it?"

"Of course I can."

Likhachëv got up, rummaged in his pack, and soon Pétya heard the warlike sound of steel on whetstone. He climbed onto the wagon and sat on its edge. The Cossack was sharpening the saber under the wagon.

"I say! Are the lads asleep?" asked Pétya.

"Some are, and some aren't—like us."

"Well, and that boy?"

"Vesénny? Oh, he's thrown himself down there in the passage. Fast asleep after his fright. He was that glad!"

After that Pétya remained silent for a long time, listening to the sounds. He heard footsteps in the darkness and a black figure appeared.

"What are you sharpening?" asked a man coming up to the wagon.

"Why, this gentleman's saber."

"That's right," said the man, whom Pétya took to be an hussar. "Was the cup left here?"

"There, by the wheel!"

The hussar took the cup.

"It must be daylight soon," said he, yawning, and went away.

Pétya ought to have known that he was in a forest with Denísov's guerrilla band, less than a mile from the road, sitting on a wagon captured from the French beside which horses were tethered, that under it Likhachëv was sitting sharpening a saber for him, that the big dark blotch to the right was the watchman's hut, and the red blotch below to the left was the dying embers of a campfire, that the man who had come for the cup was an hussar who wanted a drink; but he neither knew nor waited to know anything of all this. He was in a fairy kingdom where nothing resembled reality. The big dark blotch might really be the watchman's hut or it might be a cavern leading to the very depths of the earth. Perhaps the red spot was a fire, or it might be the eye of an enormous monster. Perhaps he was really sitting on a wagon, but it might very well be that he was not sitting on a wagon but on a terribly high tower from which, if he fell, he would have to fall for a whole day or a whole month, or go on falling and never reach the bottom. Perhaps it was just the Cossack, Likhachëv, who was sitting under the wagon, but it might be the kindest, bravest, most wonderful, most splendid man in the world, whom no one knew of. It might really have been that the hussar came for water and went back into the hollow, but perhaps he had simply vanished—disappeared altogether and dissolved into nothingness.

Nothing Pétya could have seen now would have surprised him. He was in a fairy kingdom where everything was possible.

He looked up at the sky. And the sky was a fairy realm like the earth. It was clearing, and over the tops of the trees clouds were swiftly sailing as if unveiling the stars. Sometimes it looked as if the clouds were passing, and a clear black sky appeared. Sometimes it seemed as if the black spaces were clouds. Sometimes the sky seemed to be rising high, high overhead, and then it seemed to sink so low that one could touch it with one's hand.

Pétya's eyes began to close and he swayed a little.

The trees were dripping. Quiet talking was heard. The horses neighed and jostled one another. Someone snored.

"Ozheg-zheg, Ozheg-zheg. . ." hissed the saber against the whetstone, and suddenly Pétya heard an harmonious orchestra playing some unknown, sweetly solemn hymn. Pétya was as musical as Natásha and more so than Nicholas, but had never learned music or thought about it, and so the melody that unexpectedly came to his mind seemed to him particularly fresh and attractive. The music became more and more audible. The melody grew and passed from one instrument to another. And what was played was a fugue—though Pétya had not the least conception of what a fugue is. Each instrument—now resembling a violin and now a horn, but better and clearer than violin or horn— played its own part, and before it had finished the melody merged with another instrument that began almost the same air, and then with a third and a fourth; and they all blended into one and again became separate and again blended, now into solemn church music, now into something dazzlingly brilliant and triumphant.

"Oh—why, that was in a dream!" Pétya said to himself, as he lurched forward. "It's in my ears. But perhaps it's music of my own. Well, go on, my music! Now! . . ."

He closed his eyes, and, from all sides as if from a distance, sounds fluttered, grew into harmonies, separated, blended, and again all mingled into the same sweet and solemn hymn. "Oh, this is delightful! As much as I like and as I like!" said Pétya to himself. He tried to conduct that enormous orchestra.

"Now softly, softly die away!" and the sounds obeyed him. "Now fuller, more joyful. Still more and more joyful!" And from an unknown depth rose increasingly triumphant sounds. "Now voices join in!" ordered Pétya. And at first from afar he heard men's voices and then women's. The voices grew in harmonious triumphant strength, and Pétya listened to their surpassing beauty in awe and joy.

With a solemn triumphal march there mingled a song, the drip from the trees, and the hissing of the saber, "Ozheg-zheg-zheg. . ." and again the horses jostled one another and neighed, not disturbing the choir but joining in it.

Pétya did not know how long this lasted: he enjoyed himself all the time, wondered at his enjoyment and regretted that there was no one to share it. He was awakened by Likhachëv's kindly voice.

"It's ready, your honor; you can split a Frenchman in half with it!"

Pétya woke up.

"It's getting light, it's really getting light!" he exclaimed.

The horses that had previously been invisible could now be seen to their very tails, and a watery light showed itself through the bare branches. Pétya shook himself, jumped up, took a ruble from his pocket and gave it to Likhachëv; then he flourished the saber, tested it, and sheathed it. The Cossacks were untying their horses and tightening their saddle girths.

"And here's the commander," said Likhachëv.

Denísov came out of the watchman's hut and, having called Pétya, gave orders to get ready.

# XI

The men rapidly picked out their horses in the semidarkness, tightened their saddle girths, and formed companies. Denísov stood by the watchman's hut giving final orders. The infantry of the detachment passed along the road and quickly disappeared amid the trees in the mist of early dawn, hundreds of feet splashing through the mud. The esaul gave some orders to his men. Pétya held his horse by the bridle, impatiently awaiting the order to mount. His face, having been bathed in cold water, was all aglow, and his eyes were particularly brilliant. Cold shivers ran down his spine and his whole body pulsed rhythmically.

"Well, is ev'wything weady?" asked Denísov. "Bwing the horses."

The horses were brought. Denísov was angry with the Cossack because the saddle girths were too slack, reproved him, and mounted. Pétya put his foot in the stirrup. His horse by habit made as if to nip his leg, but Pétya leaped quickly into the saddle unconscious of his own weight and, turning to look at the hussars starting in the darkness behind him, rode up to Denísov.

"Vasíli Dmítrich, entrust me with some commission! Please. . . for God's sake. . . !" said he.

Denísov seemed to have forgotten Pétya's very existence. He turned to glance at him.

"I ask one thing of you," he said sternly, "to obey me and not shove yourself forward anywhere."

He did not say another word to Pétya but rode in silence all the way. When they had come to the edge of the forest it was noticeably growing light over the field. Denísov talked in whispers with the esaul and the Cossacks rode past Pétya and Denísov. When they had all ridden by, Denísov touched his horse and rode down the hill. Slipping onto their haunches and sliding, the horses descended with their riders into the ravine. Pétya rode beside Denísov, the pulsation of his body constantly increasing. It was getting lighter and lighter, but the mist still hid distant objects. Having reached the valley, Denísov looked back and nodded to a Cossack beside him.

"The signal!" said he.

The Cossack raised his arm and a shot rang out. In an instant the tramp of horses galloping forward was heard, shouts came from various sides, and then more shots.

At the first sound of trampling hoofs and shouting, Pétya lashed his horse and loosening his rein galloped forward, not heeding Denísov who shouted at him. It seemed to Pétya that at the moment the shot was fired it suddenly became as bright as noon. He galloped to the bridge. Cossacks were galloping along the road in front of him. On the bridge he collided with a Cossack who had fallen behind, but he galloped on. In front of him soldiers, probably Frenchmen, were running from right to left across the road. One of them fell in the mud under his horse's feet.

Cossacks were crowding about a hut, busy with something. From the midst of that crowd terrible screams arose. Pétya galloped up, and the first thing he saw was the pale face and trembling jaw of a Frenchman, clutching the handle of a lance that had been aimed at him.

"Hurrah! . . . Lads! . . . ours!" shouted Pétya, and giving rein to his excited horse he galloped forward along the village street.

He could hear shooting ahead of him. Cossacks, hussars, and ragged Russian prisoners, who had come running from both sides of the road, were shouting something loudly and incoherently. A gallant-looking Frenchman, in a blue overcoat, capless, and with a frowning red face, had been defending himself against the hussars. When Pétya galloped up the Frenchman had already fallen. "Too late again!" flashed through Pétya's mind and he galloped on to the place from which the rapid firing could be heard. The shots came from the yard of the landowner's house he had visited the night before with Dólokhov. The French were making a stand there behind a wattle fence in a garden thickly overgrown with bushes and were firing at the Cossacks who crowded at the gateway. Through the smoke, as he approached the gate, Pétya saw Dólokhov, whose face was of a pale-greenish tint, shouting to his men. "Go round! Wait for the infantry!" he exclaimed as Pétya rode up to him.

"Wait? . . . Hurrah-ah-ah!" shouted Pétya, and without pausing a moment galloped to the place whence came the sounds of firing and where the smoke was thickest.

A volley was heard, and some bullets whistled past, while others plashed against something. The Cossacks and Dólokhov galloped after Pétya into the gateway of the courtyard. In the dense wavering smoke some of the French threw down their arms and ran out of the bushes to meet the Cossacks, while others ran down the hill toward the pond. Pétya was galloping along the courtyard, but instead of holding the reins he waved both his arms about rapidly and strangely, slipping farther and farther to one side in his saddle. His horse, having galloped up to a campfire that was smoldering in the morning light, stopped suddenly, and Pétya fell heavily on to the wet ground. The Cossacks saw that his arms and legs jerked rapidly though his head was quite motionless. A bullet had pierced his skull.

After speaking to the senior French officer, who came out of the house with a white handkerchief tied to his sword and announced that they surrendered, Dólokhov dismounted and went up to Pétya, who lay motionless with outstretched arms.

"Done for!" he said with a frown, and went to the gate to meet Denísov who was riding toward him.

"Killed?" cried Denísov, recognizing from a distance the unmistakably lifeless attitude—very familiar to him—in which Pétya's body was lying.

"Done for!" repeated Dólokhov as if the utterance of these words afforded him pleasure, and he went quickly up to the prisoners, who were surrounded by Cossacks who had hurried up. "We won't take them!" he called out to Denísov.

Denísov did not reply; he rode up to Pétya, dismounted, and with trembling hands turned toward himself the bloodstained, mud-bespattered face which had already gone white.

"I am used to something sweet. Raisins, fine ones. . . take them all!" he recalled Pétya's words. And the Cossacks looked round in surprise at the sound, like the yelp of a dog, with which Denísov turned away, walked to the wattle fence, and seized hold of it.

Among the Russian prisoners rescued by Denísov and Dólokhov was Pierre Bezúkhov.

# XII

During the whole of their march from Moscow no fresh orders had been issued by the French authorities concerning the party of prisoners among whom was Pierre. On the twenty-second of October that party was no longer with the same troops and baggage trains with which it had left Moscow. Half the wagons laden with hardtack that had traveled the first stages with them had been captured by Cossacks, the other half had gone on ahead. Not one of those dismounted cavalrymen who had marched in front of the prisoners was left; they had all disappeared. The artillery the prisoners had seen in front of them during the first days was now replaced by Marshal Junot's enormous baggage train, convoyed by Westphalians. Behind the prisoners came a cavalry baggage train.

From Vyázma onwards the French army, which had till then moved in three columns, went on as a single group. The symptoms of disorder that Pierre had noticed at their first halting place after leaving Moscow had now reached the utmost limit.

The road along which they moved was bordered on both sides by dead horses; ragged men who had fallen behind from various regiments continually changed about, now joining the moving column, now again lagging behind it.

Several times during the march false alarms had been given and the soldiers of the escort had raised their muskets, fired, and run headlong, crushing one another, but had afterwards reassembled and abused each other for their causeless panic.

These three groups traveling together—the cavalry stores, the convoy of prisoners, and Junot's baggage train—still constituted a separate and united whole, though each of the groups was rapidly melting away.

Of the artillery baggage train which had consisted of a hundred and twenty wagons, not more than sixty now remained; the rest had been captured or left behind. Some of Junot's wagons also had been captured or abandoned. Three wagons had been raided and robbed by stragglers from Davout's corps. From the talk of the Germans Pierre learned that a larger guard had been allotted to that baggage train than to the prisoners, and that one of their comrades, a German soldier, had been shot by the marshal's own order because a silver spoon belonging to the marshal had been found in his possession.

The group of prisoners had melted away most of all. Of the three hundred and thirty men who had set out from Moscow fewer than a hundred now remained. The prisoners were more burdensome to the escort than even the cavalry saddles or Junot's baggage. They understood that the saddles and Junot's spoon might be of some use, but that cold and hungry soldiers should have to stand and guard equally cold and hungry Russians who froze and lagged behind on the road (in which case the order was to shoot them) was not merely incomprehensible but revolting. And the escort, as if afraid, in the grievous condition they themselves were in, of giving way to the pity they felt for the prisoners and so rendering their own plight still worse, treated them with particular moroseness and severity.

At Dorogobúzh while the soldiers of the convoy, after locking the prisoners in a stable, had gone off to pillage their own stores, several of the soldier prisoners tunneled under the wall and ran away, but were recaptured by the French and shot.

The arrangement adopted when they started, that the officer prisoners should be kept separate from the rest, had long since been abandoned. All who could walk went together, and after the third stage Pierre had rejoined Karatáev and the gray-blue bandy-legged dog that had chosen Karatáev for its master.

On the third day after leaving Moscow Karatáev again fell ill with the fever he had suffered from in the hospital in Moscow, and as he grew gradually weaker Pierre kept away from him. Pierre did not know why, but since Karatáev had begun to grow weaker it had cost him an effort to go near him. When he did so and heard the subdued moaning with which Karatáev generally lay down at the halting places, and when he smelled the odor emanating from him which was now stronger than before, Pierre moved farther away and did not think about him.

While imprisoned in the shed Pierre had learned not with his intellect but with his whole being, by life itself, that man is created for happiness, that happiness is within him, in the satisfaction of simple human needs, and that all unhappiness arises not from privation but from superfluity. And now during these last three weeks of the march he had learned still another new, consolatory truth—that nothing in this world is terrible. He had learned that as there is no condition in which man can be happy and entirely free, so there is no condition in which he need be unhappy and lack freedom. He learned that suffering and freedom have their limits and that those limits are very near together; that the person in a bed of roses with one crumpled petal suffered as keenly as he now, sleeping on the bare damp earth with one side growing chilled while the other was warming; and that when he had put on tight dancing shoes he had suffered just as he did now when he walked with bare feet that were covered with sores—his footgear having long since fallen to pieces. He discovered that when he had married his wife—of his own free will as it had seemed to him—he had been no more free than now when they locked him up at night in a stable. Of all that he himself subsequently termed his sufferings, but which at the time he scarcely felt, the worst was the state of his bare, raw, and scab-covered feet. (The horseflesh was appetizing and nourishing, the saltpeter flavor of the gunpowder they used instead of salt was even pleasant; there was no great cold, it was always warm walking in the daytime, and at night there were the campfires; the lice that devoured him warmed his body.) The one thing that was at first hard to bear was his feet.

After the second day's march Pierre, having examined his feet by the campfire, thought it would be impossible to walk on them; but when everybody got up he went along, limping, and, when he had warmed up, walked without feeling the pain, though at night his feet were more terrible to look at than before. However, he did not look at them now, but thought of other things.

Only now did Pierre realize the full strength of life in man and the saving power he has of transferring his attention from one thing to another, which is like the safety valve of a boiler that allows superfluous steam to blow off when the pressure exceeds a certain limit.

He did not see and did not hear how they shot the prisoners who lagged behind, though more than a hundred perished in that way. He did not think of Karataev who grew weaker every day and evidently would soon have to share that fate. Still less did Pierre think about himself. The harder his position became and the more terrible the future, the more independent of that position in which he found himself were the joyful and comforting thoughts, memories, and imaginings that came to him.

# XIII

At midday on the twenty-second of October Pierre was going uphill along the muddy, slippery road, looking at his feet and at the roughness of the way. Occasionally he glanced at the familiar crowd around him and then again at his feet. The former and the latter were alike familiar and his own. The blue-gray bandy legged dog ran merrily along the side of the road, sometimes in proof of its agility and self-satisfaction lifting one hind leg and hopping along on three, and then again going on all four and rushing to bark at the crows that sat on the carrion. The dog was merrier and sleeker than it had been in Moscow. All around lay the flesh of different animals—from men to horses—in various stages of decomposition; and as the wolves were kept off by the passing men the dog could eat all it wanted.

It had been raining since morning and had seemed as if at any moment it might cease and the sky clear, but after a short break it began raining harder than before. The saturated road no longer absorbed the water, which ran along the ruts in streams.

Pierre walked along, looking from side to side, counting his steps in threes, and reckoning them off on his fingers. Mentally addressing the rain, he repeated: "Now then, now then, go on! Pelt harder!"

It seemed to him that he was thinking of nothing, but far down and deep within him his soul was occupied with something important and comforting. This something was a most subtle spiritual deduction from a conversation with Karatáev the day before.

At their yesterday's halting place, feeling chilly by a dying campfire, Pierre had got up and gone to the next one, which was burning better. There Platón Karatáev was sitting covered up—head and all—with his greatcoat as if it were a vestment, telling the soldiers in his effective and pleasant though now feeble voice a story Pierre knew. It was already past midnight, the hour when Karatáev was usually free of his fever and particularly lively. When Pierre reached the fire and heard Platón's voice enfeebled by illness, and saw his pathetic face brightly lit up by the blaze, he felt a painful prick at his heart. His feeling of pity for this man frightened him and he wished to go away, but there was no other fire, and Pierre sat down, trying not to look at Platón.

"Well, how are you?" he asked.

"How am I? If we grumble at sickness, God won't grant us death," replied Platón, and at once resumed the story he had begun.

"And so, brother," he continued, with a smile on his pale emaciated face and a particularly happy light in his eyes, "you see, brother. . ."

Pierre had long been familiar with that story. Karatáev had told it to him alone some half-dozen times and always with a specially joyful emotion. But well as he knew it, Pierre now listened to that tale as to something new, and the quiet rapture Karatáev evidently felt as he told it communicated itself also to Pierre. The story was of an old merchant who lived a good and God-fearing life with his family, and who went once to the Nízhni fair with a companion—a rich merchant.

Having put up at an inn they both went to sleep, and next morning his companion was found robbed and with his throat cut. A bloodstained knife was found under the old merchant's pillow. He was tried, knouted, and his nostrils having been torn off, "all in due form" as Karatáev put it, he was sent to hard labor in Siberia.

"And so, brother" (it was at this point that Pierre came up), "ten years or more passed by. The old man was living as a convict, submitting as he should and doing no wrong. Only he prayed to God for death. Well, one night the convicts were gathered just as we are, with the old man among them. And they began telling what each was suffering for, and how they had sinned against God. One told how he had taken a life, another had taken two, a third had set a house on fire, while another had simply been a vagrant and had done nothing. So they asked the old man: 'What are you being punished for, Daddy?'—'I, my dear brothers,' said he, 'am being punished for my own and other men's sins. But I have not killed anyone or taken anything that was not mine, but have only helped my poorer brothers. I was a merchant, my dear brothers, and had much property. 'And he went on to tell them all about it in due order. 'I don't grieve for myself,' he says, 'God, it seems, has chastened me. Only I am sorry for my old wife and the children,' and the old man began to weep. Now it happened that in the group was the very man who had killed the other merchant. 'Where did it happen, Daddy?' he said. 'When, and in what month?' He asked all about it and his heart began to ache. So he comes up to the old man like this, and falls down at his feet! 'You are perishing because of me, Daddy,' he says. 'It's quite true, lads, that this man,' he says, 'is being tortured innocently and for nothing! I,' he says, 'did that deed, and I put the knife under your head while you were asleep. Forgive me, Daddy,' he says, 'for Christ's sake!'"

Karatáev paused, smiling joyously as he gazed into the fire, and he drew the logs together.

"And the old man said, 'God will forgive you, we are all sinners in His sight. I suffer for my own sins,' and he wept bitter tears. Well, and what do you think, dear friends?" Karatáev continued, his face brightening more and more with a rapturous smile as if what he now had to tell contained the chief charm and the whole meaning of his story: "What do you think, dear fellows? That murderer confessed to the authorities. 'I have taken six lives,' he says (he was a great sinner), 'but what I am most sorry for is this old man. Don't let him suffer because of me.' So he confessed and it was all written down and the papers sent off in due form. The place was a long way off, and while they were judging, what with one thing and another, filling in the papers all in due form—the authorities I mean—time passed. The affair reached the Tsar. After a while the Tsar's decree came: to set the merchant free and give him a compensation that had been awarded. The paper arrived and they began to look for the old man. 'Where is the old man who has been suffering innocently and in vain? A paper has come from the Tsar!' so they began looking for him," here Karatáev's lower jaw trembled, "but God had already forgiven him—he was dead! That's how it was, dear fellows!" Karatáev concluded and sat for a long time silent, gazing before him with a smile.

And Pierre's soul was dimly but joyfully filled not by the story itself but by its mysterious significance: by the rapturous joy that lit up Karatáev's face as he told it, and the mystic significance of that joy.

# XIV

À vos places!"* suddenly cried a voice.

A pleasant feeling of excitement and an expectation of something joyful and solemn was aroused among the soldiers of the convoy and the prisoners. From all sides came shouts of command, and from the left came smartly dressed cavalrymen on good horses, passing the prisoners at a trot. The expression on all faces showed the tension people feel at the approach of those in authority. The prisoners thronged together and were pushed off the road. The convoy formed up.

"The Emperor! The Emperor! The Marshal! The Duke!" and hardly had the sleek cavalry passed, before a carriage drawn by six gray horses rattled by. Pierre caught a glimpse of a man in a three-cornered hat with a tranquil look on his handsome, plump, white face. It was one of the marshals. His eye fell on Pierre's large and striking figure, and in the expression with which he frowned and looked away Pierre thought he detected sympathy and a desire to conceal that sympathy.

The general in charge of the stores galloped after the carriage with a red and frightened face, whipping up his skinny horse. Several officers formed a group and some soldiers crowded round them. Their faces all looked excited and worried.

"What did he say? What did he say?" Pierre heard them ask.

While the marshal was passing, the prisoners had huddled together in a crowd, and Pierre saw Karatáev whom he had not yet seen that morning. He sat in his short overcoat leaning against a birch tree. On his face, besides the look of joyful emotion it had worn yesterday while telling the tale of the merchant who suffered innocently, there was now an expression of quiet solemnity.

Karatáev looked at Pierre with his kindly round eyes now filled with tears, evidently wishing him to come near that he might say something to him. But Pierre was not sufficiently sure of himself. He made as if he did not notice that look and moved hastily away.

When the prisoners again went forward Pierre looked round. Karatáev was still sitting at the side of the road under the birch tree and two Frenchmen were talking over his head. Pierre did not look round again but went limping up the hill.

---

* "To your places."

From behind, where Karatáev had been sitting, came the sound of a shot. Pierre heard it plainly, but at that moment he remembered that he had not yet finished reckoning up how many stages still remained to Smolénsk—a calculation he had begun before the marshal went by. And he again started reckoning. Two French soldiers ran past Pierre, one of whom carried a lowered and smoking gun. They both looked pale, and in the expression on their faces—one of them glanced timidly at Pierre—there was something resembling what he had seen on the face of the young soldier at the execution. Pierre looked at the soldier and remembered that, two days before, that man had burned his shirt while drying it at the fire and how they had laughed at him.

Behind him, where Karatáev had been sitting, the dog began to howl. "What a stupid beast! Why is it howling?" thought Pierre.

His comrades, the prisoner soldiers walking beside him, avoided looking back at the place where the shot had been fired and the dog was howling, just as Pierre did, but there was a set look on all their faces.

# XV

The stores, the prisoners, and the marshal's baggage train stopped at the village of Shámshevo. The men crowded together round the campfires. Pierre went up to the fire, ate some roast horseflesh, lay down with his back to the fire, and immediately fell asleep. He again slept as he had done at Mozháysk after the battle of Borodinó.

Again real events mingled with dreams and again someone, he or another, gave expression to his thoughts, and even to the same thoughts that had been expressed in his dream at Mozháysk.

"Life is everything. Life is God. Everything changes and moves and that movement is God. And while there is life there is joy in consciousness of the divine. To love life is to love God. Harder and more blessed than all else is to love this life in one's sufferings, in innocent sufferings."

"Karatáev!" came to Pierre's mind.

And suddenly he saw vividly before him a long-forgotten, kindly old man who had given him geography lessons in Switzerland. "Wait a bit," said the old man, and showed Pierre a globe. This globe was alive—a vibrating ball without fixed dimensions. Its whole surface consisted of drops closely pressed together, and all these drops moved and changed places, sometimes several of them merging into one, sometimes one dividing into many. Each drop tried to spread out and occupy as much space as possible, but others striving to do the same compressed it, sometimes destroyed it, and sometimes merged with it.

"That is life," said the old teacher.

"How simple and clear it is," thought Pierre. "How is it I did not know it before?"

"God is in the midst, and each drop tries to expand so as to reflect Him to the greatest extent. And it grows, merges, disappears from the surface, sinks to the depths, and again emerges. There now, Karatáev has spread out and disappeared. Do you understand, my child?" said the teacher.

"Do you understand, damn you?" shouted a voice, and Pierre woke up.

He lifted himself and sat up. A Frenchman who had just pushed a Russian soldier away was squatting by the fire, engaged in roasting a piece of meat stuck on a ramrod. His sleeves were rolled up and his sinewy, hairy, red hands with their short fingers deftly turned the ramrod. His brown morose face with frowning brows was clearly visible by the glow of the charcoal.

"It's all the same to him," he muttered, turning quickly to a soldier who stood behind him. "Brigand! Get away!"

And twisting the ramrod he looked gloomily at Pierre, who turned away and gazed into the darkness. A prisoner, the Russian soldier the Frenchman had pushed away, was sitting near the fire patting something with his hand. Looking more closely Pierre recognized the blue-gray dog, sitting beside the soldier, wagging its tail.

"Ah, he's come?" said Pierre. "And Plat—" he began, but did not finish.

Suddenly and simultaneously a crowd of memories awoke in his fancy—of the look Platón had given him as he sat under the tree, of the shot heard from that spot, of the dog's howl, of the guilty faces of the two Frenchmen as they ran past him, of the lowered and smoking gun, and of Karatáev's absence at this halt—and he was on the point of realizing that Karatáev had been killed, but just at that instant, he knew not why, the recollection came to his mind of a summer evening he had spent with a beautiful Polish lady on the veranda of his house in Kiev. And without linking up the events of the day or drawing a conclusion from them, Pierre closed his eyes, seeing a vision of the country in summertime mingled with memories of bathing and of the liquid, vibrating globe, and he sank into water so that it closed over his head.

Before sunrise he was awakened by shouts and loud and rapid firing. French soldiers were running past him.

"The Cossacks!" one of them shouted, and a moment later a crowd of Russians surrounded Pierre.

For a long time he could not understand what was happening to him. All around he heard his comrades sobbing with joy.

"Brothers! Dear fellows! Darlings!" old soldiers exclaimed, weeping, as they embraced Cossacks and hussars.

The hussars and Cossacks crowded round the prisoners; one offered them clothes, another boots, and a third bread. Pierre sobbed as he sat among them and could not utter a word. He hugged the first soldier who approached him, and kissed him, weeping.

Dólokhov stood at the gate of the ruined house, letting a crowd of disarmed Frenchmen pass by. The French, excited by all that had happened, were talking loudly among themselves, but as they passed Dólokhov who gently switched his boots with his whip and watched them with cold glassy eyes that boded no good, they became silent. On the opposite side stood Dólokhov's Cossack, counting the prisoners and marking off each hundred with a chalk line on the gate.

"How many?" Dólokhov asked the Cossack.

"The second hundred," replied the Cossack.

"Filez, filez!"* Dólokhov kept saying, having adopted this expression from the French, and when his eyes met those of the prisoners they flashed with a cruel light.

Denísov, bareheaded and with a gloomy face, walked behind some Cossacks who were carrying the body of Pétya Rostóv to a hole that had been dug in the garden.

---

\* "Get along, get along!"

# XVI

After the twenty-eighth of October when the frosts began, the flight of the French assumed a still more tragic character, with men freezing, or roasting themselves to death at the campfires, while carriages with people dressed in furs continued to drive past, carrying away the property that had been stolen by the Emperor, kings, and dukes; but the process of the flight and disintegration of the French army went on essentially as before.

From Moscow to Vyázma the French army of seventy-three thousand men not reckoning the Guards (who did nothing during the whole war but pillage) was reduced to thirty-six thousand, though not more than five thousand had fallen in battle. From this beginning the succeeding terms of the progression could be determined mathematically. The French army melted away and perished at the same rate from Moscow to Vyázma, from Vyázma to Smolénsk, from Smolénsk to the Berëzina, and from the Berëzina to Vílna—independently of the greater or lesser intensity of the cold, the pursuit, the barring of the way, or any other particular conditions. Beyond Vyázma the French army instead of moving in three columns huddled together into one mass, and so went on to the end. Berthier wrote to his Emperor (we know how far commanding officers allow themselves to diverge from the truth in describing the condition of an army) and this is what he said:

> I deem it my duty to report to Your Majesty the condition of the various corps I have had occasion to observe during different stages of the last two or three days' march. They are almost disbanded. Scarcely a quarter of the soldiers remain with the standards of their regiments, the others go off by themselves in different directions hoping to find food and escape discipline. In general they regard Smolénsk as the place where they hope to recover. During the last few days many of the men have been seen to throw away their cartridges and their arms. In such a state of affairs, whatever your ultimate plans may be, the interest of Your Majesty's service demands that the army should be rallied at Smolénsk and should first of all be freed from ineffectives, such as dismounted cavalry, unnecessary baggage, and artillery material that is no longer in proportion to the present forces.

The soldiers, who are worn out with hunger and fatigue, need these supplies as well as a few days' rest. Many have died these last days on the road or at the bivouacs. This state of things is continually becoming worse and makes one fear that unless a prompt remedy is applied the troops will no longer be under control in case of an engagement.

November 9: twenty miles from Smolénsk.

After staggering into Smolénsk which seemed to them a promised land, the French, searching for food, killed one another, sacked their own stores, and when everything had been plundered fled farther.

They all went without knowing whither or why they were going. Still less did that genius, Napoleon, know it, for no one issued any orders to him. But still he and those about him retained their old habits: wrote commands, letters, reports, and orders of the day; called one another sire, mon cousin, prince d'Eckmühl, roi de Naples, and so on. But these orders and reports were only on paper, nothing in them was acted upon for they could not be carried out, and though they entitled one another Majesties, Highnesses, or Cousins, they all felt that they were miserable wretches who had done much evil for which they had now to pay. And though they pretended to be concerned about the army, each was thinking only of himself and of how to get away quickly and save himself.

# XVII

The movements of the Russian and French armies during the campaign from Moscow back to the Niemen were like those in a game of Russian blindman's buff, in which two players are blindfolded and one of them occasionally rings a little bell to inform the catcher of his whereabouts. First he rings his bell fearlessly, but when he gets into a tight place he runs away as quietly as he can, and often thinking to escape runs straight into his opponent's arms.

At first while they were still moving along the Kalúga road, Napoleon's armies made their presence known, but later when they reached the Smolénsk road they ran holding the clapper of their bell tight—and often thinking they were escaping ran right into the Russians.

Owing to the rapidity of the French flight and the Russian pursuit and the consequent exhaustion of the horses, the chief means of approximately ascertaining the enemy's position—by cavalry scouting— was not available. Besides, as a result of the frequent and rapid change of position by each army, even what information was obtained could not be delivered in time. If news was received one day that the enemy had been in a certain position the day before, by the third day when something could have been done, that army was already two days' march farther on and in quite another position.

One army fled and the other pursued. Beyond Smolénsk there were several different roads available for the French, and one would have thought that during their stay of four days they might have learned where the enemy was, might have arranged some more advantageous plan and undertaken something new. But after a four days' halt the mob, with no maneuvers or plans, again began running along the beaten track, neither to the right nor to the left but along the old—the worst—road, through Krásnoe and Orshá.

Expecting the enemy from behind and not in front, the French separated in their flight and spread out over a distance of twenty-four hours. In front of them all fled the Emperor, then the kings, then the dukes. The Russian army, expecting Napoleon to take the road to the right beyond the Dnieper—which was the only reasonable thing for him to do—themselves turned to the right and came out onto the highroad at Krásnoe. And here as in a game of blindman's buff the French ran into our vanguard. Seeing their enemy unexpectedly the French fell into confusion and stopped short from the sudden fright, but then they resumed their flight, abandoning their comrades who were farther behind. Then for three days separate portions of the French army—first Murat's (the vice-king's), then Davout's, and then Ney's—ran, as it were, the gauntlet of the Russian army. They abandoned one another, abandoned all their heavy baggage, their artillery, and half their men, and fled, getting past the Russians by night by making semicircles to the right.

Ney, who came last, had been busying himself blowing up the walls of Smolénsk which were in nobody's way, because despite the unfortunate plight of the French or because of it, they wished to punish the floor against which they had hurt themselves. Ney, who had had a corps of ten thousand men, reached Napoleon at Orshá with only one thousand men left, having abandoned all the rest and all his cannon, and having crossed the Dnieper at night by stealth at a wooded spot.

From Orshá they fled farther along the road to Vílna, still playing at blindman's buff with the pursuing army. At the Berëzina they again became disorganized, many were drowned and many surrendered, but those who got across the river fled farther. Their supreme chief donned a fur coat and, having seated himself in a sleigh, galloped on alone, abandoning his companions. The others who could do so drove away too, leaving those who could not to surrender or die.

# XVIII

This campaign consisted in a flight of the French during which they did all they could to destroy themselves. From the time they turned onto the Kalúga road to the day their leader fled from the army, none of the movements of the crowd had any sense. So one might have thought that regarding this period of the campaign the historians, who attributed the actions of the mass to the will of one man, would have found it impossible to make the story of the retreat fit their theory. But no! Mountains of books have been written by the historians about this campaign, and everywhere are described Napoleon's arrangements, the maneuvers, and his profound plans which guided the army, as well as the military genius shown by his marshals.

The retreat from Málo-Yaroslávets when he had a free road into a well-supplied district and the parallel road was open to him along which Kutúzov afterwards pursued him—this unnecessary retreat along a devastated road—is explained to us as being due to profound considerations. Similarly profound considerations are given for his retreat from Smolénsk to Orshá. Then his heroism at Krásnoe is described, where he is reported to have been prepared to accept battle and take personal command, and to have walked about with a birch stick and said:

"J'ai assez fait l'empereur; il est temps de faire le général,"* but nevertheless immediately ran away again, abandoning to its fate the scattered fragments of the army he left behind.

Then we are told of the greatness of soul of the marshals, especially of Ney—a greatness of soul consisting in this: that he made his way by night around through the forest and across the Dnieper and escaped to Orshá, abandoning standards, artillery, and nine tenths of his men.

And lastly, the final departure of the great Emperor from his heroic army is presented to us by the historians as something great and characteristic of genius. Even that final running away, described in ordinary language as the lowest depth of baseness which every child is taught to be ashamed of—even that act finds justification in the historians' language.

---

* "I have acted the Emperor long enough; it is time to act the general."

When it is impossible to stretch the very elastic threads of historical ratiocination any farther, when actions are clearly contrary to all that humanity calls right or even just, the historians produce a saving conception of "greatness." "Greatness," it seems, excludes the standards of right and wrong. For the "great" man nothing is wrong, there is no atrocity for which a "great" man can be blamed.

"C'est grand!"* say the historians, and there no longer exists either good or evil but only "grand" and "not grand." Grand is good, not grand is bad. Grand is the characteristic, in their conception, of some special animals called "heroes." And Napoleon, escaping home in a warm fur coat and leaving to perish those who were not merely his comrades but were (in his opinion) men he had brought there, feels que c'est grand,† and his soul is tranquil.

"Du sublime (he saw something sublime in himself) au ridicule il n'y a qu'un pas,"‡ said he. And the whole world for fifty years has been repeating: "Sublime! Grand! Napoléon le Grand!" Du sublime au ridicule il n'y a qu'un pas.

And it occurs to no one that to admit a greatness not commensurable with the standard of right and wrong is merely to admit one's own nothingness and immeasurable meanness.

For us with the standard of good and evil given us by Christ, no human actions are incommensurable. And there is no greatness where simplicity, goodness, and truth are absent.

---

* "It is great."
† That it is great.
‡ "From the sublime to the ridiculous is but a step."

# XIX

What Russian, reading the account of the last part of the campaign of 1812, has not experienced an uncomfortable feeling of regret, dissatisfaction, and perplexity? Who has not asked himself how it is that the French were not all captured or destroyed when our three armies surrounded them in superior numbers, when the disordered French, hungry and freezing, surrendered in crowds, and when (as the historians relate) the aim of the Russians was to stop the French, to cut them off, and capture them all?

How was it that the Russian army, which when numerically weaker than the French had given battle at Borodinó, did not achieve its purpose when it had surrounded the French on three sides and when its aim was to capture them? Can the French be so enormously superior to us that when we had surrounded them with superior forces we could not beat them? How could that happen?

History (or what is called by that name) replying to these questions says that this occurred because Kutúzov and Tormásov and Chichagóv, and this man and that man, did not execute such and such maneuvers. . .

But why did they not execute those maneuvers? And why if they were guilty of not carrying out a prearranged plan were they not tried and punished? But even if we admitted that Kutúzov, Chichagóv, and others were the cause of the Russian failures, it is still incomprehensible why, the position of the Russian army being what it was at Krásnoe and at the Berëzina (in both cases we had superior forces), the French army with its marshals, kings, and Emperor was not captured, if that was what the Russians aimed at.

The explanation of this strange fact given by Russian military historians (to the effect that Kutúzov hindered an attack) is unfounded, for we know that he could not restrain the troops from attacking at Vyázma and Tarútino.

Why was the Russian army—which with inferior forces had withstood the enemy in full strength at Borodinó—defeated at Krásnoe and the Berëzina by the disorganized crowds of the French when it was numerically superior?

If the aim of the Russians consisted in cutting off and capturing Napoleon and his marshals—and that aim was not merely frustrated but all attempts to attain it were most shamefully baffled—then this last period of the campaign is quite rightly considered by the French to be a series of victories, and quite wrongly considered victorious by Russian historians.

The Russian military historians in so far as they submit to claims of logic must admit that conclusion, and in spite of their lyrical rhapsodies about valor, devotion, and so forth, must reluctantly admit that the French retreat from Moscow was a series of victories for Napoleon and defeats for Kutúzov.

But putting national vanity entirely aside one feels that such a conclusion involves a contradiction, since the series of French victories brought the French complete destruction, while the series of Russian defeats led to the total destruction of their enemy and the liberation of their country.

The source of this contradiction lies in the fact that the historians studying the events from the letters of the sovereigns and the generals, from memoirs, reports, projects, and so forth, have attributed to this last period of the war of 1812 an aim that never existed, namely that of cutting off and capturing Napoleon with his marshals and his army.

There never was or could have been such an aim, for it would have been senseless and its attainment quite impossible.

It would have been senseless, first because Napoleon's disorganized army was flying from Russia with all possible speed, that is to say, was doing just what every Russian desired. So what was the use of performing various operations on the French who were running away as fast as they possibly could?

Secondly, it would have been senseless to block the passage of men whose whole energy was directed to flight.

Thirdly, it would have been senseless to sacrifice one's own troops in order to destroy the French army, which without external interference was destroying itself at such a rate that, though its path was not blocked, it could not carry across the frontier more than it actually did in December, namely a hundredth part of the original army.

Fourthly, it would have been senseless to wish to take captive the Emperor, kings, and dukes—whose capture would have been in the highest degree embarrassing for the Russians, as the most adroit diplomatists of the time (Joseph de Maistre and others) recognized. Still more senseless would have been the wish to capture army corps of the French, when our own army had melted away to half before reaching Krásnoe and a whole division would have been needed to convoy the corps of prisoners, and when our men were not always getting full rations and the prisoners already taken were perishing of hunger.

All the profound plans about cutting off and capturing Napoleon and his army were like the plan of a market gardener who, when driving out of his garden a cow that had trampled down the beds he had planted, should run to the gate and hit the cow on the head. The only thing to be said in excuse of that gardener would be that he was very angry. But not even that could be said for those who drew up this project, for it was not they who had suffered from the trampled beds.

But besides the fact that cutting off Napoleon with his army would have been senseless, it was impossible.

It was impossible first because—as experience shows that a three-mile movement of columns on a battlefield never coincides with the plans—the probability of Chichagóv, Kutúzov, and Wittgenstein effecting a junction on time at an appointed place was so remote as to be tantamount to impossibility, as in fact thought Kutúzov, who when he received the plan remarked that diversions planned over great distances do not yield the desired results.

Secondly it was impossible, because to paralyze the momentum with which Napoleon's army was retiring, incomparably greater forces than the Russians possessed would have been required.

Thirdly it was impossible, because the military term "to cut off" has no meaning. One can cut off a slice of bread, but not an army. To cut off an army—to bar its road—is quite impossible, for there is always plenty of room to avoid capture and there is the night when nothing can be seen, as the military scientists might convince themselves by the example of Krásnoe and of the Berëzina. It is only possible to capture prisoners if they agree to be captured, just as it is only possible to catch a swallow if it settles on one's hand. Men can only be taken prisoners if they surrender according to the rules of strategy and tactics, as the Germans did. But the French troops quite rightly did not consider that this suited them, since death by hunger and cold awaited them in flight or captivity alike.

Fourthly and chiefly it was impossible, because never since the world began has a war been fought under such conditions as those that obtained in 1812, and the Russian army in its pursuit of the French strained its strength to the utmost and could not have done more without destroying itself.

During the movement of the Russian army from Tarútino to Krásnoe it lost fifty thousand sick or stragglers, that is a number equal to the population of a large provincial town. Half the men fell out of the army without a battle.

And it is of this period of the campaign—when the army lacked boots and sheepskin coats, was short of provisions and without vodka, and was camping out at night for months in the snow with fifteen degrees of frost, when there were only seven or eight hours of daylight and the rest was night in which the influence of discipline cannot be maintained, when men were taken into that region of death where discipline fails, not for a few hours only as in a battle, but for months, where they were every moment fighting death from hunger and cold, when half the army perished in a single month—it is of this period of the campaign that the historians tell us how Milorádovich should have made a flank march to such and such a place, Tormásov to another place, and Chichagóv should have crossed (more than knee-deep in snow) to somewhere else, and how so-and-so "routed" and "cut off" the French and so on and so on.

The Russians, half of whom died, did all that could and should have been done to attain an end worthy of the nation, and they are not to blame because other Russians, sitting in warm rooms, proposed that they should do what was impossible.

All that strange contradiction now difficult to understand between the facts and the historical accounts only arises because the historians dealing with the matter have written the history of the beautiful words and sentiments of various generals, and not the history of the events.

To them the words of Milorádovich seem very interesting, and so do their surmises and the rewards this or that general received; but the question of those fifty thousand men who were left in hospitals and in graves does not even interest them, for it does not come within the range of their investigation.

Yet one need only discard the study of the reports and general plans and consider the movement of those hundreds of thousands of men who took a direct part in the events, and all the questions that seemed insoluble easily and simply receive an immediate and certain solution.

The aim of cutting off Napoleon and his army never existed except in the imaginations of a dozen people. It could not exist because it was senseless and unattainable.

The people had a single aim: to free their land from invasion. That aim was attained in the first place of itself, as the French ran away, and so it was only necessary not to stop their flight. Secondly it was attained by the guerrilla warfare which was destroying the French, and thirdly by the fact that a large Russian army was following the French, ready to use its strength in case their movement stopped.

The Russian army had to act like a whip to a running animal. And the experienced driver knew it was better to hold the whip raised as a menace than to strike the running animal on the head.

BOOK FIFTEEN
1812-13

# I

When seeing a dying animal a man feels a sense of horror: substance similar to his own is perishing before his eyes. But when it is a beloved and intimate human being that is dying, besides this horror at the extinction of life there is a severance, a spiritual wound, which like a physical wound is sometimes fatal and sometimes heals, but always aches and shrinks at any external irritating touch.

After Prince Andrew's death Natásha and Princess Mary alike felt this. Drooping in spirit and closing their eyes before the menacing cloud of death that overhung them, they dared not look life in the face. They carefully guarded their open wounds from any rough and painful contact. Everything: a carriage passing rapidly in the street, a summons to dinner, the maid's inquiry what dress to prepare, or worse still any word of insincere or feeble sympathy, seemed an insult, painfully irritated the wound, interrupting that necessary quiet in which they both tried to listen to the stern and dreadful choir that still resounded in their imagination, and hindered their gazing into those mysterious limitless vistas that for an instant had opened out before them.

Only when alone together were they free from such outrage and pain. They spoke little even to one another, and when they did it was of very unimportant matters.

Both avoided any allusion to the future. To admit the possibility of a future seemed to them to insult his memory. Still more carefully did they avoid anything relating to him who was dead. It seemed to them that what they had lived through and experienced could not be expressed in words, and that any reference to the details of his life infringed the majesty and sacredness of the mystery that had been accomplished before their eyes.

Continued abstention from speech, and constant avoidance of everything that might lead up to the subject—this halting on all sides at the boundary of what they might not mention—brought before their minds with still greater purity and clearness what they were both feeling.

But pure and complete sorrow is as impossible as pure and complete joy. Princess Mary, in her position as absolute and independent arbiter of her own fate and guardian and instructor of her nephew, was the first to be called back to life from that realm of sorrow in which she had dwelt for the first fortnight. She received letters from her relations to which she had to reply; the room in which little Nicholas had been put was damp and he began to cough; Alpátych came to Yaroslávl with reports on the state of their affairs and with advice and suggestions that they should return to Moscow to the house on the Vozdvízhenka Street, which had remained uninjured and needed only slight repairs. Life did not stand still and it was necessary to live. Hard as it was for Princess Mary to emerge from the realm of secluded contemplation in which she had lived till then, and sorry and almost ashamed as she felt to leave Natásha alone, yet the cares of life demanded her attention and she involuntarily yielded to them. She went through the accounts with Alpátych, conferred with Dessalles about her nephew, and gave orders and made preparations for the journey to Moscow.

Natásha remained alone and, from the time Princess Mary began making preparations for departure, held aloof from her too.

Princess Mary asked the countess to let Natásha go with her to Moscow, and both parents gladly accepted this offer, for they saw their daughter losing strength every day and thought that a change of scene and the advice of Moscow doctors would be good for her.

"I am not going anywhere," Natásha replied when this was proposed to her. "Do please just leave me alone!" And she ran out of the room, with difficulty refraining from tears of vexation and irritation rather than of sorrow.

After she felt herself deserted by Princes Mary and alone in her grief, Natásha spent most of the time in her room by herself, sitting huddled up feet and all in the corner of the sofa, tearing and twisting something with her slender nervous fingers and gazing intently and fixedly at whatever her eyes chanced to fall on. This solitude exhausted and tormented her but she was in absolute need of it. As soon as anyone entered she got up quickly, changed her position and expression, and picked up a book or some sewing, evidently waiting impatiently for the intruder to go.

She felt all the time as if she might at any moment penetrate that on which—with a terrible questioning too great for her strength—her spiritual gaze was fixed.

One day toward the end of December Natásha, pale and thin, dressed in a black woolen gown, her plaited hair negligently twisted into a knot, was crouched feet and all in the corner of her sofa, nervously crumpling and smoothing out the end of her sash while she looked at a corner of the door.

She was gazing in the direction in which he had gone—to the other side of life. And that other side of life, of which she had never before thought and which had formerly seemed to her so far away and improbable, was now nearer and more akin and more comprehensible than this side of life, where everything was either emptiness and desolation or suffering and indignity.

She was gazing where she knew him to be; but she could not imagine him otherwise than as he had been here. She now saw him again as he had been at Mytíshchi, at Tróitsa, and at Yaroslávl.

She saw his face, heard his voice, repeated his words and her own, and sometimes devised other words they might have spoken.

There he is lying back in an armchair in his velvet cloak, leaning his head on his thin pale hand. His chest is dreadfully hollow and his shoulders raised. His lips are firmly closed, his eyes glitter, and a wrinkle comes and goes on his pale forehead. One of his legs twitches just perceptibly, but rapidly. Natásha knows that he is struggling with terrible pain. "What is that pain like? Why does he have that pain? What does he feel? How does it hurt him?" thought Natásha. He noticed her watching him, raised his eyes, and began to speak seriously:

"One thing would be terrible," said he: "to bind oneself forever to a suffering man. It would be continual torture." And he looked searchingly at her. Natásha as usual answered before she had time to think what she would say. She said: "This can't go on—it won't. You will get well—quite well."

She now saw him from the commencement of that scene and relived what she had then felt. She recalled his long sad and severe look at those words and understood the meaning of the rebuke and despair in that protracted gaze.

"I agreed," Natásha now said to herself, "that it would be dreadful if he always continued to suffer. I said it then only because it would have been dreadful for him, but he understood it differently. He thought it would be dreadful for me. He then still wished to live and feared death. And I said it so awkwardly and stupidly! I did not say what I meant. I thought quite differently. Had I said what I thought, I should have said: even if he had to go on dying, to die continually before my eyes, I should have been happy compared with what I am now. Now there is nothing. . . nobody. Did he know that? No, he did not and never will know it. And now it will never, never be possible to put it right." And now he again seemed to be saying the same words to her, only in her imagination Natásha this time gave him a different answer. She stopped him and said: "Terrible for you, but not for me! You know that for me there is nothing in life but you, and to suffer with you is the greatest happiness for me," and he took her hand and pressed it as he had pressed it that terrible evening four days before his death. And in her imagination she said other tender and loving words which she might have said then but only spoke now: "I love thee! . . . thee! I love, love. . ." she said, convulsively pressing her hands and setting her teeth with a desperate effort. . .

She was overcome by sweet sorrow and tears were already rising in her eyes; then she suddenly asked herself to whom she was saying this. Again everything was shrouded in hard, dry perplexity, and again with a strained frown she peered toward the world where he was. And now, now it seemed to her she was penetrating the mystery. . . But at the instant when it seemed that the incomprehensible was revealing itself to her a loud rattle of the door handle struck painfully on her ears. Dunyásha, her maid, entered the room quickly and abruptly with a frightened look on her face and showing no concern for her mistress.

"Come to your Papa at once, please!" said she with a strange, excited look. "A misfortune. . . about Peter Ilýnich. . . a letter," she finished with a sob.

# II

Besides a feeling of aloofness from everybody Natásha was feeling a special estrangement from the members of her own family. All of them—her father, mother, and Sónya—were so near to her, so familiar, so commonplace, that all their words and feelings seemed an insult to the world in which she had been living of late, and she felt not merely indifferent to them but regarded them with hostility. She heard Dunyásha's words about Peter Ilýnich and a misfortune, but did not grasp them.

"What misfortune? What misfortune can happen to them? They just live their own old, quiet, and commonplace life," thought Natásha.

As she entered the ballroom her father was hurriedly coming out of her mother's room. His face was puckered up and wet with tears. He had evidently run out of that room to give vent to the sobs that were choking him. When he saw Natásha he waved his arms despairingly and burst into convulsively painful sobs that distorted his soft round face.

"Pe. . . Pétya. . . Go, go, she. . . is calling. . ." and weeping like a child and quickly shuffling on his feeble legs to a chair, he almost fell into it, covering his face with his hands.

Suddenly an electric shock seemed to run through Natásha's whole being. Terrible anguish struck her heart, she felt a dreadful ache as if something was being torn inside her and she were dying. But the pain was immediately followed by a feeling of release from the oppressive constraint that had prevented her taking part in life. The sight of her father, the terribly wild cries of her mother that she heard through the door, made her immediately forget herself and her own grief.

She ran to her father, but he feebly waved his arm, pointing to her mother's door. Princess Mary, pale and with quivering chin, came out from that room and taking Natásha by the arm said something to her. Natásha neither saw nor heard her. She went in with rapid steps, pausing at the door for an instant as if struggling with herself, and then ran to her mother.

The countess was lying in an armchair in a strange and awkward position, stretching out and beating her head against the wall. Sónya and the maids were holding her arms.

"Natásha! Natásha! . . ." cried the countess. "It's not true. . . it's not true. . . He's lying. . . Natásha!" she shrieked, pushing those around her away. "Go away, all of you; it's not true! Killed! . . . ha, ha, ha! . . . It's not true!"

Natásha put one knee on the armchair, stooped over her mother, embraced her, and with unexpected strength raised her, turned her face toward herself, and clung to her.

"Mummy! . . . darling! . . . I am here, my dearest Mummy," she kept on whispering, not pausing an instant.

She did not let go of her mother but struggled tenderly with her, demanded a pillow and hot water, and unfastened and tore open her mother's dress.

"My dearest darling. . . Mummy, my precious! . . ." she whispered incessantly, kissing her head, her hands, her face, and feeling her own irrepressible and streaming tears tickling her nose and cheeks.

The countess pressed her daughter's hand, closed her eyes, and became quiet for a moment. Suddenly she sat up with unaccustomed swiftness, glanced vacantly around her, and seeing Natásha began to press her daughter's head with all her strength. Then she turned toward her daughter's face which was wincing with pain and gazed long at it.

"Natásha, you love me?" she said in a soft trustful whisper. "Natásha, you would not deceive me? You'll tell me the whole truth?"

Natásha looked at her with eyes full of tears and in her look there was nothing but love and an entreaty for forgiveness.

"My darling Mummy!" she repeated, straining all the power of her love to find some way of taking on herself the excess of grief that crushed her mother.

And again in a futile struggle with reality her mother, refusing to believe that she could live when her beloved boy was killed in the bloom of life, escaped from reality into a world of delirium.

Natásha did not remember how that day passed nor that night, nor the next day and night. She did not sleep and did not leave her mother. Her persevering and patient love seemed completely to surround the countess every moment, not explaining or consoling, but recalling her to life.

During the third night the countess kept very quiet for a few minutes, and Natásha rested her head on the arm of her chair and closed her eyes, but opened them again on hearing the bedstead creak. The countess was sitting up in bed and speaking softly.

"How glad I am you have come. You are tired. Won't you have some tea?" Natásha went up to her. "You have improved in looks and grown more manly," continued the countess, taking her daughter's hand.

"Mamma! What are you saying. . ."

"Natásha, he is no more, no more!"

And embracing her daughter, the countess began to weep for the first time.

# III

Princess Mary postponed her departure. Sónya and the count tried to replace Natásha but could not. They saw that she alone was able to restrain her mother from unreasoning despair. For three weeks Natásha remained constantly at her mother's side, sleeping on a lounge chair in her room, making her eat and drink, and talking to her incessantly because the mere sound of her tender, caressing tones soothed her mother.

The mother's wounded spirit could not heal. Pétya's death had torn from her half her life. When the news of Pétya's death had come she had been a fresh and vigorous woman of fifty, but a month later she left her room a listless old woman taking no interest in life. But the same blow that almost killed the countess, this second blow, restored Natásha to life.

A spiritual wound produced by a rending of the spiritual body is like a physical wound and, strange as it may seem, just as a deep wound may heal and its edges join, physical and spiritual wounds alike can yet heal completely only as the result of a vital force from within.

Natásha's wound healed in that way. She thought her life was ended, but her love for her mother unexpectedly showed her that the essence of life—love—was still active within her. Love awoke and so did life.

Prince Andrew's last days had bound Princess Mary and Natásha together; this new sorrow brought them still closer to one another. Princess Mary put off her departure, and for three weeks looked after Natásha as if she had been a sick child. The last weeks passed in her mother's bedroom had strained Natásha's physical strength.

One afternoon noticing Natásha shivering with fever, Princess Mary took her to her own room and made her lie down on the bed. Natásha lay down, but when Princess Mary had drawn the blinds and was going away she called her back.

"I don't want to sleep, Mary, sit by me a little."

"You are tired—try to sleep."

"No, no. Why did you bring me away? She will be asking for me."

"She is much better. She spoke so well today," said Princess Mary.

Natásha lay on the bed and in the semidarkness of the room scanned Princess Mary's face.

"Is she like him?" thought Natásha. "Yes, like and yet not like. But she is quite original, strange, new, and unknown. And she loves me.

What is in her heart? All that is good. But how? What is her mind like? What does she think about me? Yes, she is splendid!"

"Mary," she said timidly, drawing Princess Mary's hand to herself, "Mary, you mustn't think me wicked. No? Mary darling, how I love you! Let us be quite, quite friends."

And Natásha, embracing her, began kissing her face and hands, making Princess Mary feel shy but happy by this demonstration of her feelings.

From that day a tender and passionate friendship such as exists only between women was established between Princess Mary and Natásha. They were continually kissing and saying tender things to one another and spent most of their time together. When one went out the other became restless and hastened to rejoin her. Together they felt more in harmony with one another than either of them felt with herself when alone. A feeling stronger than friendship sprang up between them; an exclusive feeling of life being possible only in each other's presence.

Sometimes they were silent for hours; sometimes after they were already in bed they would begin talking and go on till morning. They spoke most of what was long past. Princess Mary spoke of her childhood, of her mother, her father, and her daydreams; and Natásha, who with a passive lack of understanding had formerly turned away from that life of devotion, submission, and the poetry of Christian self-sacrifice, now feeling herself bound to Princess Mary by affection, learned to love her past too and to understand a side of life previously incomprehensible to her. She did not think of applying submission and self-abnegation to her own life, for she was accustomed to seek other joys, but she understood and loved in another those previously incomprehensible virtues. For Princess Mary, listening to Natásha's tales of childhood and early youth, there also opened out a new and hitherto uncomprehended side of life: belief in life and its enjoyment.

Just as before, they never mentioned him so as not to lower (as they thought) their exalted feelings by words; but this silence about him had the effect of making them gradually begin to forget him without being conscious of it.

Natásha had grown thin and pale and physically so weak that they all talked about her health, and this pleased her. But sometimes she was suddenly overcome by fear not only of death but of sickness, weakness, and loss of good looks, and involuntarily she examined her bare arm carefully, surprised at its thinness, and in the morning noticed her drawn and, as it seemed to her, piteous face in her glass. It seemed to her that things must be so, and yet it was dreadfully sad.

One day she went quickly upstairs and found herself out of breath. Unconsciously she immediately invented a reason for going down, and then, testing her strength, ran upstairs again, observing the result.

Another time when she called Dunyásha her voice trembled, so she called again—though she could hear Dunyásha coming—called her in the deep chest tones in which she had been wont to sing, and listened attentively to herself.

She did not know and would not have believed it, but beneath the layer of slime that covered her soul and seemed to her impenetrable, delicate young shoots of grass were already sprouting, which taking root would so cover with their living verdure the grief that weighed her down that it would soon no longer be seen or noticed. The wound had begun to heal from within.

At the end of January Princess Mary left for Moscow, and the count insisted on Natásha's going with her to consult the doctors.

# IV

After the encounter at Vyázma, where Kutúzov had been unable to hold back his troops in their anxiety to overwhelm and cut off the enemy and so on, the farther movement of the fleeing French, and of the Russians who pursued them, continued as far as Krásnoe without a battle. The flight was so rapid that the Russian army pursuing the French could not keep up with them; cavalry and artillery horses broke down, and the information received of the movements of the French was never reliable.

The men in the Russian army were so worn out by this continuous marching at the rate of twenty-seven miles a day that they could not go any faster.

To realize the degree of exhaustion of the Russian army it is only necessary to grasp clearly the meaning of the fact that, while not losing more than five thousand killed and wounded after Tarútino and less than a hundred prisoners, the Russian army which left that place a hundred thousand strong reached Krásnoe with only fifty thousand.

The rapidity of the Russian pursuit was just as destructive to our army as the flight of the French was to theirs. The only difference was that the Russian army moved voluntarily, with no such threat of destruction as hung over the French, and that the sick Frenchmen were left behind in enemy hands while the sick Russians left behind were among their own people. The chief cause of the wastage of Napoleon's army was the rapidity of its movement, and a convincing proof of this is the corresponding decrease of the Russian army.

Kutúzov as far as was in his power, instead of trying to check the movement of the French as was desired in Petersburg and by the Russian army generals, directed his whole activity here, as he had done at Tarútino and Vyázma, to hastening it on while easing the movement of our army.

But besides this, since the exhaustion and enormous diminution of the army caused by the rapidity of the advance had become evident, another reason for slackening the pace and delaying presented itself to Kutúzov. The aim of the Russian army was to pursue the French. The road the French would take was unknown, and so the closer our troops trod on their heels the greater distance they had to cover. Only by following at some distance could one cut across the zigzag path of the French. All the artful maneuvers suggested by our generals meant fresh movements of the army and a lengthening of its marches, whereas the only reasonable aim was to shorten those marches. To that end Kutúzov's activity was directed during the whole campaign from Moscow to Vílna—not casually or intermittently but so consistently that he never once deviated from it.

Kutúzov felt and knew—not by reasoning or science but with the whole of his Russian being—what every Russian soldier felt: that the French were beaten, that the enemy was flying and must be driven out; but at the same time he like the soldiers realized all the hardship of this march, the rapidity of which was unparalleled for such a time of the year.

But to the generals, especially the foreign ones in the Russian army, who wished to distinguish themselves, to astonish somebody, and for some reason to capture a king or a duke—it seemed that now—when any battle must be horrible and senseless—was the very time to fight and conquer somebody. Kutúzov merely shrugged his shoulders when one after another they presented projects of maneuvers to be made with those soldiers—ill-shod, insufficiently clad, and half starved—who within a month and without fighting a battle had dwindled to half their number, and who at the best if the flight continued would have to go a greater distance than they had already traversed, before they reached the frontier.

This longing to distinguish themselves, to maneuver, to overthrow, and to cut off showed itself particularly whenever the Russians stumbled on the French army.

So it was at Krásnoe, where they expected to find one of the three French columns and stumbled instead on Napoleon himself with sixteen thousand men. Despite all Kutúzov's efforts to avoid that ruinous encounter and to preserve his troops, the massacre of the broken mob of French soldiers by worn-out Russians continued at Krásnoe for three days.

Toll wrote a disposition: "The first column will march to so and so," etc. And as usual nothing happened in accord with the disposition. Prince Eugène of Württemberg fired from a hill over the French crowds that were running past, and demanded reinforcements which did not arrive. The French, avoiding the Russians, dispersed and hid themselves in the forest by night, making their way round as best they could, and continued their flight.

Milorádovich, who said he did not want to know anything about the commissariat affairs of his detachment, and could never be found when he was wanted—that chevalier sans peur et sans reproch* as he styled himself—who was fond of parleys with the French, sent envoys demanding their surrender, wasted time, and did not do what he was ordered to do.

"I give you that column, lads," he said, riding up to the troops and pointing out the French to the cavalry.

And the cavalry, with spurs and sabers urging on horses that could scarcely move, trotted with much effort to the column presented to them—that is to say, to a crowd of Frenchmen stark with cold, frostbitten, and starving—and the column that had been presented to them threw down its arms and surrendered as it had long been anxious to do.

At Krásnoe they took twenty-six thousand prisoners, several hundred cannon, and a stick called a "marshal's staff," and disputed as to who had distinguished himself and were pleased with their achievement—though they much regretted not having taken Napoleon, or at least a marshal or a hero of some sort, and reproached one another and especially Kutúzov for having failed to do so.

These men, carried away by their passions, were but blind tools of the most melancholy law of necessity, but considered themselves heroes and imagined that they were accomplishing a most noble and honorable deed. They blamed Kutúzov and said that from the very beginning of the campaign he had prevented their vanquishing Napoleon, that he thought of nothing but satisfying his passions and would not advance from the Linen Factories because he was comfortable there, that at Krásnoe he checked the advance because on learning that Napoleon was there he had quite lost his head, and that it was probable that he had an understanding with Napoleon and had been bribed by him, and so on, and so on.

Not only did his contemporaries, carried away by their passions, talk in this way, but posterity and history have acclaimed Napoleon as grand, while Kutúzov is described by foreigners as a crafty, dissolute, weak old courtier, and by Russians as something indefinite—a sort of puppet useful only because he had a Russian name.

---

* Knight without fear and without reproach.

# V

In 1812 and 1813 Kutúzov was openly accused of blundering. The Emperor was dissatisfied with him. And in a history recently written by order of the Highest Authorities it is said that Kutúzov was a cunning court liar, frightened of the name of Napoleon, and that by his blunders at Krásnoe and the Berëzina he deprived the Russian army of the glory of complete victory over the French.*

Such is the fate not of great men (grands hommes) whom the Russian mind does not acknowledge, but of those rare and always solitary individuals who, discerning the will of Providence, submit their personal will to it. The hatred and contempt of the crowd punish such men for discerning the higher laws.

For Russian historians, strange and terrible to say, Napoleon—that most insignificant tool of history who never anywhere, even in exile, showed human dignity—Napoleon is the object of adulation and enthusiasm; he is grand. But Kutúzov—the man who from the beginning to the end of his activity in 1812, never once swerving by word or deed from Borodinó to Vílna, presented an example exceptional in history of self-sacrifice and a present consciousness of the future importance of what was happening—Kutúzov seems to them something indefinite and pitiful, and when speaking of him and of the year 1812 they always seem a little ashamed.

And yet it is difficult to imagine an historical character whose activity was so unswervingly directed to a single aim; and it would be difficult to imagine any aim more worthy or more consonant with the will of the whole people. Still more difficult would it be to find an instance in history of the aim of an historical personage being so completely accomplished as that to which all Kutúzov's efforts were directed in 1812.

Kutúzov never talked of "forty centuries looking down from the Pyramids," of the sacrifices he offered for the fatherland, or of what he intended to accomplish or had accomplished; in general he said nothing about himself, adopted no pose, always appeared to be the simplest and most ordinary of men, and said the simplest and most ordinary

---

* History of the year 1812. The character of Kutúzov and reflections on the unsatisfactory results of the battles at Krásnoe, by Bogdánovich.

things. He wrote letters to his daughters and to Madame de Staël, read novels, liked the society of pretty women, jested with generals, officers, and soldiers, and never contradicted those who tried to prove anything to him. When Count Rostopchín at the Yaúza bridge galloped up to Kutúzov with personal reproaches for having caused the destruction of Moscow, and said: "How was it you promised not to abandon Moscow without a battle?" Kutúzov replied: "And I shall not abandon Moscow without a battle," though Moscow was then already abandoned. When Arakchéev, coming to him from the Emperor, said that Ermólov ought to be appointed chief of the artillery, Kutúzov replied: "Yes, I was just saying so myself," though a moment before he had said quite the contrary. What did it matter to him—who then alone amid a senseless crowd understood the whole tremendous significance of what was happening—what did it matter to him whether Rostopchín attributed the calamities of Moscow to him or to himself? Still less could it matter to him who was appointed chief of the artillery.

Not merely in these cases but continually did that old man—who by experience of life had reached the conviction that thoughts and the words serving as their expression are not what move people—use quite meaningless words that happened to enter his head.

But that man, so heedless of his words, did not once during the whole time of his activity utter one word inconsistent with the single aim toward which he moved throughout the whole war. Obviously in spite of himself, in very diverse circumstances, he repeatedly expressed his real thoughts with the bitter conviction that he would not be understood. Beginning with the battle of Borodinó, from which time his disagreement with those about him began, he alone said that the battle of Borodinó was a victory, and repeated this both verbally and in his dispatches and reports up to the time of his death. He alone said that the loss of Moscow is not the loss of Russia. In reply to Lauriston's proposal of peace, he said: There can be no peace, for such is the people's will. He alone during the retreat of the French said that all our maneuvers are useless, everything is being accomplished of itself better than we could desire; that the enemy must be offered "a golden bridge"; that neither the Tarútino, the Vyázma, nor the Krásnoe battles were necessary; that we must keep some force to reach the frontier with, and that he would not sacrifice a single Russian for ten Frenchmen.

And this courtier, as he is described to us, who lies to Arakchéev to please the Emperor, he alone—incurring thereby the Emperor's displeasure—said in Vílna that to carry the war beyond the frontier is useless and harmful.

Nor do words alone prove that only he understood the meaning of the events. His actions—without the smallest deviation—were all directed to one and the same threefold end: (1) to brace all his strength for conflict with the French, (2) to defeat them, and (3) to drive them out of Russia, minimizing as far as possible the sufferings of our people and of our army.

This procrastinator Kutúzov, whose motto was "Patience and Time," this enemy of decisive action, gave battle at Borodinó, investing the preparations for it with unparalleled solemnity. This Kutúzov who before the battle of Austerlitz began said that it would be lost, he alone, in contradiction to everyone else, declared till his death that Borodinó was a victory, despite the assurance of generals that the battle was lost and despite the fact that for an army to have to retire after winning a battle was unprecedented. He alone during the whole retreat insisted that battles, which were useless then, should not be fought, and that a new war should not be begun nor the frontiers of Russia crossed.

It is easy now to understand the significance of these events—if only we abstain from attributing to the activity of the mass aims that existed only in the heads of a dozen individuals—for the events and results now lie before us.

But how did that old man, alone, in opposition to the general opinion, so truly discern the importance of the people's view of the events that in all his activity he was never once untrue to it?

The source of that extraordinary power of penetrating the meaning of the events then occuring lay in the national feeling which he possessed in full purity and strength.

Only the recognition of the fact that he possessed this feeling caused the people in so strange a manner, contrary to the Tsar's wish, to select him—an old man in disfavor—to be their representative in the national war. And only that feeling placed him on that highest human pedestal from which he, the commander in chief, devoted all his powers not to slaying and destroying men but to saving and showing pity on them.

That simple, modest, and therefore truly great, figure could not be cast in the false mold of a European hero—the supposed ruler of men—that history has invented.

To a lackey no man can be great, for a lackey has his own conception of greatness.

# VI

The fifth of November was the first day of what is called the battle of Krásnoe. Toward evening—after much disputing and many mistakes made by generals who did not go to their proper places, and after adjutants had been sent about with counterorders—when it had become plain that the enemy was everywhere in flight and that there could and would be no battle, Kutúzov left Krásnoe and went to Dóbroe whither his headquarters had that day been transferred.

The day was clear and frosty. Kutúzov rode to Dóbroe on his plump little white horse, followed by an enormous suite of discontented generals who whispered among themselves behind his back. All along the road groups of French prisoners captured that day (there were seven thousand of them) were crowding to warm themselves at campfires. Near Dóbroe an immense crowd of tattered prisoners, buzzing with talk and wrapped and bandaged in anything they had been able to get hold of, were standing in the road beside a long row of unharnessed French guns. At the approach of the commander in chief the buzz of talk ceased and all eyes were fixed on Kutúzov who, wearing a white cap with a red band and a padded overcoat that bulged on his round shoulders, moved slowly along the road on his white horse. One of the generals was reporting to him where the guns and prisoners had been captured.

Kutúzov seemed preoccupied and did not listen to what the general was saying. He screwed up his eyes with a dissatisfied look as he gazed attentively and fixedly at these prisoners, who presented a specially wretched appearance. Most of them were disfigured by frost-bitten noses and cheeks, and nearly all had red, swollen and festering eyes.

One group of the French stood close to the road, and two of them, one of whom had his face covered with sores, were tearing a piece of raw flesh with their hands. There was something horrible and bestial in the fleeting glance they threw at the riders and in the malevolent expression with which, after a glance at Kutúzov, the soldier with the sores immediately turned away and went on with what he was doing.

Kutúzov looked long and intently at these two soldiers. He puckered his face, screwed up his eyes, and pensively swayed his head. At another spot he noticed a Russian soldier laughingly patting a Frenchman on the shoulder, saying something to him in a friendly manner, and Kutúzov with the same expression on his face again swayed his head.

"What were you saying?" he asked the general, who continuing his report directed the commander in chief's attention to some standards captured from the French and standing in front of the Preobrazhénsk regiment.

"Ah, the standards!" said Kutúzov, evidently detaching himself with difficulty from the thoughts that preoccupied him.

He looked about him absently. Thousands of eyes were looking at him from all sides awaiting a word from him.

He stopped in front of the Preobrazhénsk regiment, sighed deeply, and closed his eyes. One of his suite beckoned to the soldiers carrying the standards to advance and surround the commander in chief with them. Kutúzov was silent for a few seconds and then, submitting with evident reluctance to the duty imposed by his position, raised his head and began to speak. A throng of officers surrounded him. He looked attentively around at the circle of officers, recognizing several of them.

"I thank you all!" he said, addressing the soldiers and then again the officers. In the stillness around him his slowly uttered words were distinctly heard. "I thank you all for your hard and faithful service. The victory is complete and Russia will not forget you! Honor to you forever."

He paused and looked around.

"Lower its head, lower it!" he said to a soldier who had accidentally lowered the French eagle he was holding before the Preobrazhénsk standards. "Lower, lower, that's it. Hurrah lads!" he added, addressing the men with a rapid movement of his chin.

"Hur-r-rah!" roared thousands of voices.

While the soldiers were shouting Kutúzov leaned forward in his saddle and bowed his head, and his eye lit up with a mild and apparently ironic gleam.

"You see, brothers. . ." said he when the shouts had ceased. . . and all at once his voice and the expression of his face changed. It was no longer the commander in chief speaking but an ordinary old man who wanted to tell his comrades something very important.

There was a stir among the throng of officers and in the ranks of the soldiers, who moved that they might hear better what he was going to say.

"You see, brothers, I know it's hard for you, but it can't be helped! Bear up; it won't be for long now! We'll see our visitors off and then we'll rest. The Tsar won't forget your service. It is hard for you, but still you are at home while they—you see what they have come to," said he, pointing to the prisoners. "Worse off than our poorest beggars. While they were strong we didn't spare ourselves, but now we may even pity them. They are human beings too. Isn't it so, lads?"

He looked around, and in the direct, respectful, wondering gaze fixed upon him he read sympathy with what he had said. His face grew brighter and brighter with an old man's mild smile, which drew the corners of his lips and eyes into a cluster of wrinkles. He ceased speaking and bowed his head as if in perplexity.

"But after all who asked them here? Serves them right, the bloody bastards!" he cried, suddenly lifting his head.

And flourishing his whip he rode off at a gallop for the first time during the whole campaign, and left the broken ranks of the soldiers laughing joyfully and shouting "Hurrah!"

Kutúzov's words were hardly understood by the troops. No one could have repeated the field marshal's address, begun solemnly and then changing into an old man's simplehearted talk; but the hearty sincerity of that speech, the feeling of majestic triumph combined with pity for the foe and consciousness of the justice of our cause, exactly expressed by that old man's good-natured expletives, was not merely understood but lay in the soul of every soldier and found expression in their joyous and long-sustained shouts. Afterwards when one of the generals addressed Kutúzov asking whether he wished his calèche to be sent for, Kutúzov in answering unexpectedly gave a sob, being evidently greatly moved.

# VII

When the troops reached their night's halting place on the eighth of November, the last day of the Krásnoe battles, it was already growing dusk. All day it had been calm and frosty with occasional lightly falling snow and toward evening it began to clear. Through the falling snow a purple-black and starry sky showed itself and the frost grew keener.

An infantry regiment which had left Tarútino three thousand strong but now numbered only nine hundred was one of the first to arrive that night at its halting place—a village on the highroad. The quartermasters who met the regiment announced that all the huts were full of sick and dead Frenchmen, cavalrymen, and members of the staff. There was only one hut available for the regimental commander.

The commander rode up to his hut. The regiment passed through the village and stacked its arms in front of the last huts.

Like some huge many-limbed animal, the regiment began to prepare its lair and its food. One part of it dispersed and waded knee-deep through the snow into a birch forest to the right of the village, and immediately the sound of axes and swords, the crashing of branches, and merry voices could be heard from there. Another section amid the regimental wagons and horses which were standing in a group was busy getting out caldrons and rye biscuit, and feeding the horses. A third section scattered through the village arranging quarters for the staff officers, carrying out the French corpses that were in the huts, and dragging away boards, dry wood, and thatch from the roofs, for the campfires, or wattle fences to serve for shelter.

Some fifteen men with merry shouts were shaking down the high wattle wall of a shed, the roof of which had already been removed.

"Now then, all together—shove!" cried the voices, and the huge surface of the wall, sprinkled with snow and creaking with frost, was seen swaying in the gloom of the night. The lower stakes cracked more and more and at last the wall fell, and with it the men who had been pushing it. Loud, coarse laughter and joyous shouts ensued.

"Now then, catch hold in twos! Hand up the lever! That's it. . . Where are you shoving to?"

"Now, all together! But wait a moment, boys. . . With a song!"

All stood silent, and a soft, pleasant velvety voice began to sing. At the end of the third verse as the last note died away, twenty voices roared out at once: "Oo-oo-oo-oo! That's it. All together! Heave away, boys! . . ." but despite their united efforts the wattle hardly moved, and in the silence that followed the heavy breathing of the men was audible.

"Here, you of the Sixth Company! Devils that you are! Lend a hand. . . will you? You may want us one of these days."

Some twenty men of the Sixth Company who were on their way into the village joined the haulers, and the wattle wall, which was about thirty-five feet long and seven feet high, moved forward along the village street, swaying, pressing upon and cutting the shoulders of the gasping men.

"Get along. . . Falling? What are you stopping for? There now. . ."

Merry senseless words of abuse flowed freely.

"What are you up to?" suddenly came the authoritative voice of a sergeant major who came upon the men who were hauling their burden. "There are gentry here; the general himself is in that hut, and you foul-mouthed devils, you brutes, I'll give it to you!" shouted he, hitting the first man who came in his way a swinging blow on the back. "Can't you make less noise?"

The men became silent. The soldier who had been struck groaned and wiped his face, which had been scratched till it bled by his falling against the wattle.

"There, how that devil hits out! He's made my face all bloody," said he in a frightened whisper when the sergeant major had passed on.

"Don't you like it?" said a laughing voice, and moderating their tones the men moved forward.

When they were out of the village they began talking again as loud as before, interlarding their talk with the same aimless expletives.

In the hut which the men had passed, the chief officers had gathered and were in animated talk over their tea about the events of the day and the maneuvers suggested for tomorrow. It was proposed to make a flank march to the left, cut off the Vice-King (Murat) and capture him.

By the time the soldiers had dragged the wattle fence to its place the campfires were blazing on all sides ready for cooking, the wood crackled, the snow was melting, and black shadows of soldiers flitted to and fro all over the occupied space where the snow had been trodden down.

Axes and choppers were plied all around. Everything was done without any orders being given. Stores of wood were brought for the night, shelters were rigged up for the officers, caldrons were being boiled, and muskets and accouterments put in order.

The wattle wall the men had brought was set up in a semicircle by the Eighth Company as a shelter from the north, propped up by musket rests, and a campfire was built before it. They beat the tattoo, called the roll, had supper, and settled down round the fires for the night— some repairing their footgear, some smoking pipes, and some stripping themselves naked to steam the lice out of their shirts.

# VIII

One would have thought that under the almost incredibly wretched conditions the Russian soldiers were in at that time—lacking warm boots and sheepskin coats, without a roof over their heads, in the snow with eighteen degrees of frost, and without even full rations (the commissariat did not always keep up with the troops)—they would have presented a very sad and depressing spectacle.

On the contrary, the army had never under the best material conditions presented a more cheerful and animated aspect. This was because all who began to grow depressed or who lost strength were sifted out of the army day by day. All the physically or morally weak had long since been left behind and only the flower of the army—physically and mentally—remained.

More men collected behind the wattle fence of the Eighth Company than anywhere else. Two sergeants major were sitting with them and their campfire blazed brighter than others. For leave to sit by their wattle they demanded contributions of fuel.

"Eh, Makéev! What has become of you, you son of a bitch? Are you lost or have the wolves eaten you? Fetch some more wood!" shouted a red-haired and red-faced man, screwing up his eyes and blinking because of the smoke but not moving back from the fire. "And you, Jackdaw, go and fetch some wood!" said he to another soldier.

This red-haired man was neither a sergeant nor a corporal, but being robust he ordered about those weaker than himself. The soldier they called "Jackdaw," a thin little fellow with a sharp nose, rose obediently and was about to go but at that instant there came into the light of the fire the slender, handsome figure of a young soldier carrying a load of wood.

"Bring it here—that's fine!"

They split up the wood, pressed it down on the fire, blew at it with their mouths, and fanned it with the skirts of their greatcoats, making the flames hiss and crackle. The men drew nearer and lit their pipes. The handsome young soldier who had brought the wood, setting his arms akimbo, began stamping his cold feet rapidly and deftly on the spot where he stood.

"Mother! The dew is cold but clear. . . It's well that I'm a musketeer. . ." he sang, pretending to hiccough after each syllable.

"Look out, your soles will fly off!" shouted the red-haired man, noticing that the sole of the dancer's boot was hanging loose. "What a fellow you are for dancing!"

The dancer stopped, pulled off the loose piece of leather, and threw it on the fire.

"Right enough, friend," said he, and, having sat down, took out of his knapsack a scrap of blue French cloth, and wrapped it round his foot. "It's the steam that spoils them," he added, stretching out his feet toward the fire.

"They'll soon be issuing us new ones. They say that when we've finished hammering them, we're to receive double kits!"

"And that son of a bitch Petróv has lagged behind after all, it seems," said one sergeant major.

"I've had an eye on him this long while," said the other.

"Well, he's a poor sort of soldier. . ."

"But in the Third Company they say nine men were missing yesterday."

"Yes, it's all very well, but when a man's feet are frozen how can he walk?"

"Eh? Don't talk nonsense!" said a sergeant major.

"Do you want to be doing the same?" said an old soldier, turning reproachfully to the man who had spoken of frozen feet.

"Well, you know," said the sharp-nosed man they called Jackdaw in a squeaky and unsteady voice, raising himself at the other side of the fire, "a plump man gets thin, but for a thin one it's death. Take me, now! I've got no strength left," he added, with sudden resolution turning to the sergeant major. "Tell them to send me to hospital; I'm aching all over; anyway I shan't be able to keep up."

"That'll do, that'll do!" replied the sergeant major quietly.

The soldier said no more and the talk went on.

"What a lot of those Frenchies were taken today, and the fact is that not one of them had what you might call real boots on," said a soldier, starting a new theme. "They were no more than make-believes."

"The Cossacks have taken their boots. They were clearing the hut for the colonel and carried them out. It was pitiful to see them, boys," put in the dancer. "As they turned them over one seemed still alive and, would you believe it, he jabbered something in their lingo."

"But they're a clean folk, lads," the first man went on; "he was white—as white as birchbark—and some of them are such fine fellows, you might think they were nobles."

"Well, what do you think? They make soldiers of all classes there."

"But they don't understand our talk at all," said the dancer with a puzzled smile. "I asked him whose subject he was, and he jabbered in his own way. A queer lot!"

"But it's strange, friends," continued the man who had wondered at their whiteness, "the peasants at Mozháysk were saying that when they began burying the dead—where the battle was you know—well, those dead had been lying there for nearly a month, and says the peasant, 'they lie as white as paper, clean, and not as much smell as a puff of powder smoke.'"

"Was it from the cold?" asked someone.

"You're a clever fellow! From the cold indeed! Why, it was hot. If it had been from the cold, ours would not have rotted either. 'But,' he says, 'go up to ours and they are all rotten and maggoty. So,' he says, 'we tie our faces up with kerchiefs and turn our heads away as we drag them off: we can hardly do it. But theirs,' he says, 'are white as paper and not so much smell as a whiff of gunpowder.'"

All were silent.

"It must be from their food," said the sergeant major. "They used to gobble the same food as the gentry."

No one contradicted him.

"That peasant near Mozháysk where the battle was said the men were all called up from ten villages around and they carted for twenty days and still didn't finish carting the dead away. And as for the wolves, he says. . ."

"That was a real battle," said an old soldier. "It's the only one worth remembering; but since that. . . it's only been tormenting folk."

"And do you know, Daddy, the day before yesterday we ran at them and, my word, they didn't let us get near before they just threw down their muskets and went on their knees. 'Pardon!' they say. That's only one case. They say Plátov took 'Poleon himself twice. But he didn't know the right charm. He catches him and catches him—no good! He turns into a bird in his hands and flies away. And there's no way of killing him either."

"You're a first-class liar, Kiselëv, when I come to look at you!"

"Liar, indeed! It's the real truth."

"If he fell into my hands, when I'd caught him I'd bury him in the ground with an aspen stake to fix him down. What a lot of men he's ruined!"

"Well, anyhow we're going to end it. He won't come here again," remarked the old soldier, yawning.

The conversation flagged, and the soldiers began settling down to sleep.

"Look at the stars. It's wonderful how they shine! You would think the women had spread out their linen," said one of the men, gazing with admiration at the Milky Way.

"That's a sign of a good harvest next year."

"We shall want some more wood."

"You warm your back and your belly gets frozen. That's queer."

"O Lord!"

"What are you pushing for? Is the fire only for you? Look how he's sprawling!"

In the silence that ensued, the snoring of those who had fallen asleep could be heard. Others turned over and warmed themselves, now and again exchanging a few words. From a campfire a hundred paces off came a sound of general, merry laughter.

"Hark at them roaring there in the Fifth Company!" said one of the soldiers, "and what a lot of them there are!"

One of the men got up and went over to the Fifth Company.

"They're having such fun," said he, coming back. "Two Frenchies have turned up. One's quite frozen and the other's an awful swaggerer. He's singing songs. . ."

"Oh, I'll go across and have a look. . ."

And several of the men went over to the Fifth Company.

# IX

The Fifth company was bivouacking at the very edge of the forest. A huge campfire was blazing brightly in the midst of the snow, lighting up the branches of trees heavy with hoarfrost.

About midnight they heard the sound of steps in the snow of the forest, and the crackling of dry branches.

"A bear, lads," said one of the men.

They all raised their heads to listen, and out of the forest into the bright firelight stepped two strangely clad human figures clinging to one another.

These were two Frenchmen who had been hiding in the forest. They came up to the fire, hoarsely uttering something in a language our soldiers did not understand. One was taller than the other; he wore an officer's hat and seemed quite exhausted. On approaching the fire he had been going to sit down, but fell. The other, a short sturdy soldier with a shawl tied round his head, was stronger. He raised his companion and said something, pointing to his mouth. The soldiers surrounded the Frenchmen, spread a greatcoat on the ground for the sick man, and brought some buckwheat porridge and vodka for both of them.

The exhausted French officer was Ramballe and the man with his head wrapped in the shawl was Morel, his orderly.

When Morel had drunk some vodka and finished his bowl of porridge he suddenly became unnaturally merry and chattered incessantly to the soldiers, who could not understand him. Ramballe refused food and resting his head on his elbow lay silent beside the campfire, looking at the Russian soldiers with red and vacant eyes. Occasionally he emitted a long-drawn groan and then again became silent. Morel, pointing to his shoulders, tried to impress on the soldiers the fact that Ramballe was an officer and ought to be warmed. A Russian officer who had come up to the fire sent to ask his colonel whether he would not take a French officer into his hut to warm him, and when the messenger returned and said that the colonel wished the officer to be brought to him, Ramballe was told to go. He rose and tried to walk, but staggered and would have fallen had not a soldier standing by held him up.

"You won't do it again, eh?" said one of the soldiers, winking and turning mockingly to Ramballe.

"Oh, you fool! Why talk rubbish, lout that you are—a real peasant!" came rebukes from all sides addressed to the jesting soldier.

They surrounded Ramballe, lifted him on the crossed arms of two soldiers, and carried him to the hut. Ramballe put his arms around their necks while they carried him and began wailing plaintively:

"Oh, you fine fellows, my kind, kind friends! These are men! Oh, my brave, kind friends," and he leaned his head against the shoulder of one of the men like a child.

Meanwhile Morel was sitting in the best place by the fire, surrounded by the soldiers.

Morel, a short sturdy Frenchman with inflamed and streaming eyes, was wearing a woman's cloak and had a shawl tied woman fashion round his head over his cap. He was evidently tipsy, and was singing a French song in a hoarse broken voice, with an arm thrown round the nearest soldier. The soldiers simply held their sides as they watched him.

"Now then, now then, teach us how it goes! I'll soon pick it up. How is it?" said the man—a singer and a wag—whom Morel was embracing.

"Vive Henri Quatre! Vive ce roi valiant!" sang Morel, winking. "Ce diable à quatre. . ."*

"Vivarika! Vif-seruvaru! Sedyablyaka!" repeated the soldier, flourishing his arm and really catching the tune.

"Bravo! Ha, ha, ha!" rose their rough, joyous laughter from all sides.

Morel, wrinkling up his face, laughed too.

"Well, go on, go on!"

> *"Qui eut le triple talent,*
> *De boire, de battre,*
> *Et d'être un vert galant."†*

"It goes smoothly, too. Well, now, Zaletáev!"

"Ke. . ." Zaletáev, brought out with effort: "ke-e-e-e," he drawled, laboriously pursing his lips, "le-trip-ta-la-de-bu-de-ba, e de-tra-va-ga-la" he sang.

"Fine! Just like the Frenchie! Oh, ho ho! Do you want some more to eat?"

---

* "Long live Henry the Fourth, that valiant king! That rowdy devil."
† *Who had a triple talent*
*For drinking, for fighting,*
*And for being a gallant old boy. . .*

"Give him some porridge: it takes a long time to get filled up after starving."

They gave him some more porridge and Morel with a laugh set to work on his third bowl. All the young soldiers smiled gaily as they watched him. The older men, who thought it undignified to amuse themselves with such nonsense, continued to lie at the opposite side of the fire, but one would occasionally raise himself on an elbow and glance at Morel with a smile.

"They are men too," said one of them as he wrapped himself up in his coat. "Even wormwood grows on its own root."

"O Lord, O Lord! How starry it is! Tremendous! That means a hard frost. . ."

They all grew silent. The stars, as if knowing that no one was looking at them, began to disport themselves in the dark sky: now flaring up, now vanishing, now trembling, they were busy whispering something gladsome and mysterious to one another.

# X

The French army melted away at the uniform rate of a mathematical progression; and that crossing of the Berëzina about which so much has been written was only one intermediate stage in its destruction, and not at all the decisive episode of the campaign. If so much has been and still is written about the Berëzina, on the French side this is only because at the broken bridge across that river the calamities their army had been previously enduring were suddenly concentrated at one moment into a tragic spectacle that remained in every memory, and on the Russian side merely because in Petersburg—far from the seat of war—a plan (again one of Pfuel's) had been devised to catch Napoleon in a strategic trap at the Berëzina River. Everyone assured himself that all would happen according to plan, and therefore insisted that it was just the crossing of the Berëzina that destroyed the French army. In reality the results of the crossing were much less disastrous to the French—in guns and men lost—than Krásnoe had been, as the figures show.

The sole importance of the crossing of the Berëzina lies in the fact that it plainly and indubitably proved the fallacy of all the plans for cutting off the enemy's retreat and the soundness of the only possible line of action—the one Kutúzov and the general mass of the army demanded—namely, simply to follow the enemy up. The French crowd fled at a continually increasing speed and all its energy was directed to reaching its goal. It fled like a wounded animal and it was impossible to block its path. This was shown not so much by the arrangements it made for crossing as by what took place at the bridges. When the bridges broke down, unarmed soldiers, people from Moscow and women with children who were with the French transport, all—carried on by vis inertiæ—pressed forward into boats and into the ice-covered water and did not surrender.

That impulse was reasonable. The condition of fugitives and of pursuers was equally bad. As long as they remained with their own people each might hope for help from his fellows and the definite place he held among them. But those who surrendered, while remaining in the same pitiful plight, would be on a lower level to claim a share in the necessities of life. The French did not need to be informed of the fact that half the prisoners—with whom the Russians did not know what to do—perished

LEO TOLSTOY

of cold and hunger despite their captors' desire to save them; they felt that it could not be otherwise. The most compassionate Russian commanders, those favorable to the French—and even the Frenchmen in the Russian service—could do nothing for the prisoners. The French perished from the conditions to which the Russian army was itself exposed. It was impossible to take bread and clothes from our hungry and indispensable soldiers to give to the French who, though not harmful, or hated, or guilty, were simply unnecessary. Some Russians even did that, but they were exceptions.

Certain destruction lay behind the French but in front there was hope. Their ships had been burned, there was no salvation save in collective flight, and on that the whole strength of the French was concentrated.

The farther they fled the more wretched became the plight of the remnant, especially after the Berëzina, on which (in consequence of the Petersburg plan) special hopes had been placed by the Russians, and the keener grew the passions of the Russian commanders, who blamed one another and Kutúzov most of all. Anticipation that the failure of the Petersburg Berëzina plan would be attributed to Kutúzov led to dissatisfaction, contempt, and ridicule, more and more strongly expressed. The ridicule and contempt were of course expressed in a respectful form, making it impossible for him to ask wherein he was to blame. They did not talk seriously to him; when reporting to him or asking for his sanction they appeared to be fulfilling a regrettable formality, but they winked behind his back and tried to mislead him at every turn.

Because they could not understand him all these people assumed that it was useless to talk to the old man; that he would never grasp the profundity of their plans, that he would answer with his phrases (which they thought were mere phrases) about a "golden bridge," about the impossibility of crossing the frontier with a crowd of tatterdemalions, and so forth. They had heard all that before. And all he said—that it was necessary to await provisions, or that the men had no boots—was so simple, while what they proposed was so complicated and clever, that it was evident that he was old and stupid and that they, though not in power, were commanders of genius.

After the junction with the army of the brilliant admiral and Petersburg hero Wittgenstein, this mood and the gossip of the staff reached their maximum. Kutúzov saw this and merely sighed and shrugged his shoulders. Only once, after the affair of the Berëzina, did he get angry and write to Bennigsen (who reported separately to the Emperor) the following letter:

"On account of your spells of ill health, will your excellency please be so good as to set off for Kalúga on receipt of this, and there await further commands and appointments from His Imperial Majesty."

But after Bennigsen's departure, the Grand Duke Tsarévich Constantine Pávlovich joined the army. He had taken part in the beginning of the campaign but had subsequently been removed from the army by Kutúzov. Now having come to the army, he informed Kutúzov of the Emperor's displeasure at the poor success of our forces and the slowness of their advance. The Emperor intended to join the army personally in a few days' time.

The old man, experienced in court as well as in military affairs—this same Kutúzov who in August had been chosen commander in chief against the sovereign's wishes and who had removed the Grand Duke and heir-apparent from the army—who on his own authority and contrary to the Emperor's will had decided on the abandonment of Moscow, now realized at once that his day was over, that his part was played, and that the power he was supposed to hold was no longer his. And he understood this not merely from the attitude of the court. He saw on the one hand that the military business in which he had played his part was ended and felt that his mission was accomplished; and at the same time he began to be conscious of the physical weariness of his aged body and of the necessity of physical rest.

On the twenty-ninth of November Kutúzov entered Vílna—his "dear Vílna" as he called it. Twice during his career Kutúzov had been governor of Vílna. In that wealthy town, which had not been injured, he found old friends and associations, besides the comforts of life of which he had so long been deprived. And he suddenly turned from the cares of army and state and, as far as the passions that seethed around him allowed, immersed himself in the quiet life to which he had formerly been accustomed, as if all that was taking place and all that had still to be done in the realm of history did not concern him at all.

Chichagóv, one of the most zealous "cutters-off" and "breakers-up," who had first wanted to effect a diversion in Greece and then in Warsaw but never wished to go where he was sent: Chichagóv, noted for the boldness with which he spoke to the Emperor, and who considered Kutúzov to be under an obligation to him because when he was sent to make peace with Turkey in 1811 independently of Kutúzov, and found that peace had already been concluded, he admitted to the Emperor that the merit of securing that peace was really Kutúzov's; this Chichagóv was the first to meet Kutúzov at the castle where the latter was to stay. In undress naval uniform, with a dirk, and holding his cap under his arm, he handed Kutúzov a garrison report and the keys of the town. The contemptuously respectful attitude of the younger men to the old man in his dotage was expressed in the highest degree by the behavior of Chichagóv, who knew of the accusations that were being directed against Kutúzov.

When speaking to Chichagóv, Kutúzov incidentally mentioned that the vehicles packed with china that had been captured from him at Borísov had been recovered and would be restored to him.

"You mean to imply that I have nothing to eat out of... On the contrary, I can supply you with everything even if you want to give dinner parties," warmly replied Chichagóv, who tried by every word he spoke to prove his own rectitude and therefore imagined Kutúzov to be animated by the same desire.

Kutúzov, shrugging his shoulders, replied with his subtle penetrating smile: "I meant merely to say what I said."

Contrary to the Emperor's wish Kutúzov detained the greater part of the army at Vílna. Those about him said that he became extraordinarily slack and physically feeble during his stay in that town. He attended to army affairs reluctantly, left everything to his generals, and while awaiting the Emperor's arrival led a dissipated life.

Having left Petersburg on the seventh of December with his suite Count Tolstóy, Prince Volkónski, Arakchéev, and others—the Emperor reached Vílna on the eleventh, and in his traveling sleigh drove straight to the castle. In spite of the severe frost some hundred generals and staff officers in full parade uniform stood in front of the castle, as well as a guard of honor of the Seménov regiment.

A courier who galloped to the castle in advance, in a troyka with three foam-flecked horses, shouted "Coming!" and Konovnítsyn rushed into the vestibule to inform Kutúzov, who was waiting in the hall porter's little lodge.

A minute later the old man's large stout figure in full-dress uniform, his chest covered with orders and a scarf drawn round his stomach, waddled out into the porch. He put on his hat with its peaks to the sides and, holding his gloves in his hand and walking with an effort sideways down the steps to the level of the street, took in his hand the report he had prepared for the Emperor.

There was running to and fro and whispering; another troyka flew furiously up, and then all eyes were turned on an approaching sleigh in which the figures of the Emperor and Volkónski could already be descried.

From the habit of fifty years all this had a physically agitating effect on the old general. He carefully and hastily felt himself all over, readjusted his hat, and pulling himself together drew himself up and, at the very moment when the Emperor, having alighted from the sleigh, lifted his eyes to him, handed him the report and began speaking in his smooth, ingratiating voice.

The Emperor with a rapid glance scanned Kutúzov from head to foot, frowned for an instant, but immediately mastering himself went up to the old man, extended his arms and embraced him. And this embrace too, owing to a long-standing impression related to his innermost feelings, had its usual effect on Kutúzov and he gave a sob.

The Emperor greeted the officers and the Seménov guard, and again pressing the old man's hand went with him into the castle.

When alone with the field marshal the Emperor expressed his dissatisfaction at the slowness of the pursuit and at the mistakes made at Krásnoe and the Berézina, and informed him of his intentions for a future campaign abroad. Kutúzov made no rejoinder or remark. The same submissive, expressionless look with which he had listened to the Emperor's commands on the field of Austerlitz seven years before settled on his face now.

When Kutúzov came out of the study and with lowered head was crossing the ballroom with his heavy waddling gait, he was arrested by someone's voice saying:

"Your Serene Highness!"

Kutúzov raised his head and looked for a long while into the eyes of Count Tolstóy, who stood before him holding a silver salver on which lay a small object. Kutúzov seemed not to understand what was expected of him.

Suddenly he seemed to remember; a scarcely perceptible smile flashed across his puffy face, and bowing low and respectfully he took the object that lay on the salver. It was the Order of St. George of the First Class.

# XI

Next day the field marshal gave a dinner and ball which the Emperor honored by his presence. Kutúzov had received the Order of St. George of the First Class and the Emperor showed him the highest honors, but everyone knew of the imperial dissatisfaction with him. The proprieties were observed and the Emperor was the first to set that example, but everybody understood that the old man was blameworthy and good-for-nothing. When Kutúzov, conforming to a custom of Catherine's day, ordered the standards that had been captured to be lowered at the Emperor's feet on his entering the ballroom, the Emperor made a wry face and muttered something in which some people caught the words, "the old comedian."

The Emperor's displeasure with Kutúzov was specially increased at Vílna by the fact that Kutúzov evidently could not or would not understand the importance of the coming campaign.

When on the following morning the Emperor said to the officers assembled about him: "You have not only saved Russia, you have saved Europe!" they all understood that the war was not ended.

Kutúzov alone would not see this and openly expressed his opinion that no fresh war could improve the position or add to the glory of Russia, but could only spoil and lower the glorious position that Russia had gained. He tried to prove to the Emperor the impossibility of levying fresh troops, spoke of the hardships already endured by the people, of the possibility of failure and so forth.

This being the field marshal's frame of mind he was naturally regarded as merely a hindrance and obstacle to the impending war.

To avoid unpleasant encounters with the old man, the natural method was to do what had been done with him at Austerlitz and with Barclay at the beginning of the Russian campaign—to transfer the authority to the Emperor himself, thus cutting the ground from under the commander in chief's feet without upsetting the old man by informing him of the change.

With this object his staff was gradually reconstructed and its real strength removed and transferred to the Emperor. Toll, Konovnítsyn, and Ermólov received fresh appointments. Everyone spoke loudly of the field marshal's great weakness and failing health.

His health had to be bad for his place to be taken away and given to another. And in fact his health was poor.

So naturally, simply, and gradually—just as he had come from Turkey to the Treasury in Petersburg to recruit the militia, and then to the army when he was needed there—now when his part was played out, Kutúzov's place was taken by a new and necessary performer.

The war of 1812, besides its national significance dear to every Russian heart, was now to assume another, a European, significance.

The movement of peoples from west to east was to be succeeded by a movement of peoples from east to west, and for this fresh war another leader was necessary, having qualities and views differing from Kutúzov's and animated by different motives.

Alexander I was as necessary for the movement of the peoples from east to west and for the refixing of national frontiers as Kutúzov had been for the salvation and glory of Russia.

Kutúzov did not understand what Europe, the balance of power, or Napoleon meant. He could not understand it. For the representative of the Russian people, after the enemy had been destroyed and Russia had been liberated and raised to the summit of her glory, there was nothing left to do as a Russian. Nothing remained for the representative of the national war but to die, and Kutúzov died.

# XII

As generally happens, Pierre did not feel the full effects of the physical privation and strain he had suffered as prisoner until after they were over. After his liberation he reached Orël, and on the third day there, when preparing to go to Kiev, he fell ill and was laid up for three months. He had what the doctors termed "bilious fever." But despite the fact that the doctors treated him, bled him, and gave him medicines to drink, he recovered.

Scarcely any impression was left on Pierre's mind by all that happened to him from the time of his rescue till his illness. He remembered only the dull gray weather now rainy and now snowy, internal physical distress, and pains in his feet and side. He remembered a general impression of the misfortunes and sufferings of people and of being worried by the curiosity of officers and generals who questioned him, he also remembered his difficulty in procuring a conveyance and horses, and above all he remembered his incapacity to think and feel all that time. On the day of his rescue he had seen the body of Pétya Rostóv. That same day he had learned that Prince Andrew, after surviving the battle of Borodinó for more than a month had recently died in the Rostóvs' house at Yaroslávl, and Denísov who told him this news also mentioned Hélène's death, supposing that Pierre had heard of it long before. All this at the time seemed merely strange to Pierre: he felt he could not grasp its significance. Just then he was only anxious to get away as quickly as possible from places where people were killing one another, to some peaceful refuge where he could recover himself, rest, and think over all the strange new facts he had learned; but on reaching Orël he immediately fell ill. When he came to himself after his illness he saw in attendance on him two of his servants, Terénty and Váska, who had come from Moscow; and also his cousin the eldest princess, who had been living on his estate at Eléts and hearing of his rescue and illness had come to look after him.

It was only gradually during his convalescence that Pierre lost the impressions he had become accustomed to during the last few months and got used to the idea that no one would oblige him to go anywhere tomorrow, that no one would deprive him of his warm bed, and that he would be sure to get his dinner, tea, and supper. But for a long time in his dreams he still saw himself in the conditions of captivity. In the same way little by little he came to understand the news he had been told after his rescue, about the death of Prince Andrew, the death of his wife, and the destruction of the French.

A joyous feeling of freedom—that complete inalienable freedom natural to man which he had first experienced at the first halt outside Moscow—filled Pierre's soul during his convalescence. He was surprised to find that this inner freedom, which was independent of external conditions, now had as it were an additional setting of external liberty. He was alone in a strange town, without acquaintances. No one demanded anything of him or sent him anywhere. He had all he wanted: the thought of his wife which had been a continual torment to him was no longer there, since she was no more.

"Oh, how good! How splendid!" said he to himself when a cleanly laid table was moved up to him with savory beef tea, or when he lay down for the night on a soft clean bed, or when he remembered that the French had gone and that his wife was no more. "Oh, how good, how splendid!"

And by old habit he asked himself the question: "Well, and what then? What am I going to do?" And he immediately gave himself the answer: "Well, I shall live. Ah, how splendid!"

The very question that had formerly tormented him, the thing he had continually sought to find—the aim of life—no longer existed for him now. That search for the aim of life had not merely disappeared temporarily—he felt that it no longer existed for him and could not present itself again. And this very absence of an aim gave him the complete, joyous sense of freedom which constituted his happiness at this time.

He could not see an aim, for he now had faith—not faith in any kind of rule, or words, or ideas, but faith in an ever-living, ever-manifest God. Formerly he had sought Him in aims he set himself. That search for an aim had been simply a search for God, and suddenly in his captivity he had learned not by words or reasoning but by direct feeling what his nurse had told him long ago: that God is here and everywhere. In his captivity he had learned that in Karatáev God was greater, more infinite and unfathomable than in the Architect of the Universe recognized by the Freemasons. He felt like a man who after straining his eyes to see into the far distance finds what he sought at his very feet. All his life he had looked over the heads of the men around him, when he should have merely looked in front of him without straining his eyes.

In the past he had never been able to find that great inscrutable infinite something. He had only felt that it must exist somewhere and had looked for it. In everything near and comprehensible he had seen only what was limited, petty, commonplace, and senseless. He had equipped himself with a mental telescope and looked into remote space, where petty worldliness hiding itself in misty distance had seemed to him great and infinite merely because it was not clearly seen. And such had European life, politics, Freemasonry, philosophy, and philanthropy seemed to him. But even then, at moments of weakness as he had accounted them, his mind had penetrated to those distances and he had there seen the same pettiness, worldliness, and senselessness. Now, however, he had learned to see the great, eternal, and infinite in everything, and therefore—to see it and enjoy its contemplation—he naturally threw away the telescope through which he had till now gazed over men's heads, and gladly regarded the ever-changing, eternally great, unfathomable, and infinite life around him. And the closer he looked the more tranquil and happy he became. That dreadful question, "What for?" which had formerly destroyed all his mental edifices, no longer existed for him. To that question, "What for?" a simple answer was now always ready in his soul: "Because there is a God, that God without whose will not one hair falls from a man's head."

# XIII

In external ways Pierre had hardly changed at all. In appearance he was just what he used to be. As before he was absent-minded and seemed occupied not with what was before his eyes but with something special of his own. The difference between his former and present self was that formerly when he did not grasp what lay before him or was said to him, he had puckered his forehead painfully as if vainly seeking to distinguish something at a distance. At present he still forgot what was said to him and still did not see what was before his eyes, but he now looked with a scarcely perceptible and seemingly ironic smile at what was before him and listened to what was said, though evidently seeing and hearing something quite different. Formerly he had appeared to be a kindhearted but unhappy man, and so people had been inclined to avoid him. Now a smile at the joy of life always played round his lips, and sympathy for others shone in his eyes with a questioning look as to whether they were as contented as he was, and people felt pleased by his presence.

Previously he had talked a great deal, grew excited when he talked, and seldom listened; now he was seldom carried away in conversation and knew how to listen so that people readily told him their most intimate secrets.

The princess, who had never liked Pierre and had been particularly hostile to him since she had felt herself under obligations to him after the old count's death, now after staying a short time in Orël—where she had come intending to show Pierre that in spite of his ingratitude she considered it her duty to nurse him—felt to her surprise and vexation that she had become fond of him. Pierre did not in any way seek her approval, he merely studied her with interest. Formerly she had felt that he regarded her with indifference and irony, and so had shrunk into herself as she did with others and had shown him only the combative side of her nature; but now he seemed to be trying to understand the most intimate places of her heart, and, mistrustfully at first but afterwards gratefully, she let him see the hidden, kindly sides of her character.

The most cunning man could not have crept into her confidence more successfully, evoking memories of the best times of her youth and showing sympathy with them. Yet Pierre's cunning consisted simply in finding pleasure in drawing out the human qualities of the embittered, hard, and (in her own way) proud princess.

"Yes, he is a very, very kind man when he is not under the influence of bad people but of people such as myself," thought she.

His servants too—Terénty and Váska—in their own way noticed the change that had taken place in Pierre. They considered that he had become much "simpler." Terénty, when he had helped him undress and wished him good night, often lingered with his master's boots in his hands and clothes over his arm, to see whether he would not start a talk. And Pierre, noticing that Terénty wanted a chat, generally kept him there.

"Well, tell me... now, how did you get food?" he would ask.

And Terénty would begin talking of the destruction of Moscow, and of the old count, and would stand for a long time holding the clothes and talking, or sometimes listening to Pierre's stories, and then would go out into the hall with a pleasant sense of intimacy with his master and affection for him.

The doctor who attended Pierre and visited him every day, though he considered it his duty as a doctor to pose as a man whose every moment was of value to suffering humanity, would sit for hours with Pierre telling him his favorite anecdotes and his observations on the characters of his patients in general, and especially of the ladies.

"It's a pleasure to talk to a man like that; he is not like our provincials," he would say.

There were several prisoners from the French army in Orël, and the doctor brought one of them, a young Italian, to see Pierre.

This officer began visiting Pierre, and the princess used to make fun of the tenderness the Italian expressed for him.

The Italian seemed happy only when he could come to see Pierre, talk with him, tell him about his past, his life at home, and his love, and pour out to him his indignation against the French and especially against Napoleon.

"If all Russians are in the least like you, it is sacrilege to fight such a nation," he said to Pierre. "You, who have suffered so from the French, do not even feel animosity toward them."

Pierre had evoked the passionate affection of the Italian merely by evoking the best side of his nature and taking a pleasure in so doing.

During the last days of Pierre's stay in Orël his old Masonic acquaintance Count Willarski, who had introduced him to the lodge in

1807, came to see him. Willarski was married to a Russian heiress who had a large estate in Orël province, and he occupied a temporary post in the commissariat department in that town.

Hearing that Bezúkhov was in Orël, Willarski, though they had never been intimate, came to him with the professions of friendship and intimacy that people who meet in a desert generally express for one another. Willarski felt dull in Orël and was pleased to meet a man of his own circle and, as he supposed, of similar interests.

But to his surprise Willarski soon noticed that Pierre had lagged much behind the times, and had sunk, as he expressed it to himself, into apathy and egotism.

"You are letting yourself go, my dear fellow," he said.

But for all that Willarski found it pleasanter now than it had been formerly to be with Pierre, and came to see him every day. To Pierre as he looked at and listened to Willarski, it seemed strange to think that he had been like that himself but a short time before.

Willarski was a married man with a family, busy with his family affairs, his wife's affairs, and his official duties. He regarded all these occupations as hindrances to life, and considered that they were all contemptible because their aim was the welfare of himself and his family. Military, administrative, political, and Masonic interests continually absorbed his attention. And Pierre, without trying to change the other's views and without condemning him, but with the quiet, joyful, and amused smile now habitual to him, was interested in this strange though very familiar phenomenon.

There was a new feature in Pierre's relations with Willarski, with the princess, with the doctor, and with all the people he now met, which gained for him the general good will. This was his acknowledgment of the impossibility of changing a man's convictions by words, and his recognition of the possibility of everyone thinking, feeling, and seeing things each from his own point of view. This legitimate peculiarity of each individual which used to excite and irritate Pierre now became a basis of the sympathy he felt for, and the interest he took in, other people. The difference, and sometimes complete contradiction, between men's opinions and their lives, and between one man and another, pleased him and drew from him an amused and gentle smile.

In practical matters Pierre unexpectedly felt within himself a center of gravity he had previously lacked. Formerly all pecuniary questions, especially requests for money to which, as an extremely wealthy man, he was very exposed, produced in him a state of hopeless agitation and perplexity. "To give or not to give?" he had asked himself. "I have it and he needs it. But someone else needs it still more. Who needs it most? And perhaps they are both impostors?" In the old days he had been unable to find a way out of all these surmises and had given to all who asked as long as he had anything to give. Formerly he had been in a similar state of perplexity with regard to every question concerning his property, when one person advised one thing and another something else.

Now to his surprise he found that he no longer felt either doubt or perplexity about these questions. There was now within him a judge who by some rule unknown to him decided what should or should not be done.

He was as indifferent as heretofore to money matters, but now he felt certain of what ought and what ought not to be done. The first time he had recourse to his new judge was when a French prisoner, a colonel, came to him and, after talking a great deal about his exploits, concluded by making what amounted to a demand that Pierre should give him four thousand francs to send to his wife and children. Pierre refused without the least difficulty or effort, and was afterwards surprised how simple and easy had been what used to appear so insurmountably difficult. At the same time that he refused the colonel's demand he made up his mind that he must have recourse to artifice when leaving Orël, to induce the Italian officer to accept some money of which he was evidently in need. A further proof to Pierre of his own more settled outlook on practical matters was furnished by his decision with regard to his wife's debts and to the rebuilding of his houses in and near Moscow.

His head steward came to him at Orël and Pierre reckoned up with him his diminished income. The burning of Moscow had cost him, according to the head steward's calculation, about two million rubles.

To console Pierre for these losses the head steward gave him an estimate showing that despite these losses his income would not be diminished but would even be increased if he refused to pay his wife's debts which he was under no obligation to meet, and did not rebuild his Moscow house and the country house on his Moscow estate, which had cost him eighty thousand rubles a year and brought in nothing.

"Yes, of course that's true," said Pierre with a cheerful smile. "I don't need all that at all. By being ruined I have become much richer."

But in January Savélich came from Moscow and gave him an account of the state of things there, and spoke of the estimate an architect had made of the cost of rebuilding the town and country houses, speaking of this as of a settled matter. About the same time he received letters from Prince Vasíli and other Petersburg acquaintances speaking of his wife's debts. And Pierre decided that the steward's proposals which had so pleased him were wrong and that he must go to Petersburg and settle his wife's affairs and must rebuild in Moscow. Why this was necessary he did not know, but he knew for certain that it was necessary. His income would be reduced by three fourths, but he felt it must be done.

Willarski was going to Moscow and they agreed to travel together.

During the whole time of his convalescence in Orël Pierre had experienced a feeling of joy, freedom, and life; but when during his journey he found himself in the open world and saw hundreds of new faces, that feeling was intensified. Throughout his journey he felt like a schoolboy on holiday. Everyone—the stagecoach driver, the post-house overseers, the peasants on the roads and in the villages—had a new significance for him. The presence and remarks of Willarski who continually deplored the ignorance and poverty of Russia and its backwardness compared with Europe only heightened Pierre's pleasure. Where Willarski saw deadness Pierre saw an extraordinary strength and vitality—the strength which in that vast space amid the snows maintained the life of this original, peculiar, and unique people. He did not contradict Willarski and even seemed to agree with him—an apparent agreement being the simplest way to avoid discussions that could lead to nothing—and he smiled joyfully as he listened to him.

# XIV

It would be difficult to explain why and whither ants whose heap has been destroyed are hurrying: some from the heap dragging bits of rubbish, larvae, and corpses, others back to the heap, or why they jostle, overtake one another, and fight, and it would be equally difficult to explain what caused the Russians after the departure of the French to throng to the place that had formerly been Moscow. But when we watch the ants round their ruined heap, the tenacity, energy, and immense number of the delving insects prove that despite the destruction of the heap, something indestructible, which though intangible is the real strength of the colony, still exists; and similarly, though in Moscow in the month of October there was no government and no churches, shrines, riches, or houses—it was still the Moscow it had been in August. All was destroyed, except something intangible yet powerful and indestructible.

The motives of those who thronged from all sides to Moscow after it had been cleared of the enemy were most diverse and personal, and at first for the most part savage and brutal. One motive only they all had in common: a desire to get to the place that had been called Moscow, to apply their activities there.

Within a week Moscow already had fifteen thousand inhabitants, in a fortnight twenty-five thousand, and so on. By the autumn of 1813 the number, ever increasing and increasing, exceeded what it had been in 1812.

The first Russians to enter Moscow were the Cossacks of Wintzingerode's detachment, peasants from the adjacent villages, and residents who had fled from Moscow and had been hiding in its vicinity. The Russians who entered Moscow, finding it plundered, plundered it in their turn. They continued what the French had begun. Trains of peasant carts came to Moscow to carry off to the villages what had been abandoned in the ruined houses and the streets. The Cossacks carried off what they could to their camps, and the householders seized all they could find in other houses and moved it to their own, pretending that it was their property.

But the first plunderers were followed by a second and a third contingent, and with increasing numbers plundering became more and more difficult and assumed more definite forms.

The French found Moscow abandoned but with all the organizations of regular life, with diverse branches of commerce and craftsmanship, with luxury, and governmental and religious institutions. These forms were lifeless but still existed. There were bazaars, shops, warehouses, market stalls, granaries—for the most part still stocked with goods—and there were factories and workshops, palaces and wealthy houses filled with luxuries, hospitals, prisons, government offices, churches, and cathedrals. The longer the French remained the more these forms of town life perished, until finally all was merged into one confused, lifeless scene of plunder.

The more the plundering by the French continued, the more both the wealth of Moscow and the strength of its plunderers was destroyed. But plundering by the Russians, with which the reoccupation of the city began, had an opposite effect: the longer it continued and the greater the number of people taking part in it the more rapidly was the wealth of the city and its regular life restored.

Besides the plunderers, very various people, some drawn by curiosity, some by official duties, some by self-interest—house owners, clergy, officials of all kinds, tradesmen, artisans, and peasants—streamed into Moscow as blood flows to the heart.

Within a week the peasants who came with empty carts to carry off plunder were stopped by the authorities and made to cart the corpses out of the town. Other peasants, having heard of their comrades' discomfiture, came to town bringing rye, oats, and hay, and beat down one another's prices to below what they had been in former days. Gangs of carpenters hoping for high pay arrived in Moscow every day, and on all sides logs were being hewn, new houses built, and old, charred ones repaired. Tradesmen began trading in booths. Cookshops and taverns were opened in partially burned houses. The clergy resumed the services in many churches that had not been burned. Donors contributed Church property that had been stolen. Government clerks set up their baize-covered tables and their pigeonholes of documents in small rooms. The higher authorities and the police organized the distribution of goods left behind by the French. The owners of houses in which much property had been left, brought there from other houses, complained of the injustice of taking everything to the Faceted Palace in the Krémlin; others insisted that as the French had gathered things from different houses into this or that house, it would be unfair to allow its owner to keep all that was found there. They abused the police and bribed them, made out estimates at ten times their value for government stores that had perished in the fire, and demanded relief. And Count Rostopchín wrote proclamations.

At the end of January Pierre went to Moscow and stayed in an annex of his house which had not been burned. He called on Count Rostopchín and on some acquaintances who were back in Moscow, and he intended to leave for Petersburg two days later. Everybody was celebrating the victory, everything was bubbling with life in the ruined but reviving city. Everyone was pleased to see Pierre, everyone wished to meet him, and everyone questioned him about what he had seen. Pierre felt particularly well disposed toward them all, but was now instinctively on his guard for fear of binding himself in any way. To all questions put to him—whether important or quite trifling—such as: Where would he live? Was he going to rebuild? When was he going to Petersburg and would he mind taking a parcel for someone?—he replied: "Yes, perhaps," or, "I think so," and so on.

He had heard that the Rostóvs were at Kostromá but the thought of Natásha seldom occurred to him. If it did it was only as a pleasant memory of the distant past. He felt himself not only free from social obligations but also from that feeling which, it seemed to him, he had aroused in himself.

On the third day after his arrival he heard from the Drubetskóys that Princess Mary was in Moscow. The death, sufferings, and last days of Prince Andrew had often occupied Pierre's thoughts and now recurred to him with fresh vividness. Having heard at dinner that Princess Mary was in Moscow and living in her house—which had not been burned—in Vozdvízhenka Street, he drove that same evening to see her.

On his way to the house Pierre kept thinking of Prince Andrew, of their friendship, of his various meetings with him, and especially of the last one at Borodinó.

"Is it possible that he died in the bitter frame of mind he was then in? Is it possible that the meaning of life was not disclosed to him before he died?" thought Pierre. He recalled Karatáev and his death and involuntarily began to compare these two men, so different, and yet so similar in that they had both lived and both died and in the love he felt for both of them.

Pierre drove up to the house of the old prince in a most serious mood. The house had escaped the fire; it showed signs of damage but its general aspect was unchanged. The old footman, who met Pierre with a stern face as if wishing to make the visitor feel that the absence of the old prince had not disturbed the order of things in the house, informed him that the princess had gone to her own apartments, and that she received on Sundays.

"Announce me. Perhaps she will see me," said Pierre.

"Yes, sir," said the man. "Please step into the portrait gallery."

A few minutes later the footman returned with Dessalles, who brought word from the princess that she would be very glad to see Pierre if he would excuse her want of ceremony and come upstairs to her apartment.

In a rather low room lit by one candle sat the princess and with her another person dressed in black. Pierre remembered that the princess always had lady companions, but who they were and what they were like he never knew or remembered. "This must be one of her companions," he thought, glancing at the lady in the black dress.

The princess rose quickly to meet him and held out her hand.

"Yes," she said, looking at his altered face after he had kissed her hand, "so this is how we meet again. He spoke of you even at the very last," she went on, turning her eyes from Pierre to her companion with a shyness that surprised him for an instant.

"I was so glad to hear of your safety. It was the first piece of good news we had received for a long time."

Again the princess glanced round at her companion with even more uneasiness in her manner and was about to add something, but Pierre interrupted her.

"Just imagine—I knew nothing about him!" said he. "I thought he had been killed. All I know I heard at second hand from others. I only know that he fell in with the Rostóvs. . . What a strange coincidence!"

Pierre spoke rapidly and with animation. He glanced once at the companion's face, saw her attentive and kindly gaze fixed on him, and, as often happens when one is talking, felt somehow that this companion in the black dress was a good, kind, excellent creature who would not hinder his conversing freely with Princess Mary.

But when he mentioned the Rostóvs, Princess Mary's face expressed still greater embarrassment. She again glanced rapidly from Pierre's face to that of the lady in the black dress and said:

"Do you really not recognize her?"

Pierre looked again at the companion's pale, delicate face with its black eyes and peculiar mouth, and something near to him, long forgotten and more than sweet, looked at him from those attentive eyes.

"But no, it can't be!" he thought. "This stern, thin, pale face that looks so much older! It cannot be she. It merely reminds me of her." But at that moment Princess Mary said, "Natásha!" And with difficulty, effort, and stress, like the opening of a door grown rusty on its hinges, a smile appeared on the face with the attentive eyes, and from that opening door came a breath of fragrance which suffused Pierre with a happiness he had long forgotten and of which he had not even been thinking—especially at that moment. It suffused him, seized him, and enveloped him completely. When she smiled doubt was no longer possible, it was Natásha and he loved her.

At that moment Pierre involuntarily betrayed to her, to Princess Mary, and above all to himself, a secret of which he himself had been unaware. He flushed joyfully yet with painful distress. He tried to hide his agitation. But the more he tried to hide it the more clearly—clearer than any words could have done—did he betray to himself, to her, and to Princess Mary that he loved her.

"No, it's only the unexpectedness of it," thought Pierre. But as soon as he tried to continue the conversation he had begun with Princess Mary he again glanced at Natásha, and a still-deeper flush suffused his face and a still-stronger agitation of mingled joy and fear seized his soul. He became confused in his speech and stopped in the middle of what he was saying.

Pierre had failed to notice Natásha because he did not at all expect to see her there, but he had failed to recognize her because the change in her since he last saw her was immense. She had grown thin and pale, but that was not what made her unrecognizable; she was unrecognizable at the moment he entered because on that face whose eyes had always shone with a suppressed smile of the joy of life, now when he first entered and glanced at her there was not the least shadow of a smile: only her eyes were kindly attentive and sadly interrogative.

Pierre's confusion was not reflected by any confusion on Natásha's part, but only by the pleasure that just perceptibly lit up her whole face.

# XVI

S he has come to stay with me," said Princess Mary. "The count and countess will be here in a few days. The countess is in a dreadful state; but it was necessary for Natásha herself to see a doctor. They insisted on her coming with me."

"Yes, is there a family free from sorrow now?" said Pierre, addressing Natásha. "You know it happened the very day we were rescued. I saw him. What a delightful boy he was!"

Natásha looked at him, and by way of answer to his words her eyes widened and lit up.

"What can one say or think of as a consolation?" said Pierre. "Nothing! Why had such a splendid boy, so full of life, to die?"

"Yes, in these days it would be hard to live without faith. . ." remarked Princess Mary.

"Yes, yes, that is really true," Pierre hastily interrupted her.

"Why is it true?" Natásha asked, looking attentively into Pierre's eyes.

"How can you ask why?" said Princess Mary. "The thought alone of what awaits. . ."

Natásha without waiting for Princess Mary to finish again looked inquiringly at Pierre.

"And because," Pierre continued, "only one who believes that there is a God ruling us can bear a loss such as hers and. . . yours."

Natásha had already opened her mouth to speak but suddenly stopped. Pierre hurriedly turned away from her and again addressed Princess Mary, asking about his friend's last days.

Pierre's confusion had now almost vanished, but at the same time he felt that his freedom had also completely gone. He felt that there was now a judge of his every word and action whose judgment mattered more to him than that of all the rest of the world. As he spoke now he was considering what impression his words would make on Natásha. He did not purposely say things to please her, but whatever he was saying he regarded from her standpoint.

Princess Mary—reluctantly as is usual in such cases—began telling of the condition in which she had found Prince Andrew. But Pierre's face quivering with emotion, his questions and his eager restless expression, gradually compelled her to go into details which she feared to recall for her own sake.

"Yes, yes, and so. . . ?" Pierre kept saying as he leaned toward her with his whole body and eagerly listened to her story. "Yes, yes. . . so he grew tranquil and softened? With all his soul he had always sought one thing—to be perfectly good—so he could not be afraid of death. The faults he had—if he had any—were not of his making. So he did soften? . . . What a happy thing that he saw you again," he added, suddenly turning to Natásha and looking at her with eyes full of tears.

Natásha's face twitched. She frowned and lowered her eyes for a moment. She hesitated for an instant whether to speak or not.

"Yes, that was happiness," she then said in her quiet voice with its deep chest notes. "For me it certainly was happiness." She paused. "And he. . . he. . . he said he was wishing for it at the very moment I entered the room. . ."

Natásha's voice broke. She blushed, pressed her clasped hands on her knees, and then controlling herself with an evident effort lifted her head and began to speak rapidly.

"We knew nothing of it when we started from Moscow. I did not dare to ask about him. Then suddenly Sónya told me he was traveling with us. I had no idea and could not imagine what state he was in, all I wanted was to see him and be with him," she said, trembling, and breathing quickly.

And not letting them interrupt her she went on to tell what she had never yet mentioned to anyone—all she had lived through during those three weeks of their journey and life at Yaroslávl.

Pierre listened to her with lips parted and eyes fixed upon her full of tears. As he listened he did not think of Prince Andrew, nor of death, nor of what she was telling. He listened to her and felt only pity for her, for what she was suffering now while she was speaking.

Princess Mary, frowning in her effort to hold back her tears, sat beside Natásha, and heard for the first time the story of those last days of her brother's and Natásha's love.

Evidently Natásha needed to tell that painful yet joyful tale.

She spoke, mingling most trifling details with the intimate secrets of her soul, and it seemed as if she could never finish. Several times she repeated the same thing twice.

Dessalles' voice was heard outside the door asking whether little Nicholas might come in to say good night.

"Well, that's all—everything," said Natásha.

She got up quickly just as Nicholas entered, almost ran to the door which was hidden by curtains, struck her head against it, and rushed from the room with a moan either of pain or sorrow.

Pierre gazed at the door through which she had disappeared and did not understand why he suddenly felt all alone in the world.

Princess Mary roused him from his abstraction by drawing his attention to her nephew who had entered the room.

At that moment of emotional tenderness young Nicholas' face, which resembled his father's, affected Pierre so much that when he had kissed the boy he got up quickly, took out his handkerchief, and went to the window. He wished to take leave of Princess Mary, but she would not let him go.

"No, Natásha and I sometimes don't go to sleep till after two, so please don't go. I will order supper. Go downstairs, we will come immediately."

Before Pierre left the room Princess Mary told him: "This is the first time she has talked of him like that."

# XVII

Pierre was shown into the large, brightly lit dining room; a few minutes later he heard footsteps and Princess Mary entered with Natásha. Natásha was calm, though a severe and grave expression had again settled on her face. They all three of them now experienced that feeling of awkwardness which usually follows after a serious and heartfelt talk. It is impossible to go back to the same conversation, to talk of trifles is awkward, and yet the desire to speak is there and silence seems like affectation. They went silently to table. The footmen drew back the chairs and pushed them up again. Pierre unfolded his cold table napkin and, resolving to break the silence, looked at Natásha and at Princess Mary. They had evidently both formed the same resolution; the eyes of both shone with satisfaction and a confession that besides sorrow life also has joy.

"Do you take vodka, Count?" asked Princess Mary, and those words suddenly banished the shadows of the past. "Now tell us about yourself," said she. "One hears such improbable wonders about you."

"Yes," replied Pierre with the smile of mild irony now habitual to him. "They even tell me wonders I myself never dreamed of! Mary Abrámovna invited me to her house and kept telling me what had happened, or ought to have happened, to me. Stepán Stepánych also instructed me how I ought to tell of my experiences. In general I have noticed that it is very easy to be an interesting man (I am an interesting man now); people invite me out and tell me all about myself."

Natásha smiled and was on the point of speaking.

"We have been told," Princess Mary interrupted her, "that you lost two millions in Moscow. Is that true?"

"But I am three times as rich as before," returned Pierre.

Though the position was now altered by his decision to pay his wife's debts and to rebuild his houses, Pierre still maintained that he had become three times as rich as before.

"What I have certainly gained is freedom," he began seriously, but did not continue, noticing that this theme was too egotistic.

"And are you building?"

"Yes. Savélich says I must!"

"Tell me, you did not know of the countess' death when you decided to remain in Moscow?" asked Princess Mary and immediately blushed, noticing that her question, following his mention of freedom, ascribed to his words a meaning he had perhaps not intended.

"No," answered Pierre, evidently not considering awkward the meaning Princess Mary had given to his words. "I heard of it in Orël and you cannot imagine how it shocked me. We were not an exemplary couple," he added quickly, glancing at Natásha and noticing on her face curiosity as to how he would speak of his wife, "but her death shocked me terribly. When two people quarrel they are always both in fault, and one's own guilt suddenly becomes terribly serious when the other is no longer alive. And then such a death. . . without friends and without consolation! I am very, very sorry for her," he concluded, and was pleased to notice a look of glad approval on Natásha's face.

"Yes, and so you are once more an eligible bachelor," said Princess Mary.

Pierre suddenly flushed crimson and for a long time tried not to look at Natásha. When he ventured to glance her way again her face was cold, stern, and he fancied even contemptuous.

"And did you really see and speak to Napoleon, as we have been told?" said Princess Mary.

Pierre laughed.

"No, not once! Everybody seems to imagine that being taken prisoner means being Napoleon's guest. Not only did I never see him but I heard nothing about him—I was in much lower company!"

Supper was over, and Pierre who at first declined to speak about his captivity was gradually led on to do so.

"But it's true that you remained in Moscow to kill Napoleon?" Natásha asked with a slight smile. "I guessed it then when we met at the Súkharev tower, do you remember?"

Pierre admitted that it was true, and from that was gradually led by Princess Mary's questions and especially by Natásha's into giving a detailed account of his adventures.

At first he spoke with the amused and mild irony now customary with him toward everybody and especially toward himself, but when he came to describe the horrors and sufferings he had witnessed he was unconsciously carried away and began speaking with the suppressed emotion of a man re-experiencing in recollection strong impressions he has lived through.

Princess Mary with a gentle smile looked now at Pierre and now at Natásha. In the whole narrative she saw only Pierre and his goodness.

Natásha, leaning on her elbow, the expression of her face constantly changing with the narrative, watched Pierre with an attention that never wandered—evidently herself experiencing all that he described. Not only her look, but her exclamations and the brief questions she put, showed Pierre that she understood just what he wished to convey. It was clear that she understood not only what he said but also what he wished to, but could not, express in words. The account Pierre gave of the incident with the child and the woman for protecting whom he was arrested was this: "It was an awful sight—children abandoned, some in the flames. . . One was snatched out before my eyes. . . and there were women who had their things snatched off and their earrings torn out. . ." he flushed and grew confused. "Then a patrol arrived and all the men—all those who were not looting, that is—were arrested, and I among them."

"I am sure you're not telling us everything; I am sure you did something. . ." said Natásha and pausing added, "something fine?"

Pierre continued. When he spoke of the execution he wanted to pass over the horrible details, but Natásha insisted that he should not omit anything.

Pierre began to tell about Karatáev, but paused. By this time he had risen from the table and was pacing the room, Natásha following him with her eyes. Then he added:

"No, you can't understand what I learned from that illiterate man—that simple fellow."

"Yes, yes, go on!" said Natásha. "Where is he?"

"They killed him almost before my eyes."

And Pierre, his voice trembling continually, went on to tell of the last days of their retreat, of Karatáev's illness and his death.

He told of his adventures as he had never yet recalled them. He now, as it were, saw a new meaning in all he had gone through. Now that he was telling it all to Natásha he experienced that pleasure which a man has when women listen to him—not clever women who when listening either try to remember what they hear to enrich their minds and when opportunity offers to retell it, or who wish to adopt it to some thought of their own and promptly contribute their own clever comments prepared in their little mental workshop—but the pleasure given by real women gifted with a capacity to select and absorb the very best a man shows of himself. Natásha without knowing it was all attention: she did not lose a word, no single quiver in Pierre's voice, no look, no twitch of a muscle in his face, nor a single gesture. She caught the unfinished word in its flight and took it straight into her open heart, divining the secret meaning of all Pierre's mental travail.

Princess Mary understood his story and sympathized with him, but she now saw something else that absorbed all her attention. She saw the possibility of love and happiness between Natásha and Pierre, and the first thought of this filled her heart with gladness.

It was three o'clock in the morning. The footmen came in with sad and stern faces to change the candles, but no one noticed them.

Pierre finished his story. Natásha continued to look at him intently with bright, attentive, and animated eyes, as if trying to understand something more which he had perhaps left untold. Pierre in shamefaced and happy confusion glanced occasionally at her, and tried to think what to say next to introduce a fresh subject. Princess Mary was silent. It occurred to none of them that it was three o'clock and time to go to bed.

"People speak of misfortunes and sufferings," remarked Pierre, "but if at this moment I were asked: 'Would you rather be what you were before you were taken prisoner, or go through all this again?' then for heaven's sake let me again have captivity and horseflesh! We imagine that when we are thrown out of our usual ruts all is lost, but it is only then that what is new and good begins. While there is life there is happiness. There is much, much before us. I say this to you," he added, turning to Natásha.

"Yes, yes," she said, answering something quite different. "I too should wish nothing but to relive it all from the beginning."

Pierre looked intently at her.

"Yes, and nothing more," said Natásha.

"It's not true, not true!" cried Pierre. "I am not to blame for being alive and wishing to live—nor you either."

Suddenly Natásha bent her head, covered her face with her hands, and began to cry.

"What is it, Natásha?" said Princess Mary.

"Nothing, nothing." She smiled at Pierre through her tears. "Good night! It is time for bed."

Pierre rose and took his leave.

Princess Mary and Natásha met as usual in the bedroom. They talked of what Pierre had told them. Princess Mary did not express her opinion of Pierre nor did Natásha speak of him.

"Well, good night, Mary!" said Natásha. "Do you know, I am often afraid that by not speaking of him" (she meant Prince Andrew) "for fear of not doing justice to our feelings, we forget him."

Princess Mary sighed deeply and thereby acknowledged the justice of Natásha's remark, but she did not express agreement in words.

"Is it possible to forget?" said she.

"It did me so much good to tell all about it today. It was hard and painful, but good, very good!" said Natásha. "I am sure he really loved him. That is why I told him. . . Was it all right?" she added, suddenly blushing.

"To tell Pierre? Oh, yes. What a splendid man he is!" said Princess Mary.

"Do you know, Mary. . ." Natásha suddenly said with a mischievous smile such as Princess Mary had not seen on her face for a long time, "he has somehow grown so clean, smooth, and fresh—as if he had just come out of a Russian bath; do you understand? Out of a moral bath. Isn't it true?"

"Yes," replied Princess Mary. "He has greatly improved."

"With a short coat and his hair cropped; just as if, well, just as if he had come straight from the bath. . . Papa used to. . ."

"I understand why he" (Prince Andrew) "liked no one so much as him," said Princess Mary.

"Yes, and yet he is quite different. They say men are friends when they are quite different. That must be true. Really he is quite unlike him—in everything."

"Yes, but he's wonderful."

"Well, good night," said Natásha.

And the same mischievous smile lingered for a long time on her face as if it had been forgotten there.

# XVIII

It was a long time before Pierre could fall asleep that night. He paced up and down his room, now turning his thoughts on a difficult problem and frowning, now suddenly shrugging his shoulders and wincing, and now smiling happily.

He was thinking of Prince Andrew, of Natásha, and of their love, at one moment jealous of her past, then reproaching himself for that feeling. It was already six in the morning and he still paced up and down the room.

"Well, what's to be done if it cannot be avoided? What's to be done? Evidently it has to be so," said he to himself, and hastily undressing he got into bed, happy and agitated but free from hesitation or indecision.

"Strange and impossible as such happiness seems, I must do everything that she and I may be man and wife," he told himself.

A few days previously Pierre had decided to go to Petersburg on the Friday. When he awoke on the Thursday, Savélich came to ask him about packing for the journey.

"What, to Petersburg? What is Petersburg? Who is there in Petersburg?" he asked involuntarily, though only to himself. "Oh, yes, long ago before this happened I did for some reason mean to go to Petersburg," he reflected. "Why? But perhaps I shall go. What a good fellow he is and how attentive, and how he remembers everything," he thought, looking at Savélich's old face, "and what a pleasant smile he has!"

"Well, Savélich, do you still not wish to accept your freedom?" Pierre asked him.

"What's the good of freedom to me, your excellency? We lived under the late count—the kingdom of heaven be his!—and we have lived under you too, without ever being wronged."

"And your children?"

"The children will live just the same. With such masters one can live."

"But what about my heirs?" said Pierre. "Supposing I suddenly marry. . . it might happen," he added with an involuntary smile.

"If I may take the liberty, your excellency, it would be a good thing."

"How easy he thinks it," thought Pierre. "He doesn't know how terrible it is and how dangerous. Too soon or too late. . . it is terrible!"

"So what are your orders? Are you starting tomorrow?" asked Savélich.

"No, I'll put it off for a bit. I'll tell you later. You must forgive the trouble I have put you to," said Pierre, and seeing Savélich smile, he thought: "But how strange it is that he should not know that now there is no Petersburg for me, and that that must be settled first of all! But probably he knows it well enough and is only pretending. Shall I have a talk with him and see what he thinks?" Pierre reflected. "No, another time."

At breakfast Pierre told the princess, his cousin, that he had been to see Princess Mary the day before and had there met—"Whom do you think? Natásha Rostóva!"

The princess seemed to see nothing more extraordinary in that than if he had seen Anna Semënovna.

"Do you know her?" asked Pierre.

"I have seen the princess," she replied. "I heard that they were arranging a match for her with young Rostóv. It would be a very good thing for the Rostóvs, they are said to be utterly ruined."

"No; I mean do you know Natásha Rostóva?"

"I heard about that affair of hers at the time. It was a great pity."

"No, she either doesn't understand or is pretending," thought Pierre. "Better not say anything to her either."

The princess too had prepared provisions for Pierre's journey.

"How kind they all are," thought Pierre. "What is surprising is that they should trouble about these things now when it can no longer be of interest to them. And all for me!"

On the same day the Chief of Police came to Pierre, inviting him to send a representative to the Faceted Palace to recover things that were to be returned to their owners that day.

"And this man too," thought Pierre, looking into the face of the Chief of Police. "What a fine, good-looking officer and how kind. Fancy bothering about such trifles now! And they actually say he is not honest and takes bribes. What nonsense! Besides, why shouldn't he take bribes? That's the way he was brought up, and everybody does it. But what a kind, pleasant face and how he smiles as he looks at me."

Pierre went to Princess Mary's to dinner.

As he drove through the streets past the houses that had been burned down, he was surprised by the beauty of those ruins. The picturesqueness of the chimney stacks and tumble-down walls of the burned-out quarters of the town, stretching out and concealing one another, reminded him of the Rhine and the Colosseum. The cabmen he met and their passengers, the carpenters cutting the timber for new houses with axes, the women hawkers, and the shopkeepers, all looked at him with cheerful beaming eyes that seemed to say: "Ah, there he is! Let's see what will come of it!"

At the entrance to Princess Mary's house Pierre felt doubtful whether he had really been there the night before and really seen Natásha and talked to her. "Perhaps I imagined it; perhaps I shall go in and find no one there." But he had hardly entered the room before he felt her presence with his whole being by the loss of his sense of freedom. She was in the same black dress with soft folds and her hair was done the same way as the day before, yet she was quite different. Had she been like this when he entered the day before he could not for a moment have failed to recognize her.

She was as he had known her almost as a child and later on as Prince Andrew's fiancée. A bright questioning light shone in her eyes, and on her face was a friendly and strangely roguish expression.

Pierre dined with them and would have spent the whole evening there, but Princess Mary was going to vespers and Pierre left the house with her.

Next day he came early, dined, and stayed the whole evening. Though Princess Mary and Natásha were evidently glad to see their visitor and though all Pierre's interest was now centered in that house, by the evening they had talked over everything and the conversation passed from one trivial topic to another and repeatedly broke off. He stayed so long that Princess Mary and Natásha exchanged glances, evidently wondering when he would go. Pierre noticed this but could not go. He felt uneasy and embarrassed, but sat on because he simply could not get up and take his leave.

Princess Mary, foreseeing no end to this, rose first, and complaining of a headache began to say good night.

"So you are going to Petersburg tomorrow?" she asked.

"No, I am not going," Pierre replied hastily, in a surprised tone and as though offended. "Yes. . . no. . . to Petersburg? Tomorrow—but I won't say good-by yet. I will call round in case you have any commissions for me," said he, standing before Princess Mary and turning red, but not taking his departure.

Natásha gave him her hand and went out. Princess Mary on the other hand instead of going away sank into an armchair, and looked sternly and intently at him with her deep, radiant eyes. The weariness she had plainly shown before had now quite passed off. With a deep and long-drawn sigh she seemed to be prepared for a lengthy talk.

When Natásha left the room Pierre's confusion and awkwardness immediately vanished and were replaced by eager excitement. He quickly moved an armchair toward Princess Mary.

"Yes, I wanted to tell you," said he, answering her look as if she had spoken. "Princess, help me! What am I to do? Can I hope? Princess, my dear friend, listen! I know it all. I know I am not worthy of her, I know it's impossible to speak of it now. But I want to be a brother to her. No, not that, I don't, I can't. . ."

He paused and rubbed his face and eyes with his hands.

"Well," he went on with an evident effort at self-control and coherence. "I don't know when I began to love her, but I have loved her and her alone all my life, and I love her so that I cannot imagine life without her. I cannot propose to her at present, but the thought that perhaps she might someday be my wife and that I may be missing that possibility. . . that possibility. . . is terrible. Tell me, can I hope? Tell me what I am to do, dear princess!" he added after a pause, and touched her hand as she did not reply.

"I am thinking of what you have told me," answered Princess Mary. "This is what I will say. You are right that to speak to her of love at present. . ."

Princess Mary stopped. She was going to say that to speak of love was impossible, but she stopped because she had seen by the sudden change in Natásha two days before that she would not only not be hurt if Pierre spoke of his love, but that it was the very thing she wished for.

"To speak to her now wouldn't do," said the princess all the same.

"But what am I to do?"

"Leave it to me," said Princess Mary. "I know. . ."

Pierre was looking into Princess Mary's eyes.

"Well? . . . Well? . . ." he said.

"I know that she loves. . . will love you," Princess Mary corrected herself.

Before her words were out, Pierre had sprung up and with a frightened expression seized Princess Mary's hand.

"What makes you think so? You think I may hope? You think. . . ?"

"Yes, I think so," said Princess Mary with a smile. "Write to her parents, and leave it to me. I will tell her when I can. I wish it to happen and my heart tells me it will."

"No, it cannot be! How happy I am! But it can't be. . . How happy I am! No, it can't be!" Pierre kept saying as he kissed Princess Mary's hands.

"Go to Petersburg, that will be best. And I will write to you," she said.

"To Petersburg? Go there? Very well, I'll go. But I may come again tomorrow?"

Next day Pierre came to say good-by. Natásha was less animated than she had been the day before; but that day as he looked at her Pierre sometimes felt as if he was vanishing and that neither he nor she existed any longer, that nothing existed but happiness. "Is it possible? No, it can't be," he told himself at every look, gesture, and word that filled his soul with joy.

When on saying good-by he took her thin, slender hand, he could not help holding it a little longer in his own.

"Is it possible that this hand, that face, those eyes, all this treasure of feminine charm so strange to me now, is it possible that it will one day be mine forever, as familiar to me as I am to myself? . . . No, that's impossible! . . ."

"Good-by, Count," she said aloud. "I shall look forward very much to your return," she added in a whisper.

And these simple words, her look, and the expression on her face which accompanied them, formed for two months the subject of inexhaustible memories, interpretations, and happy meditations for Pierre. "'I shall look forward very much to your return. . .' Yes, yes, how did she say it? Yes, 'I shall look forward very much to your return.' Oh, how happy I am! What is happening to me? How happy I am!" said Pierre to himself.

# XIX

There was nothing in Pierre's soul now at all like what had troubled it during his courtship of Hélène.

He did not repeat to himself with a sickening feeling of shame the words he had spoken, or say: "Oh, why did I not say that?" and, "Whatever made me say 'Je vous aime'?" On the contrary, he now repeated in imagination every word that he or Natásha had spoken and pictured every detail of her face and smile, and did not wish to diminish or add anything, but only to repeat it again and again. There was now not a shadow of doubt in his mind as to whether what he had undertaken was right or wrong. Only one terrible doubt sometimes crossed his mind: "Wasn't it all a dream? Isn't Princess Mary mistaken? Am I not too conceited and self-confident? I believe all this—and suddenly Princess Mary will tell her, and she will be sure to smile and say: 'How strange! He must be deluding himself. Doesn't he know that he is a man, just a man, while I. . . ? I am something altogether different and higher.'"

That was the only doubt often troubling Pierre. He did not now make any plans. The happiness before him appeared so inconceivable that if only he could attain it, it would be the end of all things. Everything ended with that.

A joyful, unexpected frenzy, of which he had thought himself incapable, possessed him. The whole meaning of life—not for him alone but for the whole world—seemed to him centered in his love and the possibility of being loved by her. At times everybody seemed to him to be occupied with one thing only—his future happiness. Sometimes it seemed to him that other people were all as pleased as he was himself and merely tried to hide that pleasure by pretending to be busy with other interests. In every word and gesture he saw allusions to his happiness. He often surprised those he met by his significantly happy looks and smiles which seemed to express a secret understanding between him and them. And when he realized that people might not be aware of his happiness, he pitied them with his whole heart and felt a desire somehow to explain to them that all that occupied them was a mere frivolous trifle unworthy of attention.

When it was suggested to him that he should enter the civil service, or when the war or any general political affairs were discussed on the assumption that everybody's welfare depended on this or that issue of events, he would listen with a mild and pitying smile and surprise people by his strange comments. But at this time he saw everybody—both those who, as he imagined, understood the real meaning of life (that is, what he was feeling) and those unfortunates who evidently did not understand it—in the bright light of the emotion that shone within himself, and at once without any effort saw in everyone he met everything that was good and worthy of being loved.

When dealing with the affairs and papers of his dead wife, her memory aroused in him no feeling but pity that she had not known the bliss he now knew. Prince Vasíli, who having obtained a new post and some fresh decorations was particularly proud at this time, seemed to him a pathetic, kindly old man much to be pitied.

Often in afterlife Pierre recalled this period of blissful insanity. All the views he formed of men and circumstances at this time remained true for him always. He not only did not renounce them subsequently, but when he was in doubt or inwardly at variance, he referred to the views he had held at this time of his madness and they always proved correct.

"I may have appeared strange and queer then," he thought, "but I was not so mad as I seemed. On the contrary I was then wiser and had more insight than at any other time, and understood all that is worth understanding in life, because. . . because I was happy."

Pierre's insanity consisted in not waiting, as he used to do, to discover personal attributes which he termed "good qualities" in people before loving them; his heart was now overflowing with love, and by loving people without cause he discovered indubitable causes for loving them.

# XX

After Pierre's departure that first evening, when Natásha had said to Princess Mary with a gaily mocking smile: "He looks just, yes, just as if he had come out of a Russian bath—in a short coat and with his hair cropped," something hidden and unknown to herself, but irrepressible, awoke in Natásha's soul.

Everything: her face, walk, look, and voice, was suddenly altered. To her own surprise a power of life and hope of happiness rose to the surface and demanded satisfaction. From that evening she seemed to have forgotten all that had happened to her. She no longer complained of her position, did not say a word about the past, and no longer feared to make happy plans for the future. She spoke little of Pierre, but when Princess Mary mentioned him a long-extinguished light once more kindled in her eyes and her lips curved with a strange smile.

The change that took place in Natásha at first surprised Princess Mary; but when she understood its meaning it grieved her. "Can she have loved my brother so little as to be able to forget him so soon?" she thought when she reflected on the change. But when she was with Natásha she was not vexed with her and did not reproach her. The reawakened power of life that had seized Natásha was so evidently irrepressible and unexpected by her that in her presence Princess Mary felt that she had no right to reproach her even in her heart.

Natásha gave herself up so fully and frankly to this new feeling that she did not try to hide the fact that she was no longer sad, but bright and cheerful.

When Princess Mary returned to her room after her nocturnal talk with Pierre, Natásha met her on the threshold.

"He has spoken? Yes? He has spoken?" she repeated.

And a joyful yet pathetic expression which seemed to beg forgiveness for her joy settled on Natásha's face.

"I wanted to listen at the door, but I knew you would tell me."

Understandable and touching as the look with which Natásha gazed at her seemed to Princess Mary, and sorry as she was to see her agitation, these words pained her for a moment. She remembered her brother and his love.

"But what's to be done? She can't help it," thought the princess.

And with a sad and rather stern look she told Natásha all that Pierre had said. On hearing that he was going to Petersburg Natásha was astounded.

"To Petersburg!" she repeated as if unable to understand.

But noticing the grieved expression on Princess Mary's face she guessed the reason of that sadness and suddenly began to cry.

"Mary," said she, "tell me what I should do! I am afraid of being bad. Whatever you tell me, I will do. Tell me. . ."

"You love him?"

"Yes," whispered Natásha.

"Then why are you crying? I am happy for your sake," said Princess Mary, who because of those tears quite forgave Natásha's joy.

"It won't be just yet—someday. Think what fun it will be when I am his wife and you marry Nicholas!"

"Natásha, I have asked you not to speak of that. Let us talk about you."

They were silent awhile.

"But why go to Petersburg?" Natásha suddenly asked, and hastily replied to her own question. "But no, no, he must. . . Yes, Mary, He must. . ."

# A Note About the Author

Leo Tolstoy (1828–1910) was a Russian author of novels, short stories, novellas, plays, and philosophical essays. He was born into an aristocratic family and served as an officer in the Russian military during the Crimean War before embarking on a career as a writer and activist. Tolstoy's experience in war, combined with his interpretation of the teachings of Jesus, led him to devote his life and work to the cause of pacifism. In addition to such fictional works as *War and Peace*, *Anna Karenina*, and *The Death of Ivan Ilyich*, Tolstoy wrote *The Kingdom of God is Within You*, a philosophical treatise on nonviolent resistance which had a profound impact on Mahatma Gandhi and Martin Luther King Jr. He is regarded today not only as one of the greatest writers of all time, but as a gifted and passionate political figure and public intellectual whose work transcends Russian history and literature alike.

# A Note from the Publisher

# bookfinity™

## Discover more of your favorite classics with Bookfinity™.

- Track your reading with custom book lists.
- Get great book recommendations for your personalized Reader Type.
- Add reviews for your favorite books.
- AND MUCH MORE!

Visit **bookfinity.com** and take the fun Reader Type quiz to get started.

Enjoy our classic and modern companion pairings!

Classic & Modern

9 781513 281827